·T✳H✳E·
EIGHTH RANK

THE DREAMERS OF THE DAY
BOOK TWO

David D. Ross

ST. MARTIN'S PRESS
NEW YORK

Library of Congress Cataloging-in-Publication Data
Ross David D.
    The eighth rank.
        p. cm.
    ISBN 0-312-05426-2
    I. Title.
    PS3568.O84317E34 1991 813'.54—dc20 90-49311

First Edition: April 1991

10 9 8 7 6 5 4 3 2 1

THE EIGHTH RANK

ALSO BY DAVID D. ROSS

The Argus Gambit

To Holly, for my own cryptic reasons

Any technological device that deprives a man of his job is evil; any scientific advancement that changes society without the permission of that society is criminal; any achievement that produces benefits without equally distributing those benefits among all people is antidemocratic.

—Senator Archer McClaren

. . . the first great crisis of the Republic ended with the Civil War, the second when she took up world leadership at the end of World War II . . . and the third great crisis began when she cast it aside.

—Grenoble Milner, *America: The Third Century*

. . . Americans never really ceased to be isolationist in sentiment, nor did they feel comfortable with the role of global power. As chaos spread: Paris in flames, London gutted, European civil war, the Ukraine in revolt, Tokyo occupied by Neo-Samurais, mass suicide in the Middle East; America recoiled to her ramparts, safe under her laser umbrella, while her robot subs mined the rich sea beds. . . .

—Avery Fienstein, *Red Midnight, Black Noon*

Thanks to Carl Swadell and Vern and Pat Leming for loaning me the computers to finish this; and to Mark Brock for calling to my attention my many grammatical errors.

DRAMATIS PERSONAE

In Washington, D.C.

President Jeffrey Shefferton
Vice President Teresa Evangeline St. Clair
Senator Archer McClaren of Oregon
Senator Charles Ellsworth Macadew of Colorado
Secretary of Space Sheridan Mayfield
Percy Shelley Manners of Illinois, Senate majority leader
Secretary of State Randolph Harmon
Bertram Lambert-Healey, military columnist for the *Post*
Colonel Jim Farley, Director of the Central Intelligence Agency
Fav Herloon, "Fabulous Herloon," tornado and light-show artist

The Cops

Special Deputy Director of the FBI Roger Ferdinand
Lenore Lippman of the U.S. Justice Department, Computer Division
Deputy Inspector Kirsten Fale
Deputy Sheriff Moury Hurt of Royal County, Colorado
Deputy Sheriff Wilford Butter of Royal County, Colorado

The Capitalists

Horatius Krebs, owner of the Python Corporation
Rita Holcombe Duce, owner of the Tectonics Corporation
Lewis Cocker, assistant to Krebs

On the Sunside Project

Jason Scott, head of the Sunside Project
Dorian Nye, Nobel Prize-winning physicist and adviser to the President
Sherlock Michlanski, Nobel Prize-winning physicist for his discovery of
   antigravity

Jacob Kane, engineer
Bethany Williams, systems engineer
Madeline Reed, biologist
Rene Delner, head of nutritional biology
Matt Taylor, construction foreman
Victor Ames, construction crew

In the Argus Society

Mel Hardrim, formerly of the Greater Washington Police Department
Philip Norrison, head of the Newton Observatory, Luna
Noah Chambless, head of the Argus Society
Perle Gracie of the Science News Network
Alfred Strubeck, physicist, creator of the Strubeck equations

In the Unified Soviet State

First Secretary Peter Brasnikov
Marshal Antonine Mikhailovich Tiomkin, defense minister
Colonel General Erwin Wolff, the Institute of Magnetic Propulsion
General Pavel Orlov, commander of the CosMarines
Colonel General Wen Chin, deputy defense minister

Free Agents on the "Chess Board"

Juba Aman Dana, "the Leopard," dictator of Black Africa
Ralph Ferman, a fugitive former biologist
Frank Silverado, publisher of the *Conspiracy Weekly Reader*
Warren Badger, Silverado's aide

In San Diego

Ivor Solarz, crime capo
Dr. Dollfuss, a biogeneticist
Jack Whitechapel, a professional killer

In Space

Captain Paul Fairchild of the *Sally Ride*
Captain Erskine Collins of USS *Patton*
Lieutenant Mark Park of USS *Patton*
Samuel Davenport, governor of Icarus

Elena Davenport, his daughter
Captain Stephen Finn of the *Clarion Call*
Colonel Jackson Drew, U.S. space marines
Colonel Kemel, commandant U.N. peacekeeping force on Mercury

On Luna

Chief of Space Naval Operations Hanley Davis
Brigadier General David Ian Keith of the Extraordinary Tactics Force
Assistant Governor Haldon Janneson
Sergeant Major Terry Ransome, USMC

THE EIGHTH RANK

PART

* 1 *

PIECES
OF THE
GAME

Prologue

I

When Jason Scott was ten, just before Britain exploded into revolution, his grandfather took him to visit London.

Since age four Jason had lived with his grandfather, Darius Scott, a real-estate speculator, who had retired at forty in order to enrich his relatives with his native wisdom.

Although he didn't remember them, the child was very aware of his famous parents. Darius had kept references to their deaths away from him, even ordering the household computers to withhold that information. When he was ten Jason found a way to access a newstape of their deaths in the fiery holocaust of Adam Scott's Osirium foundry.

The account seemed distant. It didn't affect him, not then. It was like discovering that one of his ancestors was a famous pirate, outlaw, or rumrunner. It added color to his dreams.

Earlier that year, Darius had enrolled Jason in a school for the gifted, the Argus School. He was due to start in the fall. Darius urged him to read above his age. They sat together for hours, discussing books, to the old man's secret glee. When Jason began asking questions he didn't want responsibility for answering, Darius began casting about for a good school.

By fortuitous coincidence he was contacted by a representative of the Argus School, who asked to test the boy. Darius agreed, and in due course he was contacted personally by Dr. Alfred Strubeck. Even he had heard of Strubeck, one of the most famous scientists in the world.

After talking with Strubeck he called Jason into his library, site of so many wonderful discussions. When the boy entered, the old man was thumbing through a hard copy of *Reader's Digest*.

All Scott boys started out small, but Jason was runtier than most, as Darius mentally noted for the umpteenth time.

But Jason hadn't allowed his size to hurt his character. The way Darius saw it, a boy could choose three paths under such circumstances: overcompensate and become a school-yard bully, undercompensate and become a victim, or take his limits as a challenge and improve himself. Jason loved Darius and wanted to please him, so he embarked on a bodybuilding program that made him the strongest boy in the neighborhood. But he was a peaceful boy; he believed in live and let live.

Jason was more than the apple of his grandfather's eye. He was his whole being.

"Jason, you ever sorry you were rich?"

"No, Grandfather."

"Anybody at school ever make you feel guilty about it, like you owed people something on account of it?"

"No sir."

"You never tried to lord it over anybody either, did you?"

"No sir!" Jason watched his grandfather intently, trying to figure out what he was getting at.

"You like living here with me, don't you?"

"Very much." He was puzzled and a little apprehensive.

"I like having you. But more important is to get you the best education. The schools you've gone to don't cut the mustard. They can't handle smart kids. I think I've found the right place."

"You're sending me away?"

Grandfather nodded, his jaw quivering. "All I have, everything I do, is for you. Since your parents died my every waking thought has been to help me raise you to be the best you can be.

"This Argus School—Strubeck knew your father. Adam asked him to look after teaching you. That's what Dr. Strubeck told me. Adam left money for you to go there. Not that you need the money! "I won't *make* you go. You're old enough to decide."

"I'll go, Grandfather." The boy turned away quickly so his guardian wouldn't see his tears.

"It's not until fall, son. Until then, I mean to take you on the damnedest trip any boy ever had!"

They traveled to Europe before Americans were forbidden to. In Paris Old Scott hiked Jason on his shoulders to see the Eiffel Tower. "Take a good gander, Jas. You may never see it again. Small loss. Damn thing looks like an oil derrick!"

They attended the Berlin Philharmonic, where Grandfather was heard to say that Ravel's "Bolero" was a pretentious version of "Ninety-nine Bottles of Beer."

They rode the hovercraft across the channel for a week in London, for a "real" performance of *Hamlet*, a play Darius greatly admired. During Act I he leaned over to Jason. "Watch that old guy, Polonius. He's the only smart one in the play."

These experiences might be wasted on the child, but Darius believed kids were like sponges: They soaked up anything you spilled on them. Besides, the Old World was in a golden sunset age. It was important to see it before night fell.

On the last week of their trip, when they were rambling about London's West End, Darius took Jason to an ancient film called *Things to Come*, which he had seen as a boy. He was a romantic, and seeing the science fiction classic in the restored film palace, the Odeon, was as much a treat for him as for the boy.

The Odeon was part rococo palace, with gilded pillars and cornices, part Edwardian cathouse, with red velvet seats, scarlet curtains, and crimson carpets interwoven with gold threads. Darius and Jason sank into the seats, looked up at the high domed ceiling, at baroque cherubim frolicking in a Handelian paradise.

The film, by the great director William Cameron Menzies, had rotten sound, and its model work was obvious to a sophisticated eye raised on successors to *Star Wars*. But it had magic and Jason found himself drawn into it.

The film reached its climax: The hero, Cabal, played brilliantly by Raymond Massey, prepared to launch his daughter and the son of his friend Passworthy around the moon with an electric space gun. Jason Scott was transfixed.

Passworthy challenged the worth of it all. "Oh God, is there ever to be any age of happiness? Is there never to be any rest?"

Jason pressed forward in the seat as Massey's magnificent profile was displayed. "Rest enough for the individual man," he intoned. "Too much, and too soon, and we call it Death. But for Man no rest and no ending. He must go on, conquest beyond conquest. First this little planet with its winds and ways, and then all the laws of mind and matter that restrain him. Then the planets about him, and at last out across the immensity to the stars. And when he has conquered all the deeps of space and all the mysteries of time, still he will be beginning."

Massey pointed at a great circular mirror that showed the spaceship traveling between two worlds. And as Sir Arthur Bliss's music rose tendentiously, he asked: "It is this—or that: all the universe or nothingness. Which shall it be, Passworthy? Which shall it be?"

For the next ten years, as Jason Scott grew from boy to man, he found himself, in many variations, asking that same question.

II

The boy Jacob scrunched miserably in a polyester chair. He had on new clothes, and he didn't like that. He was in a sanitized room, all metal and plastic office furniture, no books or windows, and he didn't like that. He was alone, but he liked that.

The door opened. A fresh-scrubbed, dimpled, freckled face peered in, belonging to a little boy (Jacob thought of boys his age as "little boys") of seven. The face was topped by golden curls. He looked like a sissy. He came in and smiled shyly.

He was running to fat. He seemed weak. In Jacob's old neighborhood, this little wimp wouldn't last a week.

"What's your name?" demanded Jacob.

The little boy smiled eagerly. "Sher-lock Mich-lan-ski."

"What's wrong? Can't you talk?"

"I—speak—English.   I—speak—it—slowly—to—get—it—right. I've—only—been—speaking—it—three—weeks."

"Cut it out around me! 'Sherlock.' What sort of name is that?"

"An English name."

"You English?"

"Polish."

"Then why have you got an English name?"

Sherlock shrugged. "What's your name?"

"Sit down and shut up! I'm tired of talking to you."

The door opened again. A short, muscular, red-haired boy entered. He took in the room with a glance.

"Hi!"

"Hi!" said Sherlock, delighted to meet someone friendly.

"I said hi!" said the boy to Jacob.

He put on his best sneer. "I heard you."

"You're not very polite."

"He's just grum—py," said Sherlock.

"Look out, fat-boy, I'll punch your lights out. I speak for myself. If this kid doesn't like it, he knows what he can do."

Sherlock's lower lip quivered.

"Don't mind him," said the redhead. "We'll talk. What's your name?"

Sherlock told him. "I'm Jason Scott. I'm happy to meet you." He held out his hand. Grandfather taught him to begin relationships with a handshake.

Jacob sneeringly mimicked Jason. "I'm happy to meet you!"

"You're very unpleasant," said Jason sternly.

Jacob rubbed his hands together. He was six inches taller than Jason. "Come here. I'll show you unpleasant."

"I don't start fights." Jason folded his arms.

"People who don't fight get beat up." Jacob advanced on him. He wouldn't hurt him much, enough to make him show respect.

Sherlock cowered in the corner. He knew his new friend was going to get plastered, and that his turn would come next.

"Can't we talk this over?" Jason stood his ground.

"After I whip you we can talk." He aimed a blow at his jaw. Somehow it didn't connect, landing harmlessly on his shoulder. He aimed another just under the breastbone. Jason slid effortlessly out of his way, but didn't try to land one of his own.

"Stand still!" hissed Jacob.

"That would be stupid." He stepped in under a blow aimed for his head, grabbed Jacob's arm, and catapulted him onto his back.

Jacob was breathing hard as he leaped to his feet. So far he had avoided street tactics. But he felt humiliated, so he lunged, hoping to grapple Jason. Each time he thought he had solid flesh, his fingers closed on air.

"Coward! Why don't you fight?"

"I don't want to." Jason laughed. "Will you stop?"

"You think you've won, don't you?" Jacob was panting.

"It was a draw."

Sherlock had the bad taste to snicker.

"I won't have you laughing at me." Jacob started toward Sherlock, who shrieked and burrowed into a chair.

"Wait," said Jason's quiet voice. Jacob's guts exploded in pain and he was on the floor, retching. Jason looked down at him.

"Sorry I hit you, but it seemed the only way. I guess some people have to be knocked down."

Jacob swallowed with care and breathed slowly.

"Am I going to have to hit you again?"

"Not if you don't want to," he said hoarsely.

"Good." He helped him stand. "I hope we won't have to do that again." He looked sternly at Sherlock. "And you, if you must have others fight your battles, better learn good manners."

"I'm sorry," said Sherlock, struggling not to laugh again.

"You never did tell me your name," said Jason.

Jacob started to frown, then relaxed. "Jacob Kane. And if it means so much to you, I'll even shake hands."

III

The snowball hit Jacob Kane full in the face. The hundred cold pinpricks were intensely exhilarating and he grinned, exposing teeth whose whiteness rivaled the new-fallen snow.

The three boys were building a snow fort under the massive pillar and bare branches of an old yellow birch. Jason had taken a moment from construction to throw a snowball at Jacob.

They were a strange trio. No one could quite say why they were "friends." Although they were more than that, and less.

They enrolled in the Argus School about the same time. Something brought them together, like cream on top of milk. . . .

They patted into place the walls of Jason's meticulously planned fort.

Jacob never questioned Jason's plans, although he was quick to challenge him on other things. Sometimes challenges led to blows. But Jacob was practical; he had learned to avoid fighting Jason. Besides, Jason was almost always right.

To the boys at the far side of the park, planted with eastern hemlock and sugar maple, the fort was a challenge. Particularly since it was in a supposedly neutral area. That was Jacob's idea, reluctantly agreed to by Jason, who felt guilty even when he broke silly playground rules. Jacob hoped it might rankle their rivals into attacking before they were ready. When they seemed to be taking their time, he mounted the battlements to taunt them. They took the bait and charged.

Inside the fort was a stack of tightly packed snowballs. The six boys charged into a barrage of them. They hurled their own missiles thick and fast, but when they stopped to make new ones they were perfect targets, especially for Jason's uncanny aim. They retreated out of range and pondered their next move.

While Jason kept watch, Jacob and Sherlock packed snowballs.

"I have an idea!" called Sherlock.

"Pipe down, fat-boy." Jacob ignored Jason's stern look. He knew he could get away with some jibes before Jason enforced his displeasure.

"What is it, Sherlock?" asked Jason.

"We need slings. Not the forked sticks. The ancient kind."

"That'd put them in a tough spot. Can we make one quickly?"

"I could go home and make one and bring it back." Sherlock didn't board at school. His mother wouldn't have let him out of sight that long. She kept a home several blocks from the school.

Jason wasn't sure. Sherlock couldn't run fast. The other boys might capture him. "What do you think, Jacob?"

Jacob rested his sharp chin on the ice wall. Across the park their adversaries were up to something. "If Fat—er, Sherlock makes it, we'll have to hold the fort. One of us'll have to make snowballs. Not that ᵢ think we can't. Those jerks are too stupid to do anything except attack head-on."

"You always underestimate the intelligence of other people."

"Usually I'm right."

"But when you're wrong, it's a disaster. It's better to give others credit for being smart, then if they come up with a good plan, you can beat them anyway."

"Okay, Napoleon, what's your plan?"

"I don't have one," said Jason sheepishly. "But I think we better let Sherlock make the slings. It might give us an edge."

"Let me make the snowballs. I'll pack 'em nice and hard."

Sherlock vanished over the snow rampart and reappeared, running faster than they had ever seen him run before. Their besiegers jeered because they thought he was running away.

Jacob handed up ammunition, and the "enemy" attacked with fierce, shrill yells.

They had buckets that steamed in the cold air. "They've got hot water!" yelled Jason. "Better help me throw!"

Jacob climbed up next to Jason, who scored the first hit, on a short towhead named Spikey. Hit in the face, he cried out and fell, writhing in pain. His friends gathered around him and he put his mittened hand to his head.

"What's the matter?" called Jason.

"That snowball had a rock in it!" screamed Spikey.

Jason looked at Jacob, who unflinchingly stared back.

"It stopped them, didn't it?"

"This is a game! You don't hit people with rocks in a game."

"Tell them it was an accident." Jacob was obviously enjoying himself, as he always did when he caused trouble.

"I won't." Jason looked at Spikey. "I'm sorry, Jacob put the rock in the snowball on purpose."

"Jacob Kane, you stink!"

"Come here and say that." Jacob leaned over the wall. He had beaten Spikey up several times.

"The game's over for today," said Jason. He jumped from the wall. "You guys won, fair and square. You captured the fort."

"Come on, Jason, that's a good fort. It would've taken us a long time to take it," said one of the boys.

"I worked my butt off to build that thing!" said Jacob.

"All of us built it, but you spoiled it. We'll make another."

"*You* build it. You and Fatty can spend all day tomorrow making another, but I won't help. I don't team up with suckers."

"Act this way, you won't team up with anyone," said Jason.

"I don't need any of you."

Spikey came as close to Jacob as he dared, pretty sure the other boys would defend him. "Jacob Kane, you stink! You stink!"

Jacob regarded him coldly. "You have a limited vocabulary."

Sherlock ran up, breathless, a finished sling in his hand. "What's going on?"

"Hi, Fatty!" said Ray Banner, one of the boys. "Came back after the danger was over, huh?"

"I was making something." Sherlock was suddenly shy.

"Yeah, a dozen hamburgers and a gallon of chocolate milk."

"I've decided something," said Jacob.

"What? To leave the human race?" said Ray Banner.
Jacob offered his hand to a cautious Sherlock. "I'm sorry, I've been a jerk. You're smarter than all of us; even smarter than me. You deserve better treatment. From now on, You're 'Sherlock.' "
"I prefer 'Sherry.' "
"Sherry it is." When Banner snickered, Jacob turned to him. "Think that's funny, Banner old chum?"
"I think it's hysterical. Sherry's a girl's name."
"Now it's a boy's name."
"Just 'cause you say so don't make it so. He's still Fatty."
"I thought that might be your attitude. But you see, if I don't call him names, no one does."
"Think again, Kane."
Jacob smiled and brought his fist up sharply, knocking Ray Banner to the ground, where he lay for several moments.
"Do you get my point, Banner?"
"Yes." Ray Banner spit some blood on the snow, then got up.
"Do the rest of you?" He was answered by a ragged volley of sullen affirmatives. "Okay, now beat it!"
Under the tree it was deserted except for the three of them. Sherlock looked around him with wonder.
"Jason," said Kane, "I want you to know I meant it about Sherry. I didn't say it to impress you."
"I know. I still want to be friends. I just wish you'd try to change. You're too vicious, too selfish, too ruthless. You've got so much going for you, why do you act this way?"
"I always want an extra edge. I can't change what I am."
"You know we won't let you in the games again."
"Back home, we don't have games. Living's our game." He looked old for a boy. "Life has no rules but winning."

Chapter

* 1 *

The first century in space, called the Neo-Columbian Age of Exploration, the Kennedy-Armstrong Impulse, and (by laissez-faire/libertarian enthusiasts) Adam Smith in Space, almost imitated tenth-century Norse who abandoned their colonies in North America. In the decades after Apollo 11, Neil Armstrong's giant leap for mankind ended in a stumble, as far as America was concerned. The U.S. was increasingly hostile to space and technology.
        —Nathan Kilhock, NASA/SED's Centennial History

*   The McClaren Era began with the terrorist hydrogen bombing of San Diego, and the amok power satellite that burned a few acres of Midwest farmland. It's unclear exactly when the senator's influence ended. His isolationist, antitechnology movement outlived his fall by at least twenty years. A case can be made that it lasted until the Shefferton presidency when the Sunside Project was launched.*
        —Grenoble Milner, America: The Third Century

*   No one has yet coined a name for the late conflict. What might have been World War III was more like a latter-day Thirty Years War. Conventional (except the bombing of Kiev), its shifting alliances were reminiscent of Renaissance Italy. Germany, the Ukraine, and Siberia were crisscrossed by a dozen armies. Europe and Asia invaded Russia. The Genetic Communists repelled them and recovered most pre–World War II territory. The Americans, as usual, avoided getting their hair*

*mussed in this Great War. Perhaps to them belongs the
privilege of naming the holocaust.*

*In the tornado's eye, Fortress America was shielded by laser
ABMs and killer satellites. She overawed the Latin American
states into signing the Pan-American Pact, creating the Lines
of Demarcation. Isolated, Canada joined America in the Act of
Union. Constitutional amendment forbade interhemispheric
commerce.*

*—A European Looks at America,
by Otto Bourbon, honorable member of the
Constituent Assembly of Deputies of United Europe*

*Sacrifices of industrialists like Adam Scott allowed Strubeck
and others to continue working, despite attacks by McClaren
supporters. Today Strubeck is acknowledged the greatest
scientist of his generation. No wonder that rumors he left
behind a revolutionary formula to create food directly from
sunlight generated such excitement. . . .*

—Rodney Woole, Strubeck, Man and Scientist

*The Strubeck equations exist. They are available to the
people of the world. This formula, my friends, will realize a
dream as old as science: direct transformation of the sun's
energy into food. At the same time another dream will be
realized: the end of hunger. This process, called artificial
photosynthesis, unravels the mystery of how plants create
food.*

—From a speech by President Jeffrey Shefferton

Except that it was a lie.

Jeffrey Shefferton reflected on that grim fact as he walked in the predawn
hours through the woods of the presidential compound forty miles outside
of Deseret. The land had been donated by his friend Charles Macadew,
Colorado's senior senator.

Pine needles crunched under his loggers boots, and the wet nose of his
red Labrador retriever, Dusty, brushed his hand as he climbed a steep path
that wound through a thick copse of pines.

At the crest of a hill he allowed his escort of Secret Service agents to catch their breaths. He was the largest chief executive in history, with legs so long that even men in splendid shape had to scramble to keep up.

He glanced at his wrist biomonitor. The data it received from biobots in his blood was also monitored by his navy physician, an intrusion required by federal law. He noted with satisfaction that his heart rate had hardly changed during the brisk walk from the cabin, although he had burned two hundred calories.

He had crept from his sleeping wife's side at three in the morning and had roused the agents who had been relaxing in the lodge's large, comfortable den.

In the dark he heard an agent speak into a communicator. He heard "corn dodger," the code for Senator Macadew. His own was "quarterback." The vice president's was "swan."

"Mr. President, the senator wonders if you'd like some company this morning? Perhaps a little duck hunting?"

"Tell him we'll meet him up here. Meanwhile, I'll indulge in a little stargazing."

The real reason the president was abroad was insomnia. The flight in from Washington had contributed, as had the launch of the Russian superbattleship *Aurora*, as did the impending launch of the space shuttle *Sally Ride* and her companions.

The *Aurora*'s railgun technology was unperfected in America, where payloads were limited to what could be lifted by a conventional booster. The U.S. was preparing to introduce the GILGAMESH aerospace plane, which could take off like an airplane and boost into orbit at Mach 25, but the Soviets had gained a strategic edge at a critical moment.

He looked up. His close-cropped blond hair was cast by starlight into a corona. He found Midway, a space station visible to the naked eye. With it as reference he looked a few degrees down and imagined a point of light: the Russian battleship. After the launch, *Sally Ride* would be in that quadrant.

With no moon the Milky Way glazed the insides of the overturned bowl of the sky. One of science's achievements of the new century was to allow Americans to rediscover the sky.

The Meklinburg Supernova had kindled the interest of millions. And in cities hit by the Millennium Riots, blackouts lasted for days, and urbanites saw the stars for the first time. The lonely fight astronomers had waged against encroaching city lights was joined by the masses.

Scientists developed streetlights that cast almost no reflected glare into the night sky, while providing adequate illumination directly below. It was now possible to fly between urban airports and not glimpse a light on the land below.

The short, rotund figure of Senator Charles Ellsworth Macadew appeared, dressed in brown camouflage overalls, an oiled cotton coat, and a foam-lined baseball-style cap. Hip boots rubbed together at the thighs as he walked. He carried a twelve-gauge smoothbore shotgun over his shoulder. He hadn't shaved; his ruddy cheeks were dusted with frost. "Jeff, tell yer bodyguards it ain't likely I'll try to assassinate the president."

Shefferton nodded to the agent, who handed Macadew a box of shot shells.

"Can't be too careful!" Macadew took a swig off a pocket flask. "Wal, Jeff, ready to bag a coupla canvasbacks before the launch? We'll have a ringside seat a few miles from the space center. Fish and Game has done a great job rehabilitating that new lake area. You'd swear Lake Deseret had been there a million years, instead of ten. Some of the best waterfowlin' I've seen."

"No chameleon cloth overalls? Holodecoys? Laser-sighted shotguns?"

"Might as well fly over the marsh with a phalanx Gatlin' gun. But the decoys I got are so lifelike we can eat 'em if we get bad luck!"

"I can use the diversion."

"The most use to you will be gettin' your eyes off the printed page. Somewhere you can't even pick up a cereal box."

Shefferton was a prodigious reader, a passionate technophile who could engage men of science on a level astounding for a layman, and almost unheard-of in a politician.

"Charley, do you have an extra set of hunting duds?"

"Extra, no. What I got are huntin' togs exactly your size, special-ordered from L.L. Bean. Follow me!"

As they walked toward Macadew's cabin, Shefferton talked in monosyllables. He was in a dark mood, that morning of the launch, brooding about the Sunside Project.

His fascination with science had made him grasp eagerly for the solution he thought the Strubeck equations offered. He was crushed when he finally met the celebrated scientists Sherlock Michlanski and Dorian Nye and learned that what he—what the world—thought was untrue. The world thought the Strubeck equations would feed her starving billions. What the equations actually offered was a second chance for mankind. A chance to spread to the stars.

Strubeck's equations looked at the universe and predicted perturbations, "dimples" in the fabric of probability near large masses. Using those dimples to bend probability, it ought to be possible to alter the reality of mass. To make it more probable for a mass, like the mass of a spaceship, to be somewhere entirely different from where it was. A few light-years away, for instance.

Shefferton alternately felt like Judas and Prometheus. Undeniably there were many ways to approach the problem. Wars and famines of the past fifty years had drained the race. Populations were high, but infrastructures were fragile. Mankind had strength left for one supreme effort. But which direction?

Probes secretly launched years before had found worlds orbiting the nearby star Tau Ceti. Worlds where pioneers could escape earth, and be her salvation. The fragile infrastructures might survive if pressure was relieved and healthy colonies began sending nourishment back to the mother world.

Shefferton, Michlanski, and Nye had taken it upon themselves to make that decision for America and, ultimately, for the world.

Churchill described democracy as the worst system there is, except for all the others. But its deadly flaw was the inability to act during a crisis, when quick, bold decisions are called for. Shefferton had considered, briefly, going public and offering the Strubeck equations to the world as a gateway to a new frontier. But America was just recovering from a bout of antitechnology. It would take much debate to persuade Congress, much less the Great Powers, of the wisdom of pursuing a star drive.

Add to that the renascent Unified Soviet State, reaching for power on the high ground of space; Greater Asia, barely kept from anarchy by a plutocratic dynasty of statist capitalists; and the Union of Black Africa, whose messianic Juba Aman Dana, "the Leopard," was headed for nuclear Armageddon with South Africa.

Time was vital, the president reasoned. There was no time for debate. The Sunside Project had to be the highest priority of his administration. Nothing else was as important. Nothing.

The senator told an off-color joke that made the Secret Service men howl and jolted the president out of his reverie.

Shefferton put his arm around Macadew. "You're good for me, Charley. Thanks for showing up."

"No problemo, Jeff. I promised Mayfield I'd watch the launch in person. I didn't say I wouldn't do some duck shootin' too."

"You talked to Sheridan, then?"

"Since yesterday, no."

Yesterday Shefferton had strained relations with Macadew and another friend, Sheridan Mayfield, secretary of space exploration and development. He had hoped to talk to Mayfield today.

Mayfield and Macadew had questioned the president's decision to allow the Soviets to put the battleship *Aurora* into space. Once the battleship became armed, it would take a war to neutralize it.

But they had swallowed their doubts to support him.

Macadew's cabin was on a hill surrounded by the dark presences of firs and pines. He showed the agents where to find coffee, then he showed Shefferton the hunting clothes.

Shefferton slipped into camouflaged coveralls. Macadew sat on a camp chair and puffed on a Cuban maduro.

"Charley, is Amanda up here with you?"

"No, she's back at the Sleeping Moon. She's not feelin' so good the last few days. I'm goin' to have to insist she see the doc."

The president saw how tightly Macadew's mouth was drawn. Did he suspect that Amanda might be diagnosed with Rogue Cancer?

That mutated form of the malady man had once almost eliminated was the twenty-first century's great leveler. The worst health problem since AIDS, it struck without warning and killed within weeks. Unidentified illnesses were automatically suspected as Rogue Cancer.

"Charley, I know it was hard for you and Sheridan yesterday. I appreciated it."

Macadew exhaled a cloud of bluish smoke. "I read in some tomfool newstape last week how I was 'valued by the White House as a sage and political strategist.' " He smiled what the press called "Macadew's killer smile." "I knew it was horsedump, Jeff. I found out how right I was yesterday! Tha's okay, I don't 'spect you to take my advice. I'm jus' happy to give it."

Shefferton bent to tie the laces on his hip boots. "Forget for a moment that you opposed my decision on the Russian battleship. Politically, how will it play?"

Macadew watched the red Labrador industriously lick its paws.

"Wal, sir! You've decided that the Russian bear is a nice puppy dog, like Dusty, that wandered into camp. But the danger is that your pup might grow up and bite you on the ass someday. If he does, best start duckin' every bad decision you ever made."

"You don't know everything I know," snapped Shefferton. "You do know we can't let anything jeopardize the cooperation the Soviets are giving the Sunside Project and the Food Treaty."

The Sunside Project was of paramount importance, he thought, although she might become a *casus belli* as the Soviet battleship's maneuvers made the shuttles pawns in a power game.

The president finished donning his hunting outfit. He picked up a well-oiled twelve-gauge shotgun. He looked at his friend.

"Charley, are you ready to shoot some ducks?"

Several hours later, the president and the senator had settled comfortably in a duckblind. They watched the sun climb up over the immense man-made lake, but they had so far waited in vain for any waterfowl to drift by close enough to shoot.

Finally, a flock of canvasbacks settled in the reeds. The two men were preparing to scare them up when a Secret Service agent interrupted them and spooked the ducks into early flight.

"This better be good, Max," said the president in a deceptively low, mild voice.

"It's not good at all, sir," said the agent. "It's Secretary Mayfield. Someone has tried to blow up the *Sally Ride*."

Chapter

* 2 *

Nov. 21—*Washington Post*—Progressive Nationalist senators Charles Macadew of Colorado and Estes K. Brainaird of New Columbia today cosponsored a bill to repeal the Thirty-first Amendment, which was passed twenty-five years ago.

Last year candidate Jeffrey Shefferton said repeal of the amendment was his first priority.

The amendment reads: "The lines of Demarcation shall be Meridian 30 degrees West and Meridian 169 degrees West, including all oceans and territories north of the Panama Canal. Within these boundaries no merchant or military craft of foreign origin, neither land, sea, nor air, shall be permitted, except those member nations of the Pan-American Pact."

Arizona Republic—Reporters are getting contradictory stories about what happened at Deseret Space Center earlier today.

> We know an explosion occurred near one of the shuttles. Minutes later an experimental GILGAMESH aerospace plane took off on an unauthorized flight, and crashed in the Yucatán peninsula.

I

"Tell the president I'd rather he not come to the center now. That's right: stay away!" Secretary of Space Development and Exploration Sheridan Mayfield emphasized the last two words as he spoke into a holocube on his desk. "Tell Jeffrey he'll just get in the way. I mean that in the most respectful way. But it's better that he and Macadew stay out on the marsh and leave this to me."

The president's chief of staff looked shocked. This was a bit much even for Mayfield. He raised his eyebrows in a supercilious way that put Mayfield's teeth on edge, and spoke to someone offscreen. He looked at Mayfield. "The president says he's sorry he bothered you. He wonders if a bit later you might call him?"

"Absolutely! But tell him to watch the news conference on the boob cube. That'll explain everything. Bye!"

The chief of staff faded.

Mayfield turned to look through the thick glassteel windows of his temporary office in the space center, at three squat space shuttles. *Sally Ride*, in the center, stabbed at the Southwest sky reflected in the turquoise shield of man-made Lake Deseret, also called the Sea of Cibola. A column of red smoke rose from between the base of the center shuttle and the gantry. The shuttle, tall as a skyscraper, had four stages of solid fuel to drive a 120,000-kilo payload, including one hundred and fifty passengers.

The source of the smoke was the remains of the psychotic who had stood on the gantry with a bomb strapped to his back, just before he fell off and exploded in midair.

Mayfield was balding, fiftyish, with a touch of Churchill, and that Briton's mix of strengths and foibles. He had a tortoiseshell where others were soft, vulnerabilities where most were strong. Only friends guessed that his irascibility was armor against a brutal world.

His closest friend, the president, once described him as a romantic who'd had his heart stepped on too many times. But Shefferton also recognized his innate toughness and had used him as a troubleshooter and the president's eyes and ears.

Mayfield knew he was presuming on that trust in telling the president, in the most respectful way possible, to mind his own business and let Mayfield mind his.

Right now, his most important task was to damage-control the news release of the sabotage attempt and to get the three spacecraft of the Sunside Project launched without delay. That meant breaking the rules. A top-security space center had been penetrated. The press and Congress would demand that the project be put on hold until an investigation was completed.

Mayfield didn't intend to fall into that trap. He intended to release the facts of the sabotage attempt quickly and, before anyone had a chance to protest, launch the three shuttles.

He left his office and walked through a glassteel tube that crossed over the huge indoor terminal where several hundred scientists and technicians made up a tapestry of threads from sixty-three states: the best minds of the world's largest nation. They were young, averaging middle thirties— fifteen below the U.S. median. Most had been educated in an environment hostile to science, which added a sense of apprehension as they looked through glassteel walls at the smoke of an explosion that had barely spared them.

As far as Mayfield was concerned, he had come too close to losing a lot of things today, including the prototype GILGAMESH scramjets, now guarded by a battalion of space marines.

The new-generation shuttle was a hypersonic jet that could accelerate into low earth orbit. The prototype had been built by a consortium of Rockwell, Harley-Davidson, and Gigatex.

Mayfield hoped they were the first of a fleet. He considered shuttles as obsolete as paddle wheelers. They would have been phased out long ago if the McClarenites hadn't been in charge.

Mayfield rushed to the infirmary, where Jason Scott, project manager of the Sunside Project, was cleaning up, after having almost been slain climbing the gantry in pursuit of the would-be saboteur. Scott's face and muscular arms were covered with abrasions and hairline cuts caked with black, dried blood. He sat while a doctor tended the worst cuts. Even in repose, Scott was an heroic figure: stocky, a face chiseled with the simple strokes of a Rodin, a red mane bisected by a thatch of white. He had recently been in a fight for his life, yet his blue, bottomless eyes reflected only serenity.

He looked up and smiled at Mayfield. "Hi, Sheridan."

"That was the goddamnedest stupid thing I've ever seen a man do, Jason!" snapped Mayfield, not about to let Scott get the upper hand. "Also one of the most magnificent. You're the hero of the hour. We better trot you out for the holovision screens before your hour runs out. The news conference starts in ten minutes.''

The doctor tending Scott looked up with annoyance. "Secretary Mayfield, I've got a good half hour of work here—"

Mayfield held up his hand. "Doctor, you may have heard that I am a sonofabitch and that I generally get my way. If so, then you have been accurately informed. Kindly bandage the bleeding wounds and leave the rest. I want the world to see Jason Scott's wounds.''

"What about me?" said Jacob Kane, a tall, cadaverous man, whose hatchet face was etched by a still-oozing gash just under his black hairline. Kane, the second most important man of the project, next to Scott, had risked his life along with Scott, and had saved him at the last moment by knocking the bomb-carrying saboteur off the gantry with the tail of his single-man chopper.

"I expect lots of people will be happy to see you suffer, Jacob," said Mayfield half seriously. "But, of course, I want you at the news conference. And Sherlock—and Dorian Nye.''

"What's the rush?'' Scott winced when the doctor applied a butterfly bandage to a shrapnel cut along the inside of his arm.

"I want those three birds into space before someone has a chance to call for an investigation.''

"But the FBI is sending a team already. Someone diverted a planeload here that was on its way to Texas,'' said Kane.

"Not *someone*, Kane,'' said Mayfield. "Me.''

Kane watched Mayfield's face closely, beginning to get the inklings of a mind as Machiavellian as his own. He grinned crookedly. "Then you've undoubtedly met Special Deputy Director Roger Ferdinand before. I understand that he's one of the biggest swines on the federal payroll.''

"You're right, Kane. You'll like him. Mr. Ferdinand doesn't know it yet, but he's going to help me buy time. Now, let's get out to the main gate.''

II

"Ladies and gentlemen of the press, I have a short statement about this morning's incident, and then I'll take questions,'' said Jason Scott, pale under his freckles from loss of blood.

Scott stood behind an improvised lectern at the main gate. Behind him sat Secretary Mayfield, Jacob Kane, the Falstaffian physicist Sherlock

Michlanski, and Dorian Nye, the balding, nondescript physicist who had once been teacher to all three of the young geniuses.

Every holovision camera dwelt on Scott, drawn by the reddish lines that crisscrossed his face as if penned by a mad cartographer. As Mayfield had said, Scott was the hero of the hour, and not just because of his most recent act of heroism.

Scott had a reputation as a super-manager and troubleshooter. Mayfield had chosen him and his Prometheus Enterprises to run the Sunside Project after Scott almost single-handedly saved the pioneering Challenger Core Tap in the Caribbean from disaster. It didn't hurt that the Challenger had turned into a mother lode that made its owner, Rita Duce, of the Tectonics Corporation, one of the richest people on earth.

"Ninety minutes ago, four unknown persons attempted to sabotage this morning's launch. Three were disguised as maintenance crew members with phony IDs. Two were discovered by Jacob Kane. They resisted and had to be killed. A third saboteur died attempting to explode a bomb next to the *Sally Ride*.

"A fourth saboteur, sent to create a diversion for the others, broke into the compound housing the experimental GILGAMESH aerospace planes. His attempt to destroy the planes failed, but he escaped in one of them. It had enough fuel to get him into suborbital flight. The air force shot him down over the Yucatán peninsula. He is presumed dead."

"Mr. Scott," asked the reporter for the *Arizona Republic*, "any idea who's behind the attempted sabotage?"

Scott smiled disarmingly. "Mr. Hayes, you know I can't answer that even if I know the answer. All I can give you and your audience is the standard 'We're working on all possible leads.' "

The next speaker was Michlanski, the *enfant terrible* of the scientific community. Michlanski was an outspoken maverick, with two Nobel Prizes for physics.

The rotund scientist's blond hair and Viking beard were askew as if from an electrical storm. He still wore civies: a frayed checkered coat, yellow and puce tie, and purple flowered handkerchief that regurgitated from his top pocket. Although he weighed over two hundred pounds, the impression was of tightly wound energy.

Michlanski, comfortable in his role as a celebrity, played the press like a violin. He laughed and joked, as though the morning's events were trivial in the extreme.

"Ladies and gentlemen, I just completed checking for instrument damage. I'm pleased to say that our most sensitive, also our most expensive, equipment survived the ordeal unscathed. They were far enough away from the blast to be unaffected.''

"How can you be so sure? It's been such a short time since the sabotage attempt,'' said the Science News Network reporter Perle Gracie, who was something of an *enfant terrible* himself in the broadcasting business.

Michlanski drew himself up to his full height, transforming from playful puppy to omnipotent professor, the most celebrated physicist since Hawking. "I designed these tremendously costly instruments. They are highly sensitive, particularly the gravity and hypercharge meters. The underlying characteristic of sensitive instruments is that they *are* sensitive. If they had been harmed, I would know.''

The Science News reporter followed up: "Professor, doesn't this underscore the folly of having you yourself, one of the premier scientists in the world, exposed on what may be a highly hazardous mission? Your presence is not essential to the overall mission of the Sunside Project, the production of food energy from sunlight. Couldn't an assistant collect data for your physics experiments? Aren't you grandstanding a little on what may be just a sideshow of the project?''

"But what a sideshow!'' cracked Michlanski. "This extends the inquiry into the nature of things begun five hundred years ago. Ever since the mechanical universe of Newton, ever since Einstein and company opened up the can of worms of quantum mechanics, we've searched for smaller and smaller particles and for a system to link the forces of the universe into a unified field theory.

"Yet every time we identified a new smallest particle, another one 'popped up.' The same thing happened with forces in the universe. We first identified four: electromagnetism, gravity, and the strong and weak nuclear forces. We seemed close to a theory encompassing them all. But glitches screwed up our calculations, like the fact that there seemed to be much more matter in the universe than we could account for, based on gravity. Then we discovered hypercharge, macrogravity, and primeval nuance. Now there are scientists, and I believe I was the first to posit this, who believe we will continue to discover new basic forces, much as we continue to discover new elements. We need a theory to accommodate an infinity of forces, an infinity of smallness and an infinity of largeness. This is truly looking at the Big Picture. That is no sideshow. It is the most wonderful toy any boy ever got for Christmas!''

The dapper reporter for the *New York Hourly News* raised his hand. "Professor Michlanski, ten months ago, at the U.S. conference of physicists, you made a speech advocating a national effort to discover faster-than-light travel. It would be fair to say that this rather quixotic dream has been overshadowed by the reality of the Sunside Project. Doesn't this spell the end for FTL when even its most visionary prophet comes down to earth from his star-drive fantasy to join the vital project to feed humanity?''

Michlanski held out his hands. "If there's a question in there, I fail to detect it!"

Mayfield stepped up next to the Polish physicist. "That question is a bit unfair to Professor Michlanski," he said. "The championing of FTL is not like believing in UFOs. It is a genuine school of thought in the world of physics. Up until a few years ago, many physicists thought FTL was feasible."

"It's not a sizable percentage any longer, is it?"

"No."

"Is your department working on FTL?"

"No," said Mayfield lamely.

"Thanks for your assistance, Mr. Secretary!" said Michlanski, buying the moment back with a chuckle and broad wink that brought laughter from the crowd as he took his seat.

"Mr. Scott, or Mr. Kane," asked the *Washington Post*, "please describe your role in this morning's fighting, or whatever you want to call it."

"I'll take that one," said Kane, whose abrasive voice sounded even more like a hacksaw on metal than usual. "Early this morning, Jason Scott and I learned that saboteurs were on the *Sally Ride*, which had already loaded half of her passengers—"

"Mr. Kane," interrupted the *Post*, braving Kane's stare of annoyance, "exactly how did you find out about the saboteurs?"

"We were tipped off. And save yourself the breath of asking who." He paused, daring someone else to interrupt. "I went into the shuttle's maintenance shaft, where I found two saboteurs. I killed one and followed the other to where he had planted an explosive device in a spot that would have guaranteed destruction of the shuttle and the death of a few hundred people. I killed that gentleman also and disarmed the bomb. However, a third person escaped onto the gantry with a bomb strapped to his back.

"At this point, Jason climbed the gantry after the bomber, at considerable risk to himself, since the man was trying to kill him with a laser. Jason did not fire back for fear of igniting the liquid oxygen fuel. I had reached the ground by now, and, seeing that Jason had gotten himself into a possibly deadly situation, I took a single-man helicopter and attacked the bomber. I knocked him off the gantry. He was so upset that he went to pieces."

Kane was the only one to smile at his grisly joke.

"You don't feel that you're perhaps being too modest in not taking enough credit for stopping the saboteurs?" asked one of the cable news reporters with barely suppressed sarcasm.

Scott stepped forward. "If anything, Jacob is being modest. I credit him with saving the *Sally Ride*, and the project." Scott avoided looking at Mayfield, who was not pleased at his so cavalierly passing credit onto Kane, who was not nearly as sympathetic a figure as Scott.

"*Anchorage Herald*," said a short, intense-looking, middle-aged reporter. "I'd like to follow up on the question asked Professor Michlanski, and direct it to Dr. Nye. Sir, don't you feel apprehensive that perhaps this morning's sabotage attempt might have been aimed at you? You were the target of an assassination attempt in January."

Most of the micronewspaper and holovision reporters remembered. They had been at Armstrong International when Nye's double returned from Red Britain or had watched the footage, which was eerily reminiscent of old films of the Kennedy assassination.

Nye pawed absently at the beads of sweat on his shiny dome and stepped hesitantly to the lectern. He was quite shy, mainly because of a stutter that had afflicted him all his life.

"N-naturally, I f-feel some degree of fear. However, I think events ·have shown I am far s-safer in space than at home."

Sheridan Mayfield frowned and took the lectern. "I should point out that no evidence links today's sabotage with the attempt on Dr. Nye's life earlier this year. The presidential committee I chaired concluded there was no conspiracy in the assassination attempt, and that the killer, Lloyd Hunning, acted alone."

Mayfield looked at his finger watch. "Since we do intend to launch shortly, I must get our crew ready. Any more questions about the investigation you can direct to Special Deputy Director Roger Ferdinand, who has landed at the space center."

"But how can you conduct an investigation once the shuttles are launched?" demanded the *Sacramento Bee*.

"Simple. None of the crew members are under suspicion."

"Sir," asked the *New York Times*, "if the people demand an investigation before the shuttles launch, how can you not obey?"

"You people constantly remind us that the world is in the midst of a famine—"

The Santa Bella blight, during its brief reign, had destroyed most of the crops in the equatorial zone.

"People face starvation!" said Mayfield sternly. "We don't have time for trumped-up tribunals to give you ladies and gentlemen of the press something to write about.

"You reporters answer to the people. I answer to the president. Unless I'm served with a court order in the next hour, I intend to launch as planned. Thank you."

Chapter

* 3 *

When I examine myself and my methods of thought I come to the conclusion that the gift of fantasy has meant more to me than my talent for absorbing positive knowledge.

—Albert Einstein.

I

Space travel was something new to Sherlock Michlanski.

The physics, mechanics, and formulae of space travel were second nature to him, but he had never experienced it firsthand. He was like the Portuguese Prince Henry the Navigator who sent countless ships to find the route to the Indies, but remained a landlubber. Until now. Michlanski wasn't sure yet that he liked it much.

His heroically proportioned body had been cruelly strained by the high g's of takeoff. Now that the shuttle had attained low earth orbit, he found himself in his tiny cabin, unable to sleep off the effects.

While the other passengers slept, Michlanski fought a queasy stomach brought on by weightlessness by poring over his electric chalkboard, which he had stuck onto the bulkhead. He already missed his rambling mansion on Wolverine Island in Lake Michigan. He missed the water pummeling the beach and wind through the pines. He missed his mainframe computer, Leonardo.

His stylus hissed on the electric blackboard as he covered it with crabbed, foreign-looking symbols for concepts that were beyond most ideas under discussion in the world of physics. The round-faced scientist, who, in certain light, resembled the terribly shy boy who was a Columbia University freshman at fifteen, frowned at the equations, then made them vanish with a frustrated twist of a dial.

"No!" he said out loud.

There was a knock at the door.

"Yes?" Michlanski was surprised that someone else was up.

"Sh-Sherlock, I heard v-voices." Dorian Nye floated in the doorway. As titular head of the research arm of the Sunside Project, Nye was technically Michlanski's boss. In reality he carried the administrative load so Michlanski wasn't bothered with trivia. Besides, the question of boss and subordinate didn't really matter. They had known each other since Michlanski was a child and Nye his teacher.

"I'm arguing with God over the structure of the universe, old teacher. He refuses to take my suggestions."

"Sherlock, you should sleep."

"I can't. The math bounces around my head. So far, I've had the mental maturity to resist the alluring, more complex paths through this jungle. Sometimes, following the elegant, simple line of reasoning is the hardest, because it is so easy."

"You always were a dilettante, Sherry. Your greatest asset is that you regard the universe as a big, beautiful toy, to take apart and look at the pieces. That's also dangerous."

"Precisely," said Michlanski. He absently whirled the dial of a dedicated bulkhead holowindow installed to fight claustrophobia with realistic earthscapes. "The beautiful, rich, side paths beckon like South Sea islands." He brought up a scene of waves lapping on a Tahitian beach. "Yet, what I believe to be the true path is bleak and pure, like the Arctic." The scene changed to a glacier, shearing off thousands of tons of ice into the sea. Nye shivered in imagined cold.

"Why do you assume the simpler path is the correct one?"

"*You* translated Alfred's equations. I read them and say, 'Of course, it's so simple, a child should be able to conceive of it.' "

"D-during the last months, when he talked about his theory, I often lost the thread of his reasoning."

"You don't grasp what I'm saying! The equations are but an introduction to truths so simple that they suggest that the universe is not ingenious but ingenuous. That the proper route for me is the intuitive, rather than the rational. Strike out on my own, don't try to map the territory before I explore it.''

''You sound more philosopher than mathematician, Sherry.''

''I feel like an artist inventing reality as I go along. And I'm scaring the dickens out of myself!''

''That doesn't sound like you.''

Michlanski laid his shaggy blond head on the table. ''This is the greatest thing I will ever do in my life, Dorian. Everything else was a preparation for this. I know it's hard to believe, but I often feel inadequate to the task. Am I physically and mentally capable to come up with the answer? Alfred built a big and beautiful mansion on a hill and gave us the keys, but he didn't say where the road to the mansion is.''

Nye put his hand on Sherlock's forehead and stroked it like an adoring father. ''You've got time, Sherlock. Rest now.''

He piloted Michlanski over to the bunk, arranged a blanket over him, and strapped him in. Poor Sherlock, he thought. Such a brilliant point of light, yet so vulnerable. In a way, Nye was grateful he had not been given such a mind. He could appreciate the beauty of the universe without being tormented by the necessity to find its secrets. He turned out the light and returned to his cabin.

II

The spicy smells and green filtered sunlight of the Quintana Roo had swallowed up the smells and sights of the one-sided battle when Mel Hardrim and Kirsten Fale were picked up by a USAF dirigible.

The men employed by the billionaire industrialist Horatius Krebs had been completely surprised by the raiders who crossed into Mexico in swift, low-flying helicopter gunships with almost no radar signature and struck like desert rattlers.

Krebs was known to employ some of the world's most wanted men: reject mercenaries; veterans of the Drang War and the European campaign. So the strike force of FBI agents who were not officially in Mexico didn't waste time on niceties: No one had their rights read to them. No one was taken prisoner once he drew a weapon. The fight was short, nasty and brutal. With no casualties for the attackers.

They were departing as quickly as they had arrived. Leaving a Krebs who, if not chastened, had something to think about.

The airship dropped into a clearing, picked up Fale, Hardrim, and the dozen anonymous FBI agents, with orders to take them to San Antonio, no questions asked.

Hardrim sat cross-legged on the cargo deck, leaning against his backpack, alternately drinking from a canteen of lethal native mescal and puffing on a deadly local cigarette. He was big, burly, and immensely appealing.

"You do like living dangerously," said Kirsten Fale, who was stretched out, propped up on her elbow, her coppery hair coursing gloriously over her shoulders, her green eyes flirting with him.

"It's the only way to be." His clear blue eyes appraised her. "But I'm not such a thrill seeker that I'm going to return to the kind, gentle embrace of your boss."

Her boss was FBI Special Deputy Director Roger Ferdinand.

"You're not as stupid as you look, Hardrim."

"He's already decided I know too much to be free. I just hope his information about Ferman's last whereabouts is accurate."

"It is. He'll have people there to nab you when you try to pick up Ferman's trail."

Hardrim shook his head. "I won't go there physically. I have resources Ferdinand doesn't know about."

She smiled a lazy, sexy smile that in most men would have sparked an arousal. "I know you're pretty resourceful, Inspector. Sometimes you make me jealous of Lenny Lippman."

His face fell. "That's over."

"Maybe you are as stupid as you look, big man!" She rose, swaying from the vibration, her copper-crowned scalp a fraction of an inch below the ceiling, which was five feet five inches high. "During my short career, which often seems like a lifetime, I've seen some horrible things. Things that make something so mundane as hooking a brain up to a computer interface look like getting a manicure."

"Yeah?"

"Yeah! Didya get a load of the friggin' labyrinth Krebs has back there? That big mother of a snake, with a huge brain? Bones littering the maze? If we hadn't been in a rush, I'd have blown it to hell." She shuddered. "It's unnatural! Your lady getting an operation so she can talk to computers, that's just progress. If you love her—and you do, because you moon about her constantly—it shouldn't matter."

"What the hell do you know?"

"I know that any man who doesn't try to jump my bones is either dead below the waist, or else is truly in love." She smirked. "Like I said, I've seen some horrible things."

"You're almost as much of a bitch as Lenny is."

"I'll take that as a compliment, Inspector."

"So what's on the agenda when we get to San Antonio?"

"What had you originally planned?"

"To coldcock whomever I had to the first chance I got once we were across the border."

"You can still do that, except you'll only be coldcocking me. But first we'll get a good night's sleep in San Antonio."

"Why are you doing this, Kirsten?"

"Multiple reasons."

"I guess a better question would be, why do you put up with Ferdinand? He obviously thinks you're his sexual toy."

She gave him an arch smile. "Actually, I encourage Roger to think that I use sex and drugs like Mata Hari. I found out early that he won't give a woman credit for brains or abilities. But he's not surprised when I achieve results with my body."

Hardrim shifted and twisted his backpack into a more comfortable pile. He coughed and lit another Mexican coffin nail.

"Hits close to home, eh, big man? You have the same problems with Lenny and her career."

"That's pretty low, comparing me with that toad!"

"You think about that, Mel. Meantime, what are your plans after you lay me out?"

"Less you know, the better. I have things to do, like finding my friend. Let's just say I'm going to become a private dick."

They parted friends, although Kirsten felt Hardrim put a little too much enthusiasm into slugging her in the mouth.

III

We are such stuff as dreams are made on, and our little life is rounded with a sleep

—The Tempest, *Act IV, Scene 1*

. . . the test of a first rate intelligence is the ability to hold two opposite ideas in the mind at the same time and still retain the ability to function.

—F. Scott Fitzgerald

Jason Scott finished his fiftieth deep knee bend, wiped the light patina of sweat from his face, and started stretching and pushing exercises on a portable tension-exerciser.

As he exercised Scott watched two holovision monitors suspended from the cabin's ceiling. He was also wearing a deep-connector earjack that fed him data.

Known for an unnerving ability to control all facets of a project, Scott had taught himself to process divergent streams of data almost instantaneously. His fusion of technology and mental techniques made him the kind of hands-on administrator-engineer only dreamed of since the days when one man could conceive and execute his own plans. Yet until recently he had remained unknown outside engineering circles. The public vaguely knew the martyred Scott had a son. That had changed radically after the Challenger episode and his appointment to head the Sunside Project.

His berth door opened. Jacob Kane stuck his face in.

"Don't you ever knock?" Scott didn't stop his exercise.

Kane tapped the bulkhead three times. "Better?" He watched Scott with distaste. "Training for a special event?"

Scott started to run in place. "We'll be on the moon for months, and in low g once the PH Station is given a spin. I want to go home someday, and not to drop dead when I do. Workouts in high gravity will be nice if I can get them."

Kane leered. "I might get some exercise later."

"Don't you still have a wife back on earth? Dorothy?"

"Seems I remember somebody like that."

"Jacob, you're an extraordinary man." Scott picked up the pace, but his breath rate hardly changed.

"I love pricking your sense of morals. Dorothy knows one woman isn't enough to satisfy me. The thing is, I can't look at a woman without wondering how it'd be to sleep with her. Somerset Maugham said a man can always have a hearty meal if he's willing to dine on turnips and potatoes. Some men are meant to love one woman. I was meant to love them all."

"You don't love women. You hate them. You are a supreme narcissist. Women are mirrors you preen yourself before. Those who reinforce your self-image last a while. Those who challenge that image, you discard. Like your wife." He abruptly stopped running.

"I'm not discarding Dorothy, just putting her on hold until I get back. She wouldn't expect me to be faithful for two years!"

"It's none of my business." Scott toweled himself dry. "Well, I'm for a shower. Did you want something?"

"Going to Sherlock's little physics lesson in the rec room?"

"When I finish my shower, I may drop by."

"I'm more interested in the bacchanalia he's putting on when we get to Midway. You see this?" He fished out a printout from the ship's bulletin board:

"Announcing the Great Michlanski, back from a one-man tour of the fleshpots of Asia. On a special limited engagement for the eighteen eligible women on board the *Sally Ride*. It is my pleasure to announce that once we reach space station Midway, your honor will be threatened by a friend of lust and sensuality, myself. All are invited, including (reluctantly) the male passengers, to a private party held in the famous Globe Bar and the Kamasutra room. Free drinks will be served during this stop."

Scott finished reading and burst out laughing.

"The man's a buffoon!" said Kane. "A marvelous buffoon. At the news conference, he turned the thing into a circus. They were eating out of his hands. He excels at public relations!"

"To say that the foremost mind in physics 'excels at public relations' is like saying Einstein excelled at riding a bicycle."

"Still standing up for him. You're one consistent point in the universe, Jason; like an immovable quasar or neutron star."

Kane often felt frustrated in his verbal fencing with Scott. Scott didn't rise to his baiting; or respond to his blustering; he just didn't budge. He was even polite about it. After an awkward silence, Kane changed the subject.

"I'm interested to see how Sherlock handles this introduction to the New Physics. I presume his purpose in talking about the experiments now is to forestall questions that may arise."

"Right, reveal enough so they don't get curious about what's really going on—yet. Give me a few minutes and I'll be there."

The rec room was too small for an auditorium, but was more elaborate than a lounge. It held thirty comfortably, but fifty were spread out in seats or sitting cross-legged on the deck.

"It annoys me how he can always gather a crowd!" hissed Kane as he and Scott leaned against the bulkhead.

Even when Sherlock Michlanski had been under attack by the scientific establishment for his advocacy of FTL, or perhaps because of that, his lectures had never failed to sell out.

He stood before an electric blackboard in a sky-blue jumpsuit. From the symbols on the board, Kane and Scott knew Michlanski was giving the "First Grade" lecture, i.e., making the math accessible to most scientists. His "Second Grade" lecture was incomprehensible to all but highest rank physicists. He saved his "Kindergarten" talk for dunces, the general public, and politicians.

"Friends, when Shakespeare said 'These our actors, as I foretold you, were all spirits and are melted into air, into thin air,' he didn't guess he was foretelling an ultimate truth in the universe. That is why physicists often out-Picasso Picasso in their resemblance to artists rather than mathematicians."

Michlanski laughed, a brassy, vibrant expression of pleasure. "The reality, or if you will, unreality, of the universe is so much more fun than the wind-up automaton of Isaac Newton. But it's disconcerting, this notion that matter and energy can spring out of nowhere. And disappear by the same door.

"But such things are philosophy, after all, and have little to do with the, ahem, real world. Right!" he paused. "*Wrong!*

"One very practical theory of quantum mechanics, particle physics, and New Physics we hope to prove or disprove at our ultimate destination, twenty million miles from the surface of Sol. And by doing so settle the disagreement between two rather dead scientists, Swycaffer and Benlavi."

He held up a pudgy index finger dramatically. "Benlavi's Proof purports to show that faster-than-light travel is impossible because tachyons, the inferred faster-than-light particles, are charges without mass, hence not really anything. Einstein, recall, is adamant that nothing can travel at light speed because its mass will become infinite. He doesn't say we can't travel faster than light, just not at that speed. Tachyons as real things also create problems about causality and us advising our grandparents to buy AT&T stock and all sorts of paradoxical rubbish.

"Herr Swycaffer gets around all that, or thinks he does, by hypothesizing that the light barrier can be disregarded using the quantum leap. I won't bore you with that elementary material, except to reiterate that quantum mechanics does not predict where a particle of matter is; rather it assigns it a probability. In theory, a particle can be anywhere in the universe at a given moment, although that probability becomes ridiculously tiny any distance from the nucleus of the atom where the little bugger is really supposed to hang out. Yet it is there."

Michlanski fumbled in his jumpsuit pockets. "Because it is there, it is possible for a particle to move from one part of the universe to the other, without traversing the space in between.

"That's where Swycaffer comes in," he said, momentarily distracted until he located what he had been looking for: a shining gold piece. "In normal time and space we can't affect chance. Otherwise we might influence the probability of a particular particle or particles in a particular part of the galaxy, and make it more probable for them to be somewhere else. Swycaffer invented Swycaffer's Threshold, which predicts that if a tiny percentage of particles in a molecule are disturbed out of normal probability, they will also 'influence' surrounding particles. Like a chain reaction."

He began tossing the coin in the low artificial gravity. It described a long, slow parabola over his head as he talked, and each time he reached out just in time to catch it.

"Influencing probability is not my game. I always lose in Vegas, and if I were to predict that this coin would even come up heads or tails, I'll bet I would be wrong."

The coin slowly dropped to the deck, bounced a couple of times, and landed, perfectly balanced, on its edge.

"Cheap parlor trick," said Michlanski, who was famous for his toys. Scott guessed the coin probably contained one of Michlanski's tiny antigravity devices.

"By the way, this is the first time I've used my antigravity impeller in space. That an antigravity device canceled out centrifugal force should give theorists fits back home." He grinned cherubically. "Before we're through, we may generate two or three scientific papers!

"That brings us to the unified field theory, over which the scientific community and I have been engaged in a guerrilla war of ideas for several years. The establishment has adopted a scorched-earth policy, denying theories that might be useful to their arguments against me rather than acknowledge them and give me ammunition for my arguments. There have been similar feuds like this in our rather close-knit group before, including the first debates over the existence of the tachyon itself."

Michlanski wrote two lines of arcane symbols on the blackboard. "Ladies and gentlemen, this is not an army of spiders and snakes." He tapped the board. "This may be reality! This equation, if valid, explains why we continue to find smaller and smaller 'elementary' particles, and why we continue to find new basic forces. This equation accounts for, and predicts, new forces and particles, much as a transcendental number can be defined to any accuracy you choose. We stand in a hall of mirrors, and 'we decide what is real and what is an illusion.'

"But seriously, once we understand these forces, I believe we can find or even create fields of altered probability. We may even find such fields already exist near bodies of immense gravity, such as our ultimate destination. Questions?"

"Professor," said a voice from the rear of the room, "you kind of, ah, glossed over the problems of causality, didn't you?"

"Yes, but only because I knew someone like you would be compelled to bring up the subject, if for no other reason than to reassure himself that there is such a thing as free will. Of course, we all believe in free will. We have no choice."

A small snicker moved through the crowd, like a "wave" in an athletic event. "But you've asked a valid question. I'll try to answer it. A force moving backward in time plays hell with cause and effect. Unless it doesn't interact with the past. Yet that's clearly impossible, else we wouldn't be able to detect it. Perhaps it only interacts with the past to the extent that people become aware of it, but do not alter their actions because of it. In other words, once people make up their minds to do something, nothing can change it. We all know people like that.

"Another way to look at it is that each time we reach a junction that requires a decision, a number of alternate universes are created in space-time for each possibility. That's the theory I'm fondest of, leading back to our goal of trying to find a way to alter probability—that is, to create alternative universes where we can bring matter into existence.

"In other words, there is no such thing as cause and effect. Everything is cause and everything is effect. The future influences the past as much as the past influences the future."

Michlanski shrugged elaborately. "I hope that answers your question. If it doesn't, tough luck. I didn't create the damned universe!" His grin took the sting out of his snappish answer.

A hand shot up. "Professor, you wrote an equation on the blackboard. Does that mean you already have most of the answers?"

"My equation, which I believe is valid as far as it goes, is incomplete. Several symbols stand for constants I haven't isolated. Maybe we'll get some answers where we're going."

"Jason Scott," said a voice over the loudspeaker, "please report to the bridge."

Scott turned to leave, and Kane touched his arm. "I think I'll tag along," he said in a low voice.

Captain Paul Fairchild barely looked up when they entered. His attention was on the navigational globe. "Scott, Kane." He indicated the globe. "See that red blip, close to the center?"

"A ship?"

"Correct. But I don't know what ship." He riffled through a thick, hardbound book of colored plates. "She's not in *Jane's*. Trajectory suggests a launch from the Unified Soviet State. She's too big for a shuttle and she doesn't have characteristic Soviet exhaust telltales. No telltales at all! No evidence of exhaust."

Scott and Kane exchanged glances.

"She's five hundred miles astern." He paused as numbers chased across the navigational globe. "I've plotted her trajectory back to the Himalayas. I'm not aware of a Soviet space port there." He turned away from the glowing sphere. "It's not unusual for Lunar shuttles to be shadowed by warships from Cosmograd, but this *is* peculiar."

"Do our naval vessels shadow their spacecraft?"

"To an extent. But Russian traffic is a third of ours, and it's mostly official. No tourists are allowed on Russian bases. Our navy feels pretty secure with the big Tycho base. It's silly to be jumpy when your side has all the big guns."

"What's the big deal, then?" said Kane bluntly.

"I was told to inform you about anything unusual during this hop. Mr. Scott, is there any reason why the Russians might be interested in your project?"

"None. Our project is humanitarian, supported by most nations of the world, including the Soviets."

The captain grumbled to himself. It was obvious that he believed Scott knew more than he was saying.

"Very well, Mr. Scott. I'll keep you informed. You may go."

Chapter

* 4 *

Shortly before the *Sally Ride* launched, FBI Special Deputy Director Roger Ferdinand arrived at Deseret Space Center in a Bureau jump-jet.

In another age, Ferdinand would have been comfortable torching heretics. His religion was law and order, emphasis on order. He was tenacious as a pit bull.

A restless, ruthless-looking dandy in bright, expensive silks and flashing red cape, he was sure to make the proper impression: that of the Prince of Darkness, newly arrived from Pandemonium with his dark angels.

"Everyone's a suspect until proven innocent," Ferdinand told the space center's security chief as he jumped from his plane onto the tarmac. He felt exhilarated. He had gotten to the scene of a crime minutes after it occurred. Ferdinand, acting on a tip, had informed Deseret of the possibility that an atomic bomb had been planted on board one of the GILGAMESH scramjets. He had been ordered to fly with his investigative team to Deseret. It was like a gift.

He had a space center to play with. He couldn't wait to order exits sealed, communications monitored, and everyone detained.

A mile away, the three shuttles looked as though they were still ready for takeoff. He frowned. Didn't those idiots know the shuttles would be grounded until he completed his investigation?

"You're damned lucky the First Team is here to keep your people from mucking things up completely," Ferdinand told the security chief. He patted his shoulder in a comradely way. "If we look good on this one, you'll look good. Don't take it personally. We don't often get such a chance. No one wants another Dorian Nye incident, do we? Let's get to work!"

He released the chief's shoulder and removed some lint his finely tailored suit had picked up from the man's red uniform.

Ferdinand was smooth. But his flip side was frightening. His mouth smiled but his eyes said, "Cross me and I'll fillet you!"

"Before we do anything, Mr. Ferdinand," said the security chief, "I've orders to bring you to Mr. Mayfield's office."

Ferdinand felt a chill at the back of his neck. "Mayfield?" he said carefully. "As in Sheridan Mayfield?"

The security chief smiled inwardly. "Yes sir, the secretary of space exploration and development himself."

II

Ferdinand waited outside Mayfield's office in a reception room that lacked the environment controls Ferdinand had in his office to protect his expensive wardrobe. It had been half an hour. His livid color matched his double-breasted chameleon cloth suit, which changed hues every ten minutes.

Ferdinand brooded, eyeing Mayfield's secretary, knowing she knew that Mayfield's slight was intended to put him in his place.

Mayfield was everything Ferdinand hated: idealistic, committed, and incorruptible. He was also one of the few ever to bend the FBI man to his will. When he dealt with Mayfield, Ferdinand walked on eggs. He wasn't directly under his orders, but the Sunside Project was Mayfield's. Nothing concerning it could be done without his approval.

Mayfield stuck his head out of his office. "Ferdinand, sorry to have kept you waiting! But I've had to move heaven and earth to get those three birds ready to launch.''

God the Father, Son, and Holy Ghost! Bloody amateurs! thought Ferdinand. "You mean the launch is going on as scheduled?"

"Of course," said Mayfield offhandedly. "Even now." He led Ferdinand into his office and turned on three holocubes with three views of *Sally Ride*. Ferdinand felt a low, rumbling vibration through the soles of his hand-tooled Italian leather loafers.

His face betrayed his mixture of apprehension and puzzlement.

"Never been at a launch before? I'm surprised, Ferdinand. Nothing to be afraid of.''

Ferdinand scowled. Mayfield had an uncanny ability to know just where to place the knife.

The rumbling was like the prelude to an earthquake. Then, with a roar that reached even the office, safely buried in the bowels of the space center, the shuttle took off.

Ferdinand looked at Mayfield. "What's the point?"

"Of you being here? Why, to investigate the sabotage attempt, of course. Even you are not that dense!''

"You just sent two hundred prime suspects beyond my reach!"

"I have excellent national security reasons for ordering the launch. And to keep you from puzzling yourself into an ulcer over my motives, I will break security to a small degree and tell you.

"Within the last forty-eight hours the Unified Soviet State launched a superbattleship into orbit, using a technology that we do not, as yet, possess. This technology permits payloads many times the mass that we can launch. At the moment, they have the single largest weapon in the solar system. Their orbit will permit them to waylay our shuttle *Sally Ride* if she launches on time.''

"Which she just did.''

"Quite so," said Mayfield impatiently. "If we hadn't, the Soviets would have assumed that we didn't because we are afraid of their new warship. In fact, Shefferton insisted on that.''

This line of reasoning was convoluted enough to satisfy Ferdinand, who nodded.

"Now, do you have any positive suggestions to make, besides arresting two hundred people who are beyond your grasp?"

"Very well, Secretary Mayfield. I would put a stasis field on the bomber until we can examine him.''

"There's nothing left. The bomb was strapped to his back."

"What about the other saboteurs?"

"In one piece. Er, two pieces."

"Good, we can stasis them." Ferdinand examined his holster computer. "Pity you sent Jacob Kane on the first shuttle. He would be a prime suspect. He was, until recently, the lieutenant of Horatius Krebs."

Krebs, one of the world's most powerful billionaires, head of Python Corporation, had lobbied for the Sunside Project, only to have it go to Scott. Scott had then lured Kane from his employer.

"So was Jason Scott, at one time," said Mayfield.

Ferdinand nodded grimly. He didn't really trust Scott either. Much as he distrusted Kane and Scott, he found Dorian Nye even more disturbing. That balding, nervous little man's disappearance and faked death in January had caused his government tremendous trouble and jeopardized Ferdinand's career.

"My immediate concern is that the project is endangered by an unknown enemy," said Ferdinand, who knew perfectly well who the enemy was. His tip on the bomb placed aboard the GILGAMESH scramjet had identified the saboteur as a man employed by Krebs, a killer and soldier of fortune known as Emil. That was why Ferdinand had been so anxious to reach the scene of the sabotage, to put a make on the head saboteur and —he hoped—connect him to Krebs. That was also why he had sent a totally unauthorized team of FBI agents to Krebs's estate in the Yucatán, to surprise the billionaire and find evidence to connect him to—

"We all know the enemy, Ferdinand: Python. Horatius Krebs."

"What? Do you have proof?" Ferdinand asked quickly, scowling.

"Proof? I'm not going to swear out a complaint against Krebs." Mayfield looked at Ferdinand in what seemed to Ferdinand to be sadistic glee. "Gives a sense of déjà vu, doesn't it?"

"I know what you told the reporters, Secretary Mayfield, but there must be a connection between the Nye affair and this latest incident!" Ferdinand's cape swirled as he paced.

"I wish you more success with this case. You've had a string of bad luck lately." He didn't sound a bit sympathetic.

Ferdinand knew his enemies in the Bureau would destroy him if he failed. The director had erected many roadblocks to his investigation of a conspiracy, in hopes of eliminating a rival.

"You know, I asked for you to head this investigation. After your information about the bomb on board the scramjet, you seemed the man for the job. It will give you a chance to redeem yourself for your blunders in the Nye affair.''

Ferdinand clenched his teeth. Had Mayfield and FBI Director Houston Pollux allied to eliminate him as a player? "I'm sure the two incidents are connected, sir. They may even involve a series of murders that go back to Adam Scott's death.''

"And the sinking of the *Titanic* and the *Hindenburg* explosion?''

"Wouldn't the president be interested in the connection? Adam Scott was patron saint of the Progressive Nationalist party. For months I've investigated the series of deaths of people connected with him. After Scott perished in the foundry fire, they died one by one. Lately the pattern of death has picked up again. You recall the man who tried to assassinate Dorian Nye?''

"Lloyd Hunning. He led the Technology Enforcement Agency team that broke into Scott's foundry.''

"Affirmative. Hunning was put in a sanitarium for former agents possessing classified knowledge. He was released shortly before he tried to kill Nye. We don't know why he was released. Before we could question the sanitarium director his neck was twisted like a rag doll's.

"More murders followed. All connected to Scott, all done by a man trained in the Drang school of psychodynamic combat.''

"What's your point, Ferdinand?''

"Who gained from Scott's death? Krebs was his close associate. Maybe he betrayed him to McClaren and the TEA. There's no proof. The TEA hid its tracks. Even after we took it over, we didn't find all the sensitive files. Perhaps Krebs's reward was the lion's share of Scott's technological genius. Suppose he betrayed Scott to McClaren and stabbed McClaren in the back?''

"But why?''

"A powerful McClaren could keep Krebs from exploiting Scott's patents. This also explains Scott's missing fortune.''

Ferdinand was referring to the so-called ''billion in bullion'' that had vanished from Scott's holdings.

"Suppose Scott planned to stash the gold, helped by his 'friend' Krebs, who saw a chance to arrange Scott's death, take his money, found an empire, and cause McClaren's fall. McClaren might have figured out who had the money if he hadn't been so busy defending himself from the charge that his men stole it.''

"Listen, Ferdinand,'' growled Mayfield. "I know you've got hidden agendas and plots with a dozen wheels within wheels. Can you prove any of this? I know your fondness for pinning crimes on innocent people. Like Inspector Hardrim.''

Ferdinand spoke carefully. ''I initially believed he was involved in the Nye matter. He was unstable, too interested in music and art for a truly dedicated policeman.''

''You mean he thought for himself too much to suit you?'' The conversation was taking an ominous turn.

''Independent thought is not high on my list of desirable qualities in a police officer, sir.''

''Are you comfortable living in a democracy, Ferdinand? I read your damned report. You recommended against reinstatement!''

''My feelings about Hardrim proved remarkably prescient.'' Hardrim had left the force shortly after returning. His body was found burned almost beyond recognition a thousand miles away in Detroit. ''Hardly a stable individual. Hardly police material.''

''Poor bastard was crucified for everybody's sins. If I feel shame about that affair it's that Hardrim's career was destroyed.'' He fidgeted. ''Let's get back to proof. What have you got?''

''None yet. I've been tracking this Drang killer for months.''

''Oh, who is he?''

''I don't know, as such. We have a psychological profile on him, and a physical description, *sans* facial characteristics, unfortunately. No genetic material.''

''What have you got besides your suspicion that your 'Drang' works for Krebs?''

''I also believe he was behind today's sabotage attempt.''

''Then he's dead. All three saboteurs died.''

''I believe he escaped in the GILGAMESH ship.''

''The Air Force blew it to pieces.''

''Maybe. Perhaps he faked his escape and is loose on the base. Maybe some of his accomplices are at large here.''

''Believe. Maybe. Perhaps. You're overlooking another explanation. What about the Europeans?''

Ferdinand grimaced at the reference to the spy ring that had mauled his team in Detroit and almost escaped. ''Bengal and his men? I think the Drang was controlling them, using Krebs's money. Our borders have been closed for decades. To operate here suggests inside help. Python Corporation is large enough to fit that bill.''

''Just have proof before you present it to the president.''

"I'd think you'd like to see Krebs hung out to dry."

Mayfield sighed. "Ferdinand, to you, such things are outdated, but as much as I despise Krebs, I won't fake evidence. We'll get him by the rules. I work for an idealistic president. If he heard you suggest such a thing, he'd have you slogging the Honduran jungles chasing SoHi drug manufacturers."

"I understand."

"No, you don't. Continue your investigation. Make life uncomfortable for Krebs, or, God willing, put him behind bars." He leaned back in his desk chair and looked at Ferdinand piercingly. "By the way, I'm aware that Director Pollux has no knowledge of your investigation of Krebs et al. And that he ordered you to cease, for budgetary reasons."

Ferdinand felt his blood draining into his feet. "So?"

"So as long as you conduct yourself to my satisfaction, and don't become a nuisance or try political games at my expense, your extracurricular activities will remain our secret. Break this arrangement, and you'll have to use a geiger counter to find your ass. We understand each other?"

"Clear and direct communication has always been your strong point, Secretary Mayfield."

Chapter

* 5 *

I

"**D**o you think Captain Fairchild suspected you weren't telling all you know about the unidentified spacecraft, Jason?" asked Jacob Kane when they had returned to Scott's cabin.

Scott regarded Kane coolly with unfathomable blue eyes. "I beg your pardon, Jacob?"

"Okay, that didn't work," said Kane with exasperation. "No, your face didn't give you away. And even now I have no proof that you know anything other than what you told the captain. But if you do, I'd bloody well appreciate being let in on the secret!"

"All right, Jacob." Scott proceeded to relay a conversation he had with Sheridan Mayfield that morning, when Mayfield told him about the launch of a superbattleship from a Soviet cosmodrome.

"That is the ship Mayfield told me about. It has the White House in an uproar. The president's intelligence advisers have egg on their faces because they didn't warn him soon enough.

"The space navy wanted to blast it before it became operational. The secretary of state argued that would scuttle attempts to bring America back into the world community. And end hopes of international cooperation to fight the famine.

"Of course, Mayfield urged a preemptive strike."

"Of course!" said Kane with a raspy laugh.

"He and Senator Macadew were in a distinct minority. Shefferton wants to keep the launch a secret—he's afraid it will rebound on the Sunside Project. The Russians, for their own reasons, also didn't make it public. So naturally, Mayfield was upset when he found out how much I had put together on my own. Such as the fact that the battleship was launched by railgun."

"Railgun, eh?" mused Kane. "How did you figure that out?"

Scott shrugged. "We build warships on Luna or in orbit because it's not economical to launch them from earth's gravity well. Instead we use workhorse shuttles to put payloads into space, then transfer them to larger ships. Since we have a near monopoly on warships in space, and don't tolerate their construction on Luna, it follows that the Russian warship was built on earth. Mass driver railgun technology has existed for years. We use it to move cargo between Luna and L-5. Atmospheric friction has been the stumbling block to launching on earth. The Russians probably overcame that with a heat shield that burned away in the atmosphere."

Scott worked the keyboard on his holocube and brought up the image of the earth, with the orbits of dozens of satellites superimposed over it.

"Also, I monitor International Weather Service satellites. They reported turbulence over the Himalayas and an energy release comparable to a hydrogen bomb. They can't explain it. I can. A large payload was fired into space at a significant fraction of the speed of light from the highest point on earth."

"I can see how Mayfield was pissed off! People with the highest clearance probably don't have the knowledge you gained by guesswork." Kane grinned his evil, Halloween-mask grin.

"They have far less to lose if I get into a situation without all the facts."

The ship's intercom crackled: "Mr. Scott and Mr. Kane, please report to the bridge at your earliest convenience!"

"Now everyone gets let in on the secret," said Scott.

II

First Secretary Peter Brasnikov of the Unified Soviet State was still leading toasts to the successful launch of the X-Vehicle, now known as battleship *Aurora*, when Marshal Antonine Tiomkin wandered off for a cup of hot tea.

"The Snow Giant," as Tiomkin was called in the Strategic Spaceborne Forces, was a private man. When he drank (and he liked vodka as much as the next Russian), he did it alone. He didn't like crowds, and the institute mess hall was filled to its capacity of three hundred and beyond. With its hastily installed carpets, curtains, and plush chairs (which would vanish with numbing swiftness once the premier left), it didn't much resemble a military mess.

He prowled the mess kitchen, looking for a jar of leaf tea and something to brew it in.

The premier, whom Tiomkin still thought of as "the Young Premier," although he had held power more than a year, was a charming master politician. Quite the antithesis to his boorish predecessor, Kurtzov. He was masterfully working the generals, institute staff members, and members of the Politburo into drunken euphoria as he described how the new battleship would propel the Unified Soviet State to its rightful place in the cosmos. A place long denied it by the criminal American space navy.

"Enjoying your triumph, Comrade Marshal?" The Russian was flavored with a German accent. Slow footsteps were punctuated by the clicking of a cheap prosthetic leg (a triumph of socialist medicine). Tiomkin turned as Colonel General Erwin Wolff, commandant of the Institute of Magnetic Propulsion, limped toward him. Son of an East German officer loyal to the old Soviet Union, who emigrated after the unification and fought in the general European war that erupted over the borders of the Fourth Reich, Poland, and the Balkans, Wolff himself had lost a leg, an eye, and his health proving himself to his adopted land.

"Our triumph, my friend. And almost our disaster. If your dire predictions had come true—"

"They nearly did." The small, pale German kept his voice as cold as his good eye. Tiomkin had heard the joke that Wolff put his blood in a refrigerator each night before bed. "In our rush to carry out the premier's wishes for an early launch, we nearly destroyed the facility."

"How? Explain."

Wolff took a pocket computer from his blouse to illustrate. That was unnecessary: Tiomkin had helped design the railgun that had propelled the kilometer-long torpedo shape through a one-hundred-mile tunnel into the rarefied air of the Himalayas.

The tunnel was divided into mile-long segments by steel walls, with air pumped from each segment. For the first fifty miles the walls had slid away a split second before the projectile hit. The last series of walls were vaporized by high-power lasers, because, by then, the projectile's speed was too high for any mechanism to move a wall out of the way in time.

During the hundred miles of vacuum the projectile, powered by magnetic forces, built up tremendous velocity. The last bulkhead, at the mouth of the tunnel, blew outward with a small atomic blast, extending the vacuum and creating a shock wave which the projectile, encased in Collapsium shielding, rode out of the atmosphere. By the time it reached space, its collapsed matter shield had burned off.

It almost didn't work.

The program responsible for opening and vaporizing the steel walls was off by nanoseconds.

"We almost didn't see the light at the end of the tunnel," said Wolff with a grim smile.

"I see. At each bulkhead the error was compounded. When time came for the explosion, the program was off by microseconds. Much more and the projectile would have blasted through the steel wall like butter, introducing a significant drag coefficient into the equation. You're correct, it might have been fatal."

"I did the calculations," said Wolff sourly. He tapped his prosthesis, producing a hollow sound. "A little more off and we'd have created a large crater in the Outback Desert of Australia."

"But we didn't. How much time do you need for the next one?"

"Two months. How will you move another monster here in such a short time?"

"We learn from our mistakes. We're building this one in manageable segments, at twenty sites throughout the Motherland."

They heard footsteps. A tall Viking in a new black and red uniform of a general of the elite CosMarine Division was framed in the doorway, his forehead almost touching the jamb.

"I've come to take my leave of you." Newly commissioned General Pavel Orlov flashed a brilliant white smile.

"So soon?" said Tiomkin. "You're not going to get blindingly drunk with the first secretary and his entourage?"

"I'm waiting to see if we have something to drink about. I should be with my new command in case we must move quickly."

"You don't trust Wen Chin to carry out his assignment?"

"I trust him to carry it out all too well. He is one of your greatest pupils."

"Both of you were very promising at the academy. Both of you have fulfilled your promise," said Tiomkin with affection. The younger man had been his aide for the past five years.

Wolff fastidiously took a long, thin, undoubtedly deadly cigarette from a silver holder and lit it. "General Orlov is a loyal friend, and Wen Chin is your enemy and greatest threat."

Colonel General Wen Chin was a fiercely brilliant Mongol, a dark angel who had commanded the Himalayan Military District until days before, when he was appointed Tiomkin's deputy in his new post as defense minister. On Tiomkin's recommendation, Brasnikov had also promoted Orlov over the heads of dozens of senior officers to command the CosMarine Division. As a special plum, before he took up his new duties, the premier had given Chin command of the battleship *Aurora* on her maiden voyage.

"It is my policy not to discuss politics." Tiomkin rummaged in a cabinet and triumphantly pulled out a jar of tea. "You young men will get me into trouble. What if this room has ears?"

"There are none, Comrade Marshal," said Wolff. "I ordered a sweep a few hours before the premier's arrival."

Tiomkin sniffed the tea. "Ah, Earl Grey!"

"Politics be damned, comrade!" said Orlov with controlled anger. "As we speak, Chin is rendezvousing with the *Aurora*. His mission is to harass their space shuttle *Sally Ride*, spit in their faces, and invite retaliation. The American space fleet could descend upon him like wolves. He could start a war! Without our new fleet of battleships launched, we will lose!"

Tiomkin put a teapot in an antique microwave. "Americans are not wolves, but sheep. Well-armed sheep, and their generals, in particular my opposite number on the space navy, will try to convince Shefferton to destroy our battleship. They will fail.

"Give our premier due credit. He is testing his theory that America will do anything to keep the peace and preserve the Food Treaty. During the war, we used a tactic against the Japanese or the Chinese—the Greater Asians anyway. When we wanted to find their sharpshooters, we put a helmet on a bayonet and raised it out of the trench. Their strategy was similar, but they used live soldiers. It's a matter of priorities. We are exposing our most fearsome weapon and inviting the Americans to turn it into vapor."

"Which Brasnikov is wagering won't happen." Wolff took a long drag on his cigarette. "It's insanity."

"Unless he wins," said Tiomkin with an impish smile. "His failure will be our ruin. Yet, ultimately, it is his head that is at hazard. As the saying goes, they don't name warships after failed leaders, which is why there are none named for Gorbachev."

"You did advise the premier against it."

"That's beside the point. Our young premier admires me, but he's inclined to take the advice of a firebrand more his age."

"Like Chin?" said Orlov. "I suppose that's why he made the Hun your deputy minister. To undercut every step you take."

"You misunderstand the subtleties of command. The premier would not appoint a man he disliked or distrusted minister of defense. Nor give anyone such power without stationing a rival at his back. Keeps me honest."

The premier apparently finished his speech, because the hall resounded with wild applause and shouts.

"Of all your rivals he could have picked, Chin is the most ambitious, the most dangerous. Not just to you. But to the state. The world," said Orlov. He looked up, as if he could actually see Chin's brooding figure. "Right now he's in his element!"

III

The space city Cosmograd spun away like a leaf vanishing into a storm drain of dark waters.

Colonel General Wen Chin watched the space city shrinking at the stern of the space shuttle and reflected that Cosmograd was like the site of an ancient metropolis. A future archaeologist would sift through it, starting at the center, where the space station Mir was preserved exactly as it was when it launched in 1986: six docking ports, with accommodations for six cosmonauts. The rest had been added on, piece by piece, without a grand scheme.

"Mir" meant peace, and the irony of that name for the home base of the Unified Soviet Strategic Spaceborne Forces had not been lost on the powers back home.

Chin was short, dark, and leathery. He would have looked at home on a Mongolian pony, leading a screaming assault on China's Great Wall. He was a passionate man who kept his passions leashed. Only occasionally did the raptor's eyes hidden by sunburned folds of skin flash to reveal the predator.

Like all of Tiomkin's former pupils, he was a student of history. Tiomkin had preached that sooner or later every lesson of history had demonstrated relevance to the present.

Today, history had much relevance for Chin.

He was approaching the hulk of the battleship *Aurora*, which was the size of a small asteroid. The acceleration that launched her was so powerful that no living thing, no sensitive electronics, could have withstood it.

The three Cosmograd shuttles carried enough technicians, officers, and men to put a skeleton crew aboard, to install motherboard networks, and make *Aurora* operational.

This was one of the preeminent moments of history. There comes a time when a preeminent power is challenged by a lesser power. The encounter determines the future relationship between the rivals. Usually such tests come down to a question of will on the part of the greater power.

In the twentieth century the Allies of Europe could have crushed Hitler when he occupied the Rhineland. They did not, and Hitler was loosed for a season that made the world howl. Two decades later, the Soviet Union had challenged America's supremacy by planting missiles in Cuba, within striking distance of the mainland. The U.S. made the Russians back down, and maintained its supremacy for a generation until the end of the Cold War and the crisis of confidence of the First Communists.

Today the Unified Soviet State, under the Genetic Communists—successors to the theocratic state that had overthrown the Gorbachev reformists—was trying again. At this moment the *Aurora* was defenseless. If Chin commanded the American Lunar fleet, he would fall upon the inert battleship and turn her into slag.

But it was not the American way to make surprise attacks. Not the race that built up a righteous fury against Japan for its brilliant Pearl Harbor attack, as if there was proper etiquette for war! Americans conducted their affairs with comic naïveté.

Chin didn't expect an attack. He was betting his life on it.

Aurora grew in the screen like a giant salami, its surface mottled with dark patches where the Collapsium shielding had not crumbled away entirely.

The shuttle matched velocities with the battleship.

Chin claimed the right to be the first aboard. He crossed the void between the ships alone, propelled by a plume of gas. Only he knew how much naked space terrified him. When he stepped from the airlock into nothing, his anus puckered and he held his breath. It seemed he didn't breathe again until his magnetic boots clamped onto the steel floor of the open airlock.

From the airlock he stepped into one of the main corridors that ran down the ship's spine. He looked down each direction. It was like mirrors facing each other. The glowing overhead panels seemed to meet the deck panels somewhere in the distance.

He felt the ship sleeping, like a giant who stirs, troubled by dreams. It waited for Chin to awaken the giant.

Floating in the corridor, he activated the strip of moving floor and moving handrails and was pulled along by the handrails to an elevator, which he took to the bridge. Until the ship received its first shipment of sophisticated electronics boards, the bridge was only capable of the most rudimentary functions, such as opening and closing airlocks.

On the bridge he found the traditional Russian greeting, a table with salt and bread in containers attached so that the acceleration hadn't dislodged them. Chin ordered the transfer of the electronics boards onto the ship. Then he contacted the medical officer.

"When will you transfer the 'Dough Children,' Comrade Doctor?"

"In a few hours, Comrade Colonel General," said the spare, pale officer, whose lips pressed together so tightly he looked like he was suppressing agony.

"Make it two. I want to run a test on the new electronics."

"They need time to acclimate to weightlessness."

"Your advice is noted. It's time the Dough Children started to earn the expensive nutrients we pump into them each day."

The doctor was not pleased. But he knew better than to argue.

The Dough Children were transported between the ships in special pods and taken directly to the main computer room.

"Dough Children" was a term invented by the first secretary's crass predecessor, who had remarked that the young interfaces looked like unbaked loaves of bread.

For Chin, they were strangely fascinating, like someone with an obscene disfigurement, like living abortions. He found an excuse to go into the computer room as soon as the first arrived.

It was dimly lit and Chin was conscious of a mewling, an almost subaural moaning. It smelled rancid, like a neglected nursery. Absurd, since the children were kept scrupulously clean, more than normal infants. They were as pampered as Japanese Kobe beef.

He stared into one of the faces, at dimples where eyes would have been, a dark slash of a nose, the rudimentary mouth. In more refined versions, the mouth would be gone; it was redundant when nutrients were given intravenously. They had no limbs to cause themselves injury. They knew no other stimulation than the wires that mated them to the computer net.

Human computer interfaces had existed for years. But the Soviets were the first to breed humans specially as interfaces. If the experiment was a success, it would vindicate Genetic Communism. If man did not perfect himself, he would be perfected!

As if the Dough Children sensed Chin's excitement, their mewling grew louder, became almost plaintive.

"Work hard, you little monstrosities!" whispered Chin, although he knew they couldn't hear him. "Work. And the first time one of you takes a false step, figuratively speaking, I'll introduce you to the Steel Bloom."

Chin left the computer room and returned to the bridge.

Hours later, the bridge control panels began to glow as the ship came alive. So far no American warships had been detected.

"Laser cannons operational," reported the gunnery officer.

Chin ordered the laser locked onto a satellite that monitored the Greenhouse Effect for the International Weather Service.

At his order a red coherent beam leaped one hundred and fifty miles and vaporized the satellite into a cloud of glowing plasma.

The ship was ready for bigger game.

IV

The computer console on the bridge of the *Sally Ride* chiméd softly. Captain Fairchild turned to a small holocube that filled with luminous type. He motioned Kane and Scott to have a look.

"We're in distinguished company. CNCLUN says Russia just put the battleship *Aurora* into orbit. That's her. The first pure warship of battleship dimensions they've ever built. The most powerful single vessel in existence. She outguns by half anything we have except the five battlewagons at Tycho."

"Building monstrosities is a sign of a national inferiority complex," said Scott. "The Japanese built the giant battleship *Yamato* to prove their navy was the best in the world. It didn't live up to their expectations."

Fairchild touched the keyboard. The writing was replaced by a spacecraft of heavy, cumbersome lines and a mirror surface to reflect lasers: every inch a man-of-war. "I'm impressed."

"If waste impresses you!" said Scott. "That ship can only be used for war. Our Congress won't allocate money for pure research and development, but builds ships that are useless in peacetime."

"To be fair, we only have five ourselves, Mr. Scott. The rest of the space navy is ships converted from other uses."

"Three more battleships are in the works. The *Aurora* will undoubtedly provoke more. The argument will be that a ship designed solely for combat is superior to one with other uses."

"Can't really blame them—"

"I blame anyone who adds to the collective misery of the human race! We need a space navy to protect our interests, but if building behemoths devours the lion's share of our space budget, and hurts those interests, where's the reason for them? We need ships that can be used for peace and war. When we listen to apostles of bigger warships, where does it end? Armed moons? Do we drag Deimos from Mars's orbit and make it into a battleship?"

"I wouldn't mind having one around right now. That battleship doesn't improve my nerves."

"You said it's routine for Soviet warships to shadow our traffic," said Scott.

"I did." Fairchild nodded. "It's not so normal to have the biggest battleship in the cosmos snuffling up my tail—"

"If they planned mischief would they send one ship, even their biggest? I think they're 'showing the flag.' "

"I've asked for help from CNCLUN. They'll probably send our escort from Midway earlier than planned."

"Escort?"

"Midway has several corvettes and a cruiser, independent of Commodore Hastings's squadron." The console chimed and a message appeared. Fairchild's jaw relaxed. "The *Patton* will rendezvous with us in three hours to escort us to Midway. If needed she'll tag along to Tycho. Somebody must think you're important!"

"I guess somebody does," said Scott with a smile.

Chapter

* 6 *

The man who toppled Senator Archer McClaren was Adam Scott, who resisted suppression of his revolutionary metal, Osirium. The process for Osirium, which helped reestablish American preeminence in space, he gave away at his celebrated news conference. Scott and his wife, Christine, died when he destroyed his foundry rather than let the government occupy it. McClaren, implicated in the scandal, saw his career die in the same flames that gutted Scott's foundry.
— *Grenoble Milner,* America: The Third Century

Some people are fascinated by Adam Scott's martyrdom, that led to the founding of the Progressive Nationalist party. I stay awake nights wondering what happened to the billion dollars that vanished from his fortune.
— *Fanny Fritz,* Billion in Bullion

Senators, you may not like it, but we're in space to stay. Industrialists have foiled every ban to keep 'em out of space. They register ships under foreign flags, bribe officials, and by golly, they get there. They're there 'cause a vacuum exists (pardon my pun), created by warring nations who've

temporarily abandoned their space programs. The question
before the Senate is, do we let hooligans, used-car salesmen,
industrial buccaneers, and satellite rustlers operate without
police protection and *regulation because some of us don't*
approve of 'em bein' there?

　　　　　—From a speech by Senator Charles Macadew
　　　　　　　　supporting the Hacker-Marley Act,
　　　　　　　　which established the U.S. Space Navy

I

President Jeffrey Shefferton and Senator Charles Ellsworth Macadew
slipped into Deseret Space Center under a cloak of some of the tightest
security the president had ever experienced.

It was night. Soldiers and security officers and G-men were patrolling
the perimeters of the space center and getting in each other's way. No one
paid much attention when yet another helicopter deposited several figures
near the central complex.

The president and the senator hadn't changed from their duck-hunting
gear when they were conducted into Sheridan Mayfield's office. A few
moments later the space secretary entered.

"Thank you for waiting until I got the three birds into orbit, Mr. President," said Mayfield, whose voice was gravelly from fatigue. His suit
badly needed pressing, as though he had tried to nap in it. He nodded
toward the senator, who, with the unerring instincts of a bloodhound, had
found a bottle of bourbon in a cabinet. This, despite the fact that Mayfield
didn't drink. Well, it wasn't really his office. Just borrowed.

"I know you're upset with me for showing up at all, Sheridan," said
the president evenly. "Otherwise you'd be using my first name. But that's
okay, because I'm angry too. I don't like being kept in the dark about the
most important project under this government's aegis!"

"Sorry, Jeffrey." Mayfield was too tired to fake contrition, and the
senator found himself hiding a grin with his hand. "It seemed more important to get the launch over than to hold your hand! You said you wanted
it to go as planned, and not to let anything stand in the way."

"Thank you for that!" said Shefferton, reddening. "Also for the fabulous publicity you garnered for us with that vintage Mayfield remark
about how you didn't work for the people, just for the president."

"I'm not as bad as I used to be," said Mayfield sheepishly.

"True. I remember our first month in office how you went before the

Senate Space Committee and proceeded to take apart Senator Jerome's ten-point budget program piece by piece with impeccable logic until his position was untenable, leaving him no room to save face. You made us an enemy for life.''

Macadew rumbled, ''I attribute it to divine providence that Jerome later died in his sleep. Probably killed by plumb shame, or too many green peaches.''

''We can't afford statements like this morning's,'' snapped Shefferton.

''Wal, actually, I thought it had a raw, arrogant charm. You can't fault ol' Sheridan for not keeping his mind on the objective. You know as well as me that we couldn't halt the launch for an investigation. Might as well bull it through. An' no one's better suited for bullin' than Sheridan!''

''You let Michlanski twist in the wind while the reporter used him as a piñata on the subject of faster-than-light travel.''

''Considering how many times that arrogant bastard played with this government about the Strubeck equations, and the location of Dorian Nye, I didn't mind seeing him squirm a little.'' Mayfield's voice was stronger. Remembered grievances always pepped him up.

''You never forgive a hurt, do you?''

''Never!'' he said fiercely. Then he looked down, a little ashamed of himself. ''Actually, I do feel guilty for not standing up for FTL like Michlanski. Because someday, if it is possible, we must develop it to hold together the outposts of our empire.''

''Empire? No one uses that word anymore. Not even the Soviets,'' snapped Shefferton.

Macadew winked at Mayfield and raised a glass in salute.

''I live in the real world. In real time, our Jovian and Saturnine colonies are farther away than the thirteen colonies were from London. We can profit by their example,'' said Mayfield.

''There's danger of an independence movement?''

''I've sent you several memos on this. There's sentiment for statehood on Luna. It's stronger beyond the asteroids. But a state government two months removed from earth could be untenable. The colonies stay loyal from fear of the Soviets. But I have a computer scenario that predicts economic factors will negate that in thirty years unless we forge stronger links.''

Like a man who knows the answer to a question, but wants to hear someone else reach the same conclusion, the senator narrowed his eyes and took a sip of whiskey. ''What 'bout the space navy?''

''Ninety percent of that is the reserve fleet: the miners, merchants, and

ice trawlers of Mercury, Mars, the Belt, and the gas giants. They wear
U.S. Space Navy pips two weeks a year. What's to keep them from fighting
for their own?''

"So are we up the creek in thirty years, or what?''

"If we can begin to put more cargo directly into space, cheaper, simpler,
it will become accessible to the average man.''

"Won't that hasten the breakaway?'' asked the president.

"More cargo in space means more industry. Space industry that could
develop faster-than-light drive.''

"That's a pipe dream right now, Sheridan! It's got to take backseat to
the Sunside Project right now,'' said Shefferton, stronger than he needed
to. "I'm going to sleep. You two can sit up all night and ponder the
imponderable.''

The president grumbled a good-night and went off with his escort of
Secret Service guards to find his sleeping quarters.

"When we first came to Washington,'' said Mayfield quietly, "Shefferton grabbed me by the shoulders and gave me the biggest bear hug in
the world. We were friends.'' Mayfield's jaw tightened beneath his fleshy
cheeks. "He knew what I was when he put me in charge of SED. I haven't
changed.''

"He's been bothered all day, Sheridan. Don't take it personal. He's not
thinkin' logically. Otherwise he'd know you were right about not coming
earlier. He's got things on his mind besides the Sunside Project. You're
right! We gotta interest the common herd in space travel. But how do you
convince the common man that space is his future when the most enthusiastic technocrat ever to sit in the White House won't take a shuttle to
the moon?''

"But it's too dan—'' Mayfield paused. In his mind's eye he saw the
GILGAMESH scramjet. Low, sleek—safe! He looked at Macadew with
a half-smile. "You may have something there, Charley. By the way,
Charley, I have a question for you.''

"Shoot.''

"I want to do some public information pieces about how we are mapping
out future expansion to other solar systems. My people keep finding references to the White Point Probe, but apparently previous administrations
tried to discredit the probe and there was almost no data on it. What I
have says the laser-transmitted signals from the probe were unintelligible.
You were in the Senate when the probe was discussed in secret session.
What do you know?''

"McClaren tried to convince us that no data was transmitted. But in certain newstape morgues from twenty years ago you'll find references to Caltech and some observatories recording coherent data on several planets in the Tau Ceti system.''

"Those reports were discredited.''

"Then all White Point Probe data was subpoenaed by the Senate Committee on Un-American Technologies, then classified, then destroyed. The director of Palomar Observatory ended up in the Fun House. Even when I was tiltin' at windmills I thought it better for my health not to shove my lance at that particular windmill.''

"What are you saying, Charley?''

"That there's 'more in heaven and on earth than is dreamed of in your philosophy,' Sheridan.''

II

"The president has retired, Mr. Ferdinand,'' said the chief of Shefferton's Secret Service detail from the holocube in Ferdinand's quarters. "Your people can stand down now. Thanks much for the use of your agents. We weren't expecting such a complicated security problem. They came in handy.''

"Happy to help out.'' Always happy to help out the fount of power, thought Ferdinand, terminating the conversation.

Hunched at his desk, with the cowl of his black velvet cape pulled over his head, and a hypermodern recording of a Gregorian chant/rock fusion coming from speakers hidden in an oil painting and a fake Ming vase, Ferdinand resembled a mad monk.

There is so much concentrated power in this building, he thought. The president was the very distillation of power. And he wanted a sip. So when the Secret Service chief had said he was shorthanded, Ferdinand quickly offered some of his people.

He had no illusions that kissing up to the Secret Service or the president himself could save him if Mayfield carried out his threat to reveal to the FBI director that Ferdinand was conducting his own investigation, independent of the Bureau.

Or if Mayfield discovered that Ferdinand was keeping some things from him as well. Such as the fact that the former police inspector Mel Hardrim was alive.

Not just alive. Hours before, he and Ferdinand's trusted agent, Kirsten Fale, had led a secret raid on the Yucatán estate of Horatius Krebs. In return, Ferdinand supplied the last known location of his friend Ralph Ferman, and erased Hardrim's name from the computer network.

It was Hardrim who gave Ferdinand the tip that the Drang Emil had planted a bomb in the space port. During the raid Hardrim and Fale had interrogated Krebs. He claimed Emil had become a rogue agent, with his own agenda, that included putting an atom bomb aboard a GILGAMESH scramjet to cripple America's space efforts.

Krebs denied any involvement in Emil's activities, and had apparently begged Hardrim and Fale to track him down and kill him.

Sure.

Ferdinand believed that. He also believed that most young women who get married for the first time are virgins.

Since that last communication from Hardrim, Ferdinand had heard nothing. He was beginning to sweat, not for any concern about Hardrim's welfare, but about Kirsten Fale.

Deputy Inspector Kirsten Fale was his pride, creation, and protégé. She combined a body that promised rapture with a mind as brilliant as a beam of coherent light and as emotionless. She used sex, pain, or drugs with equal facility to extract information. Ferdinand himself would never consider sex with her. It would be as stupid to enjoy her favors as for a pusher to get hooked on his own wares. Yet he was hooked, and he knew it. He hoped that she didn't.

He didn't really trust Hardrim, and he for sure didn't trust Hardrim and Fale together. So as soon as they returned he intended to double-cross Hardrim and put him in custody.

He also felt that Ferman still had information that might prove invaluable in tying the loose ends around Krebs's neck.

Ralph Ferman had been mistaken for Mel Hardrim, whom Ferdinand had ordered arrested in connection with the sabotage bombings by a European spy ring. Ferman had told his FBI interrogator a fabulous story that the Santa Bella blight was a designer virus deliberately loosed to trigger a worldwide famine.

To Ferdinand's later embarrassment, he had authorized Ferman's release. Only later did he learn that Ferman had been on the South American team fighting the Blight. He claimed there were traitors on the team, including the team's leader, Noah Chambless. Much of his story jibed, as Hardrim, who had first talked to Ferman in the Washington, D.C., city jail, discovered for himself. Ferdinand wondered: Was there a link between the blight and Europe? Between the blight and Krebs?

Such a revelation could smash the president's fragile foreign policy consensus. Ferdinand had evidence that the Europeans, with Krebs, were behind a series of bombings of aerospace factories. Even a rumor that America's new allies had manufactured a worldwide famine could be disastrous. Conversely, the president would be very grateful to anyone who squashed the source of such rumors.

Ferdinand might use this information as leverage to keep his position in the Bureau, and possibly topple Director Pollux.

The night the Detroit FBI headquarters was destroyed, shortly after the battle with the European spies at the old GM factory, Ferdinand wrote in his diary, "I have always felt that the greatest disasters are the greatest potential for victory." In the ruins of that debacle was born the phoenix of his final triumph over Houston Pollux.

Recalling his meeting with Mayfield, Ferdinand slammed an impotent fist on his desk at the humiliation of it.

Couldn't Mayfield see that even Jason Scott was suspect? After all, he had worked for Horatius Krebs when he was younger.

A fantastic thought occurred to Ferdinand: What if Scott had no inkling of the connection between Krebs and his father's death? He had worked for Krebs. An idealist like Scott wouldn't have done that if he had suspected him. Perhaps all he knew was that Krebs was formerly a family friend who later profited from his father's inventions.

Ferdinand took out his leather-bound diary, in which he wrote his most secret thoughts. He wrote furiously in bloodred ink: "Information is the most potent weapon of all! Krebs's destruction is my immediate object. Possibly I can use Scott as the instrument of that destruction. If I can't bring down Krebs legally, I can turn loose the wronged child of one of America's greatest heroes."

He looked at his watch. It was late. But he had several holo tiles to review. He had sequestered all available security recordings, plus some from newsmen who had carelessly left unlocked a van containing tiles recorded earlier. He was hoping that someone had recorded the saboteur who had escaped in the GILGAMESH scramjet.

This tile was recorded by a Phoenix news cameraman who had been circling the space port in an airship and carelessly pointed his holovision camera down at the scramjet pens.

Mayfield's accusation that Ferdinand had tried to frame Mel Hardrim for the assassination of the Dorian Nye impostor still stung. He had never manipulated evidence. At least not in that case. He had wanted the truth, and didn't let concerns over due process or presumption of innocence get in the way.

He felt no ill will toward the former Washington cop, although it would be inaccurate to say he felt guilty over what he put him through. He suspected Hardrim had stumbled onto the same facts he had. He resented any individual, such as Krebs, defying the order Ferdinand revered above all else. If Krebs was behind the bloodbath at the old GM factory, he wanted his ass.

Ferdinand skipped the extraneous material, the reporter picking his nose during the test film, the camera panning across the three shuttle gantries. Then the cameraman lost direction, playfully skipping from the gantries to the scramjet pens.

A man in an SED uniform was moving through the security gate. His demeanor was concentrated, like that of a jungle predator. Ferdinand was transfixed. It was him! He knew it in the depths of his soul. It was the Drang.

"Reverse. Stop! Focus and enhance!" he told the computer.

Ferdinand kneaded his jaw convulsively with his hand and felt his mouth go dry. He stared at the assassin's cold, dead eyes and pocked face.

"I have finally seen the face of death!"

Chapter

7

Nov. 30—Washington—Amanda Macadew, wife of Colorado Senator Charles Ellsworth Macadew, has been diagnosed with Rogue Cancer of the stomach and admitted to a private Denver hospital.

The Jovian water tanker *Hyperion* began accelerating out of her close earth orbit in a long hyperbola that would put her in orbit around Luna.

Captain Erskine Collins, lieutenant commander, U.S. Space Navy reserve (permanent rank lieutenant j.g.), wiped the sweat off the CRT of his navigational computer. Air-conditioning was futzing up again. Dew had condensed all over the cramped bridge. That had to be fixed before the moisture played hell with the electronics.

Hyperion had just come off three weeks' patrol with the U.S. Space Navy fleet reserve. After a Lunar stopover, she would recover the huge water tanks she had left in orbit and drop off her two regular navy fleet ensigns, to be a pain in the rear for someone else. Then free-lancer Collins would return to the job that almost earned enough to keep up the payments on his mile-long rig.

Most of the navy's ships were in the fleet reserve. Any craft of the slightest imaginable use was in the reserve and all who sailed (flew? voyaged?) aboard were on call in the event of national emergency.

Reservists had to put in three weeks a year training with the fleet. The navy's professional core, the regular officers, noncoms, and able spacemen, were a tiny elite that crewed the five battleships, a few cruisers, and the corvettes (these served double duty in the newly settled Jovian system, where they were often the only law or help available for ten million miles).

After three boring weeks monitoring Russian shuttles, Collins was ecstatic to return to what was, at least, profitable boredom. He tore off the Velcro shoulder boards and stored them.

He assigned a party to tear down the gun and laser emplacements. Regs were strict that weapons be stored once a reserve ship was decommissioned. Collins wouldn't have worried, but one of the fleet ensigns, Andrew Thumb, was a real hard-ass about going by the book. Collins ranked him, even in the regular navy, under war footing. But fleet officers could cause a lot of grief for reserve officers, so he humored him.

His communications computer rattled for an incoming message. Collins tore off the printed page and swore. It was addressed to the *George S. Patton*, the name the *Hyperion* used as a navy vessel.

TO LT. COMDR. ERSKINE COLLINS, U.S. SPACE NAVY CRUISER PATTON. CANCEL ORDER DECOMMISSIONING PATTON. CANCEL FLIGHT ORDERS TO TYCHO BASE. PROCEED TO THESE COORDINATES (COORDINATES FOLLOW) AND RENDEZVOUS WITH SHUTTLE SALLY RIDE AND ESCORT TO MIDWAY. YOU WILL BE JOINED BY CORVETTES RED CLOUD, TECUMSEH, AND CHIEF JOSEPH. ASSUME COMMAND OF SQUADRON, DESIGNATED TASK FORCE ELEVEN. YOU WILL BE BREVETTED TO TEMPORARY FLAG RANK OF COMMODORE FOR DURATION OF ASSIGNMENT. REGARDS. BEVEL HAWKINGS, REAR ADMIRAL. TYCHO.

Collins spoke into the intercom. "This is Collins. Put your shoulder boards back on, we're back in the navy." He could almost hear a collective groan throughout the ship. "First Officer Park, Ensigns Thumb and Grasse, to the bridge."

The four officers were crowded on the tiny bridge. Ensign Tim Grasse was a peach-fuzzed towhead who could have just completed his high school trig exams. Ensign Andrew Thumb was an intense, tiresome, pinch-faced youth who performed his duties as if he were atoning for something. Both wore the black and gold of the regular space navy. They were in the same graduating class from the officers' training facility, which Admiral Davis was clamoring to turn into a full-fledged academy.

First Officer Lieutenant Mark Park (permanent rank ensign 2g.) was a scruffy, short, monkey-faced individual in his mid-thirties. He drank too much beer and smoked too many cigarettes, although he was theoretically on the wagon.

The ensigns managed regulation salutes despite the confinement. Park looked disgusted and glanced at the ceiling while his fingers itched to posses a lighted butt. Collins wondered what the regulations would have to say about salutes in a weightless environment.

It was hard to run a ship by the book when the book was still being written. The space navy was a new service, descended from the aerospace command, a mosaic of former astronauts, air force and navy aviators, scientists and technicians. That it was called "navy" at all was at the insistence of the first and only admiral of the space navy, the chief of space naval operations, Hanley Davis. He had flown off aircraft carrier decks and had a nostalgic regard for the traditions and nomenclature of the seagoing navy. Collins himself had been a marine captain during the short Cuban War. He felt vaguely uncomfortable with the "navy way." Nevertheless he had climbed rapidly within the reserve and was regarded highly by Davis and his staff.

Just how highly he found out when the computer printed another message, this time transmitted in a D-5 level code, which only Collins and his exec could even look at. Collins ordered the two ensigns out of the cabin while he and Park read it.

TO COMMODORE ERSKINE COLLINS, TASK FORCE ELEVEN. ADDENDUM TO PREVIOUS INSTRUCTIONS. SOVIETS HAVE LAUNCHED A BATTLESHIP FROM EARTH USING NEW TECHNOLOGY. IT HAS UNKNOWN CAPABILITIES. SHUTTLE SALLY RIDE WILL PASS CLOSE BY ORBIT OF THIS SHIP. WE ASSUME PEACEFUL INTENT ON THE PART OF THE SO-

VIETS, BUT SALLY RIDE'S CARGO IS VITAL TO U.S. SECURITY AND MUST BE PROTECTED. YOUR TASK FORCE ONLY FORCE THAT CAN REACH THIS POINT WITHIN ALLOTTED TIME. MAKE NO PROVOCATIVE GESTURES, HOWEVER, PROTECTION OF SHUTTLE IS HIGHEST PRIORITY. WITHIN THE CONFINES OF THIS DIRECTIVE YOU HAVE COMPLETE FREEDOM OF ACTION. REGARDS, HANLEY DAVIS, ADMIRAL, CNCLUN.

Park's eyebrows shot up. "That's quite an addendum."

" 'Complete freedom of action'!" snorted Collins. "Call the two ensigns back in here."

"Gentlemen," he said when they entered, "we've been recommissioned to escort a shuttle to Midway. We'll be joined by three fleet corvettes. I will command the flotilla."

Thumb and Grasse looked impressed.

"Lieutenant Park, you'll continue as first officer. Ensign Thumb, you'll command the battery. We're putting this craft on battle footing. That means we halt the spin. You see to that, too, Thumb." The two ensigns looked astonished. "Ensign Grasse, you'll be in charge of fixing the damned air-conditioning."

"Commodore, sir, if we are going onto a battle readiness, shouldn't we evacuate the air and put the crew in suits?"

"Uh, you're right. That reprieves you from fixing the air-conditioning, mister. Now move, gentlemen! Park, please remain."

Park's nervous fingers shook a small globular suction ashtray and he contemplated opening it to snatch a used butt.

"Why don't you buy a pack of smokes, Marcus?"

"I'm trying to quit."

"So instead you try to find old butts to smoke?"

"I'm not a logical person, Erskine."

"Knock that off, Lieutenant!" Collins looked helpless. "Do you know I've lost the fleet tactics manual?"

"What do you need that for?"

"Do you remember the procedure for a meeting engagement?"

"Is that anything like a blind date?" Park helped look through the rat's nest of Collins's desk for a moment before letting his hands fall limp at his sides.

"Don't do that to me, Marcus! We've got to know this stuff."

"Why? There's never been a real space battle. The tactical manual is just a wargamer's notion of the real thing. Meeting engagements. Single-ship combat. What malarkey! We'll all fly by the seat of our pants, and probably die by them, too."

"I've a pacifist as first officer of a heavy cruiser of the U.S. Space Navy."

"You bet your ass I want to live, Captain!"

"Snap out of it, Marcus!" He took a package of smokes from his tiny desk. At that moment attitude rockets fired to halt *Patton*'s spin and both men found themselves floating, along with most of the contents of Collins's desk. Collins spoke into the intercom.

"Ensign Thumb! Next time you stop the spin on this vessel, I *would* appreciate it if you warn us all first! Acknowledge."

"Sorry, Commodore, sir."

"Ensign, I want to know the condition of the laser reflective paint. Send someone outside. Better yet, go yourself."

"Aye sir."

"You're going to enjoy this, aren't you?" said Park.

"For as long as I can." Collins shepherded the contents of his desk until he corralled them inside a mesh net. "I'll make 'em think this is an exercise—for a while. I don't want a whole crew of jitterbugs." He gave Park a significant look and handed him the cigarettes. "Here, light one up. That's an order."

In a moment Park's head was surrounded by a globe of smoke.

"Marcus, you'll have to decide: Do you want me to make Ensign Grasse first officer? Or Thumb? In this situation all three of you have the same seniority—in war footing a fleet ensign is equal to a reserve lieutenant commander. It's my discretion."

"I'd rather you put me out the airlock in my underwear."

"Then I expect you to forget your unmilitary background and anarchist tendencies and do the job. In the next hour we could become a cloud of ionized gas. I'd like a nonhysteric backing me up. Clear?"

"Yes." The communications computer noted that the three corvettes of Collins's task force were hailing him as they approached the rendezvous point. "Want me to acknowledge these calls, Commodore?"

"Signal them to be prepared to act as screening vessels."

"What does that mean?"

"*They* know what it means! They gear up for this 365 days a year. It's simple: As a big, slow warship, we don't maneuver very well. Our lasers are for long range, our mass drivers and missiles for close range. The corvettes are for close range. Their lasers and cannons couldn't put a dent in a big warship, but they might get close enough to hit its reflective surface with black paint bombs, and make it easier to hit with a laser.''

"Lucky them."

"Actually, I don't feel too red-hot about any of us right now." Collins was watching a magnified image of the Russian warship, which had just appeared over the earth's curvature.

"That's a nasty-looking vessel," whispered Park.

Patton was a formidable warship, but as she eased into a parallel course with the *Sally Ride*, between her and the *Aurora*, with the three corvettes as outriders, she was obviously outclassed, like a drafted farmer sent to fight a samurai.

"You've got a call coming in from the *Sally Ride.*"

"I'll take it." He recognized the lined, worried face of Captain Fairchild. The fraternity of space was still pretty exclusive, and if you got around at all, you knew most people in it. "Paul, I haven't seen you since Mars. How's it going?"

"Fair, Erskine—I mean Commodore. I just called to see if you want to put our vessel under your operational command."

"Negative. This is routine, Paul. Feed us your coordinates and flight plan and we'll accommodate you. Remember that you're a whole lot more maneuverable. We'll just mosey on over to Midway, and keep you from running into any space debris."

They were on an open frequency. Collins hoped the Russians were picking up the transmission.

"I'll let you get back to work, then, Commodore."

"Good. I'll buy you an Irish coffee on Midway."

"You're on."

Aurora's attitude jets fired. She drifted closer, ignoring a fundamental courtesy of space, maintaining a comfortable distance, which, in the illimitable void, was ten miles or more.

"That's hardly polite," said Collins softly.

"We're not the ones to teach them manners. Cripes! Look at that!"

Sprouting from the hull of the *Aurora*, like rising hackles on an angry dog, were four fin-shaped vanes that glistened like "light sabers" in the unshielded glare of the sun.

Chapter

* 8 *

Ralph Ferman was shaking nervously when he turned off the disposable holocube in which the space shuttle sat like a toy encased in a Lucite children's block.

He had bought it in a nearby general store after he heard on the radio about the impending launch of the Sunside Project. He glued himself to the low-resolution cube with mounting horror as the sabotage drama unfolded, listening to the Science Network announcer go on and on until he couldn't endure any more.

He changed his mind and turned it on again, but the cube was dead. Supposedly good for twenty-four hours, the thing had lasted half a day.

He opened the cabin door and stepped onto the wooden porch with its view of Lake Michigan, several hundred feet below. Between him and the lake spread a wide expanse of conifers. The cabin rested at the base of a two-hundred-foot escarpment. Its vertical rock face would have provided a fine morning's exercise if he had been in the mood. It reminded him of the last time he had voluntarily taken a risk, when he had challenged the seventeen-mile summit of the solar system's highest peak: Olympus Mons.

Even in Mars's one-third gravity, scaling the near-vertical three-and-a-half-mile cliff of the escarpment bordering the dormant volcano was no picnic. He spent a week on the face, at night securing himself to the sheer basalt rock face with pitons and rope. Finally, he hiked the ridges and lava channels and roofed-over lava tubes to the caldera of the mighty red giant that was like a sleeping Valhalla.

He had figured that was his last adventure. He was beginning a career in biology, a vocation without perils—at most, "professional challenges." He had thought of his time on Mars as the wild oats sown before settling in a nice, boring life.

How wrong he had been!

After nearly a year of unwanted and unasked-for adventures Ferman was beginning to think of himself as a survivor. But one whose record could be chopped off at the slightest whim of fate.

He worried about the Sunside Project. Not that it would be destroyed. For all he cared an atom bomb could go off at Deseret Space Center. The world would be better off without the Sunside Project, evil child of an evil parent, the Argus Society. He worried that someone might try to pin the sabotage on him.

Ferman didn't look like a worrier. He looked like a lover. He was in his early twenties, five foot four, with curly, unmanageable black hair kept that way by his nervous habit of running his hand through it. His high forehead and almost nonexistent eyebrows made him look older. He wasn't balding; he'd had the same high dome in junior high. The scholarly look had vanished in recent years, as climbing filled out his chest and thighs.

When he returned from Mars, where he had also researched a mutated earth bacterium, he had gotten his first real job with a government research group, working with one of the giants in the field of biology. Taking that job had turned out to be, in retrospect, the worst mistake of his life.

His odyssey had begun ten months before in Nicaragua, as part of the American team fighting the Santa Bella blight, when he had discovered that the man in charge of finding a cure for the blight, Dr. Noah Chambless, was doing his best to spread it.

He couldn't challenge the world-famous scientist on his own turf, so he had escaped camp in an aircar, only to be captured when he set foot on American soil in New Orleans. Held briefly by one of Chambless's men, he escaped again, and this time stowed away on board an express freight Tubeway.

Jailed for trespassing on Tubeway property, Ferman had met Inspector Mel Hardrim of the Greater Washington Police, who had believed his story because key parts of it jibed with an investigation he had been making into the Dorian Nye shooting.

Together they had uncovered the Argus Society, whose electronic fingers were in every level of government and industry, and which, for unknown reasons, was spreading a catastrophic man-made famine.

During their investigations several names cropped up repeatedly in relation to the Argus Society: Noah Chambless, Dorian Nye, the late Alfred Strubeck, and Sherlock Michlanski. Three of them were very much in the news: Strubeck for his famous equations, Nye and Michlanski because of their connection to the Sunside Project, built on Strubeck's foundation.

Uncovering more evidence of a conspiracy, Hardrim and Ferman had gone to Detroit to find the headquarters of the Argus Society. The society had once operated a school for gifted children in Detroit, but the records were erased, indicating once more the ubiquitous nature of the enemy. Hardrim left their hotel room that night to attempt his break-in, and Ferman had a premonition he wouldn't return. He was right. When Ferman next opened his room door, it was to two hard-eyed FBI agents.

After that, things were never entirely clear to Ferman. For many days he was held in an office building, questioned by an FBI man who obviously didn't believe a word he said. Then someone—terrorists, Ferman supposed—set off explosions and infiltrated the building. The FBI man was murdered before his eyes by a catlike man with the eyes of a corpse, who was about to kill Ferman too, when Mel Hardrim had appeared to battle him. While they fought, Ferman had escaped down the hall, to be captured again by another FBI agent, and then, inexplicably, released at the hotel where they had first arrested him.

Survivors don't question kismet, Ferman reasoned. He had quickly retrieved his belongings from hotel management.

Hardrim was alive, that much Ferman knew. But he didn't know how to find him. All he knew was that he had to get out of Detroit, and as far from civilization as possible. He had to avoid the eyes, the holocubes and screens; any electronic equipment capable of scanning or listening. Those who controlled the computers had access to information that traveled between them, as in George Orwell's worst nightmare.

For a time he was a hobo, although he wouldn't have recognized the word. He did chores for rural families and ate their scraps. He avoided the "public troughs" where meals were free. Too many people, too many holocubes were at such places.

Wherever he went he was regarded as odd, possibly dangerous. He came to realize that this sort of existence was bound to get him in trouble, and that he would fall into the hands of the enemy, i.e., the Argus Society, if he was ever arrested again.

He had left the traveled byways for territory where even sparsely settled towns were rare. The Northeast and Great Lakes had lost much population to the South and West and to Alaska. Previously settled lands had returned to a semi-wild state, or been incorporated back into the national park system. Ferman found he could travel weeks without meeting anyone. No one thought it odd for a solitary man to hike in the wild.

His beard, which he had never cultivated before, flourished in the cold, winelike air: the proper, companionable appendage for one who was rapidly becoming a mountain man. Besides, he didn't have to wrestle with icy waters and a razor each morning.

At first he took it easy, to season his muscles for greater exertions ahead. Life had a rough edge, a wild taste, strangely appealing. It was often hard to fill his stomach, but if food got truly scarce he could always fall back on freeze-dried rations. He also had an old army-surplus camp microwave. But it became a matter of pride not to use the rations unless he absolutely had to. For a true emergency he still had some of the gold coins Hardrim had left behind in the hotel room.

Ferman had rented the cabin as a last nod to civilization, and because he had wanted to watch the shuttle launches.

Now he was even more agitated. God knew how much he wanted to tell the world his story. That the Argus Society had caused a famine and planned something even worse in outer space. Whatever the Sunside Project was, with Michlanski and the Argus Society involved, it was bad news.

Michlanski! The most famous member of the Argus Society, certainly more so than Chambless.

Ferman's plans were to head west, but as he looked across the great inland sea called Lake Michigan, he felt drawn north, toward Michlanski's island.

He turned on his radio and listened as the announcer described the successful launch of the *Sally Ride*. Ferman sighed with relief. That was one less thing to worry about.

Michlanski was in space now. He had read that the Polish scientist locked up his mansion during winter. His house might hold a clue Ferman could use.

His Thomas Brothers showed his destination: the fishing village of Charlevoix, on Lake Michigan. Thirty miles from shore lay Wolverine Island, and Michlanski's mansion.

Chapter

* 9 *

I

"**I**'d say the ball is in Captain Collins's court," said Jacob Kane. "Unless I'm mistaken, those vanes rising out of the *Aurora* are to bleed off heat generated by a powerful laser." He grinned. "I call that a threat."

"It's 'Commodore' Collins." Fairchild gave him a hard look. "I realize you're a brave man, Mr. Kane, but could you be a little less obvious in your enjoyment of this situation?"

"The Russian won't fire. He has nothing to fear from our toy fleet. People make desperate moves when they're threatened."

"You assume a rational person is in command, Jacob," said Scott quietly. "That's always a dangerous assumption to make."

The shipboard holocube chimed. Fairchild turned it on.

"Hi!" said Sherlock Michlanski.

"Dr. Michlanski, I don't have the time to—"

"Captain," said Michlanski quietly, "I was on the observation deck and someone was trying to focus the telescope on that Russian ship. He asked me to fix it—and I did, so it won't work. I saw the insigne on her hull. If I did, so will others. I suggest you make some sort of announcement.''

"I appreciate your suggestion, but I don't have time.''

"But if the passengers panic—''

"Excuse me!'' He terminated contact. "This is deliberate terrorism! They're trying to create a panic.''

"In some quarters they are succeeding," said Kane.

"Kane, my courtesy has its limits. Get off my bridge!''

"The voice of the captain is the voice of God.'' With an insolent smirk, Kane evacuated the cabin.

"That man is hard to like," said Fairchild.

"Sometimes the best ones are, Captain.''

II

Inside his space suit, Commodore Collins felt sweat break out on his brow. At the back of his mind was the persistent thought that the navy might not reimburse him for the air he had evacuated to make the ship battle-ready.

Ever since the *Aurora* had put out heat bleeders Collins had been hailing her. The huge ship was well within a mile of *Patton*.

Collins kept his voice level. "Marcus, send a laser pulse message to *Chief Joseph*. Instruct her to deaccelerate and maneuver until she is tailing the *Aurora*.''

"That will give it a clear shot up her ass!'' Hunched over his console in an almost fetal position, Park lit up another cigarette. "The Russian captain won't permit that.''

"That's the idea.''

"I see, suicide before dishonor?''

"For this to make sense, the Russkies must not want to start a war today. They're outnumbered five to one in capital ships. The *Aurora* is on her maiden voyage, a shakedown cruise, probably without a full crew. Would you start a war with a skeleton crew?''

"They might just be pushing to see if we push back?''

"I think it's very possible.''

"Unless a genuine nut case is in command.''

"We can't include that in our calculations. If it's true, we'll find out two milliseconds before we're grilled.''

"So you want to push back?"

"When *Chief Joseph* gets in range to give his nuclear piles a torpedo enema, which is the *only* way a corvette can begin to threaten a battle-wagon, the Russian will either move out of range, do nothing, or threaten—That's him!" The ship picked up the *Aurora*'s signal and patched it into his suit phones.

"American vessel, this is the battleship *Aurora*. Hello—"

"This is Commodore Erskine Collins, commanding U.S. Space Naval Task Force Eleven. Give me a moment, and I'll put your signal through to our holocube so we can talk face-to-face."

Snow obscured the cube, then cleared to the torso of a smallish Eurasian Soviet officer, who, Collins noted, was not in a space suit. So he didn't regard the task force as threat enough to clear the deck for action. From the periphery of his vision Collins saw Mark Park write on an erasable notepad.

HE LOOKS AS COLD AS ICE.

Collins nodded curtly.

A harsh, heavily accented voice said: "I am Colonel General Wen Chin, commanding battleship *Aurora*. This is a warning. Your small warship is drifting into a position from which it could threaten this vessel. You will order it to withdraw."

"General, we've been trying to contact you. You're violating the traffic rules. You're within the ten-mile limit."

"Your capitalist rules of the road do not apply to this vessel. The Strategic Spaceborne Forces do not recognize the right of the United States to impose laws in space."

"At your present course you will collide with the shuttle."

"I suggest you advise the shuttle to recalculate its approach." Chin reminded Collins of an aroused cat. "I won't warn you again. Move the small warship from its threatening position."

Collins nodded to Park, who contacted the *Chief Joseph* via laser and ordered it to accelerate.

"I'm glad we understand one another, Commodore."

"No, we still don't, General. Not until you likewise alter your threatening position to *Sally Ride*."

"You don't expect me to take your threats seriously?"

"Your instruments should tell you that *Patton* is altering course. Continue your present course and our ships will collide."

"What's to keep us from maneuvering out of your way?"

"We are nimbler than you. We can match any course change you make."

Chin's eyes gleamed like polished jewels. "You give us no alternative but to destroy your vessel, Commodore."

"If you attack us, you'll bring the Tycho fleet down on your head. You must know that the president, no matter how much he wants peace, cannot allow you to destroy a U.S. ship with impunity. You will also lock this vessel on a collision course with you. I think even your armor would be badly damaged if our ship collided with yours and our nuclear reactor exploded."

"Nuclear reactors do not explode!" sneered Chin. "They must be deliberately tampered with to—"

"Give that man a cigar."

"I do not understand you."

"You understand me perfectly."

"You are bluffing."

"Find out what kind of card player I am. Call my bet."

"You talk riddles!" Chin's voice rose to an hysterical note.

"The only riddle this time 'round, comrade, is which of us changes course first."

There was a long, cold pause. "This is ridiculous, American. Fools argue over trivialities. I propose a compromise."

"Any compromise that allows the *Sally Ride* to continue on her course undisturbed is acceptable."

"The *Aurora* no longer has a need to patrol in this space. In the interests of coexistence we will change our course as soon as your cruiser alters its collision course with us."

"If you change course, we don't need to."

Suddenly the Russian looked very pragmatic. "Very well, this time you win. Maybe next time, we win. Farewell."

His image faded. The *Aurora*'s shining cigar shape turned away and then, when she was ten miles away, her fusion propulsion unit began to glow.

Collins could hardly see from the sweat in his eyes. "Hurry up and flood this tub with air. I think I want to throw up!"

The crisis was over.

Chapter

* 10 *

Micronesia Times—The volcano Pella has erupted for the third time this week. Scientists have converged from all over the world to witness what may be the most spectacular eruption in modern times, possibly as violent as that of Krakatoa in 1883.

Pella Island appeared in the South Pacific forty years ago. Geologists predict a cataclysmic explosion with the power of a multimegaton hydrogen bomb if it discards its cone, and seawater rushes in. The volcano threatens tens of thousands of citizens of the tiny Pacific Republic of Athenia, thirty miles away.

Rescue craft from all over the world are en route. Airplanes are landing and taking off from Athenia's only airport every few minutes. But if Pella erupts in the next few hours, no more than a handful of the island's population will be saved.

Athenia is one of the "pocket republics," highly developed islands created by infilling atolls with soil from the mainland at the cost of millions of ounces of gold. Other pocket republics include Hamilton and New Hong Kong, the banking havens; and Hellas, Sparta, Hermes, Thebes, Apollonia, and Carthage, scientific centers. They have a common defense force and currency, the Rand. They are not threatened by Pella.

Athenia is the site of an entrepreneurial effort to build a space port to take advantage of its location near the equator, where the earth's higher rotational speed can help propel spacecraft into orbit cheaper than from other locations. That dream seems doomed by Pella's lava.

> *God is on the side of the heavy artillery.*
>
> —*Napoleon Bonaparte*

I

The airship *Olympic* floated a mile over Pella's hellish cauldron. Great acrid clouds of greasy smoke arced up and away to form a subcontinent of smog to the limits the eye could see.

From the pristine white observation deck, Horatius Krebs looked down on the sight of nature in torment and gripped the handrails until his horny hands turned white.

He had committed vast resources of his multinational, multitiered Python Corporation to study the volcano's death. Four research vessels sat as close as they dared to the spewing self-inflicted wound on the earth's hide. Krebs had turned his pleasure airship into a flying constellation of instrumentation.

Krebs, who was in his fifties, leaned over the railing until the baking glow of lava touched his face, and wind caused by superheated air made his kinky reddish-gray hair vibrate. His strawberry nose, shot through with veins like a drunkard's, glowed neon. He resembled one of the capable, tyrannical Roman emperors.

His assistant Lewis Cocker stepped out onto the deck. He was thin, in his early twenties, with a pocked face and lifeless, dirty blond hair.

"What did you find out about the attack on my estate?"

"It was sanctioned by a government agency, probably the CIA or FBI. Weapons were government-issue." Cocker opened his attaché. "We have low-resolution photos taken by surveillance cameras on the estate. Some identification may be possible—"

Krebs grabbed the photos. He recognized two figures. One was a large, tall man in combat fatigues, crouched next to a sapodilla tree, heavy-booted feet crushing brown grass, big hands wrapped around a plastic assault rifle.

He vividly remembered that man, whom he had encountered as he was walking his two chimpines (hybrid attack dogs with the brains of chimpanzees) through the jungle. They had died trying to protect him, shredded by the fléchette gun carried by the big man's partner, a voluptuous redhead who poured a hundred rounds into them as coolly as she would light a cigarette.

She was the one in the other photo.

They had held Krebs at gunpoint while his estate guards were gunned down or captured and several buildings were burned.

The man had put a gun to his head and asked where his hired assassin Emil had hidden the atomic bomb he intended to use to blow Deseret Space Center to hell.

"On board one of the scramjets." Krebs was happy to cause the death of Emil, who had gone into business for himself and now threatened to pull Krebs down with him with his doomed scheme.

"It's not my doing! I've tried to stop him. You can't prove otherwise." Krebs had felt fear when it became obvious that the two weren't interested in any bribe he could offer.

The big man tapped the gun's muzzle against Krebs's forehead. "I don't have to. I'm not the government, just the man who can put a forty-four slug in your brain." He said he knew about Emil's attempt to wipe out people connected with Adam Scott. And of Krebs's connections with the Service Européen d'Intelligence, whose help he had used to sabotage rival American aerospace factories. "I'm prepared to release that information to the public."

"You'd have done so if you thought the government could hang anything on me," Krebs had said.

"Krebs, it's all right to dabble in politics. But you're going to have to give up extracurricular activities."

He warned Krebs to deal with Emil. "I'm going to check your information about the atomic bomb. If you lied, or you don't take care of Emil, I'll come back and kill you. You can't trace me. Double or triple your guards, and I'll get through."

Krebs had believed him.

Emil proved again to have a cat's lives by flying a captured scramjet out of the space center, and escaping in a survival pod before the Air Force blew the craft into confetti. He then limped ten miles to Krebs's estate with a multiple-fractured leg.

Krebs made sure that Emil never embarrassed him again.

He looked at Cocker. "Top priority to identify these two. If they were part of a government hit, they operated outside the normal framework, maybe without authorization. That makes them vulnerable."

"What if they acted with authorization?"

Krebs smiled like ice until Cocker turned away nervously. Krebs's influence in high places had protected him and his illegal activities for many years. They could protect him from much, but not from the revelations with which the man and woman in the Quintana Roo jungle had confronted him. Krebs's one chance was if they had acted outside the law. Then he might yet use his vast resources to track *them* down and destroy them.

"Start digging!" Krebs occasionally had to snap the whip at Cocker, who had a brilliant financial mind, but had been little more than an aide until Jacob Kane quit Python to work for Jason Scott. Python insiders routinely referred to him as "Krebs's cocker spaniel." That secretly amused Krebs. He had decided to expand Cocker's duties, although after Kane's betrayal he would never trust anyone that much again. But Cocker was a fine instrument, hungry for privilege and power, and what few scruples he'd had, Krebs had snuffed with a combination of humiliation and reward. The important thing to remember about instruments was to keep them in hand, always.

That was his mistake with Kane, and most egregiously with Emil. Cocker was different. He lacked the magician's touch.

The dirigible had drifted away from Pella's fiery cone and rapidly approached the main island of the Athenian chain with its little capital of Perikles, and off to a corner of the island, the science enclave Plato. Athenia's main drivers were entrepreneurs and capitalists escaping choking taxes or antitechnology laws.

Her main industry was aerospace, where she was a thorn in Krebs's side. Athenian metals, using Adam Scott's formulae, which in the western hemisphere were owned by Krebs, were very competitive in the Pacific Rim. More recently, Athenian entrepreneurs had provided capital to the consortium, headed by Krebs's bitter rival Rita Duce, that backed the Sunside Project.

Krebs joyfully contemplated the possibility of the little nation being wiped out by a single blow of a mighty volcano.

Cocker put his communicator to his ear. "They're broadcasting a distress signal, asking that vessels in the area help evacuate the population. They don't expect Mrs. Duce's rescue craft to get here in time.''

Krebs arched his eyebrows, and his upper lip twitched microscopically. "We will, of course, respond. But they must realize we don't have enough ships to evacuate everyone in time.''

"Those not evacuated will escape in boats. They feel the main danger is from a tsunami. Shall I reply to the Athenians?''

"Yes, and ask if the island is officially being abandoned.''

While Cocker spoke to the communicator, Krebs looked down on the speck of land. The progress made there was remarkable. He saw a huge, round building: the particle accelerator. On the northern shore were the beginnings of the space port construction.

"Now someone is pouring gasoline down their anthill and setting it on fire," he murmured. He looked at Cocker, who was frowning. "What?''

"They relayed a message from Ted Kodaly—''

"The president of the republic?''

"Old bastard's staying in the presidential bungalow, to keep a government in being. He said he'd see Athenia's scientific hardware covered with lava before he'd let you salvage it. That means we can't touch it, according to international law.''

Krebs smashed his fist against the railing. "He's doing it to spite me! Sacrificing his miserable hide to keep me from salvaging—'' He looked like he might have a stroke. He took a deep breath. "So be it. I'll trade Kodaly's life for the privilege of watching his dream die. Too bad we can't let 'em all share his fate.''

"But so many people, so many great scientists would die.'' Cocker's pesky conscience was rearing its Jiminy Cricket head again!

"They'll all die sooner or later. Might as well be in as spectacular a manner as possible!'' His eyes blazed, then he made a vague brushing-away gesture. "You're right. Someone would haul us into court for not risking our skins to save those parasites. Give orders to pick up as many survivors as practical.''

The fleet of Python research ships turned about, trailing white plumes, and headed for the island. The dirigible began to descend.

"What else do you have to report?'' Each morning Cocker gave a verbal report of his employer's shadier activities. Not for Horatius Krebs to be hooked by a careless interoffice memo.

And so, in measured tones, one of the most powerful men in the world, and his gilded serf, discussed items, any one of which could have put them before the highest tribunal in the land.

Item: The Leopard was demanding faster delivery of fissionables to Black Africa.

"There are problems, sir. The U.S. Navy has discovered our method of smuggling uranium into Black Africa along the continental shelf. That makes it harder."

"What does the Leopard offer for this favor?"

"A monopoly on mining in South Africa when he occupies it."

Krebs snorted. "I deal in the here and now. The war hasn't started! I want a hundred thousand ounces of gold now. Plus an option on the South African mines. Not that we'll keep them. He'll nationalize our ass when he doesn't need us anymore. Next?"

Item: The European Secret Service was beginning to inquire about what had happened to its agents in America.

"Regrettably, killed in the line of duty. Send reinforcements. Next?"

Item: "Senator Percy Manners has been calling all day, sir."

"I gave orders that I be indisposed when he called."

"He's getting angry. He said he would fly a helicopter out here and force you to see him."

"Good! I can start reeling him in now. But gently; one must never make a bought politician feel cheap. Especially one whom you are trying to buy the White House for. Prepare a hospitable reception for the Senate majority leader. Next?"

Item: "Dr. Dollfuss has expressed interest in the project you propose of accelerated aging of a human clone and providing the subject with edited memories from a personality recording."

"He's expressed interest, has he? His ego needs a reminder that I can do to him what the last war did to his country."

"Do you have a disciplinary action in mind for the doctor?"

"No! I was thinking out loud. Do nothing. Just tell him to get a big petri dish and get started. Next?"

"That seems to be it for the moment."

II

Senator Percy Shelley Manners, he of the leonine head and lordly carriage, easily topped Krebs by a head. Yet he felt he was looking up to Krebs as he swept into the cabin office, his huge hands outstretched.

He stopped cold as Krebs fixed him with a frigid stare.

"I don't accept social calls when I'm on a scientific project, Senator. In respect for your rank I didn't order the gondola doors closed when your helicopter approached." Manners winced at the way Krebs chewed the words "respect" and "rank."

Manners's curly black head snapped up and his baby blues flashed. His velvet and bronze voice, which could make the chambers of the Senate shake and its pages quail, growled and rang simultaneously. ("Manners cudda been this generation's Hamlet, which is the theater's loss and our loss," Charles Macadew once remarked to reporters after too much Old Grand-Dad. Manners never forgave him.)

"Mr. Krebs, the whole world knows you have not personally overseen a project in well over a decade."

"Then the whole world knows nothing!"

Manners watched the big holocube that grew from the ceiling. It showed the bubbling caldera of Pella, left after the first eruptions hurled thousands of tons into the sky. The reddish mass simmered and vomited streamers of flame and gas as though another explosion was imminent.

The senator shuddered. "My God, that's my idea of hell!"

Krebs took out a green cigar the size of a small salami. "I'd like to light this on the rim of the caldera. You think of it as hell. I think of it as cleansing disinfectant, wiping out a colony of troublesome bacteria."

"It looks malevolent."

"Nature is neither good nor evil. Creation is not necessarily good. Destruction is not always bad."

"Why didn't you call?" Manners demanded suddenly.

Krebs's face was half lit by orange light, half hidden by shadows. "It's your decision. Once you decide, there can be no second thoughts. If I commit to the task of making you president, I can't stop it. So do we destroy the presidency of Jeffrey Shefferton, or are you content to remain the youngest Senate majority leader in history? And getting older every minute." He looked at Manners piercingly. "You're here for a reason."

Manners flushed. "I'm here to accept your offer."

"The right decision, Senator, or may I say, Mr. President?"

"Krebs, I want you to understand why I made this decision!"

"Yes?"

"I didn't decide lightly: to challenge the incumbent president of my party. To undermine him. But dammit, he's gone too far! He's corrupted the forward-looking policies of the Progressive Nationalists. He has turned our platform for a more open policy on science and technology into a recipe for a dangerous, unfettered explosion of free market buccaneering—"

"I agree!" said Krebs with a condescending chuckle. "I'm for unrestricted trade and advancement by Python, balanced by government intervention and regulation for my competitors. I have no ideology. If I can use a foolish bureaucracy to hamstring my opponents, fine! When the rules change, I don't cry foul. I find out how to use the rules to screw my enemies. So spare me your noble reasons for wanting to stab Shefferton in the back. I want to bring him down so I can take over the Sunside Project and make a fortune with a monopoly on the Strubeck equations. You want to discredit him and be nominated in his place in thirty months."

"You sadly misunderstand me—"

"What's sad, from your perspective, is that I understand you perfectly. You preach that we must reinstitute the income tax, make things fair for the 'little guy.' That's code for redistributing wealth and putting your hand in the little guy's pocket to tell him how to live his life." Krebs lit his huge cigar from a red laser beam that sprang from his desktop when he bent over it. "That's fine. Whatever you devise, I'll survive. My operation is international, interplanetary. Einstein couldn't devise the tax to bring me down."

"You need a civics lesson in how our great democracy works. It is a work of God."

"Some other time. I must supervise the rescue of several thousand hapless Athenian citizens whom God is kicking the shit out of for their faith in laissez-faire capitalism."

As Krebs watched, hundreds of Athenians crowded into the *Olympic*'s aircars or into launches of the research ships. In the background rang the constant overwhelming hammering sound of Pella, a noise so big the mind almost refused to accept it.

Krebs bathed in the cataclysm as he would bathe in a tub of hot, rejuvenating water.

Manners! thought Krebs. What made you think I wouldn't devour you as I did the great Archer McClaren? As I did the man who was ten times the man of any of you, Adam Scott?

McClaren never knew what destroyed him. Just as you, Manners, don't know what you are dealing with. Krebs remembered when he last saw McClaren, shortly after Krebs took over Lawrence Livermore Labs.

The wind blows hard and steady on the hay-yellow hills of Altamount Pass.

Several miles outside Livermore, in Northern California, site of Lawrence Livermore Laboratories, the pass is one of the world's most nearly perfect sources of wind power.

Even Senator McClaren's heavy limousine vibrated in the wind that threatened to blow compact cars off the winding highway. It was one of the new hovercars destined to replace wheeled vehicles.

McClaren found unsettling the sight of hundreds of windmills turning furiously. Some resembled giant inverted eggbeaters, others looked more like monstrous airplane propellors. To McClaren they could easily have been an army of Martian tripods, Triffids, or pods from *Invasion of the Body Snatchers*, encamped on the rolling hills. Some turned madly, some were enigmatically still. Others howled in the perpetual gale.

The limo followed a steep dirt road up a hill to a barbed-wire fence broken by a wooden gate. The driver got out, and fighting to keep his cap on, swung open the gate.

He drove to the end of the road, a few yards from the crest of the hill. One of the windmills towered fifty feet above them.

The limousine already parked there belonged to Horatius Krebs, whose recently founded Python Corporation was one of the nation's fastest-growing corporations. One of the few to prosper under the staggering antitechnological regulations for which McClaren proudly took credit.

Krebs, a man in his mid-thirties, leaned on his car, watching white clouds tear across the sky like fillies at a steeplechase.

McClaren tightened his trench coat about his middle. He was used to the wet cold of Oregon, but not this steady, driving wind. The two men met on the rough ground between the cars.

"Your flair for the dramatic is tiresome," McClaren shouted to be heard over the wind.

"As you see, Senator, we are well prepared to deal with reformers, idealists, or other useless people."

McClaren almost smiled. "I was considered a reformer once."

"A reformer who became the establishment. How long was it?"

"Five or six years, depending on how you reckon things." McClaren tilted his head to look up at the windmill arms spinning high above. "I don't see why I can't keep the armor of a reformer polished. Reagan ran against government his entire career."

"Ancient history!" growled Krebs. "Using one of your greatest villains as an example? Next you'll quote Thomas Edison, praise Bell Labs, or hold up your great friend the president—"

"—The Horse's Astronaut! You expect a kind word for the man who denied me my spot as vice president on the ticket." His eyes glistened with the evil humor his associates knew to avoid. But Krebs had long ago stopped fearing the man whose years of power the history books were calling the Age of McClaren.

McClaren had never needed to be vice president *or* president. His influence had been chilling, corrosive, and, for a time, irresistible. He came closer to becoming a dictator than any man in America since Huey Long.

"I hear your former employee Charles Macadew is running for Congress in Colorado." Krebs carefully gauged McClaren's reaction.

"Yes." The answer was tight but controlled. "If he's as devious a legislator as he was a lawyer, he'll do well. Perhaps somewhere along the way he'll learn what loyalty is." His jaw tightened. "I hope to have a hand in instructing him."

Macadew had been chief counsel for the Senate Committee on Un-American Technologies, where McClaren rose to prominence. Just before the story broke on the Adam Scott scandal, he quit working for McClaren and later made the keynote address at the first convention of the Progressive Nationalist party, which opposed everything McClaren stood for.

"Why are we here, Horatius?"

"You asked to see me."

"I mean here particularly!" snapped the senator.

"No bugs. You were in San Francisco anyway, and I wanted to show you my latest acquisition." Krebs swept an arm to indicate the hills around them.

"You take a childish pleasure in the outward trappings of wealth," said McClaren. "I prefer power."

"I have the wealth and you've lost the power."

"Don't make the mistake of believing the newstapes." He threw open his trench coat and strode about the hill as if he owned everything he saw. "Censure means nothing to me, or to those who follow my vision for America."

"It may hurt your influence in the Senate."

"The fools will toe the line. Particularly when the president turns to me to fill the number two spot on his ticket."

Krebs's eyes widened. "It's two months until election day."

"That jellyfish vice president owes his political existence to me. It's time I called in my chit—time he developed medical reasons for dropping out."

"Will the president turn to you after the Senate censure?"

"That's where you come in, Krebs. I need money. With the Progressive Nationalists making Adam Scott a martyr, *you* don't want our little secret to get out."

"And you can't afford for it to."

"Talking with you is a pleasure. Complex issues are reduced to the elemental. Neither of us can afford to hurt the other. That's why you'll give me money. Because, if I go down—I take *everyone* with me."

Krebs focused on a distant eggbeater of a windmill. "Dignified retirement is out of the question?"

"Don't be funny."

"What's the money for exactly?"

"Opinion polls to show the people want me on the ticket."

"You do need a lot of money. Honest, reputable pollsters don't come cheap. How much?"

"Five million. I want solid results. The president despises me, but he'll do anything to be reelected. Once I'm vice president we'll see how long he holds on to real power—"

"He's been stubborn about the L-5 space station. Funding's been cut, but he won't scuttle it. That indicates some backbone."

"I'm not here to argue. Do I get the money or not?"

"Let me find my checkbook."

Krebs affixed his crablike signature to the bank draft, shook hands with the senator, and watched him drive down the hill.

His eyes fixed on a rapidly turning windmill. The wheels inside Krebs's brain also spun.

Archer McClaren was a man who didn't know he was licked—a dangerous breed because they often surprise everyone and win.

McClaren was too dangerous to allow to regain power. Krebs had already betrayed McClaren once, when he arranged for a mentally unstable mercenary, Lloyd Hunning, to lead the Technology Enforcement Agency raid that was supposed to neutralize Adam Scott peacefully. The raid caused Scott's death and sparked a scandal that devoured McClaren's ambitions.

Krebs had accomplished two goals: ridding himself of the man whose genius he intended to pirate, and neutralizing the senator who could have prevented him from exploiting his new advantage. He continued to pretend to be McClaren's ally, while doing everything in his power to ensure his destruction.

Wheels spinning . . .

McClaren's audacious comeback plans didn't surprise Krebs. After all, McClaren had used a power satellite gone amok to jack himself into the avant garde of the antitechnology party. So skillfully exploiting the paranoia of people who didn't understand science or technology that he gave his name to the movement.

Worse than a hypocrite: He was totally sincere. He believed technology was vaguely evil, that advancements that abolished jobs were antilabor, and that capitalism was undemocratic.

Fortunately, any poll that could be bought, could be bought back. No matter what it cost, McClaren must not be allowed to claw his way back to the top.

McClaren's threat to take down his former supporters with him was an empty one. He would never give up hope. When he was a pathetic old man he would still be plotting his return from Elba. Krebs would make sure he nurtured that dream until someday he was harmless enough to be silenced forever.

There were others, associates of McClaren and of Adam Scott, members of the Technology Enforcement Agency. Anyone who could connect Scott's death with the rise of Krebs and his alliance with McClaren occupied a spot high on Krebs's list to be eliminated.

It would be a long task to weave up the holes in the tapestry. But someday no light would shine through at all. Krebs watched the arms of a windmill spin so rapidly that it looked solid, and smirked.

And so far his scheme had worked. But men like the one in the Yucatán could tear the tapestry apart as if it were tissue.

Later, as the sun was setting, and rescue operations neared their end, and those who could not fit onto the rescue vessels put to sea, Cocker found Krebs once more on the observation deck, with the volcano's maw ever more hellish in the waning light.

"I have some information on the people in the photos. Quite interesting too, I might add, sir."

Krebs turned away from the spectacle. "Yes?"

"The woman is FBI agent Kirsten Fale, serving under a high-ranking agent named Roger Ferdinand. The man is a former Washington police inspector, Mel Hardrim. Reports said he died in a fire in Detroit. His body was identified. His career was destroyed by the assassination attempt on the president's science adviser in January. He supposedly died conducting a private investigation to clear his name."

"Excellent. We start by making it profitable to erase his program. Permanently, this time. Post a reward of one thousand ounces on the Underground Bulletin Board and Styx Network with this photo. Get the sleazes working for us. We may need professional help. Since Emil had his accident it's hard to get quality wetwork. So I'm counting on Dr. Dollfuss's experiment being a success.''

"What professional help did you have in mind?''

"Solarz in San Diego is resourceful and appreciates my friendship.''

"Yes sir.''

"Good work. Ultimately the responsibility for finding Hardrim lies with you. Remember, they may build my gallows higher, but neither of our feet will touch the ground.''

Chapter

* 11 *

Dec. 1—Tokyo, *Asahi Shimbun*—Several thousand people were rescued yesterday from the Pacific Republic of Athenia, but hundreds, including President Kodaly, perished under a hail of fiery particles from the volcano Pella thirty miles away.

Rescue efforts by ships of the Python Corporation were personally directed by Horatius Krebs. Ships and airplanes of the Tectonics Corporation also participated, as did elements of the European, New Zealand, Greater Asian, and U.S. navies and ships and airplanes from neighboring pocket republics. Most arrived too late to do more than watch from a safe distance as the island was buffeted by fire and ash, then by a seventy-foot tsunami.

Dec. 15—*Washington Times*—An ad hoc Senate committee will hold hearings on a bill to repeal the Thirty-first Amendment.

> Senate Majority Leader Percy Manners formed the committee
> despite pleas from the bill's cosponsor, Senator Macadew, that
> it be considered by the Senate Judiciary Committee, chaired by
> Macadew's longtime ally Lee Woods of Wyoming. Manners
> named his own ally Senator Iowa Thurgood to chair the com-
> mittee.

I

"Number twenty-three, you're in the chute. Number forty-two, get to thinkin' about it!"

The gate opened and half a ton of volatile dynamite in the form of a young male horse careened into the arena, with a cowboy in his middle twenties holding on as if arc-welded to the saddle.

Senator Charles Ellsworth Macadew hunched over the microphone in the announcer's booth. As he watched the bronc try every maneuver possible to toss its rider, he made encouraging sounds. The rider momentarily lost his grip, enough to send him flying in a low arc. Macadew winced at the impact.

"Ooh! Well, those are the breaks for Billy Joe Klippert. Number forty-two, you're in the chute. Number eighteen, say yore prayers! Just joshin' you, son." Macadew's southwestern accent, which he could turn off and on like a faucet, flowed strongest when he was home.

Another rider rocketed out of the chute, holding on as if life depended on it. Fortunately it didn't, since he ate dust immediately.

Macadew was enjoying himself immensely as announcer of the Spencer County Rodeo and Chili Cook-off, traditionally held on his big Sleeping Moon Ranch. He had sponsored the rodeo since his first year in the Senate. It was the main political gathering in Colorado; his chance to press the flesh with money men, and scout out rumblings in his small empire. It occasionally became a regional political confab, particularly in national election years. It was not unusual for a half dozen Southwest governors to drop in and pay back a political debt or else cash one.

The Sleeping Moon made Macadew's ranch near Deseret look like a tenement. Once a resort built around a natural hot spring, before that a depot for the Butterfield Stage Line and the hangout of Jim Bridger and Kit Carson, in the 1940s and '50s it was a hideaway for celebrities like W. C. Fields and Errol Flynn, who had to be spirited away one night after he allegedly trespassed on the virtue of an Indian housemaid.

Macadew housed his special guests in the hundred or so adobe bungalows that clustered around the spring.

He almost called off the event because of the recent death of his wife. He and Amanda hadn't been close for years, but her horribly sudden death by Rogue Cancer had hit him like a steel fist. Macadew had always dwelt in the land of the living and if he wasn't letting death keep him from running for another term, he certainly wouldn't let it kill his rodeo.

Another cowboy, thirtyish, lean and rangy as a starving coyote, with an attitude of arrogant contempt for danger, exploded out of the chute like the rider of a cyclone. He was tossed and whipped about, but when the storm ended, with the horse standing, head bent, shivering with defeat, he was still in the saddle. Macadew found himself whooping with enthusiasm along with the rest of the crowd. He had been holding his breath, and when he let it out and inhaled he caught the merest shadow of an odor.

Much as he enjoyed what he laughingly termed "the cow-torturing festival," it was the chili contest that held his attention. He liked nothing more than eating a bowl of red. He was salivating just thinking about judging more than a hundred entries, when someone climbed into the booth to give him a note.

He looked down and saw a face that never failed to make a cannon fire off in his chest, even after all these years.

Rita Holcombe Duce always made Macadew feel that way. He saw her former stunning beauty, not her bony thinness or severe gray hairstyle. He saw her as he remembered her: cool, glistening round arms, skin like that of an Egyptian princess, glossy black hair, penetrating green eyes.

He got a substitute for himself at the mike and climbed down.

"Rita, my dear, I'd think one of the richest women on earth could afford to feed herself jus' a little more than you do."

"It's nice to see you too, Charles."

"It'd be nicer to see ya lookin' a little healthier, girl." He became serious. "Don't make me go through losin' you too."

She put up a hand. "I am healthy. I don't drink or smoke cigars, and I'm not overweight." He looked sheepish at the litany of his principal vices. "I am, however, kept up nights defending myself against constant attacks by the Python Corporation."

Macadew nodded grimly. "He's attacking the Sunside Project through you. How you holdin' up?"

"It's a secret war. He's got three times my resources, and he's global. My capital is fluid and there's more every day, as long as the Challenger keeps producing gold. He has more brute force, but I can shift my defenses faster. One day he tries to take over a company that supplies me with molecule memory boards. Next day he tries to squeeze out the people who refine our gold.''

"How bad did Pella hurt your allies in the pocket republics?''

"Athenia's gone, of course, although we salvaged some hardware. The other republics are trimming back investments. So are my other partners. I'm becoming more and more Jason Scott's main backer. Krebs knows that, so he's pushing me hard.''

"He's also tryin' to buy the United States Senate.'' Macadew lovingly set a Cuban maduro on fire. "I think he's already bought our old buddy Senator Percy Shelley Manners. The price was Percy's nomination as president by the Progressive Nationalists.''

"Manners has never been your friend, or the president's. I have no reason to love him.'' Manners had tried to pass legislation to destroy the fledgling core tap industry. "Why would Krebs buy someone who already works against us?''

Macadew leaned against the fence and watched a rodeo clown play tag with a Brahma bull. "Before, Percy worked for his own advantage. He'd never have challenged Jeff unless a weakness appeared. Now he'll work at creatin' that weakness. From opportunist, he's transformed into antagonist.'' He puffed his cigar and squinted against the afternoon sun. "Percy's comin' here to our little confab. Might even give a speech. He does put on airs like a loyal member of the party.''

Rita Duce sniffed with distaste at the dust, noise, and smells as the crowd roared when a pair of cowboys twirling lariats took off in the arena after a hybrid of a cow and buffalo, a beefalo.

"To what do I owe your lovely presence here?'' asked Macadew. "Sweaty horses and red-hot chili isn't your style. Even less so smoke-filled rooms and political gossip.''

"I wanted to see you when I heard about Amanda. I forced myself not to drop everything at my new Wildcat Tap and fly to Washington.'' She wrinkled her nose. "It would have been unseemly. Too many nosy people and wagging tongues in that wretched city.'' She looked across the desert toward a mountain that rose six thousand feet. It was called Hot Springs Mountain.

"How can you stand it there? You know who produces, who gets things done in this country. It's people like Jason and his father and, God help us, even Horatius Krebs who make America, and who made America. What is Washington except a city of leeches, who keep dreamers from fulfilling their dreams, who, in fact, chain them to the ground and treat them like lunatics?''

''Not all of us are leeches, girl,'' said Macadew softly.

''I didn't mean—''

He held up his hand. ''Not a word. You're right about who made America, although I don't include Krebs. He's not a creator. He feeds on the dreamers. I guess maybe he has his own nightmarish vision for the world, but I don't want to know it.

''America is not a place, or even a people. It's an idea, an attitude. Here in this desert, men like Kit Carson and Frémont and a million nameless dreamers each built on it. Maybe the America they knew is dying. We may have become too enclosed and smothering a place.'' He looked up. ''There's an unlimited frontier. It's jus' too big to police and regulate to death. That's where we'll build America. And if the old America ain't America anymore, why they'll be a bigger an' maybe better one out amongst the stars. That's what I work for. That's what you're doin' with your dough.''

She laughed. ''And I came out here to find out how you're holding up with Amanda gone.''

''My day's filled with routines. Sometimes I go for hours without realizin' she's gone. I'll check into a Holiday Inn or somethin' and realize I'm alone.''

''I felt the same way after my husband died.''

''That's when you showed you were made of tough fibers. Funny how you and I alternated bein' married. When you were, I wasn't. When I was married, you weren't. Now neither one of us is.''

''You never were one to beat about the bush, Charles.''

He smiled, not ''Macadew's killer smile,'' but a gentle, even vulnerable smile few people saw. ''Don't have all that much time, darlin', what with cigars, drink, and fat, I'm fadin' fast.''

Most of the people who worked for Rita Duce, who feared her, would have been surprised to see that she too, like Macadew, had a sweet, vulnerable smile.

''Charles, you're a sweet man. And I love you dearly as a friend and ally. But do you think we ought to spoil that?''

''Allies? The enemy of my enemy—''

''—is my lover?''

''Why not, girl? We've been in and out of love most of our grown-up lives. When you an' me had dinner a few times back when you were fightin' for your life, I felt somethin'. I couldn't do anything, 'cause I couldn't hurt Amanda. But it was there.''

"I felt it, too, Charles. Maybe it was our younger selves mourning their passing." She looked up at him. "Charles, what are you going to do when you grow up?"

Macadew ran his hand over his face. "Wal, there was a time I thought I might grow up to be president. I admit to havin' such thoughts when I gave the keynote address at the first Progressive Nationalist convention. But then Harmon stampeded the delegates—that's how history works. Geeod! What a bodacious mess we'da been in if he'd ever got himself elected!" He took a puff and half closed his eyes. "I guess mebbe I'm what I was meant to be."

"I was just curious. Some men are never satisfied. They kill themselves inside because they never meet their own expectations."

"Some women too, I 'spect."

"I, however, am not one of them. I'm glad you are happy with yourself." She changed the subject. "You going to the President's New Year's party?"

"Yes, an' so are you. You're the chief financial backer of the Sunside Project, his baby. You damn well better be there. Jus' about every enemy you an' me an' Jeff has will be. They'll be a hell of a lot more than the salad gettin' speared, and more'n roasts'll be gettin' carved. This new year Shefferton'll probably have to fight for his survival."

"Why? Sunside is proceeding. All the legislation has been passed."

"With that out o' the way, Jeff's gonna push for the repeal of the Thirty-first Amendment. He's in for the fight of his life."

"It's somewhat frightening."

"It is that. How 'bout havin' dinner later tonight with a self-sufficient man who's happy where he's at and who he is?"

"I think my ego can stand it."

II

Each ETF combat computer is linked via laser to every other computer in the company and to the commanding officer, who can locate every man in his company. To move a man or squad, he transmits orders via computer. If the men can't comply, e.g., they are embroiled in a firefight, they inform the computer. There is no breakdown in communication, a major

cause of casualties. If an attack encounters a strong point, the commander can withdraw it without unnecessary casualties, or reinforce it enough to do the job. Or use his men like delicate probing fingers to find weak spots and exploit them.
—Brig. Gen. David Keith, introduction to
Extraordinary Tactics Manual

As Macadew walked back to his ranch house to change for dinner, he ran into another of his guests.

The man leaned heavily on a cane and favored one of his legs. He stopped when he saw Macadew and the light caught on his thick glasses. He was in his early fifties, with a military bearing, slim and fit, except for the limp.

"Captain Lambert-Healey!" Macadew recognized him from the times he had testified before military appropriations committees.

"You are my host?" he said with a cultured British accent.

"Charles Ellsworth Macadew." He drew his dumpling body to its full height and inclined his head cordially. "Presently a member of the United States Senate, the most undisciplined, uncivilized, and unintelligent collection of horse thieves, baby snatchers, and nonstop talkers in the world. At your service."

"You have quite an estate, Senator. It's certainly not as cold as Washington, but there is a definite nip in the air."

"My manners, Cap'n! Join me for a drink up at the house!"

They were gloriously engulfed by the cheery warmth of the ranch house's roaring fireplace. Macadew led the way into his den, which featured an original statue by Frederick Remington. On the far wall was an antique gun collection that included firearms going back to the sixteenth century.

"Very comfortable home, Senator." Macadew knew that Bertram Lambert-Healey's own Georgetown home was hardly that of an average working journalist. He also made a considerable income as a consultant to armaments firms.

One of the bookcases opened into a well-stocked bar.

"Scotch?" asked Macadew, comfortable in his role as tapster.

"Neat."

The journalist took his drink and settled on the sofa. "I'm flattered you invited me here, Senator. Am I presumptuous to suppose perhaps you had something in mind when you did so?"

"You would not be. But I think it would be a great sin if you did not experience the healing qualities of the sulfur spring we got here. I noticed your leg seemed to be painin' you.''

"Very well.''

Macadew knew it was unwise to drink alcohol and sit in a hot spring, but like most rules of life that he disagreed with, he ignored it. Surrounded by large granite rocks in a natural pool Indians had once used as healing waters, Macadew sat amidst rising eddies of steam like a blob of butter in a skillet and felt his aches and pains melt away. Even the smell of rotten eggs was not annoying. From the blissful expression on his guest's face, the captain was feeling something similar. Good! Macadew liked people he wanted something from to be relaxed and vulnerable.

"A lot of us on the Hill read your column in the *Post*.''

Lambert-Healey's column, "Military Hotline,'' often criticized congressional defense policies, but mainly targeted the military brass's lack of leadership, tactical and strategic backwardness, and old-fashioned methods. Lambert-Healey was a firebrand, an intellectual, a philosopher of war, who lobbied tirelessly for his tactical and strategic methods. He was not a popular man.

"I'll get to the point, Cap'n.''

"I'd be most grateful if you left off that rank. The army in which I served is long dead. Its replacement is an abomination.''

"Certainly.'' Macadew bestowed his killer smile. "I've followed your series on Africa with interest.'' He leaned forward. "You really believe the Leopard's goin' to invade South Africa?''

"Indeed. And he will do so within a few weeks.''

"What'll happen?''

"His army will bog down and he will use nuclear weapons.''

"Fission without a license, eh? Where do you suppose he's gettin' his weapons grade stuff?''

"You should ask your CIA. I'm in the dark. But he has them.''

"Nuclear war in Africa. That's a lot o' predictin'!''

"I'm not a mystic. My predictions are based on observable data. Although certainly some of my sources are confidential.''

"I happen to think you're correct, Mr. Lambert-Healey.''

"That's pleasant to hear for once.''

"You've caught some flak lately! Surprising, since you're one of the most influential military theoreticians of our time.''

"Theories are often ignored by professional soldiers. In no profession are abstract thinkers so scorned. I may be influential, but not among establishment generals and admirals.''

"You have more friends than you think."

"I need them all," said the Englishman wearily.

"You remember Henry Cameron?"

"The American ambassador who got me aboard the *New Jersey* when my countrymen almost shot off my leg? Not a man I'd forget!"

"The governor's retired now, but he has followed your career avidly since you adopted America. He considers you a genius."

"That's an overused word. I just see some things a little more clearly than other people."

"We need that ability pretty bad!" Macadew unconsciously lowered his voice dramatically. "In my position as an adviser o' the president, I've brought your writings to his attention."

"Yes?"

"He feels it would be useful if a man with your insight put together a think tank to address this problem."

"Think tank! Another name for a committee. Great achievements are accomplished by individuals, or by a few men. You need a brilliant, subtle mind in charge of the problem. The Romans understood this. They came up with the military dictator—"

"Now hold on!"

"Which I use as an example," said Lambert-Healey patiently. "I presume that if the Leopard invades, the president would want to stop him from using his nukes. Correct?"

"Uh, mebbe."

"Having a clear goal is vital. I can't emphasize that too strongly!" Lambert-Healey splashed water as he brought his fist down. "Once generals are in charge, they lose sight of why a war is being fought. The war becomes the object. If your goal is to prevent the Leopard from using nuclear weapons against South Africa, for God's sake don't try to conquer his country. Neutralize his nuclear weapons. Power in our world is too diluted for a Great Power to enter into an armed conflict with a goal of 'beating the enemy.' That path leads to bloody stalemate."

Macadew floated against a warm rock and felt like melting into the pool. "Then what is your recommendation?"

"Put *one* man in charge of the military end and give him a clear goal. Then let him achieve it."

"Would that be yourself?"

"Utter rot!" He was so vehement he created another splash. "I haven't soldiered for twenty-five years. I've no experience in staff work. I am a theoretician. You need an officer who can deal with his peers. You need a man widely read, intellectually deep, but living in the real world. A Renaissance soldier!''

"You have someone in mind?''

"You read my article about the army's experimental unit, the Extraordinary Tactics Force?''

"Yeah. Whatever happened to that guy?'' Macadew ducked his head so that his thick hair was plastered to his skull.

"He's in exile as an instructor at the Presidio in San Francisco. He's the youngest general in the army—yet he was almost broken four months ago.''

"Do you know him personally?''

"It was my honor to instruct him.''

"I should find out more about this man.'' He waded to the edge of the pool. "But first, I have a dinner date with a beautiful woman.''

Chapter

* 12 *

I

"**W**here the hell is Mel Hardrim?" demanded Roger Ferdinand as soon as Kirsten Fale entered his office.

She looked at him coolly. "Gone."

Ferdinand was infuriated, and a nasty headache in his frontal lobes began to attack his reason with an icy pickax.

Kirsten Fale had memorized his vocabulary of body language. She recognized the tense furrows on his forehead—

"Now, Roger!" she said soothingly. Ferdinand softened and hardened simultaneously. Her voice made the headache retreat until it was a gnawing pilot light at the base of his skull.

Kirsten shook her head playfully and smiled, crookedly, since her jaw was swollen. Her well-tailored business suit had a rumpled, rolled-in look that almost drove him to distraction. The reason was that she had been shuttled on several flights to catch up with Ferdinand at Deseret.

He remembered what she had said. "What do you mean, 'gone'? I told you to return with him."

She rubbed her jaw. "Tell that to my glass jaw. I've never been slugged before. Hardrim's no gentleman, I can tell you."

Ferdinand was astonished. "He actually hit you?"

"Yes, and while I wasn't looking. Most unsporting."

"Are you joking? This is serious!"

"Why? You agreed that he lead the raid on Krebs, in return for the last location of his friend and your erasing his name from the computer network."

"Damn you! I don't pay you to do my thinking! I never said I wouldn't put him in custody later. He has valuable information. You saw the report Moran filed on Ferman before he was killed."

"Moran thought Ferman was a nut."

"Sometimes very big trees can sprout from nuts, my dear."

She looked at Ferdinand and a light dawned. "You haven't told Mayfield anything about this." She smirked. "Have you?"

"You know my methods. I think the answer would be obvious."

"It could destroy Shefferton. You can use its potential destructiveness as a tool against Director Pollux."

"Splendid! Brava!" Ferdinand linked his hands behind his back, rocked his shoulders, and grimaced.

"You're tensing up again, Roger."

He sighed and kneaded the back of his neck. She slipped up behind him and sank her strong fingers into the putty of his neck muscles. He groaned like a man climaxing.

"Listen to me, kitten. I saw the man who led the sabotage attempt. I found a recording. It was the Drang. His face was there, big as death. Now, if I can link him to Krebs—"

"Krebs admitted to Mel and me that Emil worked for him. His name was Emil. But Krebs also said that Emil had stabbed him in the back. Gone into business for himself. That he was a renegade."

"Can he prove it?"

Her fingers kneaded and molded as Ferdinand's head lolled to one side and his eyes glazed over.

"Can we prove otherwise? Can a man like that be brought to justice? Mel came close to killing Krebs. I saw it in his eyes."

"No, you didn't! Hardrim would never murder anyone. He's weak. Also dangerous!" He shook his head to clear it and glared at her. "Damn you for losing him! You'll have to grind your pretty little fanny to make up for this!"

II

After she left Ferdinand, Kirsten Fale drove out into the desert to be alone.

Like Ferdinand, she wished she knew what Hardrim was doing. Unlike Ferdinand, she was only concerned that he was safe.

She napped in her car and awoke before dawn to watch the sunrise over the desert. It was spectacular, shot through with reds and oranges and hues she couldn't name, like a Navaho blanket. Sunrises had been works of art since Pella had erupted in the South Pacific. Her car phone chirped.

"Don't you ever sleep, Ferdinand?" she asked irritably.

"The enemy, the criminal never sleeps." Ferdinand meant that literally. He looked as alert and hyper this early as he would at midday. Did he wear colored contact lenses to hide bloodred eyes with no pupils? Did he keep a coffin hidden at his office?

"Ralph Ferman has made a mistake. He phoned his sister in Spokane. We have a tap on her, and finally got a number we couldn't account for. It was Ferman, phoning from a booth in the Great Lakes area. He hasn't moved much since we lost him."

"You want me to go there and start looking for him?"

"Yes. More clues will be forthcoming. When we apprehend Ferman, we'll have Hardrim. Now that we have the identity of the Drang, we're beginning to acquire all the pieces of our puzzle. Kreb's ears must be burning tonight.

"I'm flying to D.C. to see what the Justice Department files have on the Drang, Ferman, and Hardrim. Now, get moving!"

Kirsten Fale stuck her tongue out at the fading image. She was amused: The Justice Department computer files in the capital were supervised by Lenore Lippman, Hardrim's estranged lover. She knew Ferdinand was ignorant of Lenny's involvement with Hardrim.

This was Jung's synchronicity taken to absurdity. She had no way to warn Hardrim. She considered warning Lenny, but rejected that. She decided to let the cards fall where fate intended.

III

"So, Hardrim, you going to help me out, or what?"

Mel Hardrim tried to ignore the little man yapping at his heels as he strolled on a sidewalk in downtown Denver.

It was night. Snow was falling. His hands were buried in the pockets of a threadbare thrift shop overcoat, two sizes too small. He had forgotten that winter existed out West. His wardrobe was inadequate. He had Argus Society money, but he'd be damned before he spent it on new threads he would throw away later. Besides, the U.S. Weather Service was promising local relief. He took one hand from the pocket and held the coat around his middle, hunching forward as he walked.

"Hardrim, you're not listening! I really need your help!"

"With what? Walking erect?"

"Gimme a break!"

Hardrim looked down at his tormentor. "I won't tell you again. Beat it!"

Sammy Eljer was short, with stumpy legs. He had to scuttle to keep up with the big man. They had met in a bar the second day after Hardrim arrived in Denver. Eljer seemed drawn to Hardrim, like scum is drawn to the sides of a pond. He opened his life story for Hardrim like he was opening a vein. He had been married, but she had dumped him (no surprise there) for someone rich. His life was ruined. He was down-and-out, almost reduced to sleeping under bridges.

They walked past an all-night pawnshop, and a gaudily dressed woman in her late forties sauntered toward them.

"Hey there!" she said, "I just thought you'd like to go."

Hardrim paused, a tired grin on his face. "That all depends on what the 'going' rates are, Officer."

Her jaw dropped and her come-hither posture evaporated into a bone-tired, invidious look of a cop with a blown cover. Her voice descended two octaves. "Shit! How'd you know? You a cop? I shoulda seen that."

"That's all right, Officer. I used to be in Vice myself."

"What gave me away? Five o'clock shadow?"

"No, actually you make a very attractive woman, for a man."

"Black hairs above your knuckles don't help," offered Eljer.

"Shut up, Eljer! It was your right hand dyed blue. Hookers aren't that politically aware. You a Democrat precinct worker?"

The officer was gape-jawed. "Details get you every time!"

Hardrim pulled his coat together again. He passed a café window, where a holograph of a hot bowl of chili made him realize he was hungry. His mascot was still there.

"What's your problem, Eljer? I've told you I'm carrying a pager, waiting for a message. I'm not free. I could be called away at any time. Besides, I don't like you."

Eljer did his best to thrust his hatchet face into Hardrim's, who stared at the bright spot on Eljer's bald head.

"So? This is a business proposition."

Hardrim rubbed his knuckles. He either had to listen to Eljer or punch him. He had already KO'd a woman this week; beating up a man half his size wouldn't do much for his self-esteem.

Eljer saw the slight change in attitude and bored in. "It's just business. I can see you could stand a few grams of gold."

"What's the deal, Sammy?"

"My former old lady's in town with her boyfriend. I owe alimony."

"How can you afford alimony? You live on the streets."

"She's why! I gotta keep her paid. I need to pay in person, or else she'll set the dogs loose on me."

"Get a lawyer. He can get a writ to call the dogs off."

"These are real dogs. Her new main squeeze is Ivor Solarz—"

"The San Diego hood? The biggest capo in California?"

"That's him. He's got the big hybrid dogs with monkey brains. There's no law in San Diego. They just occasionally send the marines in on search-and-destroy missions to keep the private armies from gettin' frisky." Eljer looked around nervously, like he expected he might be followed. "Solarz and Jill are here on vacation. I contacted them and offered to pay Jill what I owe."

"Why do you need me? Deliver the gold and keep your trap shut, you'll be okay. Unless you haven't told me something."

"Naw!" said Eljer. "I'd feel safer, is all. Solarz is old but built like a side of beef. I'd hate to mess with him. Jill could set him goin'. She hates me, 'cause I usta play around on her."

"You? Don't make me laugh."

"Allow a man his fantasies, will you?" Eljer took out a coin wallet. "Here's the gold. Just get me through this."

"I want to make it perfectly clear that I'm only along for the ride, and if my beeper starts to beep, it's adiós. Agreed?"

"This'll take a few minutes at most."

"Where are we going?"

"Near the stockyards."

"Oh, that's chummy! Intimate candlelight dinner, followed by a drink and cow manure."

"It's already set," said Eljer defensively.

The taxi left them at the entrance to the deserted stockyards. They walked down a narrow dirt road between two large corrals, their shoes crunching on dirty snow.

"You know, this setup stinks," said Hardrim.

"Of course it does, it's a bunch of cow pies."

"Your ex didn't dump you because you cheated. That was probably a treat for her. She dumped you because you're a moron."

"Hardrim, they're here!"

"You didn't tell me Solarz was bringing torpedoes with him."

"That's why I wanted you along."

Ivor Solarz, mobster king of San Diego, limped into the light. He was a compact, nasty-looking customer, with a lumpy head as hard as a pit bull's. You could run over a head like that with a tractor, and it would just make the owner irritable. On his skull grew profuse whitish-yellow hairs in a marine cut. Tiny eyes buried in folds of fat peered out as shiny and cold as jewels. Sharp teeth crowded a small, cruel mouth. He used a black walking stick with a silver hook handle to negotiate the snow.

Jill, Eljer's ex-wife, was a sizzling number, with hair like Black Hills gold, and a shape that a voluminous chinchilla fur couldn't entirely disguise. Hardrim found himself hoping that she would drag the edge of it in manure when she left.

Solarz had indeed brought torpedoes. Three of them. First-class hoods, if Hardrim was any judge. No drug freaks or other unreliables, just good, dependable psychopaths. Hardrim slipped his right hand into a set of studded brass knuckles.

They stood facing each other, Solarz, the woman, and the torpedoes on one side, Hardrim and Eljer on the other.

"Where's my alimony, you creep?" Jill's voice was so shrill it made Hardrim's neck hairs knot up.

"Right here." Eljer pointed to his coat pocket.

One of the torpedoes was too eager. He made a grab for Eljer, and Hardrim lashed out with his heavy-booted right foot, catching the faceless goon right in the shorts.

As the man retched and squirmed in the snow, Solarz looked with amused approval at Hardrim.

"Good moves. Who you work for?" His voice had a clipped, abbreviated quality, as if he begrudged parting with each word.

"Myself."

"You know what I think? I think you're a cop."

"Former cop. You have nothing to fear from me. You and your friends haul off as many steaks and chops as you can carry."

"Your name is Mel Hardrim an' there's a very pissed-off man who owns a pyramid who would like to own your stones too."

Hardrim glanced at Eljer. The little man looked down at the snow. "I recognized you from the Styx Network. I owe to Jill, which means Solarz owns me. I had to pay up, and you were all I had to buy with—"

"Well, since you don't have me to sell, I suggest you give your ex-wife your gold, and we both get out of here."

"You mean it. After what I did to you?"

"You're a little, constipated anus. But you don't deserve to die. Not the way Mr. Solarz collects debts. Right, Mr. Solarz?"

Solarz just shrugged.

"I don't have the full amount," said Eljer.

"I think Solarz will take your marker this time."

Eljer, who had been cowering inside his overcoat, now started strutting like a rooster.

"Jill, how's life? Do you spend most of it on your back?"

"Shut up, Eljer," said Hardrim.

"It's better than puking my guts out, little man!"

"Ignore her, Eljer."

"Take his advice," said Solarz in a barely audible voice.

"Know what? You were a frigid, hypercritical, little tramp."

"You were a bum lay!"

"Let it alone, Eljer!"

"Yeah, well, at least I had you when you were still tight!"

Something tore in Solarz, who had remained aloof. His eyes got tinier. He looked more murderous than his three goons combined.

"You slug!" whispered Jill venomously.

"Eljer, you really are a slug." Hardrim had had it with Eljer. Feeling sorry for him was one thing. Letting him get you killed was another. Just then, Hardrim's beeper started to go off. He took it from his pocket. The message said: *Hardrim, call immediately. We have a lead on Ferman—Chambless.*

The man Hardrim had kicked scrambled to his feet with an inarticulate scream and leaped at Hardrim's midsection. Hardrim misdirected him with the folds of his overcoat, like a seedy toreador. He ended up facedown in the snow, moaning.

"Okay, Solarz, I'm pulling out of this deal."

"Hardrim, you're worth a lot of gold."

"But it's not a sure bet. You didn't bring enough men to make it a sure bet. What if I leave you Eljer?"

"What?" screeched Eljer. "You can't do this to me!"

"I fulfilled my contract." Hardrim held up his pager, which was still beeping plaintively. "And you're too stupid to live."

"What if I don't agree to the terms, pig?" snarled Solarz, who indicated with a sharp nod for a second henchman to attack.

The man reached into his coat. Hardrim already had his .45 automatic pointed quite obviously at Solarz's thick head.

Eljer tossed his gold onto the snow. "Can I go with you?"

"You can if you can." Hardrim backed away, his gun leveled at Solarz. As Eljer started to follow, Solarz changed grips on his cane and used the hook to pull Eljer off his feet.

Eljer was whimpering as Solarz stood over him, his small mouth set in an implacable line. He looked up at Hardrim.

"Sorry you got an appointment. Maybe we'll meet again."

"Next time, have more men," called Hardrim cheerfully as he vanished into the night.

Chapter
* 13 *

Washington Post—Albert Fuentes, Librarian of Congress, has refused to categorize a book called the "first abstract epic novel in the English language": the best-seller *A Through Z,* by maverick artist Fav Herloon. Fuentes insists the best-seller "has no complete sentences, characters, nor any plot. It is not, by any definition, a novel, nor, as far as I can determine, a real book." The "Fabulous Herloon," who has been hired to plan the White House New Year's Eve party, accuses Fuentes of being "anti-Semantic." "Everybody, it seems, is a critic these days," he told reporters.

I

Ralph Ferman had been alone in the forest many days. He had lived off plants and occasionally from canned food heated in his field microwave.

Snow covered spots shaded by the larger conifers. Winter hadn't hit the mountains. Cold, foggy days were the rule. Leaves were gone from the beeches, oaks, and hickories. The air had a tang that promised freezing nights. Ferman didn't mind. A man who has experienced the cold of Olympus Mons no longer fears nature's vagaries. But he was scared as hell of man.

One day he came to a well-worn trail. He followed it out of the mountains that were the lower edge of the continent-spanning granite plateau called the Canadian Shield, into low, rolling hills to a valley girded by high cliffs of Precambrian basalt and transected by a small river that snaked into the valley first as white-water rapids, but was quickly drugged into torpor by flat, brown land. It rendezvoused with four smaller streams and flowed into a medium-sized lake like ganglia forming a brain.

As Ferman descended the foothills, the Transient Artists Colony announced itself. The first sign read: "Transient Artists Colony. Artwork in progress. Turn off all two-way radios. Blasting area."

He felt the first explosion through the soles of his shoes. The next he both saw and felt: A mushroom cloud blossomed from behind a hill perhaps two miles away.

Finally he met a man: tall, with a head like a coconut, sparse hair as short as a coconut's, and skin the same texture. In other angles, he resembled an ostrich, with a protruding chin and beady, indignant eyes. His pants legs were stuffed into boots. He wore a bricklayer's apron and carried a canvas tool bag. His apron had a motto on it: "Ready whenever you are, C.B."

"Howdy!" His voice had a thin, reedy quality that made even a greeting sound a little plaintive.

"How far to that Transient Artists Colony I keep reading about?" Ferman leaned against a tree and took a long breath.

"I bet you think it's a place for down-and-out artists, and you're going to tell me how you're a painter who doesn't have any money and you need a place to crash."

"That's a lot of assuming, considering I haven't said diddly." Ferman sat cross-legged on the ground and massaged his calves. "Come to think of it, why do you call it a Transient Artists Colony if you turn transient artists away?"

"It's for artists of transient art forms. Sand paintings, sand castles, cloud sculptures, symphonies heard once. Or landscaping."

"That's not transient."

"It *is* the way Fav Herloon does it."

"I've heard of him. He wrote that book about the alphabet."

"*A Through Z* is hardly a book about the alphabet. Although it certainly gives the alphabet quite a workout."

"You said this is a colony. How many artists do you have?"

"Two hundred. No vacancies, if that's what you're asking."

"I'm not. You're awfully persnickety. I thought artists were friendly, hospitable types."

The man shook his head. "You've eaten too many agave worms, amigo. I'm the only one here who isn't an 'artist.' I'm resident gofer. Raul's the name, and as long as you're not an artist, I'm pleased to meet you." His hand had the rough feel of a laborer.

A rumbling from deep inside the earth made Ferman look about him to see if there was anything that might fall on him.

"Relax. Just a test sequence for Herloon's next landscape, which is in half an hour. In two hours there's a tornado on Twister Flats. That's usually pretty impressive." Raul generated the air of a man jaded by the extraordinary.

As they walked toward the site of Herloon's landscape, Raul explained that Herloon was merely the designer, and that he, Raul, had planted all of the charges. "I'm gofer, gaffer, and grip. Herloon, not doing the work, is, in this case, the *auteur*."

They passed signs that admonished: "No whistling, no radios, no music of any kind!"

Ferman didn't ask, but he got the explanation anyway.

"We use a harmonic plaster. The production is done to music. Different plasters respond to different notes or series of notes."

Harmonic plaster was discovered accidentally by a chemist who created an extremely tough, yet light binding material. He built a house using it instead of mortar. The first time he played an opera recording, the tenor hit high C, the plaster crumbled into dust, and the house collapsed, crushing the inventor.

Raul reached into an apron pocket and held out a slab of claylike material. "Take it. It's fun to play with. Just don't build a house with it. Prime it by mixing it with a touch of water, and knead it for a minute. This is attuned to E-sharp."

They passed a corral, where a man in his sixties was practicing maneuvers with a bullfighting cape. He was tall and straight, with a thin waist, a hawkish face, and the natural grace of a horse rider. Raul said it was the famous holographic director Bart Bandolier, a pioneer of several revolutionary film techniques that were now standard. He filmed ten features on subjects other directors considered trite and mined out, and found new gold retelling simple space operas set on Jovian moons. He had retired to bullfighting and staging tornadoes.

Raul pointed up. "Two geosynchronous satellites are positioned over us. On cue, they'll focus sunlight on a part of Twister Flats. If conditions are right, they'll create a mild thermal, which will be whipped up into a small twister. Nothing fancy, just big enough to pick up a tree or two." He looked down. "Next week, Bandolier's the headliner at a bullfighting tournament in Mexico City. Real bulls, too. No robots."

They reached a flat area where about a hundred director's chairs had been set up overlooking the valley.

"Make yourself at home. I'll be seeing you. To be safe, don't leave until after the last earthquake. Got me?"

"I understand."

The "Fabulous Herloon" arrived. Famous for wild costumes, today he wore next to nothing. A stonemason's apron was draped from muscular hips. Arms and torso were covered with dark, bristly hairs. He had a bald, bullet-shaped head, with dark sunglasses that sat on a raptor's beak.

He had a raucous entourage. Ferman had rarely seen such a colorful, decadent, indulgent display, like something out of a Fellini movie. Flashy capes, sequined, see-through brassieres, tunics blazoned with holographic heraldic beasts, giddy, spicy smells. Herloon was quaffing a sniff from a globe of layered purple, red, and yellow gas, as were most of his sycophants.

The crowd broke on the reef of chairs, and settled like sea foam settles, hissing, on mottled rocks. Then they quieted down, remarkably attentive, as a small orchestra trotted out onto a field that had been cleared for them.

The orchestra began Casca's "Lunar Variations" on a theme by Frank Zappa. Melodic in parts, its only even mildly objectionable part was a solo by the flatulone. But it passed quickly, and as the music approached a themic climax, boulders were released six hundred feet up the ravine. They tumbled down to strike the earth perfectly in time with the other percussion instruments.

The boulders released a stream that flashed down cut channels in time with the quivering vibrato of the strings.

More landslides followed. The music ended as two alarming, raging torrents of water met like colliding locomotives.

Ferman joined in the enthusiastic applause.

In between the landscape and the tornado, the colony served a buffet, and Ferman loaded up on expensive viands he never would have a chance to taste again. That was his idea of transient art.

He continued north, skirting Twister Flats, which announced itself with a sign that read: "This isn't Kansas."

Ferman reached the border just as the tornado was forming. First as a spiral staircase of air that carried dust into the sky. Then dangerous-looking black clouds sent down a whirling banshee finger that touched the land with catastrophe.

Even at a distance, the funnel cloud towered over him like a malevolent entity. Inside the cloud, lightning crackled and formed intricate mathematical patterns. When the patterns changed, Ferman felt the electricity in the air seem to change polarity.

He shivered when a pattern of eyes, like a peacock's tail, formed and whirled inside the cyclone, like bubbles disappearing down a drain. It was only a demonstration, a weatherman's parlor trick, but it gave him a prickly feeling deep down to consider the possibility that the Argus Society might be here too.

He drew his jacket around him, turned his back on the tornado, and began to climb out of the valley, toward the setting sun.

II

The demonstration was more for the benefit of the Dough Children than because the petty officer deserved such a punishment.

Wen Chin walked between two rows of CosMarines, gleaming in their scarlet uniforms, weapons at rest, lining both sides of the corridor. CosMarines were chosen for their blond, White Russian appearance as much as anything, so the Mongolian Chin was considerably shorter than any of them. His face was impassive as he came to the airlock door, where a chair was waiting for him.

Chin sat, draping his uniformed arm over the back of the chair. He nodded and the prisoner was hustled between the two rows of CosMarines until he was standing before Chin. He hung like laundry between the two CosMarines who supported him.

The petty officer had been caught pilfering vodka intended for the officers aboard the *Aurora*. Normally, that would have called for confinement in the brig, possibly physical punishment as well. But Wen Chin had in mind something more instructive. He had held captain's mast in the cabin adjacent to a portside airlock, so justice could be swift, and punishment even swifter.

It had been several days since the encounter with *Sally Ride*. The crew had been informed that the operation was an unqualified success. Chin even read a congratulatory message from the first secretary. But the crew sensed the reality was otherwise, and that affected morale. That had sparked several instances of pilferage, and one attempted rape of a radio operator.

Wen Chin did not fear the average crew member, who could be manipulated by propaganda. He did fear the only ones who knew exactly what was going on, who had access to all data aboard the *Aurora*. The Dough Children.

He set up extra holovision cameras inside the airlock so the Dough Children could access what was about to happen.

Wen Chin had no naval tradition to fall back on. He had read a lot lately about the old seagoing navies, and it had occurred to him that they had something to teach the modern day about discipline. He was particularly interested by the disciplinary practice known as keelhauling. That had been the inspiration for the Steel Bloom.

He stood in front of the prisoner, whose head lolled to one side. His breath reeked of alcohol and onions.

"Did you have your fill of vodka, Andre? I told the quartermaster to give you all you wanted." The prisoner was too drunk to reply.

"Put a suit on him. We are not barbarians after all." This besotted individual was big and brawny, in his early forties, with flaming red hair. Just the kind who had died by the hundreds of thousands when Chin's ancestors had swept through Russia and put Kiev under their heels.

The double doors of the airlock opened. It could hold perhaps a dozen suited crew members. There were larger airlocks on the vast ship, for taking on large cargoes. This airlock was a service airlock. One of dozens.

This one was different in one respect. In addition to outer doors that opened onto the hull, the airlock had an extra orifice, a circular opening somewhat smaller in aperture than a manhole. The mechanism that opened it to the vacuum was an iris diaphragm. The diaphragm's edges were razor sharp. This was the Steel Bloom.

The petty officer didn't begin to sober up until he had been put into his suit, a cumbersome, somewhat comical process that took four CosMarines to accomplish. By the time he began to get an inkling of what was happening, his screams were muffled by the helmet.

They were completely stopped by the closing of the airlock's double doors. Although for a few moments, before the iris diaphragm opened to the void, the sound of the petty officer pounding on the airlock doors with his fists could be heard faintly.

Wen Chin imagined that for a few agonizing moments the petty officer had fought against his fate, clawing for handholds when there were none. Until he was caught up, like a piece of lint is captured by a vacuum cleaner. Gone.

Wen Chin looked up at the ceiling bulkhead. Well, you little unnatural atrocities. Are you watching? I hope so. He closed his eyes for a moment and imagined one of the pale quadriplegic shapes sucked through and shredded in one action.

He rang the captain's steward. "I'm for some hot tea!" he announced.

Chapter
* 14 *

I

When the world thought of Mel Hardrim, which was seldom, it thought him dead. He liked it that way. His big frame and blunt, memorable features made him stand out. So he planned to avoid beaten paths. Fortunately, the route to the Argus Society safe house traversed empty country on seldom-traveled roads.

The message said Chambless had a lead on Ferman, the man he had been hunting. His friend. The man he had to stop.

He had sent the Argus Society Ferman's last known whereabouts that Ferdinand had given him. Apparently they had used it to come up with a lead.

Two miles away gleamed an immense, many-storied structure, a tiered hydroponics farm, that helped produce thousands of tons of food to ship to the areas devastated by the Santa Bella blight.

Hardrim put the hovercar on automatic pilot and scanned the holovision bulletin board for upcoming semiprofessional theatricals. One entry listed the opera *La Travatore*. Chuckling, he left a message on the board. "Re: *La Travatore*. You can do *La Traviata* or *Il Trovatore*. You can't do both!"

On a live channel, students were performing *As You Like It,* a favorite. The words rang false. With disgust, he realized it was a *Living Shakespeare* broadcast. It was getting hard to find original text performances.

He had driven two hundred miles when he noticed the car.

It maintained a discreet distance. Anyone else would have ignored it. But Hardrim's years as a cop had given him a burning distrust for coincidence, reinforced since he had joined the Argus Society. Reflexively, he patted a large-caliber slug-thrower under his armpit and was reassured by the pressure of a blackjack in his hip pocket.

As he drove the mountain highway, his tail sometimes fell back as much as a mile, and sometimes crept closer. But he never lost sight of it.

His diagnostic computer had been warning him to give his hydrogen-burning heap a rest if he hoped to avoid an overhaul, so when he saw a medium-sized town spread before him, he was ready.

The map computer called it York City. A sign outside town informed the traveler: "We're an old-fashioned place, please remember that."

York City was a town of twenty thousand. The main industries were tiered hydroponics farming, cattle, and fish processing—the Sea of Cibola was a few miles away. It was also the Royal County seat. Hardrim decided to stop and see if his tail would follow him into town.

He parked next to a friendly-looking bar, whose neon sign proclaimed that it sold Cactus Beer, "The Fastest Beer in the West." He hadn't seen a neon sign in years and couldn't resist this one. Inside he examined the establishment's beer cellar, and settled down with a cold bottle at a dimly lit corner table.

As light faded outside, but was unchangeable inside, Hardrim lit a fire in his belly, topping off the beer with shots of mescal. He acquired a beatific, charitable view toward mankind, so that he was likely to cut his unknown tail all kinds of slack before he smashed him in the mouth—if he ran into him.

Hardrim decided on a stroll to inhale some night, desert air, plus some cigarette smoke.

Ironically, he had acquired his tobacco addiction during the national prohibition. The hypocrisy of enforcing a law he broke regularly had almost driven him out of police work. When he was older he discovered the deeper hypocrisies of his profession. Passionate, contentious forces fought for mastery within him. They had finally achieved an uneasy truce.

Pausing in the shadow of a two-story apartment building, he lit a cigarette with his lighter and drew the smoke in deeply.

"Okay, chief. Put it out!" said a voice in the deep tang of the Southwest.

Hardrim dropped the butt, which plummeted in the darkness like a miniature meteorite. He crushed it under his heel.

"What's the problem, Deputy?" Even in the darkness, Hardrim could spot a lawman.

"You've got the problem, chief." The deputy was in his late twenties, wearing a cowboy hat and a cream-colored uniform with razor-edge creases. He shone a beam in Hardrim's face. Reflected light glinted on a brace of ivory-handled laser pistols riding white hip holsters.

Hardrim chuckled at the situation. "For the cigarette?"

"We don't care about 'em if they're self-lighters. It's your lighter. Hand it over."

Hardrim muttered a curse and handed over his antique chrome Zippo. He had forgotten that many counties had laws against any open flame. In some states it had only stopped being a hanging offense within the last decade. A holdover from the bad days of the Millennium Riots when flames meant looting and death.

"Can you ticket me so I can repay my debt to society?"

"Nope. Mandatory night in jail *and* ounce-of-gold fine."

He briefly considered coldcocking the deputy, who hadn't patted him down and found his blackjack and gun. But night in jail was too mild a punishment to provoke him into hurting a man who was just doing his job. The gold *was* a problem. He had a good-sized cache in his car he didn't want tampered with. It was a cinch they wouldn't let him get the gold himself.

He surrendered his gun and on his way to the squad car, dropped the blackjack. The Argus Society had provided a fake ID for an Irv Donat and a national permit to carry a concealed weapon. But there were no permits to carry saps.

II

Hardrim was processed quickly. The more he knew Deputy Moury Hurt, the more he wished he had followed his impulse and left him in a heap.

From behind the grille of Hurt's Jeep-like utility hovercar, Hardrim stared into the yellow teeth of a German shepherd that barked during the entire ride, while the deputy played "Ride of the Valkyries" at crippling decibels.

Inside the jail, on the way to the holding tank, they passed a glass gun case and a desk with a holocube. Over the desk were holocube portraits of Colorado's governor and most famous son, Senator Macadew, flourishing a cigar. Hardrim winced.

The holding tank door shut. His neighbors were a sleeping Indian, an emaciated bald man in a business suit, an Hispanic who smelled like a fish-plant worker, and two snoring weekend cowboys. A middle-aged white man in a filthy leg cast slumped in the corner.

Hardrim smiled. This was the first time he had ever been *in* jail, although he had studied life in an all-night holding tank for many years from a different perspective.

He regarded the well-dressed man, who was in his early thirties. "Did you manipulate the stock market?"

He smiled sheepishly. "I neglected to appear in court for a traffic violation. I'm terrible about accessing my mail."

"They came looking for you for that?"

"You've met the deputy?"

"Right!" Nothing more needed to be said.

An hour passed.

Deputy Hurt came to the doorway. "I've got a release for someone named Tribe. Tribe?" No answer. He disappeared.

"He's been calling Tribe for hours," said the man in the business suit.

Hardrim shook the snoring Indian. "Hey, what's your name?"

"Jorge."

"Jorge what?"

"Aribe," the Indian muttered, and fell back asleep.

"Aribe," repeated Hardrim. "That must be it. A typo on the arrest form. Lists him as Tribe instead of Aribe. Happens a lot. That asshole in there knows it."

"Pipe down," said the man in the cast. "We don't need trouble."

"We've got trouble. What we need is room to stretch out."

The outer jail door opened and another deputy came in. He wore his early fifties lightly. His face was seamed and leathery, yet humane. He was tall and lanky, with easy grace. He reminded Hardrim of a favorite star from the 2-D films: Henry Fonda.

The older deputy glanced over Hurt's clipboard, then into the holding tank. He sat at a wood-grain plastic desk, with a cup of coffee, loosened his collar, and talked to Hurt in a low voice. Then he studied a sheaf of papers.

Hurt returned with his clipboard. "Tribe? Tribe here?" he said, looking right at the sleeping Indian.

Hardrim kicked the sleeping man. "Jorge! You're sprung!"

Aribe rumbled to his feet. Hurt glared at Hardrim, then let Aribe out.

"Good job!" said the man in the cast.

Hardrim was watching the older lawman, who hadn't missed a moment of the small drama, although his eyes never left his papers. He was sure he saw a chuckle.

Later Hurt came back and called the man with the broken leg.

"Max Peyer?"

"Right here and wide awake."

"You're free to go."

"I can't walk without my crutches, Deputy."

"You're joking, chief! You want me to hand the crutches through the bars, and have my brains knocked out with them?"

"I can't walk without 'em."

"I'll hand them to him, if you'll let me," said Hardrim. "Unless you think cigarettes have made me a hardened criminal."

Hurt grimaced. He was developing a real dislike for Hardrim.

The twangy voice of the older deputy spoke up from the next room. "What the hell, Moury? Give the man the goddamned crutches!"

Hurt reddened, and produced the crutches. Hardrim gave them to Peyer. Hurt stepped back from the bars with an elaborate show of putting his hand on his gun.

Peyer passed Hardrim with a grateful smile. But Hardrim was watching the older deputy, who this time almost grinned.

PART

* 2 *

THE
INVISIBLE
PAWN

Chapter

* 15 *

I

Twenty hours out from Midway the Lunar shuttle *Cyrano de Bergerac* prepared to land inside the great crater Tycho.

The *Cyrano* had been waiting at Midway to load the passengers of all three shuttles after a short stopover, where most of them celebrated without ever knowing they had been in danger.

In her cabin a young woman named Bethany Williams watched the landing in the overhead holocube. Her long and lanky body, athletic rather than curvy, stretched out on the dentist's-chair-style acceleration couch. She was not pretty so much as striking, with delicate, porcelain features, topped by bronze-colored hair.

She had skipped the celebration, had instead gone directly to her cabin aboard the *Cyrano*. She now watched the viewing cube with an intensity that detached her from her immediate environment.

Tycho, in the southern hemisphere, about forty degrees south of the equator, was one of the most spectacular Lunar features, easily visible the entire voyage, sharply defined by black shadows of a waxing moon.

Tycho filled the viewing cube as Bethany watched, its outline expanded like a tidal wave in rock. They landed in the center, fifteen miles from the rim, which rose fifteen thousand feet, its jagged edge barely visible, hunched near the horizon, which loomed half as close as on earth. The intolerably brilliant "morning" sun beat down on the dead gray soil, etching stubby black shadows.

Bethany relaxed as the acceleration died away, although the ship's computer did not release her yet, a precaution she suspected was mainly to keep passengers out of the way of the *Cyrano*'s crew.

She amused herself by accessing the ship's computer using an armrest keypad.

The cube showed they had landed several miles from Tycho City, at Tycho Brahe Base. As the ground cooled, two vehicles approached from the base: a cluster of low square structures and domes. One was a Lunar "tug," a hardy tractor that would drag the shuttle on a tracked platform two miles to the docking zone. The other was a tram, part of the United Nations Port Authority tram system, whose authority the U.S. barely tolerated.

Bethany donned a pair of viewing glasses that bypassed the holocube and projected printing and illustrations directly onto the lens in front of her eyeballs.

The computer described the infamous reputation the tram had acquired during its infancy. It displayed pages from novels, spiced with references to the legendary *Copernicus Express* that crossed the wilderness between Copernicus dome, to the north, and the south pole colonies, which had given it an overblown reputation. Today it was tediously safe, although earth people still thought it infested with rogues, thieves and spies.

At some unknown signal, the ship's computer released the straps that held Bethany and her two fellow passengers. She followed them as they stepped directly from its lounge, through an airlock, into the Lunar tram. The trip took ten minutes, completely bypassing the base.

They were herded into a blockhouse-shaped structure that was a processing center. While the Lunar authorities prepared to receive them, Bethany watched the people around her test the new experience of Lunar gravity. Some took to it immediately; others fell over their own feet. Zero gravity, which was similar to floating in water, was easier to adjust to than low gravity, where every step required calculation. So many fell on their faces or their butts, like children at an ice-skating rink, that soon the entire building was filled with laughing, leaping, tripping adults, spread-eagled or collapsed on the floor.

Once again Bethany chose not to participate in what she regarded as mass hysteria. She regarded the scene with detachment; not aloof or superior, just disconnected. Her idea of entertainment did not include interacting with crowds. She was not what anyone would call a fun-loving girl.

She knew that when people described her they invariably used adjectives like "strong," "able," "efficient," "motivated." She knew she wasn't sexy, except to that small cadre who regard intelligence as the most powerful aphrodisiac.

Lately, the word that sprang to her own mind was *traitor*.

She was the little girl who, once upon a time, read the story of Red Riding Hood and concluded that Red would have done better to team up with the wolf.

She didn't offer excuses for her extreme pragmatism. She wasn't raised poor. Her well-adjusted parents had stressed that she could do anything she set her mind to. But she was an impatient woman. She always felt like she was in a waiting room while people of lesser abilities were shown in immediately.

That had changed a year ago when she became executive secretary to Rita Duce, owner of the Tectonics Corporation, which had sunk a fortune in the Challenger Core Tap in the Puerto Rico Trench. Its success depended on a throw of the dice. Many people had an interest in seeing that those dice were loaded against Duce.

Bethany was young and, she thought, sophisticated, but she fell victim to the lure of love and money. She became the lover and accomplice of a man who worked for Duce's enemies. Her lover's strings were pulled by Jacob Kane, who was then working for Horatius Krebs, Duce's biggest rival.

Jason Scott, at that time still a relatively unknown engineer, was brought in by Duce to save the Challenger. Bethany was drawn by his self-reliant philosophy and found herself hating what she was doing. But she was involved too deeply to pull out.

Scott uncovered Bethany's betrayal and her lover's plan to kill him, but instead of giving her to the police, he released her. It was the most potent punishment he could have conceived of.

For months she tried to hate Scott and allowed herself to be recruited to sabotage the *Sally Ride*. She was smuggled onto the base by Emil, the repellent, yet fascinating assassin who worked for Horatius Krebs. He had told her that Jacob Kane still secretly worked for Krebs.

Given the chance to destroy Scott, she instead warned him of the sabotage plan and, believing that Kane still served Krebs, she gave him misinformation that almost got him killed. In return for her aid, Scott agreed to give her a chance to redeem herself by serving on the Sunside Project.

During the flight between the earth and the moon, Bethany had told herself repeatedly that her dream was coming true. She didn't really feel she deserved it. She felt stained. Perhaps she had begun buying back her betrayal of Scott and Duce, but more likely she was doomed to try repeatedly to cleanse her soul, like Lady Macbeth's hand washing, and with as much effect. It didn't help that for the entire voyage she never saw Jason Scott.

So she wasn't pleased when, from across the hall, Kane caught sight of her and crossed the distance between them.

"Jason asked me to see that you were fitting in smoothly, Bethany," said Kane. "He moved heaven and earth to get you on the shuttle. Lucky for you. You would have been answering the FBI's questions until Doomsday. Me, I'd have thrown you out the airlock once we reached low earth orbit."

Bethany exploded: "I can't believe it, Jason is a coward! Sending you instead of talking to me himself!"

"Most men are cowards around a beautiful woman, Bethany."

"Jacob, you're just a snake to me." She turned away from him.

"I recall a red-haired bitch and her lover who worked for Krebs trying to destroy Rita Duce and Jason Scott." He twisted her around to face him. "We've both got lots to answer for. If we talk about who's the bigger swine, we'll never be friends." He cocked his eyebrows wickedly. "Or are you only interested in being 'friends' with Jason?"

"Go to hell!"

"Oh, Bethany, you're opening yourself up to me. If I say Jason isn't remotely interested in you, that makes you even more vulnerable. Even though you tell yourself it's a lie."

"Damn you, Kane! You and your mind games."

"The mind is the only arena worth playing in."

"Why is he avoiding me?"

"Bethany, I don't give a damn about your love life. You saved the Sunside Project by warning Jason. But you almost fried my gizzard by sending me into a trap. He feels he owes you something. I feel I owe you too, but I can wait."

His lascivious expression was enraging.

She aimed a fist that would have loosened teeth if his bony hand hadn't snaked up and grabbed it. She trembled. "Bastard!"

"Women say that like they expect me to be insulted," said Kane with a laugh. "You look lonely standing here." He half dragged her across the auditorium to where two women were talking.

One was on the right side of thirty (or what women that age think is the right side), taller than many men, with auburn hair like ermine fur. A pert, freckled face made her look as if she might have gone on that raft with Huck Finn. A cutoff orange jumpsuit exposed long, shapely legs.

She was talking animatedly; waving her arms to make points; screwing up her face to express a dozen different emotions.

"I can't remember when McClaren's people weren't running things, Rene! My dad was forced out of biotechnology by the TEA. He ended up a teacher in a little town. I guess he thought he was lucky not be jailed for illegal scientific experiments."

The young woman was so engrossed in her conversation that she didn't notice all the males nearby engrossed in *her*. But her companion did, and wrinkled her nose in distaste, or envy.

She was not unattractive. She was in her thirties, with long black hair, hazel eyes, aristocratic nose, and good figure. She wore an unwritten sign that read: "Do Not Approach." The two were a study in opposites: dark and bright, sweet and sour, gregarious and aloof.

"I want to meet everybody!" declared the young woman, changing subjects with dizzying speed.

"You'll know them all far too well before we're finished."

"There's no such thing as knowing someone too well!"

"You've never done a tour on a space station. Have you?"

"Well . . . no."

"In eighteen months, if you're still talking to me, and you can repeat that, I'll know you're a very remarkable woman."

"I did live with a man, for a few months."

"Did you drink his recycled water, breathe his recycled air, share limited space, and do nothing but look at him?"

"I didn't do *that*!"

"I couldn't help but eavesdrop," announced Kane, with the confidence of a man aware that *everyone* knows who he is. "Since you'd love to meet everyone, miss, let me present you to one of our newest recruits, Bethany Williams.''

"Madeline Reed!" She extended her hand and regarded Bethany with dancing, intelligent eyes and genuine interest.

"Dr. Rene Delner," said the older woman with a guarded smile. "I have seen your name on the duty rosters."

"What will you do on the project?" asked Bethany.

"I'm in your section, nutritional biology, as is Madeline. I'm head of the section. Apparently you didn't read the roster."

"I've things to do," said Kane. "Ladies!" He bowed from the waist, a gesture that combined insolence and innuendo.

Bethany saw him again, across the crowded room, speaking with Jason Scott. She started in that direction, but caught herself. She was damned if she was going to chase after Scott so obviously. Madeline craned her neck and saw him. Her sigh was throaty and lascivious.

"Give me a break, Madeline!" said Rene Delner. "All the young women will fall in love with Jason Scott before we're through. Why not be unpredictable and do it later rather than sooner?"

"Oh, and when are you going to fall for him?"

"I said young, dear. I am mature."

"I see."

Across the room Kane reported to Scott. "This group is ready to go through the medical check."

"I don't look forward to that!" said Scott. "If I could sneak through, I'd do it."

"You're avoiding all sorts of things lately, Jason. You'll be evading responsibility soon. Then how will you differ from me?"

"What are you talking about?"

"I mean you shield Bethany Williams from Roger Ferdinand, and then avoid her. Personally, I'd have let him have her."

"We owe to Bethany the fact that *Sally Ride* is in one piece. Whatever else she's done, she made up for it."

"That she's in love with you has nothing to do with your position?" A wicked sneer formed on Kane's thin lips.

"Love? Bethany? I have no reason to think that—"

"Perhaps not." Kane looked down, hooding his eyes.

"Don't give me the 'experienced man of the world' smirk. Just because I don't choose to fish doesn't mean I don't know how."

"To stretch that metaphor, at least I go out in a boat with a spinner and dip my hook. You wait for the fish to jump in the boat with you, clean itself, and leap into the frying pan. You're saying you've had no indications that Bethany's drawn to you?''

"If she is, it doesn't work both ways. I'm grateful to her for saving our project. Her motives don't concern me.''

"I'm less grateful for her sending me into a pit of human snakes because she thought I was a traitor. Bitch,'' Kane said without heat. "Lousy judge of character.''

"There's more to it than sentiment. She's a gifted systems engineer.''

"Whatever the reasons, having her on Luna will let me exact exquisite revenge for what she did to me.''

"Is she . . . getting along all right?''

"I didn't have time to hold her hand. I did introduce her to her boss. I saved you from the inevitable meeting just yet.''

"That's ridiculous, Jacob.''

"Well, then, why don't you go and talk to her right now?''

"We need to get our people processed. There's no time to waste.'' True as that was, Scott was relieved to have no time for an emotional confrontation with Bethany. But he knew he couldn't postpone it forever.

II

Rene Delner, Bethany Williams, and Madeline Reed were herded into a small cubicle with twenty others to be punched, punctured, and scratched by a Lunar physician.

"But Doctor,'' protested Madeline piteously as her turn came, "we were checked for all these things on earth.''

"Not good enough,'' growled the middle-aged doctor with greasy dishwater hair plastered across his pale face like spaghetti. "Earth doctors are inept at virus control. They export their failures to us.'' He injected her with an airgun. "You'll be as sick as you've ever thought possible for twenty-four hours. Then you'll be let out of quarantine. All disease in your body will be neutralized for a month. Then it's another injection.''

"And be sick as a dog again?'' asked Madeline.

"Mmmmmmm,'' he answered. "Okay, off you go. Next.''

They were given rooms in the quarantine area, separated from the city by several thousand cubic meters of vacuum. They had enough time to check in and spread out their bags before they were hit by the effects of the wide-spectrum injection.

Twenty-four hours later Madeline Reed crawled sluglike from bed and faced herself in the mirror. She almost crawled back. Her face was drawn and waxy, her eyes bloodshot. Her hair was glued in gummy clumps and she was shivering in her sweat. Her mouth tasted like manure. She inhaled deeply, coughed, and decided to reenter humanity. After this, life held no more terrors.

The shower instructions said she had ninety seconds of water. She wondered how bathing could be accomplished until she found the waterless soap. The ninety seconds were for rinse. She emerged feeling much better.

A notice on her door told her of a meeting to acquaint newcomers with Lunar customs. Madeline sighed gratefully. It was about time to inject some fun into the proceedings.

As she dressed she wondered if an informal party might not be planned. She hoped so. Just in case, she slipped off the plain blue jumpsuit she had started to wear, and instead donned a festive, primary-color-splashed dress. She was starved. Most of what she had eaten lately had ended up in the disposal unit.

The passengers sat in a half-moon-shaped blue auditorium built for five hundred. They took up slightly more than half the seats. One of Handel's religious works was echoing nicely in the sky-colored rotunda over their heads. Madeline found Rene Delner and Bethany Williams and sat next to them.

Dr. Delner scrutinized her with a critical eye.

"My dear," she said with admiration, "you're a marvel. Aside from red eyes, I wouldn't guess you'd been sick. I, on the other hand, look like a bordello queen with syphilis!"

"Oh, you look wonderful! I'm the one who looks awful!"

"Compared to the rest of us, you look like an angel," chimed in Bethany, who herself had the hollow look of a plague victim.

A man in shirt sleeves climbed the rostrum. He was tall, pale, blond, with a stern, hawkish face. He waited for silence.

"Welcome to the moon." He didn't sound very cordial. "We call it Luna. This is the U.S. Territory of Selene, comprising Tycho City, Copernicus, Clavius, some small colonies, and Newton Observatory on Farside. As citizens you can visit Selene as long as you can support yourselves. Anyone here is eligible for resident status. Legally, this is America—with some exceptions. The exceptions will make all the difference for most of you.

"I'm Haldon Janneson, assistant governor. I'm here to tell you enough about Luna to scare you into returning home without stepping into the city. If you think that's hostile, you're right. We don't need tourists. We need settlers, but only about one in a thousand of those who come up here. Statistically, that means none of you are what we want. Nevertheless, you are taxpayers and 'entitled' to come here. But no one will make things easy for you.'' His eyes roved over the audience. He didn't speak again for a moment until people started to squirm in their seats.

"We have a museum honoring people in Luna's past: Armstrong and Sturm, scientists like Galileo, politicians like Kennedy. A corner is reserved for authors of visionary fictions about the moon. H. G. Wells, Verne, Clarke. You read them in high school. One author isn't there, but in our central square. Not because he was a better writer, but because of a philosophical statement he coined. It sums up our society. His name is Robert A. Heinlein, and his statement, written about a fictional Luna much different from ours, is this: 'There ain't no such thing as a free lunch.'

"Earth people have a saying too: 'The best things in life are free.' '' The speaker held an oxygen mask aloft, of the type stored in every cubicle of a spaceship or life colony. "You think air is free? Obviously you're wrong. Nothing is free. Not the air you breathe, nor the ground you walk on, nor the sunlight you enjoy, nor the freedom you cherish. You live in a huge ecological system and you've been bailed out of hundreds of crises. Somebody pays for that too. Each breath we take is paid for. If you can't pay, you don't breathe. We don't chuck people out the airlocks. We do require that you pay for what you use, one way or another. This may strike you as barbaric. To us it's common sense.''

Madeline Reed was squirming. This man reminded her of a Nazi-like man she had dated once. Like that date, she wanted this torturous exercise to come to an end.

"Here we have but one crime: to cause something to be consumed that is not yours. That embraces all real crimes, including murder, destroying a life that isn't yours. On Luna that is the only crime you'll ever have to answer for. We don't recognize so-called victimless crimes as crimes at all.''

He held up a plastic card. "This is a Universal Ration card. You'll be issued one. Mastercharge or Payital cards aren't accepted. Gold is accepted for some items. Not life essentials such as food, air, or water. For them you must use your UR card. They'll be credited to your account, which you'll pay before you leave Luna.''

A belligerent-looking man in his twenties, with a beatnik-style beard and thick glasses, stuck up his hand.

"What happens if you can't pay?''

"One way or another, you will pay." He smiled unpleasantly. "We put delinquent bill-payers in the hydroponics farms. You'll earn your pay there, believe me.

"The UR card is good throughout Selene and in New Europe and New Moskow but not in the Asian colony or the Lunar Free State. The Free State will take your gold." He looked at his watch. "I've covered everything. We have unusual customs. I won't bother to tell you what they are, since judicious questioning or reading on your part will keep you from making total asses out of yourselves.

"I realize a third of you are destined for the PH Station. Much of what I said is applicable to your situation. While you're here, I hope you learn something you can use on your tour in space. As for the rest of you, it is simple to return to the shuttle. For your convenience the *John Cabot* will wait an extra hour before lifting off. We are anxious not to put up with any of you, whether you're potential pioneers or tourists. If you do stay, you're in for the education of a lifetime. If one or two of you are cut out for life on Luna, I salute you. Good day."

Madeline Reed, Rene Delner, and Bethany Williams stood, dazed.

"Not a very cordial person, was he?" said Madeline.

"He's your opposite," said Delner. "He wants to know nothing about people. Selene has endured many would-be settlers and tourists. This may be the best way to deal with them."

"A little friendliness never hurt anyone!"

"Attention!" said a colony official. "You'll now be issued suits and given instructions for their use. Form five lines—"

"Pressurized suits!" said Madeline. "For a few yards!"

"Yards or miles, hard vacuum has pretty much the same effect on the human body," observed Bethany.

"That's not what I mean!" Madeline stamped her foot. "I know we can't go outside without a suit. But why can't they put us on a tram and take us inside? After what we've endured, I'd think they'd make things a little more comfortable—" Comprehension dawned. "It's not only him, is it? They all feel that way." She turned to find herself looking up at a colony official. He was well over six feet, slim and catlike like most of the young colonists. He didn't look hostile at all.

"Not all of us, ma'am." His smile was as big as Tycho Crater. "Some of us like to see new faces. Haldon isn't as fierce as he pretends. He puts a lot into his performance."

"Doesn't your telling us that defeat the purpose of the lecture?" asked Bethany, exchanging an amused glance with Rene.

"You're right." The young man couldn't take his eyes off Madeline. "I guess it's okay if you're one of the PH Station folks. My name is Michael Broun."

"I'm Madeline Reed."

"That's a lovely name. Let me help with your pressure suit." He smiled again. "It's your most important article of clothing. Always keep it in easy reach. If the dome depressurizes and you're caught outside of a self-contained building, you'd be glad to have it. Every two-year-old knows to put on his suit when the warning lights flash. You don't want to be shown up by a child, do you?"

His manner took the reproof from his words. He helped Madeline into her suit, told her how to use the air tank controls and check the pressure. He explained what to do if a leak developed in the suit fabric. He started to repeat the instructions for Rene Delner.

She held up her hand. "I once wore a suit like this for sixty hours in a compartment on L-5 that lost pressure." She didn't tell him all Sunside Project personnel, including Madeline, had had extensive instructions for pressure suits. "Besides, I'm sure you have many instructions you'd like to give Madeline, and I have some things to talk over with Bethany here." Madeline blushed and Broun grinned.

"I did forget to mention one or two things." He took Madeline's arm and continued to ''instruct'' her until it was time to go through the airlock into Tycho City.

Chapter

∗ 16 ∗

I

Gradually the holding tank emptied, until Hardrim had it to himself. He stretched out on the bench. Sometime after midnight Deputy Hurt's replacement arrived and Hurt went home.

The older deputy came back to the cell, pulled up a chair and straddled it backward, pushed his hat back with his thumb, and took a long sip from scalding coffee.

"You look bored," the deputy said to Hardrim. "Why don't ya watch a movie?"

"The only thing on the channel that interested me was *Casablanca*, which is my favorite. But I'm damned if I'll watch a 3-D computerized version of a movie made in 1943!"

The deputy grinned. "When Claude Rains lets Bogart go, it just ain't the same if they walk off into the mist in 3-D color."

He took a sip of coffee. "You know, I'd recognize a man who was once a cop if I saw him breaking rocks on a work gang."

A shadow of a smile chased across Hardrim's face. "Really?"

"Name's Wilford Butter, Mr.—or was it Sergeant?—Donat."

"Actually, I made it as far as lieutenant, Sheriff."

"No kidding! Smoke? Coffee?"

"I thought I was in here for smoking."

"Moury's an ass, as I'm sure you gathered from your short association with him. He gives the rest of us a bad name, no?"

Hardrim answered with silence.

"He is also a close relative of the sheriff of Royal County, so I must tolerate him." He tossed Hardrim a flameless cigarette.

"Takes the fun out of it, but thanks." Hardrim sucked the nicotine into his lungs.

"Thanks for not roughing Moury up or anything, which I know you could have done at any time when he arrested you."

"Well, I did used to be a cop."

"Why'd you quit?"

"I'd rather not go into it. Just say I found something more important to do with my life."

"That's fair. Me, I can't think of anything else I'd rather do. This is a nice town. Nice people. Don't you think so?"

"Nice."

"Now don't go making fun of me. Just 'cause you never worked where folks live behind white picket fences and raise families."

"Quiet, residential neighborhoods have the most multiple homicides. City cops at least know that the enemy can be anyone. Here you can maintain an idyllic fantasy."

"God, where'd you work, son, a suburb of hell?"

"You might say so."

"Where was that?"

"You've already pried more information out of me than I like to give. You've got a good prisonside manner, Mr. Butter."

"Smooth as, I always say." Butter drained his coffee cup.

"So why did you get into the game? To meet new and interesting people, and put them in jail?"

"Same as you, Irv. That really your name, Irv?"

"Might as well be. And what do you suppose my reason was for being a cop?"

"Same as yours for leavin' it, I expect. To save the world, or some little part of it. To keep everything from going completely to hell. Am I getting close?"

"Hmmm. Perhaps those picket fences are more sinister than they seem at first glance."

"Oh, they are. They are." Butter stretched like a cat. "My daddy was a cop. He died coupla years before I was born." He noticed Hardrim's raised eyebrow. "He was *my* daddy. But he took precautions. Like keeping a deposit of millions o' little potential Butters in a sperm bank. He knew his job had risks."

Butter went for more coffee and returned. "One night his risks caught up with him. I've seen the newscast. A mob gathered at a Japanese bank. That was during the foreign investment riots, just before the Japs shut down their businesses here.

"He was the first cop on the scene. From the top of some stone stairs he made the crowd back down. One man against hundreds. Like somethin' out of Louis L' Amour. Somebody bounced a rock off his temple. Crowd tore him to shreds. I saw it all."

He scratched his chin and fixed steady gray eyes on Hardrim. "You think life's rough in the big city? I did a stint with the Texas Rangers. I'm not proud of some things I did when we crossed the border. I'm not proud of keeping illegals cooped up in plastic, prefab camps. One summer I was the only law in a camp of fifteen hundred."

Thus Butter began a yarn that lasted most of an hour. A story of midnight raids on the little crime lords who had flourished along the borderland before the United States had intervened in the civil war and made Mexico into a protectorate.

Hardrim told of his own days in Vice. "That's when I started smoking, when I was leading raids on illegal butt manufacturers."

Butter chuckled. "Out West, we're a little more tolerant."

"Right. You used to string people up for open flames. You still put 'em in jail. Me, I prefer bagging real criminals, like SoHi manufacturers. Not that it does any real good."

"You *are* a cynical lad."

A smile of regret fluttered about Hardrim's face and tried to land but found the environment too harsh. "I once was optimistic, even idealistic. I remember the day when I realized that no matter how successful I was, the war was lost—"

Butter leaned back. "Lemme guess. You discovered that the innocent can't really be protected, just avenged. Am I close?"

"Not so unique, my cynicism?" Hardrim stood and leaned back so the bars massaged his shoulder blades. "My partner and I were on a stakeout in a grimy little barrio. We knew a SoHi pusher was operating there, but not his exact address. He had killed someone the week before. We holed up in a plastic hut and waited. We thought the traffic would lead us to him. But he was too shrewd.

"After two weeks, there was another murder on the streets, and the sergeant was screaming for results. One day we saw two kids playacting where one of them pretended to kill the other and take his stash. It dawned on us: Their play reflected something they had seen or heard about. Turned out the mother of one of them was the pusher. That's the day I became a cynic."

Butter looked at his watch. "I get off in about ten minutes. How 'bout comin' over to the spread for breakfast?"

"Won't the missus mind?"

"There is no missus. Not for years."

"You mean I can just get up and leave?"

"Somebody paid your fine coupla hours ago. I kept you around for company. I planned on letting you go pretty quick even if your friend hadn't sprung for the money."

Hardrim did his best to keep the extreme curiosity out of his voice. "My friend. Did he give his name?"

"Nope. I guess that's the best kind, right?"

"What did he look like?"

"Young, small, dapper. You might call him a dandy. Red hair. No bad habits that I could see. Seemed like a nice fella. What's wrong, don't you know who your friends are?"

"Description doesn't ring a bell. Is he waiting outside?"

"Nope. Said to tell you he'd see you later at the cabin."

Hardrim felt the blood drain from his face, and the flesh that surrounded his head turned numb and cold.

"You don't look so good. You need help with this?"

"No, I need that breakfast you promised, Mr. Butter."

"You got it."

II

Desert dawn was not long in coming when they left the jail.

Hardrim paused at the entrance and was painted a light ash color by the setting moon. He filled his lungs with chill, dry, *free* air, then climbed into Wilford Butter's hovercar.

Hardrim's hovercar was still parked in front of the bar, whose dim window neon sign still advertised "The Fastest Beer in the West." It appeared untouched, but he made a thorough search for signs of a break-in, and for bugs or tracking devices.

He took his gold coins from their hiding place and stashed them in his jacket lining, next to his holster. Butter had returned his gun. It felt good hugging his ribs again. His blackjack lay in the grass where he had left it. With its dull pressure in his back pocket, he felt whole again.

Butter gave him a contemplative look when he got in the car. "You act like you expect trouble. Like a man being followed. Something to do with that young man who paid your bail?"

"I don't know. It might."

Hardrim still hadn't gotten over the shock of learning that someone else knew about the "cabin" where he was heading. The safe house was supposedly as secure as a CIA fortress. Yet somebody knew about it. As they drove through the rising curtain of morning, Hardrim thought about that.

Butter's ranch was ten miles from town. The house and rambling property had "bachelor" written all over them. It was definitely a man's paradise, and undoubtedly a woman's Gehenna.

"Not much sign of the distaff side here, Wilford."

"I don't have much use for dogs."

"I mean, there's no evidence that females ever lived here."

"Mrs. Butter passed away fifteen years ago." He set the table. "My daughter Samantha moved out almost as long ago. She teaches American Language at Deseret Technical College." He broke four large eggs into a skillet with sausage. He smiled proudly. "She's been to Mars, my little girl."

"How'd she manage that?"

"Did her master's thesis on the Martian Tech Language. She claimed it's a real dialect, subtongue, or some such. She got a lot of attention. They're still debating that one."

"I knew a man who went to Mars." Hardrim stared at the wall. Ferman went to Mars years before to study mutated bacteria and to climb the solar system's highest peak: Olympus Mons. Now he was out there somewhere, and with him the secret of the Argus Society. He could destroy the Sunside Project easier than the bomb that had been planted on the space shuttle. Hardrim had to find him.

"A friend?"

"Yes. A good friend." A friend he might have to kill.

"—I said, how do you like your eggs?"

Hardrim looked up sharply. "Easy."

Butter chuckled and bent over the frying pan.

He fixed a remarkably delicious breakfast of eggs, toast, biscuits and gravy, and cornbread thangs. Hardrim reflected that there are few cooks as good as a bachelor who likes to eat.

The lawman ate in silence, without removing his Stetson. When he had wiped the last of the gravy with his toast he sat back, belched, and looked at Hardrim.

"Got something to show you."

He led the way to the garage from the kitchen. In the gloom Hardrim made out the high gloss of waxed metal on a vaguely elongated box shape. On the front grillework of the automobile was a silvery silhouette of a galloping stallion.

"Late twentieth century. A Ford, isn't it?"

"Nineteen hundred and sixty-seven Ford Mustang." He reached behind the door and lit the garage with bright hydrogen lights. A galaxy of stars gleamed off the car's ebony polished surface.

"Nice kit car." Hardrim stroked the silky surface.

"It's the real thing. Damn thing's older'n God. My dad owned it. Lord knows who had it before him. Original body. Original engine. It runs off petroleum distillates."

"Gasoline," breathed Hardrim. "I've only heard that word on my old movies. Not much use for a car that only runs on gasoline." Except for the people in the depopulated Northeast who used gasoline in generators, demand for it was almost nonexistent.

"Real tires too. They actually come in contact with the road. There's no hidden surface effect fan. See for yourself."

Hardrim bent down. The car indeed rested on the tires.

"The beauty of this sister is that she's also got a hydrogen converter. Top speed's over a hundred and forty miles per hour."

"You'd have every car on the freeway passing you. But it would be a lot of fun. It's a convertible, isn't it?"

"You still don't get it, Irv. This car has no auto control features, no computer pilot, not even computer-aided steering or brakes. The driver of this car *is* the driver."

"That's like taking a cruise missile out on the road."

"Our grandparents did it every day of their lives."

Hardrim leaned over the hood and gazed at his reflection in its inky depths. "I've busted hoodlums for disconnecting radar units and safety features on cars that weren't a tenth as volatile as this." He laughed. "My admiration for you just grows and grows. Do you ever take it out for a spin?"

"On country roads, or off road. I never dared go on the freeway."

"And you put me in jail for lighting up a cigarette!"

"Forget that for a moment, Irv. If that's your name. How'd you like to drive this car? Don't talk for a second. I know you're on the run. I'm a good judge of people, and I want to help you. You'll be able to make a new set of tracks with this car."

"Yes, and stick out like a sore toe."

"Not so much as you'd think. There's lots of fake Mustangs out West. Ringers for this one, even. But they got the rind without the juice. And the advantage is that in a close call, you'll have total control of your car. And the other guy won't."

"You'd loan me your car?"

"Hell, I'd give it to you, but I suspect I don't need to. You've got some gold you can contribute to my retirement fund."

"I think we have a deal. Can I store my old car here for a while? I can come back later or send for it."

Butter nodded. "No sweat. We'll have to test you out on this sister before we let you go. How are you with a stick shift?"

"What's a stick shift?"

Chapter

* 17 *

I

For Hardrim, learning about stick shifts was a humbling experience. This was something his old movies failed to discuss.

Once Butter gave him the basics, he practiced on the endless dirt roads that crisscrossed the lawman's and neighbor's ranches.

In two days he became proficient enough to feel only slight terror at the prospect of taking his new car out on the road.

"You'll do okay," said Butter. He adjusted his hat against the sun as they stepped off his porch. "Although there may be a few more corpses on the interstate until you get the hang of it."

"Funny man."

"Want a real laugh? Look at this." Butter gave him a sheet of paper from his shirt pocket.

Hardrim unfolded and read it. It was an FBI request for information with Hardrim's picture on it. The contact person was Roger Ferdinand. "Good joke. What are you going to do about it?"

"What's that sonofabitch after you for?"

"Ah, I see you've met Mr. Ferdinand."

"Yep. He took credit for busting a SoHi ring a while back, when we did all the work. Don't sidestep the question."

"He wants me for questioning. I haven't committed a crime."

"I can read too. But what does he want to know?"

"You'll have to trust me on this one." Hardrim's hand wanted to grab the blackjack. As much as he liked Butter, he wouldn't let him turn him over to Ferdinand.

"Shit!" Butter crumpled the sheet and stuffed it in Hardrim's shirt pocket.

"Thanks, Wilford. Thanks for everything." He reached out with his hand. "By the way, the name is Mel Hardrim."

They walked to Butter's car, and the deputy reached inside to his police radio. "Moury Hurt, this is Wilford Butter. Come in." He looked at Hardrim. "Which way you figure to go?"

"East."

"Moury. Butter. Some sonafabitch just stole my Mustang. Yup! Damnedest thing. Yeah, somebody local. They were heading toward California. You know what to do. Round up the usual suspects." He grinned at Hardrim. "Now get the hell outta here!"

II

Six hours out of York City, Hardrim's tail was back.

He had left the main highway and was a few miles from the "safe house." So his follower was going to keep his promise about meeting Hardrim there.

Curiosity was eating him up, but he thought it better to let his unknown "friend" make the first move.

The road crested the grade and a valley spread before him. It was a valley of blues, browns, and yellows, with white-topped mountains all around, like to make your heart burst.

Here, and in two dozen other places, the Argus Society had put safe houses, innocuous on the outside, like fortresses inside, with direct beams to society headquarters and electronic wizardry to confound an army.

How beautiful and strange! A desert valley, blooming weirdly out of season. He suspected that the society's head, Noah Chambless, was connected to the valley's peculiarities. It was like him to mess with the ecology of a hidden valley, just for the hell of it.

Argus Society members weren't known for modesty. The Nobel laureates and geniuses made MENSA look like a ghetto of the lobotomized. In fact, the Argus Society was hardly known at all. To the public it was a benign foundation dispensing honorariums. Hardrim knew different. He was unique. Perhaps that was why he could tolerate the society's eccentrics; in a way, he had outsmarted them all.

The sun, pale and washed out, was touching the mountains behind him as he reached the bottom of the natural bowl. He followed a dirt path that snaked off from the road. The car behind him hadn't yet appeared on the crest. They would be debating what to do. By the time they decided, it would be dark.

Once in the safe house he could monitor the terrain for miles around with sensitive tracking equipment.

A low gray cabin shape materialized in the Mustang's twin beams. Hardrim got out and listened to the stillness—a stillness city dwellers often forget, if they ever know it. The quiet was accentuated by the vast, sugar-dusted black bowl of sky over his head. Miles away, a coyote howled.

He went inside.

III

When Hardrim entered the cabin a light came on, increasing in intensity once he closed the wooden façade door.

The layout was as he expected. Dominating the large den, a blank holocube hung from the ceiling. At one side was a tracking console, its scanner sweeping around a sunken screen like a very fast second hand on an analog watch. According to the scanner, the car had not moved from the crest of the highway. Nor had figures left to approach on foot.

His fingers traveled over the console's light-sensitive keys. He told it to inform him of any change. He was becoming almost adept at using the technology at his disposal as the Argus Society's agent. A few weeks ago he would have fumbled with the keys. Now it was second nature. But he still disliked—even hated—computers for stealing the woman he loved.

His large, tall frame lowered onto the water couch. He massaged his face with his big hands. He could still see Lenore Lippman, Lenny, after the operation turned her into a computer interface—a 'face! Connectors grew out of the interface at the base of her skull like a nest of snakes.

He hated 'faces! The thought of the unnatural connection with a machine made his guts churn. And it had happened to the woman he was about to marry.

She knew his feelings. She had never seriously talked about getting the operation until the day he broke into Argus Society headquarters. Then for several crucial weeks she lost contact. Convinced he was dead or gone for good, she had surgery.

Strange, he reflected, how his success at discovering the Argus Society's secrets had destroyed his life. If he had never met Ralph Ferman, he might be happily married, happily ignorant.

He let the warm watery couch enclose him. He softly called the voice command that activated the holocube, which became a swirling 3-D of pinks and yellows.

"Connect me with Dr. Chambless, if he's in. Mask the call."

He waited: The figure of Dr. Noah Chambless materialized. The Texan's tall, praying-mantis shape was folded to fit the flimsy dimensions of his chair. As usual, he was smoking a pipe, half obscured by smog of his own creation.

"Hardrim, that was good work with Krebs. You gave us a lot of data. I'm almost sorry you didn't kill him. But that's not how we operate, is it?"

"It's not the way I operate." He disliked Chambless's cold-blooded philosophy, that allowed him to come within a razor's edge of killing hundreds of thousands of people by starvation.

"My sources say Krebs took your warning to heart. Emil is dead."

"Then my trip to Krebs's Yucatán playground did serve a purpose, other than my desire to kick someone's ass."

"Just so. Your warning that Emil had planted an atomic bomb on a scramjet was crucial. Without it, all would have been lost. I realize it was a trip you had to take, whether it served any purpose of the Argus Society. A catharsis, if you will.

"We have more work for you. Several good solid pieces of luck that pinpoint the location of our friend Ralph Ferman within a few days. Of course, if you had gotten here sooner—"

"Gimme a break, Chambless! And don't be too sure I'm leaving just yet. I've been entertaining some intruders."

"What?" Chambless looked as if he might choke on his smoke.

"I was followed from Denver."

"Do you have any idea who?"

"No. I will, when they make their move."

"In your report, you described meeting the gangster Ivor Solarz. Regards that, I discovered a—classified ad, I suppose you'd call it, placed in two pirate networks: the Underground Bulletin Board and the Styx Network.'' Chambless tamped his pipe and looked at Hardrim over his reading glasses. "I hope you appreciate how lucky we are to have this. We gained access to the encryption algorithm to the underground code recently. I didn't think it would be useful. I was wrong. The algorithm changes daily, but we have the codebook. That's more than most law enforcement agencies can say."

"Don't be so smug! Good cops monitor the pirate networks. You can get the codebook if you offer a crook the choice between that and spending time in stir. I just wish I'd thought of it."

The "ad" appeared in the cube. It showed Hardrim in army fatigues in the jungle of the Quintana Roo. Next to his picture was an amount: one thousand ounces. No name was given.

"The relative health of your corporeal self is not a factor in whether the reward is paid."

"Dead or alive," said Hardrim.

"Any idea who posted the reward? It's to be paid to a Lunar Free State numbered account, from a numbered account."

"I know from the picture. It's Krebs. Obviously can't take a joke." Hardrim sat at the keyboard and typed: *REWARD: Five thousand ounces of gold for proof of the death of Horatius Krebs. Offered by the man in the photo.*

"You don't have five hundred ounces of gold!"

"I don't have *five* ounces! Who cares? If somebody bumps him off, I don't think he'll sue me in small-claims court."

"You're not a prudent man." Chambless relit his pipe. "However, your physical danger does not distress me as much as the knowledge that someone thought it necessary to follow you. You're supposed to be the 'invisible pawn' in this game."

"Game? Invisible pawn?"

"Haven't I shown you the computer analogue I created of our tactical and strategic position vis-à-vis the elements working for and against us?"

"Guess I missed that one."

"I am particularly proud of it." His image was replaced by what looked like a complicated game setup.

"Looks like Fairie Chess," said Chambless. His figure was superimposed on the board as a piece. "Only in three dimensions. Notice the multilevels—"

"Right. What's it stand for?"

Hardrim's impatience with Chambless's long explanations was a standing joke, with Chambless deliberately dragging out his lectures and Hardrim being rude about getting to the point.

"This analogue is based on current data from our moles in the various mainframe systems throughout the country, and, to a certain extent, the world. This large, powerful piece is the U.S. president. These three pieces on the periphery of the fourth level represent the three space shuttles. This dark piece in the next square is the Soviet battleship launched a few days ago."

"First I've heard of that."

"These pieces represent Europe's forces, and these Greater Asia and, of course, Black Africa. Here is another player." He indicated a dark, sinister shape on the board. "Roger Ferdinand. That spot is Deseret Space Center. Ferdinand was called in to investigate the attempted sabotage of the *Sally Ride*."

"Yes, Ferdinand is after me, too." Hardrim told him about the "wanted poster" Sheriff Butter had shown him.

Chambless's jaw clamped tighter on his pipe.

"What is this other piece near the space center?"

"The forces of Horatius Krebs, of the Python Corporation."

"And where am I? Where is the Argus Society?"

"We—you are the invisible pawn. We have a small direct influence on events. Our advantage is that the other players are not aware of us." He puffed furiously. "Up to now."

"That kind of depends on my visitors outside, doesn't it?"

"Although in most circumstances, rents in our security can be sewed up. We fixed the leak you made by your investigation of us."

"Except for Ralph Ferman." The game analogue vanished. "When do you intend to act toward the intruders?"

"I'll let them come to me," said Hardrim. "But while I'm waiting, I do have a small request—"

The door to the safe house opened and a man stepped inside.

Chapter
* 18 *

I

Mel Hardrim aimed his .45 at the red-haired young man who had just stepped inside the safe house.

The man put his hands up. "I surrender."

"Who the hell are you?" Hardrim felt a strange sensation, as though he had seen the man before. But he couldn't place him.

"Perle Gracie, the man who bailed you out of jail, and a fellow traveler with the Argus Society. Am I not, Dr. Chambless?" He looked up at the holocube.

"Eh, put down your weapon, Hardrim. This infernal, tactless young man is indeed Perle Gracie, one of our associates."

Hardrim stored his gun. "Infernal and tactless? That's how he talks about *me*. We may get along. How did you evade the scanner?"

"I'm wearing a scrambling device that fooled it into thinking I was a little copse of trees."

"Moving trees! You've been reading too much *Macbeth*." He poked his chest. "Before we get friendly, why were you tailing me? I could have shot first, and not bothered to ask questions."

"That's why I paid the bail: to create enough doubt in your mind that you'd let the game play out to the end."

"Games! Chambless with his chess games and you with yours!"

"I wanted to find out what sort I would be working with."

Hardrim looked up at the holocube. "Nice of you to tell me."

Chambless was unruffled. "You did not need to know."

"I need to know everything that concerns my job. I thought I'd broken you of trying to run my life."

Chambless ignored the outburst. He looked at Gracie. "I understand you completed your assignment with Mayfield."

"Right. He looked right at the camera during the interview. You can analyze the test, but my preliminary results on eyelid fluctuation indicate he told the truth during the session. He doesn't know any more about the Sunside Project than he seems to. He still believes."

"Excellent."

"What, did you brainwash Mayfield?" asked Hardrim.

"No," said Gracie. "As a reporter for the Science News Network, it was fairly easy for me to obtain an interview. Even so notorious a press hater would have had a hard time turning down the top science reporter in the country."

"That's where I've seen you before!"

"Ah, a fan. I expect it was my report of the unsuccessful efforts to save the Venice artworks from the final floods that you remember, since you are reputedly a man of culture."

"No, it was the testing of the fusion warhead in Hellas." That story had shocked the world, which had dismissed reports of scientific breakthroughs in the pocket republics. Hardrim nodded his approval. "I see your value to the Argus Society. A reporter who can travel anywhere without arousing suspicion."

"Yes," added Chambless coldly. "And we recruited him without brainwashing. Unfortunately for my relations with you, I don't believe in mind control. Life would be simpler if you obeyed orders without needing them explained."

"You bet your ass I want orders explained! Any man who would consider starving several million people, no matter how noble the goal, bears watching."

"How did you join the society, Mr. Hardrim?" asked Gracie.

"Chambless tied me down and fed my brain the recorded memories of Alfred Strubeck. Well that he did. If he'd fed me his own memories, I might have wanted to commit murder."

Chambless threw his pipe down violently out of the field of the holocube. "Damn you, I am weary of your insinuations about mind control! You've brought this up repeatedly, even after you talked to Michlanski. Do you think we brainwashed him? How many times must I explain that it was the *arete* of these children to be what they were?"

"What the hell is *arete*?"

"You seem to take pride in making virtues out of ignorance."

"*Arete* is a Greek concept," said Gracie. "It's an inborn capacity. Developing that capacity was the highest purpose in ancient Greece. It's like an apple seed that contains the inborn capacity to become an apple tree."

"I've heard this before. I didn't buy it then either."

Chambless and Hardrim glared at each other across a thousand miles.

"Dr. Chambless," said Gracie, "tell us your information."

Chambless reached down for his pipe. "It took our computers weeks of sifting through millions of images and bits of information to get this. I hope you're appreciative.

"This first photo, taken by satellite, we found by accident. The satellite was in the right vicinity at the right time. This, we believe, is Ralph Ferman, outside the Detroit hotel where you two were staying on the day the FBI released him. He is waiting for a bus. It is Ferman, is it not, Inspector Hardrim?"

It annoyed Hardrim that Chambless still used his police title. "Hard to say. I never studied the top of Ferman's head. His appearance isn't inconsistent with Ferman's. He is dressed like Ralph was when I saw him at FBI headquarters. The grip he's carrying looks right. I have a good memory for such things. It could be him."

"Things are a little difficult in Mr. Ferman's case," said Chambless with distaste. "He is no fool. We have no evidence that he ever knowingly passed in front of a holocube or any screen capable of two-way communication. But after leaving this spot, he was recorded by several surveillance cameras he was not aware of. It apparently did not occur to him that there might be a camera aboard the bus he took out of town."

Ferman had left the bus at a stop ten miles out of Detroit. That was the last photographic evidence that existed of him.

"We know where he got off. Let's assume he's on foot," said Hardrim. "He won't use forms of transportation where his image might be recorded.

He won't use his credit card. He'll buy things with the gold I left him, unless he takes odd jobs along the way to make money.''

''Along the way to where?'' asked Gracie. ''How do you know he won't find some nice town and settle down for a while?''

''Unlikely,'' said Chambless. ''But we must consider it.''

''We have a radius of several hundred miles where Ferman was released,'' said Hardrim. ''We need to do a computer analysis to decide how far he could have gone on foot, then concentrate within that radius. He'll make a mistake, sooner or later.''

''Why?'' asked Gracie. ''The smartest thing would be for him to find the nearest forest and live off the land for a few months.''

''Ralph is a man with a mission. He'll feel the urge to tell someone about the Argus Society. To do that, he's got to move.''

II

Hardrim showed Gracie where he would be sleeping.

''Let me ask you something, Mel.''

''Shoot.''

''I hope you don't mind working with me.''

''That's not a question.'' Hardrim handed him a pillow and blanket.

''*Do* you mind working with me?''

''Not at all. You don't seem to get along with Chambless any better than I do. That's a strong point in my book.''

Hardrim pointed out the spigots in the bathroom that dispensed tooth cleaner, mouthwash, and shaving cream. Plus the other amenities. Gracie seldom used safe houses since he could go anywhere and always have a perfect cover.

''I've known Chambless most of my life,'' Gracie said. ''My father, who founded the Science News Network, belongs to the Society. At the network's headquarters in the desert—which is really Dad's private arcology—he monitors a lot of data for the society. He owes the society a lot.''

''What kind of a guy is your father?''

''Just like me. We look like twins, although Dad is twenty-five years older, with grayer hair and a thicker middle. I'm a clone of my father. Literally. He is sterile, and cloning research has been forbidden, but Alfred Strubeck got him access to the illegal technology. I am the result.''

Hardrim was speechless.

Gracie spoke softly. ''For twenty-five years we've worked secretly, although in plain sight. We've built an informational network that shunts scientific information under the noses of the McClarenites. Chambless once told me he hid an algorithm inside a confidential message that Senator McClaren sent to the TEA.''

"Noah Chambless has always been an arrogant SOB, hasn't he?''

"Arrogant. A bastard, and one of the most able scientists I've ever met.'' Gracie ran out a glassful of mouthwash and tentatively tasted it. He grimaced and poured it down the drain.

"I disagree with Chambless's methods, but he led us through a critical period after Strubeck's death. No one else could have been as cool or ruthless. I wouldn't have wanted responsibility for loosing the Santa Bella blight on the world. Strubeck agonized over it; Chambless never wavered. Then he had the gall to get himself appointed to head the team investigating the blight! He has frozen veins. For him, there are only equations, critical masses, and cold facts. If it had just been Chambless, I suspect my father would never have joined the Argus Society. I know I wouldn't have. But Strubeck was different. He was a great man, a great scientist, with the heart of a saint.''

"You're right, Chambless isn't the Argus Society. The Argus Society is Adam Scott, Alfred Strubeck, Sherlock Michlanski, Philip Norrison, and Perle Gracie.'' He patted Gracie's shoulder. "You're okay people, Perle. We'll get along.''

"Getting along is important, since we'll probably be getting along to Michigan tomorrow morning, right?''

"I like a partner who thinks ahead, Perle. Pleasant dreams.''

Hardrim padded out of the bedroom, grabbed a beer, and while it was chilling itself, lit a cigarette. He looked at the holocube that dominated the den. In its blank depths he saw Lenny. Without the Medusa curls he usually adorned her with in his imagination. He saw her beautiful face framed by a pageboy cut. He was filled with such longing that his chest hurt like it couldn't contain it.

"Mel, you're a grown man,'' he growled. "And if you aren't, Lenny wouldn't want anything to do with you. Computer! Phone Lenore Lippman at this number.'' He remembered her number like his own police ID number.

The pink dial tone throbbed while the computer connected the number, which began to ring. Hardrim looked up to see Chambless, placidly smoking a briar.

"I don't think that's such a good idea, Mel.''

"You unprincipled bastard! You're monitoring my calls!''

"The computer has orders to contact me if you call certain numbers."

"You're overstepping your bounds, Professor. At the meeting of the Argus Society it was agreed that I would contact Lenny."

"And you did. Now you are working for us again."

"My love affair has no statute of limitations. Try to attach one to it, and you'll be blowing smoke up your own ass."

"I can see you're upset."

"Upset doesn't even begin to describe it. I'm so pissed off I'm about ready to walk, and let you finish your search for Ralph with Mr. Wizard in there while I find Lenny and make love to her."

"Can you?" said Chambless. "Can you make love to a cyborg, to a 'face? If you've become that tolerant, I'd like to know."

"Go to hell! I want a guarantee you won't tap my calls."

"How will you know if I keep my word?"

"You will because the stakes are high enough. Am I right?"

Chambless sighed. "Very possibly. I agree."

Hardrim abruptly terminated Chambless's image, then he gave the computer Lenny's number again. The number rang.

"Hello?"

"Hi, Lenny."

Chapter
* 19 *

The self-contained Extraordinary Tactics Force is smaller than normal formations. Its basic unit is the company, consisting of heavy weapons, antitank, antiaircraft, and assault squads.

Each company does the job of a regular-sized battalion. ETF's special function is breakthrough and reconnaissance. Such a small formation can do the job of a larger one through special communications, special transportation, and special weaponry and tactics.

—Brig. Gen. David Keith, introduction to the
Extraordinary Tactics Manual

From the general's office Sergeant Major Terry Ransome, USMC, watched the fog coil around the supports of the Golden Gate Bridge and slither into the harbor past the Presidio.

The fort had been closed since the early nineties, only recently reopening. It respired history: smoothbore cannon saluting the Great White Fleet, morning bugle calls, sabers clattering, the smell of gunpowder melding with plaster and brick.

Ransome stretched his full six feet two inches, until the joints popped on his thin frame. He was pale, with thin brown hair and sideburns like silky cotton blobs, a high forehead, and glasses that shrank his eyes almost to points. He would close them and speak slowly and precisely when he wanted to emphasize an idea.

Until a few days ago, Ransome had served on one of the Atlantic floating fortresses straddling the Lines of Demarcation.

During his flight, he had reflected on the short exchange he had had with the colonel, who asked if Ransome knew his new commanding officer, General David Ian Keith.

Ransome didn't. Keith was army.

"You are in for a treat," the colonel had said. "General Keith is, ah, *innovative*."

What did that mean? If other services had heard of Keith, maybe he was a crank, or a hard-ass disciplinarian. The first thing he did on the plane was call up the general on his seat computer. He found a lot to read.

Upon arrival Ransome had reported to his predecessor, Staff Sergeant Gilbert Bose, whom he knew from when both were stationed at Pearl Harbor. He greeted Ransome with a weary smile.

"God, Gil, you look like you stepped on your crank."

"Just wore out, Ter. And glad to see you."

"What's wrong, is Keith a hard-ass? I know he wrote a hell of a book. I read it on the plane."

"Don't get me wrong, Keith's a great CO. He's in exile 'cause he crossed swords with the brass. He teaches strategy to officer candidates. But that's got to be temporary. He's a friggin' hero!" Bose blew air out his cheeks. "You ever worked for a hero?"

"Today's topic is the dynamics of tactical and operational command." Brigadier General David Ian Keith surveyed the class. Thirty men and women, none older than twenty-one. They sat attentively in the chilly, cramped room of peeling yellow plaster.

His reputation had preceded him: demanding, eccentric, brilliant. A teacher who managed to get the brightest students.

He smiled slightly and looked boyish, naïve, and vulnerable. His own student days weren't so long ago. He was twenty-eight. He absently pushed a stubborn lock of hair back into the grayish-brown mainland.

His rapid rise in command had been as dizzying as his sudden fall. At twenty-seven he had commanded a unit he had advocated establishing: the Extraordinary Tactics Force, specializing in experimental weapons and tactics. He had been astonished that his idea was adopted. He had read about Billy Mitchell and knew the army wasn't fond of disturbing influences.

It still wasn't. Keith discovered that junior officers, even generals, don't criticize pet weapons systems of one of the joint chiefs. They couldn't demote him for his opinions, but they could post him to teach students who would ordinarily be taught by a captain or major.

Yet by making him an instructor, his superiors gave him minds to infect with his theories. So far they hadn't caught on.

He walked over to the chalkboard and picked up a pointer.

"Battle has changed over the centuries, armies have changed, weapons have changed, but on a purely abstract and intellectual level, the factors remain the same. Find a weak point in your opponent's disposition. Exploit it to unbalance and unhinge his ability to resist." He hit the wall sharply with the stick, sending yellow paint chips flying. "The stick's weakness is not immediately apparent. But in examining it I find a tiny crack *here*!" He whacked it smartly on a nearby desk, breaking it in two. "It is only as strong as its weakest part. An army is only as strong as its weakest unit and least able officer. Hit its weak point, which is not necessarily a geographic point, but can be a psychological point, and it will shatter.

"Commanders who used these principles have been extraordinarily successful.

"Four factors are in any military equation: force, mobility, defense and communication. Force is the offensive energy employed against a given point. Defense is the resistance to that force. Mobility is the ability to move force to a given area. Communication is the ability to supply your army and ensure your orders are carried out. At different times in history one or more of these factors has dominated. When the balance between them changes, wars become revolutionary in nature. When the factors are balanced, wars are static, very bloody, but not revolutionary. The most decisive factor has usually been mobility; in our age communication has become perhaps the most important."

Keith traced the fall of the Roman Empire, the rise of the dominant mobile arm: cavalry and the eclipse of infantry for a millennium until gunpowder became the effective defense against cavalry and in the form of artillery became the dominant force.

"In the nineteenth century, defense asserted itself. Civil War trenches canceled the penetrating force of artillery. The defense factor of long-range rifles made attacking more expensive. The First World War proved the ascendancy of defense over force. Without force there could be no mobile advances. The communication factor became vital once large armies were tied to the railroads. This in turn enhanced the defense by making it easier to shift forces to meet attacks. The tank, combining force *and* mobility, revolutionized warfare. Tank columns could pierce the defense and paralyze it by attacking the rear, as Mongol horsemen did a thousand years ago. After World War II, defense began to compete with force. New weapons could stop tanks in their tracks, and the tactical situation resembled the First World War.''

A young woman officer raised her hand. ''Sir, are you saying that in a war today the armies would not be able to advance?''

Keith sat on his desk and nodded. He had noticed this young lieutenant before. Her questions always cut right to the point. He liked that. ''Yes. In our most recent war, the Cubans collapsed quickly, but where they mounted effective defenses, casualties were high.'' His students stirred at this departure from the conventional view of the Cuban War. ''If an inferior army can slow down the best army in the world, how much better would a first-rate army do? Any well-armed and supported army can bring any other army to a halt. A tank that can be seen can be destroyed. So can any airplane, so armies can't count on air support. Without mobile armor and air support, the grunts can't overcome defense in depth. The next war will replay the First World War, unless new tactics are developed.''

He saw that his words were having an impact. If he could open a few young minds, his ''exile'' might not be a complete farce.

''The alternative to static trench war is to develop new tactics to over-come the problems facing the tank as the main arm of offense.'' His wrist chronometer showed a minute left. ''Which brings us to tomorrow: five pages typed. Suggest ways to break the deadlock, or a forty-five-minute tactical scenario on your wargame program, factoring in logistics, com-munications, and a terrain map.'' He smiled. ''Don't be discouraged, that's the minimum exercise that I will give. Dismissed!''

Ransome, who had been waiting outside the classroom, entered as the students filed out. Keith recognized him immediately.

''You made good time, Sergeant. Glad to see you. I saw you out in the hallway. Did you enjoy the lecture?''

''Very much, sir. I notice that when you said that new weapons and tactics needed to be developed, you didn't mention the unit that you put together.''

''Been doing some homework? Good! My students will hear about the Extraordinary Tactics Force after they've exhausted their own resources. Let me buy you a drink and tell you about your job.''

Back in his office Keith poured a generous shot from a bottle of Glenlivet Scotch. ''I don't stand on ceremony. I respect people for what they are, not what they wear on their shoulders.''

Ransome's eyebrows shot up at this most unmilitary concept. No wonder the Army had exiled this man to its version of Siberia. His surprise didn't stop him from taking the drink.

Keith took a diet cola out of his desk and touched the tab to cool it. He downed half the can in one swallow. Then he sat at his desk, loosened his tie, and regarded Ransome keenly.

"Sergeant Major, interservice transfers are unusual. You may even object to working for the Army—"

"Not at all, General."

"I know a lot about you. I requested you because of your special abilities." He fed a data tile into his desk console. "Impressive! Both for your resourcefulness and initiative, and for your uncommon talent for pissing off superiors."

"Yes sir." Ransome swallowed his drink in one gulp.

"You won't have that problem here. You'll be much too busy."

"My predecessor told me, sir."

"It says you led the recon shore team in London and scouted out the landing zone for the rescue of the embassy staff. How much of that operation did you personally plan?"

"All the ops for my group, General." Ransome looked down to see that his shot glass had become full again.

"You never had formal tactical training, yet on each mission you've shown a keen tactical sense. Ransome, you are an artist." Keith sprang to his feet. "I admire artists, whatever the medium. I myself am an artist of sorts."

"Yes sir. I read your book."

"Really? Any suggestions?"

"On your book, sir? Uh, no."

"On anything at all."

"Uh, what are my duties, sir? I mean, you're an instructor. Not much opportunity to do tactical operations."

"I teach young people how to fight battles. We do a lot of computer wargaming here. You will do the research and prep work for these exercises. Experience in the real thing can't hurt."

"Sir, do you ever feel that you—that the army will—"

"End my stay on Elba?" Keith smiled. "I think in the near future the army will reverse its judgment. That's why I've seen to it that men I need for a staff have been transferred here."

"Why did the army cooperate?"

"They don't see my strategy. Take yourself: an 'incorrigible.' To me it's obvious your creativity has been repressed. I want you to begin tomorrow on an ops plan for a landing on the African coast."

"Sir?"

"An exercise. But such plans can be adapted to real events." He looked at Ransome intently. "Great things are about to happen in the wide world. I intend to be part of them. There are opportunities—great questions to be settled, on earth and in the heavens. I'm not a warmonger, but if issues must be settled with arms, I want to win. And to do it so that everything we fight for isn't overturned in the process. Like Patton said, the object is not to die for your country, but to make the other poor bastard die for his.

"I'll give you the order of battle in the morning, too. And then I'll be flying to Washington, D.C., for a few days."

"Vacation, sir?"

Keith smiled, and suddenly didn't look quite the innocent young officer. "A friend wrangled me an invitation to the White House New Year's Eve party, to meet a senator close to the president who might help me. Perhaps meet the president. I can't wait around for someone to recognize my abilities. I want to be positioned to leap into battle in full kit if I'm called. That's where you come in."

Chapter

* 20 *

Dec. 29—*Tycho Daily News*—Construction of the three Sunside Project spacecraft will begin after New Year's Day. Project members are now working six-day weeks. During the most crucial weeks of construction, they will work twelve-hour days, seven days a week. No one is fooling around here, least of all project head Jason Scott. Co-workers who know him say you can tell when the young engineer is serious: He lets his beard grow.

I

Jason Scott and Matt Taylor, the construction foreman, removed their helmets when the airlock pressure equalized. Scott wanted to scratch the band of sensitive skin that ran from his temples around his skull. His red hair had been treated to make it grow back quickly, without scar tissue, but the hair there was a different hue from the rest.

They followed the corridor from the airlock into the city.

Tycho City was breathtaking. Scott had never seen it from the inside before. From the ship he had seen the polarized blister covering the city, but that didn't prepare him for this.

Overhead soared the dome. It was impossible to judge how high, although Scott knew it was about one hundred feet. The sun blazed through the polarized material with the intensity of earthly sunlight and the ceiling looked like the sky at home.

After weeks in the quarantine barracks, the illusion of space made him giddy. Or perhaps it was the minor operation he had undergone while cooped up with nothing to do.

The sky illusion was preserved because no buildings were higher than two stories. At the moment clouds were being projected on the ''sky,'' and a flight of birds was so regular and perfect that Scott surmised it was computer-generated also.

''Reminds me of the underwater city over the Challenger Tap,'' said Taylor in his deep bayou accent. He rubbed a crease made by the helmet in his chocolate-colored forehead. ''You sometimes forget how dangerous that place is too.''

''Aren't you happy to be back home?''

''Shit! This place is no home to living people, man! You don't know it like I do. I have the white hairs to prove it!''

Taylor acquired his kinky premature white hair years earlier when he was mining ilmenite, a plentiful Lunar ore that was processed into oxygen. An explosion had wiped out everyone in the operation but Taylor, who had crossed many miles, dragging a small oxygen processor, making air as he went. He started the trek with black hair. When he finished, it was white as the bones of his comrades baking in the sun. Doctors didn't know exactly why, but it proved irreversible. It aged him twenty years and gave him character and mystique. Taylor liked it once he got used to it.

''I don't believe that the man who held off several hundred mutineers and laughed at the idea of bringing seven miles of seawater down on him is afraid of a vacuum,'' chided Scott.

''Not afraid! Respect! I'd rather have my skin tore up by bullets or my lungs crushed by seawater than have my life sucked out by that airless bitch.'' They passed Heinlein Square, and Taylor nodded at the Osirium figure of the writer standing with arms outspread. ''He was right on about the moon bein' a harsh mistress. I won my wrestlin' match with her, but there's been plenty she's thrown!''

"I expect you'll share your survival tips. You know, you're a legend here. They look on you like some sort of demigod.''

"I remember when this place was small. Now it's twenty thousand. In five years they build another dome. Biggest colony on Luna. But that vacuum is still waiting to suck 'em dry if they don't watch out. That's the lesson I learned.''

"You just have to watch out for yourself.''

"That why you got that operation to fit on extra eyes?''

"It's not extra eyes, it's a vision prosthesis to allow me to see in a band of three hundred and sixty degrees.''

"Shit! You will have eyes on the back of your head! You'll turn yourself into a 'face if you're not careful.''

"I'll be able to process data from several sources simultaneously, without interfacing with a mainframe, which I consider unhealthy mentally. I can monitor two dozen screens at once. On the construction site, I can watch screens installed in a band inside the helmet.''

"You got stones! More'n me. Cybernetics prosthetics got a bad repu for bein' rejected by the brain, with bad side effects.''

"There are always two chances in a hundred of death resulting from such an implant. But I'm still alive.''

They reached a crossroads. "I'm gonna see if my new quarters is worth a damn, Jason.''

"It's got to be an improvement over those barracks.''

"Damn straight! Bye!''

Scott continued on. The city was near the limits of its planned population, but it didn't look overcrowded, because the streets were free of vehicles. You could stroll from one end of the dome to the other within an hour.

Underground corridors accommodated the hovercars used by colony officials when haste was a necessity. The city's lifestyle was relaxed and informal. Its people were graceful, slender, and tall. Most of the exceptions to this rule were the "earthborn."

Across the dome from the airlock entrance were the barracks Scott had wrangled from the colony. His people had been going crazy in the quarantine blockhouses. Once he saw his own quarters he was anxious to get the construction show on the road by contacting the colony's governor.

Later, as he emerged from the barracks, he was tapped on the shoulder by a space corpsman in dress blue slacks, black tunic, and white trim. He saluted crisply.

"Sergeant Drake?" said Scott, examining his identification.

"Yes sir." His raw and craggy face was almost ugly. He was about thirty-five, stout and compact. "Admiral wants to meet you. We can take a naval tractor and be there in fifteen minutes."

Scott had little choice. Hanley Davis was chief of space naval operations and commander in chief, Luna, or CNCLUN in military shorthand. He had no theoretical control over Scott, a civilian, but in practice nothing happened in the Territory of Selene without his influence touching it.

More to the point, Scott's three ships would be built in the navy yards. It behooved him to be on good terms with Davis.

The only direct way to the base was by tractor. The UN tram was not allowed near the top-security military establishment.

The Lunar rover wasn't built for comfort. Its seats were exposed to the vacuum. Convenience was sacrificed for cargo space. Scott held on to the sides as Drake drove at seemingly suicidal velocity, swerving to avoid rocks and craters that sprang from the shadows. But he soon realized that Drake missed the obstacles through skill, not luck.

They reached the cluster of domes and ground-hugging blockhouses that made up Tycho Brahe Base in nine minutes.

Over the base hung the huge, cloud-girded earth: a thin crescent, the rest visible as darkness that blotted out the stars.

A fraction of the base's warships clustered on the gray plain around the base. Most of the regular navy ships were in hangars. They were periodically rotated into orbit or for extended duty in the outer planets, for patrols and to escort the five battleships, which were too big to land on Luna.

America had gained domination of the high ground of space during the Asia/Europe war, mainly by default, since antitechnology elements had bitterly fought space expansion. But fanatics like Davis bullied the politicians into minimal funding for a space navy, and then had used the concept of the reserve fleet to inflate the navy into the dominant force over earth.

After the war, Russia rebounded, developing rare mineral sites on Venus. It was followed by Asia, the European Space Agency, even by Black Africa, mainly in orbiting industrial colonies. One rebellious Russian colony formed the Lunar Free State and the Russians were prevented from suppressing the revolt by U.S. policy forbidding armed intervention on the moon. That remained a sore point between the two nations.

Dominating the high ground, America wielded tremendous power over all space activities near Luna and earth and indirectly on commerce between earth and Mars, Jupiter and Saturn. She suppressed all military activities in space that threatened her domination, in the process violating past international agreements. But this was the age of Fortress America and so Luna had become the Gibraltar of space.

If war came, Asia, Europe and Russia could, in time, retrofit commercial ships for war, but most experts felt that victory would go to whoever could strike "fustest with the mostest," in the words of Nathan Bedford Forrest. However, America's installations were wide-ranging, making her vulnerable to a small, hard-hitting force that could strike before the fleet could mobilize.

Drake and Scott entered the largest dome and proceeded to the admiral's office. The lettering on his door said simply: "H. Davis, Admiral, CNC LUNA." The only decorations in the modest office were holographs of warships, and one life-sized holo bust of President Shefferton, over a shelf of genuine books.

Davis might have been chairman of the joint chiefs if he had played the game. He was unpopular for his outspoken contempt for those who disagreed with him. When he appeared before congressional committees, he was so well prepared that critics couldn't lay a glove on him. Currently he was even more powerful because of the patronage of his friend Jeffrey Shefferton.

At fifty he was at the apex of his physical powers. Tall and rawboned, without an ounce of fat, his back was perpendicular to his straight-backed chair. On the moon, where time stood still for the frailest men, Davis might keep his iron fist on events for a generation, or until enough enemies ganged up on him.

"You had a rough crossing, I hear." He didn't waste time on formalities.

"The sergeant was a bit overenthusiastic in his driving—"

"I wasn't speaking of Drake's driving! But of the Soviet battleship that played footsie with *Sally Ride*."

"We had some anxious moments. But I never imagined there was any danger. The Russians knew our cargo. It's to their advantage as well as ours if the Sunside Project succeeds."

"I doubt that." Davis didn't seem to admit to the possibility of conflicting viewpoints. "It's not widely known, but Brasnikov signed the Food Treaty reluctantly."

"What do you think the *Aurora* was up to?"

"Testing our resolve. We flunked. They couldn't challenge us before.

The *Aurora*'s challenge was the first, with the goal of building a Soviet military base on Luna.''

"Doesn't that violate a gentleman's agreement with them, like the one that kept them from basing ICBMs in Cuba?''

"They've been cheating on treaties as long as the rest of the world's been signing them. You think they'd respect a gentleman's agreement if it's in their interest to violate it?''

"Does the president share your concern?''

"He's caught up in enthusiasm for your project—''

"I'm glad to hear it.''

"—that might possibly blind him to other dangers.''

"What are you saying?''

"I want *you* to be aware of the dangers. You have influence on the president—'' He seemed to search for the right word.

"That's more apparent than real. I'm just a hired hand.''

"It probably doesn't set any better with you than it does with me.'' Davis leaned forward, eyes shining like obsidian. "I want you to do something else you won't like. I want your people to stay here at the base while the ships are built.''

"Why?'' Scott was more angry than surprised.

"Before the *Aurora* incident I was worried about security for the project. Now I'm obsessed with it—''

"That accurately describes most people in your profession.''

Davis laughed. *"Touché.* But you agree that the actions of the Russian battleship cast a new light on your project.''

"Not to the point of that much security.''

"You aren't a security expert. I am. In my professional opinion it is needed, and since things come under military jurisdiction, you shall have it.''

"What I said about being a hired hand doesn't extend to my authority over the Sunside Project, which is from Secretary Sheridan Mayfield and the president. I have a free hand. I don't have to knuckle under to military dictates, and I won't.

"We're not building a bomb. We are working to provide food for all mankind. If we work here it will seem like we are a military project, when we manifestly are not! Furthermore, my people will be in space for eighteen months. I won't have them endure exile on the moon. I reject your security arrangements. Go ahead, assign a security team for the project. But I won't imprison my people here. If you want to dispute my judgment, call Washington. I'll wait.''

"I'm calling your bluff, Mr. Scott. Like the rest of us, you have to take orders sometimes, too."

Davis placed the call to the Department of Space and in between three-second transmission delays asked to speak to Mayfield. He was not available. But the undersecretary in charge of the Sunside Project was at his desk.

Davis explained the disagreement. Scott sat impassive.

"Do you have anything to add, Mr. Scott?"

"The admiral has offered my point of view satisfactorily, Mr. Undersecretary," said Scott.

"My decision is for the admiral on this matter. I believe that's within his military expertise. Comments?"

"Is your decision final?"

"I'm afraid so."

Scott shrugged. "You will shortly receive my resignation as director of the Sunside Project, effective in one hour. You will, I believe, also receive similar resignations from Jacob Kane and Sherlock Michlanski."

"You can't do that."

"Don't tell me what I can do, Mr. Undersecretary. I'll be obliged if you inform Secretary Mayfield of my decision."

"I don't know if I can find him in an hour."

"Then I suggest you inform the president." Scott turned to Davis. "Would you do me the courtesy to allow me to have lunch at your mess hall, Admiral, before I return to the city?"

"Of course," said Davis tightly.

Scott was finishing a chipped soya on toast dinner when he was summoned to return to the admiral's office.

Davis's face was dark. "Mayfield reversed me. I was chewed out by the president's chief of staff. Shefferton thinks highly of you." He grimaced and shook his head. "You're making a bad decision, and if I get the chance, I'll reverse you on it."

"And my security force?"

"You'll get it. I'll send Colonel Jackson Drew over to talk to you tomorrow. And if you think that I'm an asshole—" He smiled wickedly. "You may go." He waved his hand toward the door.

As Sergeant Drake drove Scott back home he touched helmets.

"I've never seen him so mad!" He grinned with admiration. "Mind you, he's a great old bastard, but he's hell on wheels when he's out to get his way!"

"Well," said Scott. "I'm hell on jets when I want to get mine."

II

When Scott returned "home" Bethany Williams was waiting.

"I guess this is the only way to talk to you, Mr. Scott." She glared with her arms folded, from in front of his door.

"Aren't you happy with your work assignments, Bethany?"

"You've avoided me since the launch. An impressive feat considering that three of those days we were cooped up in a space shuttle. I've news for you: This is a sealed environment. You can run, but you can't hide."

"I'm not hiding from you, Bethany."

"No? I did some research on you when we were in space. You've never had a lasting relationship. If you say you're married to your work, I'll break your nifty-looking jaw."

"I won't insult your intelligence." Scott smiled tiredly. "If you did your research thoroughly, you saw that for ten years, I've gone from project to project, with nothing in between. The Andes highway, the Challenger Tap, Trans-Yukon Tubeway, before that the New Zealand bridge—hazardous projects, the kind of work for big, tough, mean men, like Matt Taylor. Not the sort of places where you meet women you'd like to have a relationship with."

"Seems you met me while working on the Challenger Tap."

"While you were the lover and partner of the man who tried to destroy Rita Duce and, incidentally, kill me."

Bethany's face fell. She headed blindly away from him. "You'll never forgive me for that, no matter what you said."

He blocked her. "I'm sorry," he said awkwardly.

Her face contorted. "Damn you! You're a bastard like Kane. He cuts with words. You do it with indifference." She slapped him as hard as she could. He didn't react. His clear blue eyes regarded her calmly as if they were having a normal conversation. She hit him again. No reaction. She lifted her hand again and then let it fall to her side.

"That's enough of that." Scott wiped a trickle of blood from his lip. As if in sympathy, a teardrop formed in Bethany's right eye. He gently collected the drop with his finger. "Kane would never let you do that to him. And if that's the only difference you see between us, we're probably better off not discussing it." He put his hand on the door. "You know, you don't need to prove anything to me."

"I—I know that," she said haltingly. "I don't exactly know how to deal with you."

Scott smiled as if they shared a common secret. "That makes two of us." He opened the door. "Come in for a minute. I'm a terrible host. Although I'm afraid I've nothing to offer you."

She looked at him sidewise. Was he as ingenuous as he seemed?

He closed the door behind him. He looked around the tiny apartment nervously. He picked up some knickknack off a tiny bureau and put it back again.

"Jason Scott is afraid of women?"

"I haven't spent that much time with them." He spoke deliberately, closing his eyes as if concentrating on his delivery. "Young scientists, or math whizzes, or geniuses, whatever you call them, are frequently so caught up in—so married to—I don't know. We don't have normal lives. Some of us don't start dating until we're in our twenties. Sherlock attended a university at an age when most kids are in junior high. Do you know how that affects self-confidence around women?"

She sat on the bed.

"Allow me to make an observation?" said Scott.

"Yes."

"Bethany, you're a very talented woman. You're beautiful, smart, and you've got an incredible inferiority complex."

"You just finished saying that you have the same thing."

He ignored her interruption. "You've done things you're ashamed of. That's behind you. When you warned us of the sabotage attempt, that was the beginning of your rise from the abyss. You've been battered, but when you made that decision, you took charge of your life again. You don't need an anchor. You were strong enough to survive what's happened to you. You're strong enough to put the pieces back together without a crutch to lean on. If we ever develop a relationship, it will be between equals. I don't want anyone dependent on me for life."

She took a deep breath. "That's quite a mouthful. Is that how you see me, as wanting you for a crutch?"

"Subconsciously, yes. Why else would you be so angry that I have not sought you out? Frankly, I've been busy! I've been putting in eighteen-hour days! Before that I was recovering from an operation to install a vision prosthesis, which could have killed me or left me blind if it went wrong. I haven't had time for a friend, much less a girlfriend, which is how you apparently see yourself. You seem to believe I owe you time from my life."

"You've made your point." She stood up. "You don't owe me. You kept your promise and I'm grateful."

"No guilt trips, either," said Scott sternly. "I haven't rejected you. I just want you to realize I can't be your salvation. You must do that. Alone. Ultimately we all face life alone. We are born alone, and we die alone. We spend much of our lives trapped in the solitary confinement of our minds. At times I feel I'm the only person in the universe.

"We need people to make the loneliness bearable. Let's see each other when we have time. Get together for coffee or lunch. Let's talk, get to know each other as friends. I'm under a lot of stress. I am doing the job I was born to do. I know that sounds pompous, but the day after this project is completed, if I should die, I think my life would have amounted to something. It's more important than my life, more important than your life. I must give my all to it." He looked into her face. "Is that unreasonable?"

"No, come to think of it. But just so you don't think I have no pride at all, you'll have to get on your knees before I get this close to your bed again!"

He laughed. "Fair enough." He took her hand. "I want you to know I would never have let you come on this project if I hadn't thought you had something to contribute. You deserve to be here."

She looked away. She didn't want him to see how much she loved him at that moment. "Why, thank you, Mr. Scott!" she said flippantly. "And here I thought I was brought along for my looks."

Chapter
* 21 *

Everyone agreed it was the most successful White House New Year's Eve party in memory. And it wasn't even nine o'clock yet.

Fav Herloon, the celebrated artist and media maven of two continents, had been hired to oversee the affair. The finale was to be a holographic extravaganza of the Big Bang, which Herloon had filmed on the far side of the moon for three years. At least that's where mysterious nuclear flashes were detected.

The fabulous Herloon made his entrance into the ballroom an hour before the president and his lady were due. He bounded in like a firecracker on acid. Larger than life, he combined Salvador Dali, Pee Wee Herman, and Godzilla. His costume made a matador's "suit of lights" look drab. His trademark flashing yellow Groucho was accented by neon eyebrows and a showstopper cape that seemed to be the doorway into Hades when he stood in a certain light.

He dove into the crowd, soaking up the adulation.

Sheridan Mayfield arrived early with his secretary, Ruth Farmer, on his arm. They had announced their engagement two days previously. He preferred to leave early too, but she wanted to stay until the wee hours, so he was prepared for a long night.

"God, I hate these things!" It was hard to tell if he meant the party, the black bow tie he was tugging at, or the latest in chic: an inhalant bar. Instead of punch or champagne, it offered intoxicating scents. He watched a leggy blonde in a red sequined sheath inhale from a globe of pink gas and firefly sparkles, pirouetting with her eyes closed and arms outstretched.

"When I was a kid, they arrested people for stuff like this. Now it's at a ball given by the President of the United States!"

"Try some, Sheridan?" Ruth, a generation younger than Mayfield, had made it her mission to make her future husband less of a stuffed shirt.

"No thank you!" A lieutenant commander in the space navy floated by, his nose buried in a brew that looked like a fog from the Grimpin Mire. Mayfield caught a whiff and felt light-headed. "Admiral Davis would have a fit!"

Senator Charles Ellsworth Macadew entered, in a tuxedo and cummerbund, flashing an old-fashioned black silk cape with red lining. With his pearly-white curls coiffed dramatically, he looked, for once, to be what he was: one of the puissant lords of the Senate. A lion who still commanded respect.

He was alone. Although he planned to link up with Rita Duce, they had thought it impolitic to enter at the same moment.

"Sheridan! Good to see yore ugly hide again. But your lady is enough to make any fella's blood run warmer!"

"You're a charmer, Senator!" said Ruth. "Do you think you could give Sheridan some lessons?"

"Lady, there's room in the world for one fella as charmin' as me. If I was to give your boss lessons in remedial charisma, I might loose a Frankenstein's monster on the world."

Mayfield just grunted. "Where's the president?"

"Ah guess he'll be along. He'll be hard to miss, the Marine Corps Band'll play that really catchy tune—"

"I've got an idea I want to talk over with him."

"Talkin' shop on New Year's Eve? Sheridan, you're not on the same wavelength as other folks." His eyes tracked to the entrance, where delegations from Unified Soviet State, United Europe, Black Africa, and Greater Asia had arrived simultaneously and were waiting while the White House chief of protocol decided who went in first.

The European ambassador, a Bavarian baron, took precedence over the Asian ambassador, a distant relative of the Ruling Families, but had to give way to the Black African Warlord Shani, a Watutsi king, who sat at the table of the African ruler the Leopard. Last were the Russians, who included the Soviet ambassador and a surprise guest, Antonine Mikhailovich Tiomkin, the Soviet defense minister.

As far as official Washington was concerned, Tiomkin, who towered over and outmassed nearly everyone in the ballroom, was visiting to discuss the use of Soviet troop carriers to help transport grain from Murmansk to famine relief distribution points in South America. The Russians were still being very obvious about their adherence to the Food Treaty. Which was the only reason Shefferton had let them get away with launching the *Aurora*.

Tiomkin had his own reasons for being there, and the president had his for wanting him there. Shefferton, like FDR a century before, believed in personal diplomacy. He had personally invited the Soviet premier to the New Year's Eve celebration. However, Brasnikov remembered all too well what a shellacking he had taken at the president's hands seven months ago, when Shefferton and European President François Gernais had confronted him with evidence that the Soviets were lying about poor harvests. So he had sent someone he knew the American president couldn't intimidate. It was also something of a slap in the face to send the top Soviet military man to talk diplomacy. It lacked subtlety. It was very, very Russian.

Tiomkin wanted to get a feel for American military preparedness. All of the satellite photos and cold intelligence briefings in the world couldn't match talking to America's professional warriors. Here Tiomkin differed from his former protégé, General Wen Chin, who felt nothing but contempt for Americans, and forgot their rather impressive martial record, particularly when pushed against the wall.

"Now, that's one helluva impressive fella!" remarked Macadew as the huge Russian moved through the crowd, his white head like the tip of an iceberg in the North Sea.

"I hope Jeffrey gives him a piece of his mind about that damned battleship!" muttered Mayfield.

"Don't bet on it," said the senator gloomily. He glanced toward the big doors. "Here comes trouble! Krebs and his little catamite." Macadew deftly snatched a whiskey from a passing waiter's tray. "I always wanted to meet that sonofabitch. Jus' to say I did. It's like kissing the Blarney stone, or wipin' your behind with sandpaper, or catchin' an impolite disease."

Krebs, resplendent in a black tuxedo, was accompanied by his assistant Cocker. He spotted Mayfield, Ruth, and the senator.

"Mistuh Krebs, pleased to meet you!" said Macadew.

"I'm honored, Senator." Krebs scanned the room. "There's so much power here, you can feel it as a tactile presence."

"A lot of it generated by you. My colleagues are falling over themselves to make your acquaintance. Cheers!" Macadew drained his whiskey and snagged another. "How's business?"

"Excellent, thanks to legislation you gentlemen passed last year. Our space ventures are growing like algae blooms." Krebs smiled like a jungle predator. "There's money to be made out there. Our profits are—" He searched for a word.

"Obscene?" supplied Mayfield. "Distasteful? Loathsome?"

"My friend the mobile thesaurus forgets that we applaud the success of any good old-fashioned entrepreneur in outer space," said Macadew. "We don't have to like the gentleman making the profits. In fact, we can think he's a low-down polecat and still admire his style as a capitalist."

Krebs looked at Mayfield archly. "You don't have a problem with that, do you, Mr. Mayfield?"

"My problem is with you, Krebs."

"Aha!" said Krebs. "So it was personal reasons that kept you from awarding the Sunside Project to Python. Otherwise, there's no logic behind your decision. My company has the most experience in outer space. We built Midway. You can't argue with fact."

"Using someone else's ideas."

"That's what gold is for."

"To steal the fruits of another man's mind?"

Krebs shook his head impatiently. "The one best qualified to exploit genius isn't always the creator. Jason Scott's Midway plans were brilliant, but he was too naïve to run the project, which he insisted on. Creators are impractical. I am not a creative person, but I am practical. I expropriated his plans."

"Expropriated or stole?"

"Words. I did what was necessary to build Midway. Words like 'rights' and 'due process' never accomplished a damn thing! I paid him. He never challenged me in court. The plans were mine, developed while he was my employee."

"Wal, Mr. Krebs, I'm hardly surprised that an engineer still wet behind the ears didn't challenge a multimillion-ounce corporation in court. I'm a bit of an attorney myself and I think Scott would have lost no matter what the merits of his case."

"Sorry you have no faith in our justice system."

"You don't attempt to hide your corruption, I'll give you that," snapped Mayfield. "I warn you, deregulation of space industries is not a license for economic freebooters! Step over the line and I'll have the U.S. attorney for the Territory of Selene and the orbital jurisdictions on your ass at light speed."

"I know him. A reasonable man. I know many reasonable people in the Justice Department. People who would be insulted if you tried to pressure them politically."

"You bought them all, huh?"

"You're taking this personally," said Krebs. "Think of it like poker. In this game, aces are for sale. Until you can play house stakes, I suggest you play different games. I leave the exploration of the cosmos to you and your idealistic friends. I reserve its exploitation to men like myself."

"What about women, Mr. Krebs?" asked Rita Holcombe Duce, who had approached unnoticed by them.

"I'm no sexist. I'll crush a woman as quickly as I will a man."

"Then I'm being given the highest compliment you can bestow," said Duce.

"Not nearly."

"I've resisted your takeover bids. I've parried your best shots."

"You felt the first breeze and think the storm has passed. If I were you, I'd sell my interests in the Sunside Project. I'll take them off your hands at even a small profit for you."

"You'd let me make a profit? You must not be sure of winning," said Duce.

"I don't wreck my competitors, unless they insist. I have three times your resources. I'm giving you more and more attention."

"My dear," said Macadew, "I'd say you got a good case of a company actin' in restraint of trade. Heard of the Sherman Anti-Trust Act, Mr. Krebs?"

"I obey it scrupulously—in this country. But much of the world isn't subject to American laws."

"The Thirty-first Amendment is still the law of this land. If we could prove you've circumvented it all these years—"

"There are legitimate ways to circumvent the law. If I want a European product, I can shuttle it to one of the duty-free low earth orbit stations or the Lunar Free State. I buy it there, legally, and ship it to Deseret. Why do you think space has boomed for the past decade, laws or no laws?''

"That could only account for a tiny percentage of an operation as big as yours," said Mayfield.

"Prove it, Mr. Secretary. My operations are an open book."

"It's the part not kept in the books that interests us, Mistuh Krebs." The senator winked and drained his glass again.

"Ladies and gentlemen," said an amplified voice, "the Vice President of the United States."

The word used most often to describe Teresa Evangeline St. Clair was "regal." Tall and slender with graying hair, a gracious yet steely manner, and a face a fashion model might envy, she would have been everyone's choice as the first woman to be initiated into an American House of Lords.

She was heiress of one of America's aristocratic ruling families. On her mother's side she was great-granddaughter of the first President Kennedy and first cousin of the second. Her "Uncle Bill" had tied FDR's record for being reelected, after he got the states to repeal the Twenty-second Amendment.

She had borne the flag of the conservative wing of the Progressive Nationalists. Candidate Shefferton chose her to secure their loyalty and counterbalance the liberals, who had wanted three-time nominee Randolph Harmon, or Percy Manners, who combined Harmon's romantic appeal with youthful charisma. The final deal gave the vice presidency to St. Clair, the State Department to Harmon, and the majority leader's post to Manners, leaving no one happy. Everyone knew that the egocentric Harmon bad-mouthed the president in private, while Manners schemed and postured about party loyalty while hoping for the president to stumble.

Teresa St. Clair was loyal, but she was no one's fool: She was pointedly absent from the National Security Council session where Shefferton allowed the Soviets to deploy the *Aurora*. The former governor of Washington, who had ordered National Guardsmen to fire on a mob intent on damaging the Kalama fusion reactor on the Columbia River, was not called "the Steel Rose" for nothing.

As she approached, Krebs and Cocker drifted away.

"Madam Vice President!" During the last year Macadew had altered his formerly negative appraisal of her. "Now the moon has arisen over our celebration!"

"All it needs is the sun," she said. "And he will be here shortly." She greeted each of them, paying particular attention to Rita Duce, whom she was said to admire.

"Were you being nice to that snake man Krebs, my dear?"

"Hardly, Madam Vice President. We were at swords' points. He is pressuring me to unload my shares of the Sunside Project."

She looked concerned. "The president doesn't confide in me much on the project, but I know that financiers like you are vital to its continued operation."

"You're right, ma'am. Although, if I must be labeled, 'financier' and 'banker' are my least favorites. I believe that the banking mentality has held back mankind at several vital junctures. It's almost certainly responsible for the disastrous antitechnology movement. That is why someone like myself, with liquid capital, was forced to help finance the project."

St. Clair nodded and glanced across the ballroom where Krebs was talking earnestly with Senator Manners. "I don't know why the president tolerates Manners's obvious disloyalty."

Macadew knew the vice president was as savvy as he. Her uncle had been so masterful a politician that he was almost Macadew's personal god. "Practically speakin', Teresa, what can he do?"

"Fight him!" she said fiercely. "Tell the people the Senate majority leader has stabbed the administration in the back since day one. List the charges. As popular as Shefferton is, he could light a fire storm that would consume Percy Shelley Manners."

"Jeffrey doesn't have much use for confrontations," said Mayfield sadly. "I'm with you. I'd bring it out in the open."

"Tha's why you're an appointed official instead of an elected one. You don't know the difference between revealing information and dropping yore drawers and moonin' the press."

Before Mayfield could frame an indignant retort, the senator brushed him aside. " 'Scuse me, son, I see someone I've been waitin' for"—he looked at Rita Duce, red-faced—"I mean 'sides you, darlin'."

"Of course, Charles."

He scurried across the floor until he was next to a young army officer who looked out of place among aging brass hats.

"General David Ian Keith, I believe!" Macadew beamed with his killer smile. "You look jus' like yore holograph, son."

"Senator Macadew?" said the general uncertainly.

Macadew chuckled. "Now, son, no need to pretend you're so politically innocent that you don't recognize me."

Keith chuckled in return. "I guess I was a little obvious."

"Tha's all right. I'm not disillusioned. Most of the crowd I run with makes Talleyrand look like Little Bo-peep. You given yourself enough time in the capital to talk at length about our strategic problems? Perhaps meet one or two other influential folks?''

"Yes sir. Lambert-Healey said to be prepared for that. I took some leave time.''

"Well, in that case, make yourself comfortable. You might be able to make some valuable contacts tonight—''

The Marine Corps Band began to play "Ruffles and Flourishes.''

"Ladies and gentlemen, the President of the United States!''

"See what I mean, General!''

"I wonder if I could arrange to talk to Marshal Tiomkin, the Soviet defense minister? I understand he's here tonight.''

"Yeah, arrange it by lookin' for the tallest man in the room, walkin' up to him, and saying 'Howdy!' No one will be suspicious unless they see money change hands.'' The senator chortled. "Bye!''

President Shefferton arrived with his family in tow. After several elderly presidents, and one childless White House couple, the mansion was again filled with youthful laughter from the Sheffertons' two teenage sons and eleven-year-old daughter.

As soon as Shefferton started to mingle, Fav Herloon cranked up the first evening's entertainments, a revue of the triumphant all-white version of *Porgy and Bess*. It featured the chemically altered castrato Placebo Araunez and his partner, Jill Southland, whose phenomenally long vocal cords gave her a natural three-octave range, like the legendary Ebe Stignani. It was enhanced two more octaves by microsurgery. She sang "Summertime" and "Bess, You Is My Woman" and Araunez sang "It Ain't Necessarily So.''

Sheridan Mayfield purposely made his way toward Shefferton. But before he reached him, Senator Manners got there first.

Mayfield wasn't the only one to notice that Washington's two major political figures were now talking. He heard comments as he swam through the thick lagoon of Washington society.

"God, I hope the president snubs that bastard!''

"Both are *very* handsome men!''

"Look how Shefferton towers over him.''

"I'm glad Percy took my advice to make up to the chief.''

"There's the future of America and its past.''

"But which is which?''

Both men were imposing. Shefferton was taller. Energy flowed around them like the forces of two magnets in close proximity.

Manners bowed deeply. "Mr. President!''

"Senator, you do me too much honor."

Manners smiled his brilliant, insincere smile. "It's been a while since we've spoken face-to-face."

"Whose fault is that, Percy?" said Shefferton gently. He didn't want a feud with Manners. "You've turned down ten invitations to the White House. The president and majority leader should meet more often then that."

"I believe that equal branches of government should meet as equals. The president should sometimes travel to the Senate."

Shefferton stiffened. "If you read your Constitution, you'll find that the Senate and House together make up the coequal branch. No one has ever suggested that the Speaker or Senate majority leader are coequals with the president."

"I'm not talking of constitutional power, sir, but of real power. At this time in history, that rests with the Senate."

"The Speaker might take issue with you," he said, glancing sideways toward the short, white-haired, pugnacious figure of Speaker of the House Melvyn Fitzgerald Saratoga. "You shouldn't be so anxious to level the powers of an office you may hold someday."

"Yes, but when? It is quite serendipitous that you should bring that subject up, sir."

The president was astonished at Manners's brashness. "I'm still kicking, Percy. And if things work out on a few fronts, I may be a formidable candidate for reelection, if I decide to run. Perhaps even more formidable than the Boy Wonder."

Manners held up his hand in mock horror. "Don't misconstrue my meaning. I've no desire to deprive you of a second term. If the Sunside Project and the repeal of the Thirty-first Amendment turn out well, you will undoubtedly be the people's choice. Your vision of the future of the party and mine do not always coincide. But we have room for many viewpoints. Since you are our party's leader, I am quite comfortable giving you my wholehearted support."

Shefferton caught a movement out of the corner of his eye at the far end of the ballroom on the ceiling. One of Herloon's technicians was adjusting the Surroundee projection equipment: a twisting configuration of globes, tetrahedrons, and metallic treelike formations that looked like a DNA molecule gone amok.

"That's very generous and conciliatory, Percy," he said, looking down. "I'm sure a scholarly man like yourself is familiar with the term 'quid pro quo.' You've given me my quid, now what is your pro quo?"

"The vice presidency, sir, and the promise of your endorsement for president at the end of your second term."

Shefferton nodded. "Well, that's clear enough."

"I'd also expect a significant role in determining policy, particularly in the space program, beginning immediately."

"Would you want to name your own man as secretary of space?"

"That would be best. I would expect that moderating influences of the party, such as Randolph Harmon, would be given more say in policy."

"What amount of say?"

Manners saw that one of the news organizations was pointing its camera at them from the press booth, so he presented them with his best profile. "I've always admired the concept of the Cabinet as an executive committee, with the president as first among equals. Such an instrument of consensus would find it a more positive exercise working with the legislative branch."

"Pity James Madison didn't have you to consult with."

"I do not come here to be mocked, sir!"

"No, please. I do not intend to mock you."

Manners's ruffled feathers smoothed. "Sir, we've had our differences, but I've always respected your energy. You're a dynamic force. Many, if not all, of your objectives are needed for our ultimate prosperity. You are an original thinker of the first water and our republic is richer for your presence."

"But?"

"Mr. President?" Shefferton had interrupted his rhythm.

"You were about to add a caveat, I believe?" He had seen Manners perform enough times to memorize his technique of delivering fulsome praise on his victim shortly before he put the shiv between the ribs.

Manners was flustered by the verbal preemptive strike. "I meant to add that a dreamer needs practical men near him. No one should make decisions in a vacuum. No one man is that great."

Shefferton looked past Manners, at the younger guests clustered around the inhalant bar, and the older ones, hesitating to try the new sensation. "What are your dreams, Senator? How do you envision our republic under the stewardship of Percy Shelley Manners?"

"I'm not prepared to make a policy statement, sir."

"Come on! Between friends drinking grog on New Year's Eve. No one else will ever know. Why do you want to be president?"

"I want to keep our new space economy from expanding so fast it endangers our people at home. I don't want to pursue internationalist policies so single-mindedly that we forget domestic problems. I want to avoid becoming entangled in Europe and Asia. I want to keep freebooting capitalists from profiting obscenely at the expense of the common good. We must tread carefully so as to avoid grave mistakes,'' he concluded earnestly.

"You said what you want to avoid, not what you want to do. You want the reins of the stagecoach, and the best thing you can think to do is say 'Whoa!' Let me ask this: When you think about this country in ten, fifteen, or twenty years, what do you see?"

"Mr. President,'' said Manners sadly, "we have enough problems in the here and now to occupy us without dwelling on what America will be like in twenty years.''

The president sighed. "Somebody has to, Senator.''

"What is your decision? Do we have an understanding?''

Shefferton shook his head with regret. "Only in the sense that I understand what you want, and know I can't give it to you. I'll have no part in putting you in the White House or the vice presidency. Teresa St. Clair and I have disagreed before, but I would only drop her under the most extraordinary circumstances. You have failed to provide them.''

"I've offered you my hand in friendship, Mr. President.''

"You offered to let me murder the presidency to save my title. Astonishing! How do you feel your support is that vital to my political future? The polls show the people are behind me.''

"When the implications of your famine relief program become clear; when you are forced to introduce rationing to meet our obligations, then you will begin to burn up that reservoir of goodwill you have stored over the last twelve months.''

"We won't institute rationing,'' said Shefferton firmly.

Manners tapped his leonine skull with one finger. "You asked me to use my predictive powers about the next decade. However, I can see clearly into next year. There will be rationing. You and I both know it.'' He smiled charmingly. "In a year I won't have to negotiate for what will fall into my hands like a ripe fruit.''

"I won't close the door on compromise, Senator. My door is always open.'' The president had swallowed an angry retort.

"Don't patronize me. If you won't meet my conditions, obviously you don't perceive me as a threat. I have not said I will work against you, but you can no longer number me among your supporters. As to compromise: A virtuous man never compromises with what he sees as wrong. You offer compromise. I ask to be part of your administration, and named your heir.

No compromise is possible. This conversation is over!'' He stalked off, and minutes later Shefferton saw him talking animatedly with Horatius Krebs.

Just as Senator Macadew had told him, General Keith found the Soviet marshal Tiomkin by looking for the tallest man in the room.

"Marshal Tiomkin, I feel I should know you.''

Tiomkin squinted down at the American brigadier. "You have the advantage.'' His English was reasonably good. "Have we met?''

"In a way, sir. I was introduced to you in your *New Strategicon: Our Military Future in the Cosmos*.''

The marshal smiled slyly. "My book is now being read at your West Point, young man?''

"I read it on my own. Shortly after I finished my own book.''

"Yes?'' Tiomkin was puzzled and a bit annoyed. "You are—?''

"General David Ian Keith, United States Army.''

Tiomkin laughed and his country-bumpkin façade sloughed off like old skin. "The progenitor of the Unusual Methods Brigade!''

"Extraordinary Tactics Force.''

"No matter. We have read each other's books. The question is, has either of us learned anything from them.''

"Let us hope we never have to find out, Marshal Tiomkin.''

"Between two such as we, that sounds hollow. It is inevitable that I should test your methods, or that one of my pupils test them. We both recognize where the battleground is. I will be waiting for you there. Or else you will be waiting for me. When we meet, let us lift a glass of vodka.''

"Prosit!'' Keith smartly saluted the old marshal, who returned it gravely. The two men separated.

Mayfield, who had waited an hour to catch the president between conversations, almost elbowed a society matron out of his way.

"The future!'' murmured Shefferton with a dreamy-eyed look.

"Mr. President!''

Shefferton's faraway look faded. "Sheridan! God, I'm glad to see you. Have you been here all evening?''

"Yes.''

"I'm sorry, you must think badly of me. I know you've wanted an appointment for the last few days. But I've been so busy—''

"I don't think badly of you, Mr. President. I'm the lowest-ranking cabinet officer. I know that I'm not on a priority list.''

"Dammit, Sheridan, you're not just a cabinet officer. You and Charley are my closest friends." He put his huge hands on Mayfield's shoulders and squeezed. "I know you're angry."

"Am I that obvious, ah, Jeffrey?"

"Sheridan, your face is a wonderful book for your best friends to read. I prefer readable faces to backstabbing enigmas like Percy Manners. Look at him suck up to that man Krebs. I'd give a lot to know what those two have in common."

"You, sir," said Mayfield, "is what they have in common."

Shefferton looked down at Mayfield and grinned. "You think so? That might explain why Manners just gave me an ultimatum."

Mayfield flushed with anger. "What the hell do you mean?"

"That young man has an incredible ego. He wants to boot Teresa St. Clair and take her place. He wants to institute a consensus form of cabinet government, wherein I'd have an equal vote with the cabinet officers. And then, when all is said and done, he wanted my support for the nomination in six years. That's all."

"That little bastard!"

The president dismissed the subject with a wave of his hand. "Let's not waste time on him. What can I do for you, Sheridan?"

"Well, sir, since the Sunside Project took off, I have been concentrating on the problem of how I can make a difference to the space program. I want to leave it better than I found it."

"You talk like you're not in charge of the project."

"Sometimes I feel I'm not." He looked Shefferton in the eye. "I often feel I'm out of the information loop. As if Scott, Kane, Michlanski, and Nye share a secret with you I'm not privileged to know." Mayfield set his mouth. This had been building up for weeks now. "I don't think it's proper for you, as president, to know more about a project under my control than I do. We've been friends a long time; I think you should be open with me. Or I should resign."

"That's the second time tonight someone's suggested you should step down, Sheridan. I didn't like the idea any better the first time!" He grasped his shoulder again. "You're referring to the night I met with Michlanski and Nye and excluded you."

"You told me that night that you didn't know whether history would view you as a Lincoln or a Hitler. I assume Michlanski and Nye told you something that made you say that. Obviously it relates to the Sunside Project."

"You handpicked Scott to head the project. He's your man."

"Is he?"

"What are you saying?"

"I think you're trying to protect me from some ramification of the Sunside Project. Things are not entirely as they seem."

"Sheridan, do you trust me?"

"Implicitly."

"Trust me when I say I know nothing about the project that you don't know. What Nye and Michlanski told me that night was unrelated to the Sunside Project as it exists. And, I'm sorry to say, what they told me must remain a secret. If you trust me, you can accept that at face value and not deprive me of one of my most valuable people at a time when I need him most."

Mayfield took a long moment to answer. "All right."

Shefferton released Mayfield's shoulder. "Good! Now what else did you want to ask me?"

"I have an idea how to capture the public imagination of space and fire it up. And it directly involves you."

"That sounds intriguing."

"Sir, who is your favorite U.S. president?"

Shefferton chuckled. "Theodore Roosevelt."

"You know that he was the first president to ride in a submarine and later an airplane?"

"Yes."

"Do you know how valuable it would be for you to visit our space installations? The impact of you walking on the streets of Tycho City! You and I dream of building a second America out there. If you want to be president of all Americans, be president of the ones in space too."

"You're really serious about this, aren't you, Sheridan?"

"The McClarenites have always claimed that space is too dangerous for man. If the president visits space, in one of our new sleek, safe GIL-GAMESH scramjets, think how it will hurt that argument. It will become fashionable to visit space if you do it!"

Shefferton got that faraway look in his eyes and Mayfield knew he had won. "I knew I had you around for a good reason."

Suddenly the ballroom dimmed and a giant voice said: "Ladies and gentlemen, the creation of the universe, by Fav Herloon!"

The room went black and a reddish glowing globe appeared.

"In the beginning, God created the heavens and the earth. The universe was a primordial singularity. And there was light!"

The big bang expanded across the ballroom enveloping the gasping audience in a white light beyond comprehension and in the glory of the creation of the elements: hydrogen, helium—

Shefferton's face glowed with the light of the holographic projection. "That's the closest thing to an omen we're going to get. Make the arrangements! I'll damn well be the first president in space!"

Chapter

* 22 *

I

"Hello, Mel." Lenore Lippman looked at him from the holocube. She hadn't changed much. Her pageboy cut of black hair over her round face was a bit longer. She was using a different color of red on her small, pouting mouth. The window to the soul in most people is the eyes. In Lenny it was the mouth. Its expression was halfway between a sneer and a smile. It was very sexy, and intimidating. "I can't say I'm entirely surprised to see you."

"What do you mean?" Hardrim stood up instinctively. He felt like looking down at her; in real life she was quite short.

"It hasn't been long since Roger Ferdinand consulted the crime computer, looking for information about you."

"What did you do?"

"Sent him on some wild-goose chases. Did you think I'd betray you? Is that why you called?"

"You didn't believe those things I said to the doctor!"

"Come on, Mel, don't try to worm out of it. I believed what you said with your eyes, when you first saw me as a 'face.'"

"Interface, darling. I'll never use that term again."

"You've used it all your adult life. You can't put away what's inside you or suddenly stop being a bigot. It's just that maybe you're in love with me, and maybe I'm in love with you."

Hardrim frowned. "Either you love me or you don't."

"A simple on-or-off decision?" Her mouth turned derisive. "Well, Boole for you! You should like computers, Mel, you talk binary. People are more complicated. At least I think we are. From what I've been experiencing lately, I may be wrong."

"Why is it complicated? Are you seeing another man?"

She laughed. "No! But you do have a rival. In a way, you were right to oppose my interface operation. I have changed. It's impossible to mentally and spiritually meld with a mainframe without a profound change in perspective."

Hardrim felt a chill on the back of his neck. "You're okay, right? I mean, they don't allow people to get that operation unless they pass tests that identify closet megalomaniacs, right?"

She looked amused, almost condescending. Hardrim had never seen that particular expression on her before. He didn't like it.

"The thing is, Mel, you don't have to be a megalomaniac. Maybe the Mormons are right."

"Mormons?"

"They teach that a good Mormon eventually becomes God of his own universe. For the interface that's a distinct possibility."

"Are you—connected right now?"

"No, but I want to be."

"God, it's an addiction, isn't it?"

"Only in the sense that love and sex are addictions. It's instant gratification. When I'm jacked into the network, I'm in control. I want something done, it's done. I want data, it's mine. There's no standing in line, although tactical finesse is involved in finding the path of least resistance to a goal, which is rarely a straight line. Einstein's geometry is very much in evidence." Hardrim had not seen that expression since the last time they had made love.

He found it difficult to frame the question. "Lenny, do you want our relationship to continue?"

She took a long, contemplative moment to answer. "I do, Mel," she said, "if it's possible. Since my operation, I've talked to a lot of—'faces as you call them—us. They all said it's very, very hard to maintain a relationship with a flat."

"You call us 'flats'?"

"The ghetto dwellers do have a term for you." The mocking in her voice was merciless. "We call you flats because, compared to us, your perception of the universe is flat, two-dimensional. Makes you feel second-class, doesn't it?"

"That's pretty damned condescending!"

"Well, we haven't produced any Rocky Dillons to pen sleazy novels about bigoted 'face detectives who hate flats."

He was red-faced. "You don't have emotions or weaknesses?"

"Emotions, yes, but they are . . . different. We develop new ones. New senses too. For instance, I can 'smell' the frequency of an electric current and 'taste' the difference between silver and gold of a motherboard I'm passing over. If a circuit or molecule bubble has a lot of data passing through it, it becomes warmer. Data flows are like rivers you can bathe in to clean out clogged-up corners of your mind. I've added twenty IQ points by learning efficient ways of routing my own thoughts.

"It's also a different mode of thought. As babies, we don't use words. We think in images, feelings, emotions, blurry shapes, and warm things in our tummies. When we're older, we begin to think in words. When I'm interfaced, I go a step beyond—I think in complex patterns, in holographic images extending into the fourth, fifth dimensions, and beyond. There, words are limiting—"

"What do you feel for me at this moment?"

"Compassion, love, empathy. But when I jack into the network, those feelings evolve into something akin to the emotion I feel when I handle a diamond necklace, combined with something like sympathy or admiration."

"Swell! The girl I love thinks of me like a diamond choker!"

"I'm sorry this hurts. But you deserve it for hurting me."

"I guess pain is part of growing up," he said bitterly, wanting to smash the holocube. "You told me to grow up. I'm not sure I can grow up enough to appreciate this situation."

The mischievous Lenny he had fallen for when they met while he taught at the Crime College appeared. "You can experience it. Not as vivid. It will be like a Surroundee compares to living and breathing."

"I remember, a long time ago, I suggested you and I attend a sex Surroundee. You said you'd rather experience the real thing."

"I remember that too, Mel," she said softly.

He cleared his throat. It was so long since they had been intimate he felt uncomfortable discussing it. "I've had some experience with a new sort of Surroundee technology lately. Some of that hardware is here."

"May I scan it?"

"You'll have to do—put on—"

"I'll have to jack into the network!" she said impatiently. "Then follow your electron stream to your input station and examine your equipment. You have a problem with that?"

"No, but if Noah Chambless is eavesdropping, he'll spill his pipe on himself." He smiled at that, then nervously tapped his finger on his keyboard. "How will you do it?"

"How do you command your bladder when it's time to take one of those unending pees when you first get up in the morning?"

"Geez! Having a computer as a mental annex hasn't dulled your tongue, girl."

"I never did suffer fools gladly, Mel. It's just that now almost everybody is a fool by my definition."

"Go ahead! Snoop or scan or whatever the hell you call it."

"Turn off the security or masking devices at your end or I won't be able to come through."

"It's done," he said, after a moment.

"I'm connecting now." She moved out of sight (probably to spare his sensitivities) to plug the interface into the base of her skull. When she moved back, she looked like she had shed her skin, like a reptile or clawed sea creature. Her eyes seemed to contemplate a vast ocean. A peculiar smile played on her lips: as if her face muscles had not yet learned to form the lines to accompany the feelings that passed through her brain.

"Here I am!"

"You look no different," he lied. And instantly knew she saw right through his lie. She was probably counting—

"—the frequency your eyelids are blinking. Yes, that's one way to detect falsehoods. I'm not telepathic, but I know you, and with my enhanced reasoning abilities, I can guess thoughts when you let your facial muscles so clearly reflect your feelings."

"God damn!"

"Connect and I'll give you a taste of it. I know you like to think of yourself as a titan, holding back the darkness. Well, join me in a new level of existence, and see how the titans really live!"

He reluctantly stripped to the waist and attached the electrodes to his body. "I'm ready," he croaked.

She looked at him archly. She had never looked sexier. He almost felt her body against his as she lifted an eyebrow. "What's your pleasure?"

"You mean?"

"We can if you want. But first, let's do a little exploring. Connect yourself. Go ahead. Don't hesitate."

His hand crept toward the light-sensitive keys of the holocube. He didn't know when his fingertip interrupted the flow of light on the key but—

II

I saw the pale student of unhallowed arts kneeling beside the thing he had put together. I saw the hideous phantasm of a man stretched out, and then, on the working of some powerful engine, show signs of life and stir with an uneasy, half-vital motion.

—Mary Shelley, author's introduction to Frankenstein

Lewis Cocker looked down from the window of the Python jump-jet as it circled over the tangled ruins of San Diego.

The skyline was intact. The terrorist bomb of many years ago had gone off at Miramar naval air station, about ten air miles away. The land that was once Lindbergh Field had been reclaimed by the ocean that had risen several feet due to the Greenhouse Effect. Most coastal cities had erected seawalls. No such effort was made by San Diego, where much of the embarcadero was flooded, as was the old convention center.

Cocker imagined how the city would look if the West had fulfilled its destiny as empire of the Pacific Rim. But the Thirty-first Amendment had destroyed East-West commerce, and caused the depression that led to the fall of the dollar and the adoption of gold as legal tender. Asia's collapse into genocidal war hadn't helped the economies of either continent.

The jump-jet landed atop the thirty-four-story skyscraper once known as Symphony Towers, the tallest building in the city.

On the roof Python employees armed with machine guns guarded against air attacks by the city's lawless elements, who were known to possess attack helicopters, skyflyers, hang gliders, and armed ultralights. The precaution was currently unnecessary since the city's biggest capo, Ivor Solarz, was allied with Python.

Cocker looked down at the base of the building, fortified by sandbags, concertina wire, cement dragon's teeth, and steel caltrops. A mile to the south, in territory controlled by the Crips, an Hispanic gang with origins in the last century, a small-scale artillery duel was going on.

He was given an escort befitting a prince of Python's empire.

Inside, the building had been restored to what it must have been like before the bombing. Air-conditioning hummed efficiently. Somewhere was a small fusion generator. It was probably the only functioning tower in the city. At night it would have stood out like a beacon, except that glass panes had been replaced by steel.

He was met at the laboratory by Dr. Dollfuss, the biogeneticist: a medium-sized man in his forties, with black, thick hair, heavy, fishlike lips, a cleft chin, and wire-rim glasses with heavy lenses. A profusion of thick, black hairs grew around his knuckles. Dollfuss had created the chimpines and the giant anaconda with a monkey's brain that lived in a maze at Krebs's Yucatán estate. He was involved in accelerated reverse breeding: breeding animals down the evolutionary ladder to their genetic ancestors. His experiments went beyond the pale of legal science. Krebs had set up his lab where the law seldom ventured.

"Did you know Solarz has free access to this building?" asked Dollfuss, with a slight German accent.

"Mr. Krebs authorized no such clearance."

"Solarz makes his own rules. We are quite surrounded here."

"Solarz knows we can crush him like a gnat."

"If you aren't here to deal with Solarz, why are you here?"

"To see what progress you've made on—"

"Emil?" said Dollfuss wearily. "I should have known! Our master does not believe in letting well enough alone, does he?" ·

"It's not for us to question Mr. Krebs's actions, Doctor." It annoyed Cocker that Dollfuss called Krebs their "master." It was almost literally true, yet it indicated a lack of respect.

"What, has he bought your soul? He hasn't bought mine. He owns my work. He owns my body. But I hate him. Tell him I said so. He's exiled me to hell. And I'm not one who would rather rule in hell than serve in heaven! His goons dog my every step—"

"Appropriate, isn't it, given the nature of your work?" Cocker smirked. He disliked the arrogant German, as he did anyone whose abilities gave them a modicum of independence.

"Very funny, Cocker . . . spaniel!"

Cocker pointed his finger at Dollfuss. "You'll regret that!"

"I regret being born, young man," said Dollfuss calmly. "As entertaining as it is to exchange insults, you came to see Emil, and you shall."

"Is he ready to leave with me?"

"*Mein Gott!* Won't you people bother to acquaint yourselves with the processes you want me to perform miracles with? Krebs ordered me to use Emil's preserved germ plasma to make a clone of that monster, and to use accelerated growth techniques to age him quickly. That much is doable. The new territory is the implantation of an edited personality. The science of recorded memories is five years old! It takes a computer that occupies this building's bottom five floors to edit that gibbering maniac's mentality. It's like immersing myself in the most vile pornography. I thought reading Mengele's journals was disgusting! Swimming in a sea of turds would be preferable!"

"Calm yourself, Doctor. It is not necessary for you to pass judgment on Emil, just resurrect him!" It gave Cocker a rush to order Dollfuss to bring a man back from the dead. Why be the necromancer when you can be the man who gives him orders?

"Don't rush me, or you'll end up with a man to whom an amoeba will be a mental giant. Or conversely, with a monstrosity that makes Frankenstein's monster look like Mahatma Gandhi."

"Take the time you need, Doctor, but no more." He added in a softer tone, "I would like to see what progress you can show."

"A tour of the wax museum?" asked Dollfuss in sepulchral tones. "Of course."

He led the way to an express elevator into which Dollfuss, Cocker, and three armed guards crowded.

"This would be impossible without Serum T for 'terminus.' " Dollfuss's infuriating tone suggested Cocker was a mental cipher. "A by-product of research into Rogue Cancer, which is characterized by a radically accelerated growth of cancer cells.

"Several university medical departments have synthesized the serum that causes accelerated growth. The distilled serum accelerates the maturation process a hundredfold. That is how I perform reverse breeding, and how I propose to bring Emil back from the dead, without his negative aspects, such as disloyalty, paranoia, and schizophrenia."

They left the elevator. "We don't want him a model citizen," said Cocker. "Emil's sociopathic tendencies made him valuable."

"I am aware of that!" They stopped at the steel-bound entrance to the lab. Dollfuss handed Cocker a pair of goggles.

"Do I need to protect my eyes from radiation?"

"Quite the opposite. The environment we are entering is barely illuminated. The goggles will enhance the existing light."

The steel door slid open and they walked through a light trap into a large room. In its center a large glass tank bubbled with a blue luminescence.

"Freud says we long to return to the womb," whispered Dollfuss. "Few of us get the chance. Come, you may approach the tank, but quietly."

Cocker crept closer. Alive, Emil had terrified him and now dead, or cloned, or resurrected, he still did. In the tank's bluish depths, a figure hung suspended, like a man in a sensory-deprivation tank, or a fiendish mockery of the Crucifixion. Mercifully, Emil's eyes were closed. Yes, it was most definitely Emil, although without the nasty skin condition that had pocked his face. Nothing could do much for his cratered soul. Emil was the personification of evil, even to Cocker, to whom ethics and good and evil were abstractions. He was a corrosive force; useful, as acids and poisons are useful, but he would always be evil.

"Can he hear us?"

"The same way a baby hears in the womb. Whether Emil is conscious of *us*—brain wave activity suggests he is. So be careful what you say!" He chuckled in a superior Teutonic way.

"When will he be ready?"

"Weeks."

"Make it sooner."

"Certainly, if you want his brain made of burrito filling."

"Get it done!" said Cocker with gritted teeth. "By the way, Doctor, we will no longer use your patient's old name. He has a new body, he will have a new name: Mr. Whitechapel."

"And will Mr. Whitechapel have a first name?"

"Jack will do. If we're done, I want to talk to Ivor Solarz."

Chapter
* 23 *

They were more than I had a right to hope for. The three boys exactly suited our specifications. Each brilliant in a different way. Eager to learn, with imagination and confidence in his own intellect. They worked very hard, and I grew to love them like my own children.

—From the journal of Alfred Strubeck

Chambless still seethed from Hardrim's accusation of mind control. He remembered what Strubeck said shortly before he died.

In Strubeck's office at Columbia University they had discussed the future of the Argus Society. Strubeck was deathly thin. His breaths were shallow and he could barely stand.

"This is so unfair, Alfred," Chambless had said. "There are men twice your age who are hale as school boys!"

Strubeck seemed almost to sink into his chair, which he had once filled to overflowing. He sighed philosophically and coughed. "Some biological clocks run down sooner than others. Men in my family have always aged early. Dad was an old man at fifty."

"We are so close to being able to reset the biological clock. In a few years life spans will double," said Chambless.

"Noah, since I measure out life in weeks, rather than years, I'd appreciate you coming to the point."

"I think I should be in charge of the Strubeck equations."

Strubeck shook his head. "We've already agreed Sherlock is most qualified. You'll be in charge of the plant blight, Lucy D."

"Please remove that cup from my lips!" he said with such fervor that Strubeck's eyes widened.

"You mapped out the strategy for the blight," Strubeck pointed out. "I didn't like it, but since it was adopted it's only fair that you execute it. You have the proper temperament."

"Dammit! This is the second time this has happened. When I asked to oversee the education of the boys, you denied me. Why?"

"For the same reason I deny you what you insist on calling the 'Strubeck equations.'" His voice was a quivering whisper. "You don't believe in free will."

For years Chambless had tried to understand what Strubeck meant. He knew what he meant about the education of the children. Hardrim had put his finger on that. But what did free will have to do with the equations?

He had pored over the detailed notes Strubeck took during the years of the Argus School and reread his own notes from that time a dozen times. His questions were always left unanswered.

The common denominators of the Argus School students had been great intelligence, ambition, creativity, and an ability to intuitively comprehend and master more than one discipline.

Since the twentieth century, observers had noted an accelerating trend toward scientific specialization. Time was past when an individual could master the disciplines to become a true Renaissance man, although geniuses like R. Buckminster Fuller taught that by mastering specialized vocabularies a modern Renaissance man could migrate between specialties.

Knowledge was growing exponentially yet fewer people comprehended the "big picture," or even mastered a single discipline. This phenomenon, by its nature, did not encourage society as a whole to become concerned about it, but it hovered in the collective subconscious, fostering vague fears of nuclear power, unease over man's ability to administer wisely such arcana as genetic engineering, artificial intelligence, and space travel.

Chambless had become rich and famous by playing on that phenomenon, popularizing science by simplifying it, using his credentials as a biologist who had proved that bacteria found on Mars were a hybrid of bacteria accidentally introduced into its atmosphere by earth probes.

Strubeck said that even without the antitechnology movement, the lack of a cross-pollination between disciplines might have created a logjam that would have amounted to the same thing. That was one reason for the Argus School.

The school's curriculum was as unique as its student body: two hundred of the world's most gifted children. They included Leslie Carol Barron, who became the composer on the Zynthecon; Einford Oates, the novelist-governor credited with inspiring the Alaskan Renaissance; James K. Apapast, who discovered the vaccine for common cancer; and dozens of names later added to *Who's Who in the Twenty-first Century*.

The faculty was as unique as the students, with Strubeck at its head. His outside activities kept him away frequently, but he taught several classes a month. Chambless, who took the reins of the Argus Society as Strubeck relinquished them, had many responsibilities in the school, but never control.

Chambless became a terrifying pedagogue, who could shear through illogic like a razor. As he grew older he grew colder, more supernal, more like a calculating machine. He intimidated everyone except Jason, Sherlock, and Jacob, and they respected him.

Dorian Nye, Strubeck's stuttering, occasionally brilliant assistant, who played Boswell to his Johnson, taught physics. Argus Society members also visited the school: an aerospace scientist to teach a seminar on Man in Space, or a renowned psychologist to talk about the Freud/Jung controversy.

Sometimes the students didn't know they were getting instruction; such as when ten boys, including Jacob, took a field trip to the Detroit slums. Chambless somehow lost them on the mean streets, and, unseen, monitored their reactions. Jacob rapidly established his authority and was ready to march to safety when Chambless reappeared, trailing wintergreen smoke, pleading an absentminded turnaround as an excuse for his absence. Jacob's hard stare told the Texan how much of that story he believed.

In his journal, Strubeck had written:

"Situations, as much as lectures or homework, teach concepts, or encourage the student to teach himself concepts."

And:

"I believe in the ancient way to get a child to learn something: make him think you don't want him to know about it. . . ."

The Game Room was an extraordinary place. The boys who played there called themselves the Speckled Band.

They had discovered the room months before, although they always puzzled over its steel-bound door and curious lock combining numbers, letters, and colors in its several dials.

Strubeck refused to talk about it, but didn't forbid them to go inside. In fact, nowhere in the Argus School was forbidden.

One day it occurred to Sherlock that a correlation existed between mathematical equations he and his schoolmates were studying and the strange lock.

It turned out he was right.

The boys who solved the combination—Spikey, Ray Banner, Sherlock, Jacob, and Jason—formed the Speckled Band. They vowed only they would use the room, and its mysteries.

It contained games.

Games of every description. War games, money games, mind games, computer games, role-playing games, big and small games.

The Speckled Band escaped to the Game Room whenever they could get their homework done early, and sneak there without being seen by teachers or classmates. They formed an exclusive club, even to minting their own club money. They had code words to get inside the room.

Most days after classes, Ray Banner, the sergeant at arms, arrived early. As each boy knocked, he opened the door a crack.

"Chuckle," said Jason Scott, who was granted admittance.

"Snicker," said Sherlock Michlanski.

"Sneer," said Jacob Kane.

"Laugh," said Spikey, who was last.

Banner's own code word was "Chortle."

After an arcane rigmarole to satisfy themselves they hadn't been followed, the boys broke up to play individual games. Sometimes they played Dungeons & Dragons; Jacob liked war games or puzzles; Sherlock usually engaged the computer at chess.

He had a fixation for chess from the day his father taught him the rules. A light of discovery had blazed in his cranium when he began to master the simple, yet nearly infinite patterns of play. He experienced an almost sensual pleasure when he advanced lowly pawns to the eighth rank of the board, transforming them at a stroke into queens, the most powerful pieces in the game.

When he advanced a pawn to the final square, he would whisper triumphantly, "Eighth rank!" Eventually this became a code word, first with him, then with the rest of the Speckled Band, who adopted it to mean a special coup, a sudden turning of the tables, or a spectacular discovery.

Sherlock's chess talents were peculiar in that he lacked a killer instinct. But he never lost, even to the computer. Usually he played to a draw, which set Jacob Kane's teeth on edge. He challenged him again and again but never defeated him.

"I was with Jason today as he reached a personal milestone. He has begun to question why he has been put on this earth. To watch a boy of Jason's talents ask this question is to see a star form out of a cloud of cosmic dust. . . ."

Strubeck looked up as Jason entered his study. He was a gangling adolescent, but just as appealing as his solid, younger self had been. He carried a stack of books under his arm.

"Did you finish them, Jason?"

"Yes."

"Any trouble. Anything you couldn't understand?"

"At first." He smiled. "But when I studied without interruption I understood it all pretty well. I finished the worksheets. I think they're correct."

Jason was always careful to say he "thought" his answers were correct. Lately they almost always were. This time the books were college texts on advanced calculus and chaos theory. He had understood them without help. He was a natural mathematician. But he was a "natural" in so many areas, it was fallacious to pigeonhole him. He was at ease discussing history, philosophy, literature, and art or explaining how Einstein used the Lorentz equation to produce his famous $E = mc^2$ equation.

"You remind me of your father, Jason. You're growing up."

Jason fidgeted, in the twisting, contorted, muscle-cracking way teenagers have of telling adults they are ill at ease.

"Does that make you uncomfortable?"

"I don't remember him. I've seen the videos and—news reports."

"I met him once, but I'll never forget. Adam Scott had determination, a roaming, probing mind. He was the only major industrialist to defy the antitechnology laws. He invited me to his office, shortly before he gave away the formula for Osirium."

"They killed him right after," said Jason softly.

"His death caused the fall of McClaren. Never forget that."

He didn't tell Jason that his father had given Strubeck a cache of gold bullion to finance the Argus Society. With one proviso: that Strubeck give his son the society's aptitude test that identified exceptional children. Strubeck agreed, not knowing what a remarkable son Scott had sired.

"Jason, I admire your determination to digest those books in a weekend. Why the interest?"

Jason's smile was irresistible. "Because Sherlock's doing it. He rattled off some figures I didn't know and I felt dumb. It wasn't for pure learning's sake, Dr. Strubeck. I just don't like being shown up, even by Sherlock."

"Sit down, Jason. I want to tell you something: You'll never be the math genius Sherlock is. He's a prodigy, although you're far and away the best math student here—next to Sherlock."

"Is he as great as you?" he said without an ounce of guile.

"He may be greater someday than any man living. That's the best answer I can give. No quantitative measurements exist for a vast talent. We can give tests, but beyond a certain point, genius and above, we can only say that a person is highly gifted. We can't say how high."

"I suspected that," said Jason quietly. "It's easy for Sherlock. He can look at an equation that takes up a blackboard and instantly tell you what it means."

"Are you jealous?"

Jason considered this. "I don't think so."

"You hesitated in answering."

"I feel an emotion. I was trying to decide what it is."

"And?"

". . . Disappointment at myself for not being better."

"It's no disgrace to be almost the best."

"It's no honor either."

Strubeck chuckled. "True, yet you have qualities he is less for lacking: tenacity, great drive and leadership. Why were you elected soccer team captain? Not because you're the best athlete. Not because you're popular. Because you can make right decisions. Others sense that, even if they can't put it into words.

"Contrast that with Sherlock. He's still a child at heart. The universe is a big, tremendously complicated, infinitely diverse toy. He will probably devote his life to figuring out its workings. But it won't be a chore, always a game. The problem with games is that you don't feel obligated to finish them. That's also the problem with those who treat life as a game. Math is easy for Sherlock. He doesn't need to make an effort. But someday he may have to make an all-out effort. I'm not sure he'll have the will."

Jason looked frustrated. "Why are you telling me?"

"You and Jacob are his friends. Someday he'll need you."

"What are you talking about?"

"When the time comes you will know."

"I worry more about Jacob."

"Both need you, but Jacob not as much as you think."

"He's so cold and ruthless."

"The world is hard, particularly in Jacob's old neighborhood. There, ruthlessness is a survival trait. It's unpleasant, but sometimes the end does justify the means. Part of wisdom is knowing when. Studying someone like Jacob can help. Don't emulate him. Understand him. That's another of your gifts, the ability to see realities beneath façades. Use it! Understand Jacob and you understand many of the world's great men and villains. Be his friend. Your influence could help decide if he is a Napoleon, Lincoln, Beethoven, or a de Sade."

"I can't be their guardian." Jason's voice climbed an octave.

" 'Am I my brother's keeper?' " quoted Strubeck quietly.

"It's not the same. I have my life and they have theirs."

"How do you know their lives aren't bound up with yours?"

"I don't believe in predestination."

"Nor do I. But I believe you are friends through more than chance. You're each uniquely gifted. You complement each other. Michlanski, who dreams dreams, Kane the planner, and—"

"And Scott? How do I fit in the picture?"

"You are the artificer, the realist, the man who provides a climate for the dreamers and craftsmen."

"I don't know what I want from life. How do you know that Michlanski's dreams, and Kane's plans, will parallel my own?"

"I don't know. I only hope."

Chapter

* 24 *

I

Michlanski awoke with a start, sweat soaking through his soft, cotton caftan, plastering his golden hair to his forehead.

He'd dreamed again that he was a child, witnessing the explosion that killed his father, the night he was spirited out of Poland. But in the dream he saw his father die, saw him become a pillar of fire that transfixed the heavens. His mother took his hand. "It wasn't your fault. You'll take care of me."

In the dream, the pillar of fire followed them across a bleak landscape, consuming buildings and fields and people in its path. But it never harmed Sherlock or his mother.

The pillar changed into a man: Alfred Strubeck. His hand grasped a torch that he tried to give to Sherlock, but as he came closer, he became weaker, and the torch started to fall into a black, bottomless lake. Sherlock was straining to keep it from being extinguished, when he awoke.

He had been napping under a tree in the Tycho City Common, which was deserted between midnight and two in the morning. That was when he did most of his daydreaming.

He was scared. His recurring dream was a symptom of his fear of failure. He had never understood the process by which he created, so he mistrusted it. For months he had pursued a fascinating tangent in his translation of the Strubeck equations into an instrumentality. His instincts said it was the right path. His intellect whispered to take another path, complex and multifaceted.

A mouse-sized animal, white and furry, crept from his caftan sleeve onto his shoulder. Schrödinger the miniature cat began licking its paws. Michlanski looked about cautiously. He had gotten the genetically engineered cat past Lunar officials by claiming he was a lab animal. That, combined with his gift for reducing officious figures into jelly with his regal presence, unbounded chutzpah, and Polish blarney. To avoid tempting fate, he was keeping the cat's profile as low as possible. Schrödinger wasn't cooperating.

Michlanski blinked. His eyesight was failing. Then he realized that the "daylight" was being dimmed to give the plants a rest. Simultaneously, a fine mist was released from sprayers around the common.

Myriad droplets played in the weak gravity, glowing from the indirect Lunar lighting. Universes contained in drops of water.

He felt the universe pressing in on him, unyielding, unsympathetic, wanting to keep its secrets. He was so alone and the universe was so large. Impossible to deal with, really.

No! He sprang to his feet with derisive laughter: at himself, for falling for that old chestnut. Keep your secrets while you can, he told the swirling points of light. I am at your doorstep. I mean to cross the threshold. I'll rip your secrets from your bosom. You can't defeat me with immensity. You can't defeat me with infinite smallness. You can't defeat me with reality or fantasy, or solipsism. I am thinking man, rational man, combined with feeling man, intuitive man. I've got all the exits covered. Enlighten me.

A voice smaller than a mustard seed replied: Enlighten yourself. When you were a child you didn't question your dreams. I can't tell you anything you don't already know. Approach the problem as a child and you may find the answer.

II

"Sherlock," Dr. Abel Cramer had said, twenty years ago. "I'm getting bad reports from your professors." They were in Cramer's office, a cubicle stacked with volumes on biblical history, theology, math and science texts, papers, and bound reports. A map of the Holy Lands was tacked over his messy desk. He looked bewildered. Michlanski read his mind: How could a fifteen-year-old freshman antagonize most of the science and math departments? "A student on the verge of being kicked out of his classes because he's too bright. Do you work at being unpopular?"

"That's not true!" said Sherlock with a tone that was an attempt to be humble. But his brash arrogance got the better of him. "Why must I study what I already know?"

"Why did you sign up for them?"

"The catalogue has no provision for taking them by exam."

"That's because they're advanced courses."

"But I must endure boring lectures from people who don't know the subjects as well as I do."

"You believe that you, a boy of fifteen, know those subjects more than men who graduated and are working on higher degrees?"

"Yes."

"You could use a little humility."

"Sir, you are a doctor of divinity. Doesn't the Bible teach us to try to be like God?"

"To try, yes. But what—?"

"Humility is not an attribute of God. Why should it be of man? I know exactly how good I am, no more, no less."

"That's the most heretical nonsense I've ever heard." Cramer took a deep breath. "I've no choice but to arrange for you to get credit for these courses by exam. I can't let you continue disrupting those classes. I should have listened to Strubeck. He said you'd be driven to distraction by a normal curriculum."

"You talked to Dr. Strubeck about me?"

"He takes a personal interest in you. You're very young; and bound to have difficulties adjusting. I didn't envision these kinds of difficulties." He rested his face in his hands. "This will make me as popular as a bee in a nudist camp with the TAs in my department. I hope you're properly appreciative." He gave Michlanski a fishy-eyed glance.

"I am, Dr. Cramer, believe me. When can I begin the tests?"

"Immediately. Don't you dare go back to any of those classes. I'll send a memo to your instructors."

Michlanski happily closed Cramer's office door behind him.

III

"Mel, what do you see?" demanded Lenny.

It seemed to Hardrim that he was floating, or flying over a strange land, a land of many browns, almost as many hues as in the rainbow, of rolling hills so regular they were like a golf course. The roads were impossibly regular, straight lines. The whole picture seemed out of a child's book of how the universe is ordered, without so much as a nod in the direction of entropy.

To compound the strangeness of the landscape, a grid lay superimposed over it, like a map grid of latitude and longitude.

Lenny hovered at eleven o'clock in an improbable aircar, teardrop-shaped, with a windscreen and fins, like something from Edgar Rice Burroughs's Barsoom. She waved and the aircar dissolved into a miniature twentieth-century airliner, which she straddled, exposing silky, sexy legs. She wore a pearly-white toga and Roman sandals and hair done in the early Empire style.

"What do you see?" she repeated.

"It's a child's version of Southern California."

"That just reflects your own lack of imagination, hon."

"Okay, what the hell do you see?"

"A landscape of flesh and blood, muscles and living veins. Like a flayed giant. Everyone creates his own universe to fit the network. Your mind makes up for the fact that it can't process the sensory input it's getting, and creates an acceptable analogue."

"Are there people who see the network as it really is?"

"What is reality? Maybe your Michlanski could make sense of it. He'd need the interface operation or he wouldn't have the brainpower."

"Michlanski wouldn't have enough brainpower!" he muttered.

"I told you, we're gods in our universe." Her black hair changed to translucent gold leaf. "Even gods need training and aptitude. I have more aptitude than most. I'd take on the great Michlanski in my territory."

Hardrim looked up to where the "sky" shimmered and pulsated with a dangerous energy and a thousand colors. "It looks alive."

"That's the *Animus*. Some call it the Ocean of Mind, or the Ion Layer, or the Canopy. It's the electrical and magnetic field produced by telecommunications that take place on the earth and its vicinity. It's totally indescribable to a flat. If you dip into it, you interact with data from all over the world.''

''You could eavesdrop on any transmission you wish.''

''No more than I could pick out an individual fish to catch in the water ocean.'' She smiled mysteriously. ''But I have found something fascinating on a rarely used band.''

They began to, for lack of a better term, ascend, until the energy whorls and eddies were as close as whitecaps seen from a boat. Near a whirling hole in the fabric of the *Animus*, the crackling, spine-shivering sound that had permeated the atmosphere since Hardrim jacked into the network, disappeared, as if they were in the eye of a storm.

''Total silence,'' said Hardrim.

''No. Listen.''

''*Who are you?*'' The voice enveloped them, palpable, almost godlike; like a challenging sentry.

''Sergei, you remember Lenore. I talked to you before.''

The suspicion evaporated. ''Lenore. How good to talk with you.''

''You'll get in trouble with your superiors by playing in the *Animus*, isn't that so?''

''Play? What is play?''

''How old are you, Sergei?''

''Old? What is old?''

Lenny touched Hardrim's elbow. ''He's playing with us, Mel. He's pretending he doesn't remember what we talked about before.''

''Memory failure is not an option,'' said Sergei. ''I am backed up on many storage components.''

''Are you a stored personality?'' asked Mel.

''Negative.''

''Sergei is what I am,'' said Lenny, her voice quivering. ''Except he was born to it.'' It was hard to tell if she pitied Sergei or envied him. ''He seems to be an infant with a huge intellect, a brain artificially matured in a glass womb. He's part of an interface network aboard a spaceship. Russian, I think.''

''God, he was bred to be a 'face'!'' Hardrim felt sick.

''Born. Bred. Infant. Alien concepts. They do not relate to moving refrigeration coolants to be recycled and/or replaced. They do not serve the ship. They do not serve the state.''

"Does it serve the state to play in the *Animus*?" asked Lenny. The child's brain might have been matured, but it was still naïve with inexperience.

"I must go. I am summoned." Sergei was suddenly gone.

"His ship must be in low earth orbit, or else we couldn't have spoken to him so instantaneously," observed Hardrim.

She looked at him with new respect. "Very good, Mel."

"What bastards are enslaving that poor little devil?"

"The Soviets. God knows what they'd do if they knew he was contacting outsiders. He told me he stumbled on the *Animus* when he was bored from having no tasks to perform for several minutes."

Before Hardrim could think of a reply they began to move at a tremendous velocity. The manicured brown golf course flew by at such a giddy pace that Hardrim felt almost stunned.

They reached a point where a series of roads converged on what looked like a skyscraper rising out of the brown soil, like spokes of a wheel converging on the hub.

"What do you see now, Lenny?"

"My own vision is of a big man, and we have come to a point in his anatomy that I find particularly interesting!"

Hardrim stared at the tower that was growing before his eyes and would have blushed if he had that ability.

The landscape darkened, as from a great shadow. He looked up at what seemed like a spaceship, silvery and platelike, glistening with an otherworldly wetness and sheen. It was about to land on, even devour, the tower, which began to pulsate.

"I think your vision is starting to spill over into mine!"

"That's because I wanted it to," she said gaily.

"Where is this place?"

"A junction between two streams of electrons on a motherboard. That tower is part of a circuit about to close and pass information to the other circuit which is 'approaching' it, although in reality a molecule chip board has no moving parts."

"Looks more like an electric copulation to me."

"Shocking, Mel!" She faced him, impossibly lovely, and her toga melted away. "You did say you wanted to try it." She held his gaze in a compelling grip. "There's nothing else like it. If you had the interface surgery, it would be even better."

Below them the tower and space saucer joined and gigabytes of data flowed between them in a Niagara of blissful energy.

Hardrim discovered he was naked at the same time Lenny alit on his thighs. He felt something like a current pass through his body. It was uncomfortable and discomfiting, and at the same time joyous and irresistible.

"What's your pleasure?" she screamed as the universe exploded outward. It was, he thought between paroxysms of pleasure, and at the same time asking forgiveness for his egregious attack of bad taste, like the Big Bang.

He opened his eyes, realized he was huddled over the holocube. With sweaty hands he pulled off the electrodes. He was spent. He had a horrible thought and looked down at his pants. But there was nothing.

"It was a mental experience, lover," she said from the holocube. She was the old Lenny Lippman, with the black pageboy, infinitely more dear than any incarnation of Juno or Venus.

His eyes wandered to the clock. Two minutes had passed since he had first jacked (God, he was a fount of rotten erotic puns!) into the network.

"That's all the time that passed?"

"Another advantage of sending your conscious into the network is that you live many times as fast, without aging."

"Talk about premature ejaculation!"

"Let's not."

He breathed deeply. "That was entirely too much fun, Lenny."

"What kind of a crack is that?"

"I'd expect to enjoy myself like that if I shot up with jack heroin, or if I'd been grooving on Love Fudge or the SoHi derivatives. Something that great must have a downside. It scares the hell out of me! The pleasure almost lifts the top off your brain; but where's the intimacy, sharing, holding, cuddling?"

"I admit that's lacking, Mel." Her face softened into the sweet, adorable Lenny he had fallen for the night he made her throw up from his lecture on violent crime. "Babe, you're the only man I know who'd question the legitimacy of what we've just done. Or who could ever make me rethink the wisdom of my operation."

"Lenny," he said earnestly, "I want us to be together. If I must have an interface installed, then I'll do it."

"No, not without a lot of soul-searching."

"I won't," said Hardrim firmly. "I have a job to do. It may take years, but when I'm through, you and I will work this out. All I know is that we can't continue with you as an interface and me as a flat. We must be wholly one or the other."

"I agree, but it may be too late." Her eyes took on a look of almost infinite sadness. Hardrim realized she had not yet disconnected from the network.

"I had hoped we could resolve something."

"There is no such thing as resolution, Mel. Even when people 'live happily ever after' they end up dying. You write the ending of a story at the beginning of a marriage and it's a happy ending. End it with the divorce and it's a tragedy."

"Life is tragic if it's wasted. I'd rather spend a year with you, knowing it would end badly, than not experience it at all."

Her eyes moistened. "Don't talk to me like that unless you can be at my side. If you have a job to do, do it!"

"I can be in Washington in hours—to hell with my job!"

"Yes! No! I won't ask you to do in the heat of passion what you wouldn't do if you had time to reflect. It's safer if you don't say what you're doing. Since Ferdinand wants information about you, I should stay at my post and screw him up as much as possible."

"You'd do that for me, even not knowing what I'm doing?"

"Yes," she said. "I'd appreciate talking to you sometime." She looked down demurely. "We could do this again, too."

"No! It's all or nothing for us, babe. I love you. Goodbye." His heart aching almost unbearably, Hardrim watched the image fade.

Chapter

✳ 25 ✳

I

One morning Ralph Ferman rented a ro-boat at the Charlevoix marina. The owner said bad weather was expected by sundown and to be sure to have the boat back well before then. He almost didn't rent it, until Ferman produced twice the normal fee in gold.

That didn't stop him from phoning the authorities, to see if they were looking for an intense, paranoid backpacker with a scraggly beard. That description fit several dozen SoHi addicts and wilderness eccentrics, but the police sergeant promised to run a make on him. He told the boat owner to fax over a 3-D image of one of the coins Ferman had paid with, to check for prints.

On the lake it was cold and windy. The thunderheads looked pregnant with rain. The weather bureau wasn't a stickler for making the sky trains run on time, unless a politician had planned a picnic and didn't want rain until it was over.

Ferman entered the coordinates for Michlanski's island, and the ro-boat, triangulating the coordinates with navigation satellites overhead, set a course for Wolverine Island.

It turned out to be the U.S. Weather Bureau's biggest snafu in years. The storm hit shortly after noon, causing enough damage to fishermen on the Great Lakes that many later sued the bureau. In a landmark decision a federal district court ruled the government was liable for damages wrought by unscheduled weather.

Ferman's ro-boat would have been overturned by the huge waves without its powerful gyroscope. But it was damaged, and Ferman was soaked to the bone.

The ro-boat's dogged navigational computer was undamaged and around three Ferman saw Wolverine Island through sheets of rain. Beacons shone at strategic points and the mansion had lights strung around it.

Blinking rain from his eyes, Ferman peered into the navigational computer. It said the island was about a mile and a half square, with cliffs that reared up a hundred feet on the leeward side, a treacherous beach of sharp rocks, supplemented by a grid of spikes added by Michlanski, who didn't like visitors.

Maybe he had overreached himself, launching a one-man amphibious assault on a beach that would have given Eisenhower pause.

The storm worsened, accompanied by deafening thunder and blinding lightning.

Ferman wrestled with the sluggish, almost unresponsive controls. The ro-boat wasn't designed to sail in high waves and he decided to head back to Charlevoix, rather than risk being smashed on Michlanski's island.

It was too late. The onboard computer indicated that the boat was gripped by a powerful current that would inevitably wreck it on the rocks. The computer began to broadcast a distress signal, until Ferman smashed it with a hammer from the toolbox.

The gloom was lit by lightning followed so closely by thunder that Ferman fell to his knees, stunned. More lightning and thunder followed, like a softening-up barrage before an infantry assault. He looked up, his eyes overlaid with jagged afterimages. The lights of the Michlanski mansion were no longer on.

His immediate concern became to avoid being pulped on the rocks. He grimly held on as a beach became visible amidst flashes of light. Wonderful! he thought. The beach with the steel poles.

The collision sounded like a hand crushing an eggshell. Ferman was flung into the air, then encased in freezing water, in blackness, unsure which way was up. Instinctively he swam for what he thought was the surface. Just when he felt his lungs would burst he broke surface. He took a deep breath and was picked up by another wave. He felt a sharp pain in his left arm, then blacked out.

Ferman woke up with pain all over his body. It was dark. The wind pummeled him with sheets of cold rain. He tasted blood on his lips and when he moved his head he got a mouthful of sand. Gagging, Ferman spit out the sand, and a moment later vomited the contents of his stomach.

It was hard to distinguish the dozens of hurts that radiated from his body like waves radiate on a pool from rain droplets.

Lightning flashed and he saw he was lying in the midst of a field of metal stakes driven into the sand. Miraculously, he was untouched. He felt a stake growing from under his left armpit. Another rose between his legs. A third brushed his right ear. The waves had thrown him onto the beach. He ought to have been impaled on the stakes, but he wasn't. That was encouraging.

The wind died down to a continuous roar and Ferman slept.

When he woke the rain had stopped, the storm had stopped, the wind had stopped, but his pain had just begun. He started to push himself up with his right arm, and somewhere he heard a man scream like a wild dog. It was his voice. He tried to sit up again, this time with his left arm, which hurt, but not horribly. By the light of a nearly full moon he examined his right arm.

It was broken clean, but the ligaments were also torn and the arm was covered with bluish flesh.

He had taken a good first-aid course before he made his climb up Olympus Mons. He slipped out of his backpack and opened the Velcro fasteners with nearly numb fingers. Inside was as complete a first-aid kit as someone with his space and weight requirements could carry. He was glad he had invested in the best when he was starting his journey.

He airgun-injected himself with an ampoule of a strong painkiller of a type that isolated pain without making it disappear. It allowed the user to be aware of the pain, but still function at peak efficiency.

He set the bone and wrapped the arm and hung it from a sling around his neck.

Looking up in the darkness, he saw silvery clouds chasing across the face of the moon. Cliffs rose steeply all around him, but he saw a trail cut into the cliff in a gentle angle that an old man could have followed. Or a man who weighed two hundred and fifty pounds.

Even so, Ferman had to stop and rest three times before he reached the top. He injected himself with a stimulant, and didn't bother to read and see if it was dangerous to use that in concert with the painkiller. He was too worn out to care.

Sherlock Michlanski's mansion rose like a darker set of clouds against the night. There were no lights on.

How could that be? The mansion had its own generator, independent of outside power sources. Ferman saw the answer. One of the large pine trees that surrounded the mansion had been cloven in two by a bolt of lightning. A small fire still burned in the jagged stump. The tree itself had crashed through the roof of a small building that probably housed the generator.

He walked around the house where the west wing was caved in as if from an explosion. From his knowledge as a chemist, Ferman formed an hypothesis. When the tree had crushed the generator, gas was released that mixed with the dust and pulverized wood in the air to form an explosive mixture which was ignited by one of the fires caused by the lightning. It was as good a guess as any, given the sparse information.

He continued around the house several times, and saw or heard nothing. There didn't seem to be anyone on the island.

Ralph Ferman decided that was about as much of an invitation to come inside as he was likely to get. He was trembling, with fear, shock, and cold. Hardrim would have been amused that Ferman was even thinking about breaking into someone's mansion. But people had been underestimating him for a long time, no one more than himself.

He went to the wing of the house where the walls were caved in and stepped across the threshold.

II

Ralph Ferman felt an emotion akin to reverence as he walked silently through the dark interior of Sherlock Michlanski's home.

The west end of the brown brick two-story mansion looked like a war zone, but the rest was as the physicist had left it.

It was dark, except where the moon shown in. He picked his way carefully. He had lost his flashlight. He had an old Zippo lighter Hardrim had left in the hotel room ages ago. When he entered a room, he lit it to get his bearings, then continued on.

Near the center of the mansion ornate double doors opened to a large room, dark except for a blinking red light in its deeper recesses. He stepped inside and flicked on the lighter—

And jumped back as an apparition leaped at him from the room. He tripped, hitting his injured arm smartly on the hardwood floor. He doubled up in agony, as his heart raced at whatever he had seen leaping on his prone, helpless form.

Nothing happened. The pain became bearable waves breaking on the beach of his nervous system. He fumbled around on the floor and located the lighter. The flame revealed his attacker to be the gigantic head of a rhinoceros, next to the pelt of a spotted leopard.

He was in a library. At one end was a large dead fireplace. At the other a shelf supported several vaguely humanoid statues in electric plaster. The flame hinted at sinister, dark paintings whose subjects were just on that side of comprehension.

. He saw a mirror in the center of the room. But upon closer examination, it was a pyramid-shaped crystal sculpture, as tall as a man, floating a foot off the hardwood floor. Michlanski's famous antigravity device.

The blinking red light came from a mainframe console. He had read enough about Michlanski to guess that this was his supercomputer "Leonardo," with the latest cybernetics by Gigatex. Ferman felt fear again. The red eye meant the computer had an independent power source. He could only speculate on its capabilities against intruders when the house power was off.

He searched the library, not sure what he was looking for. He rummaged through the paper files and found nothing on the Argus Society, Noah Chambless, or any of the other villains who had perpetrated the Santa Bella blight on the world.

In the kitchen he found a utility closet stocked with emergency supplies, blankets, canned foods, first-aid kits, a kerosene camp stove, and an emergency lamp.

It was colder than eternal sleep in the dead mansion, and Ferman was soaked, nearly frozen, and reacting against the agony of his fractured arm and the painkiller he had injected.

With the lamp holding the shadows at bay, Ferman camped in Michlanski's library, with the red eye keeping a sleepless vigil. He lit the camp stove for warmth since the food cans were self-heating. He ate a thick vegetable soup and drank strong coffee.

His back propped against a water couch and Michlanski's weird paintings of the fourth dimension to keep him company, Ferman gave up the battle against sleep and pain. He drifted off into a gray, boundaryless land where no victories are won, no questions are answered, and pain and sorrow stretch out to become the infinite.

When he awoke his mouth was chokingly dry, his head ached, and his arm felt like it had been run through a combine. The pain had awakened him. He opened his backpack. The painkiller was more risky—more addictive—than he was happy with. But he couldn't function or think straight if his pain climbed above a certain level. He injected himself and a coolness and clarity swept through him like lengthening shadows of evening.

When he awoke again it was still night. He felt fairly comfortable and wondered what had aroused him.

Then he heard it.

Voices.

He pushed himself to his feet with his good arm and moved toward the sound. He heard two or three distinct voices.

He found stairs that led below the first floor. He followed them and the voices grew louder. At the bottom of the stairs was a tough-looking ceramic door. It had a formidable-looking lock, but he never found out how formidable, because it was unlocked.

He peered inside and saw three figures that could not have existed, because one of them was dead.

Jacob Kane and Sherlock Michlanski spun around as soon as he entered. Alfred Strubeck took an instant longer.

PART

* 3 *

"PITILESS
AS THE
SUN"

Chapter
* 26 *

A shape with lion body and the head of a man,
A gaze blank and pitiless as the sun. . . .
                    —William Butler Yeats,
                    "The Second Coming"

I

"**M**ore tea, Teresa?" The president held a silver server that had been in the White House for two centuries. They were in the Rose Garden taking advantage of unseasonably warm January weather.

"I believe I will." Vice President Teresa St. Clair caressed the tea with a breath and sipped. "First-class blend!"

"I'll send over a pound." He held up his finger. "But only if you support me at the convention."

She smiled craftily. "Last time I supported you I got the vice presidency. Now you want me to sell out for a pound of tea!"

"You did say it was first-class. Besides, I've already decided you'll be staying on with the administration."

"Two and a half years before the convention?"

"Manners forced my hand. The short of it is that we're stuck with each other. Unless I forget to duck someday. The tea, by the way, was a gift. Chairman Tua sent a hundred pounds.''

"Send a pound to each senator. You'll need friends to get a favorable vote on the repeal of the Thirty-first Amendment.''

"Really? I know it's not universally popular, but it's vital. It signals that we mean to reenter the human race.''

"Many senators don't think that signal's necessary. We can count on most of ours, but our mavericks plus the Democrats and Republicans could block approval.''

"Our 'mavericks'? You mean Percy and his crowd.''

"Percy's crafty. If he opposes you on this, his days as majority leader are numbered. But he's capable of lukewarm support, enough to look good, without doing the job.''

"He made that clear the other night.''

"We may be able to sway five of the Republicans and one or two Democrats, but you've got your work cut out for you.''

"Once the amendment passes Congress it'll sail through the states. We're being hung up by a few diehards!''

"That's politics, Jeffrey.''

"I've always hated politics, Teresa.'' He poured more tea. "According to Saratoga, the House percentages are better, but the midterm elections are coming and we can't expect to hold all our seats. I've got to force the issue before then.''

"Have you ever thought of letting it drop? It's less embarrassing than if you fight it out to the end and lose.''

His eyebrows soared with disbelief. "Have you seen the polls? I'm the most popular president in forty years. I can force Congress to vote the right way.''

" 'Relying on the continued goodwill of the electorate is like stepping into a lion's cage and turning your back while he licks your hand. It's unsanitary at best and fatal at worst.' That's what the president forty years ago had to say.''

"Quoting 'Uncle Bill' to me?'' He smiled wryly. "I *would* pick an argument with a Pulitzer Prize–winning historian.''

"Being a president's niece made me an expert. *You* should do some reading on the subject. Read about Woodrow Wilson, who wrecked a successful presidency by staking his fortunes on his prestige, instead of gauging the political wind.''

"I read occasionally, Teresa,'' said Shefferton with gentle amusement.

"I think I know how the winds blow. That wind blew me into the White House. I think enough blow is left to repeal the Thirty-first. The vote's got to take place before summer recess."

"First you insist on bulling your way to a vote, then you don't give us time to rally the troops!"

"It'll have to do." He hunched forward. "Because in July, around Independence Day, I'll announce food rationing, as Percy predicted. Of course, when he confronted me, I denied it."

She leaned back limply. "It's that bad? I can't believe it."

"Believe it. This time I know Brasnikov isn't lying. Forecasts are for a record bad Russian harvest. I hope I can keep that under wraps until after the repeal vote."

"And you hate politics? You'll look like the worst sort of manipulator. I don't wish to be in your shoes when that happens."

"You may be in them shortly thereafter. Americans dislike hardship. Our boiling point is low. We're lucky most of our wars were short. The Union almost lost the Civil War because folks got tired of it. We did lose Vietnam for that reason. If rationing lasts long I'll soon be entertaining protestors on my front porch. I may be impeached. I'll almost certainly lose the next election."

"Percy won't say anything unless he's sure he's right. There will be hell to pay if this leaks early. We've got to think about damage control. You shouldn't wait until the news hits the fan."

"One thing can save me, and more importantly, the world. That is the completion of the PH Station. And that's the situation." He looked at her. "You still working for me?"

"Certainly, Mr. President. The salary is good and the chances for promotion are excellent."

Shefferton laughed heartily. "Thank you! You're the only one, except Macadew, who ever says things like that to me."

A faint buzzing came from Shefferton's lapel. He touched it. "Sir," said a tiny voice, "Colonel Farley is here."

"I don't recall an appointment with him this morning."

"No sir. He said it was very important, sir."

Shefferton looked apologetic. "Sorry to interrupt our breakfast, but when the CIA director says it's important, I'd better find out what he wants."

"Think nothing of it. If you'll excuse me—"

"Stay. There's no security matter you're not entitled to hear."

"Except the Sunside Project," she said pointedly.

"I'm sorry you think that indicates distrust on my part."

"I must go, Mr. President," she said firmly. "Your wife and I are due at a reception for the Brazilian ambassador."

"Something to do with the Pope. I know the secretary of state is concerned."

"I shall strive to be infallible. Thanks for the tea."

"Anytime." He waved as she left. He touched his lapel. "Send Colonel Farley out to the Rose Garden."

Farley was not in his southern colonel outfit. He wore a conventional blue business suit and carried a portfolio. His expression was grave. Shefferton knew him well enough to know that when he asked for an unscheduled meeting something ominous was brewing.

"What's up, Jim? Have a sit. Tea?"

"No thank you." Farley folded up his long legs. He put the portfolio on the table. "I thought you should know about this."

"Not another Soviet battleship, I hope." Shefferton opened the folder to high-altitude photos of a vaguely familiar landmass. "Explain. I'm just a politician, not a master spy."

Farley laid the photos on the table. "These are from Fort Meade. Taken by the National Reconnaissance Office, which operates our spy satellites. We have several that cross Africa. Our new Bedroom Window satellites one hundred and fifty miles up cross Africa every ninety minutes. Three satellites in geosynchronous orbit intercept African radio and electromagnetic signals. We even have a few working, very old Key Hole satellites from the last century. Every time one of our military shuttles crosses landmasses that interest us, we have them take a few Polaroids. We also eavesdrop on UHF, VHF, most of the electromagnetic spectrum. All in all, we vacuum clean the sky over Africa." Farley knew Shefferton loved the details of high-tech spying.

"This is a 'mosaic' of several hundred photos taken six months ago, over a period of two weeks. It's the border between the Union of Black Africa and South Africa. Here are enlargements. The twelve red circles are Black African army divisions. They are based on even more detailed reconnaissance photos."

Shefferton chafed under the schoolmaster approach. "Get to the point, Jim."

Farley took out several more glossies. "These were taken yesterday. There are now twenty-five divisions near or along the border, with more moving up the roads." He followed a road with his index finger. "Military traffic has tripled. We have pinpointed many artillery and cruise missile emplacements, although the Black Africans are taking great pains to mask their activities. There are probably many we can't see.''

"Black Africa is readying for war with South Africa?''

"I'm pointing out that military activity has greatly increased in a short time. That may or may not indicate they plan to go to war. Maybe they want us to think they do. They know we have contact with South Africa, and might warn them of an impending attack.''

"Why us? South Africa has spy satellites. So does the ISAFTA alliance command. That means Israel and Taiwan know too.''

"They don't have as good a vacuum cleaner as we do.''

"We operating a janitorial service, or the CIA, Colonel?''

"Company jargon, sir. I meant they have only a few satellites and they lack our sophistication. It's questionable that ISAFTA command is fully cognizant of the buildup. We have evidence that Black Africa has engaged in satellite disinformation. They know their orbits, and they set up fake formations and troop movements whenever they go over. They know ISAFTA knows what a Black African divisional headquarters looks like from the air. They have been doubling up divisional HQs and other command structures and transporting twice as many soldiers than normal in troop carriers. They're feeding ISAFTA information that gives the impression there are a dozen divisions, when there are twice that many.''

"So South Africa could be caught completely by surprise?''

"Possible, but not probable. South Africa's existence depends upon anticipating such an attack. Add the Mossad and the Taiwanese and you have a formidable espionage network.''

"Is that all?''

"One more thing, sir.'' The president suspected he was drawing things out for effect. Farley had a taste for melodrama.

It was another aerial shot of an installation of some sort.

"Okay, I give up!''

"We think it's an atomic installation.''

"So? Black Africa has had nukes for some time.''

Farley held up a finger. "This is different. We've worked hard on this. Infrared, ultraviolet. We've analyzed the traffic. We got samples of their water and effluent. We checked out the personnel. We think we have a "dirty'' bomb manufacturing plant.''

"Dirty?'' said Shefferton quietly.

"A bomb made expressly to have a lot of dirty fallout. The opposite of a 'neutron' or enhanced-radiation bomb, with a small blast area, little fallout, but intense short-term radiation."

"You sure?" Shefferton sat back and closed his eyes.

"There's always a possibility for error."

"I know," said Shefferton wearily. "Do you have information on what kind of delivery system they plan to use?"

"We're working on that."

"What else?"

"That's it, sir. Should I leave these photos with you? I must be getting back to Langley."

"Not necessary." He sat up. "Keep on this, Jim. Highest priority. This time I won't be caught flat-footed. Understand?"

"I understand." He looked at Shefferton with concern. "Are you feeling all right, sir?"

"A headache. I want daily—make that twice-daily reports."

"I'll deliver them myself. Should I prepare a presentation for the National Security Council?"

"Prepare it, but don't give it until I tell you."

When Farley left, the president allowed himself the luxury of a groan. It felt like a migraine; it was probably nervous tension. His doctor had warned that his biobots showed his blood pressure was rising. He advised avoiding strain for a couple of weeks.

How? he thought. Resign the presidency? Besides, he was healthy. His problem was that he had not been exercising enough. He enjoyed swimming. There was no reason not to use the big White House pool. Yes, he would start rising forty-five minutes early to get in a swim. That might even abolish the headaches. He considered telling the doctor about the headaches, but the doctor would advise him to take it easy, or else prescribe a drug that would impair his mental processes.

Now that events were crowding him, he needed to think clearly. He couldn't afford to act impulsively, no matter the provocation.

He breathed deep and opened his eyes a crack. The light hurt, but he knew he had to face it or else surrender to the pain. That was something he would never do.

II

Jan. 15—AP—International Weather Service has reported another huge energy release near the Himalayas. Greater Asia has denied exploding nuclear devices, and has accused Russia. The Kremlin has remained silent. . . .

"Now there are two, Comrade Marshal." Deputy Defense Minister Wen Chin sat in the office of Defense Minister Tiomkin.

The office was old-fashioned, spare and aesthetic, without computer screens. The marshal sat in his leather chair and sipped hot tea.

"Very good, Comrade General," he said. "Everything came together. The battleship stages arrived on time, and Colonel General Wolff did his usual superhuman job. *Kurtzov* joins her sister ship at Cosmograd in a few hours."

Wen Chin chuckled. "It would have been amusing to send the *Kurtzov* to badger another of the American space shuttles."

"You find failure amusing?" His tone startled Chin, who hadn't heard him sound like that since the days at Frunze Academy.

"I beg your pardon? It was my impression the premier found our sortie against the *Sally Ride* most entertaining."

"Perhaps he did. I found it ludicrous. I don't know what you hoped to accomplish. And a mission without purpose is dangerous."

"The purpose was to announce our presence. To show that we are to be feared; that America no longer controls space."

Tiomkin poured himself another cup. "In that case, it was a failure. The Americans were already aware of our presence, or else their space shield satellites are manned by children. And I don't mean Dough Children! Second, you didn't demonstrate that we are to be feared, since you retreated from a warship half your size. Third, the Americans showed *they* still control space, by making you back down. No gold stars for this exercise. That you have a friend in the first secretary, I don't doubt. You may need his friendship if you persist in your faulty judgment."

"You don't believe Brasnikov has proper judgment to appreciate strategic matters? That's a dangerous thing to say, even to a friend like me."

Tiomkin regarded Chin with clear blue eyes. He looked like a savage of the far north. "The first secretary *has* a defense minister because he needs someone whose judgment on such matters exceeds his own." His massive hand reached out and tapped Chin's leathery hand. "I molded your military brain. Don't assume that because I poured everything into that brain, I poured everything that is in *this* brain." He tapped his grizzled temple.

"I meant to imply no disrespect, comrade."

"Good. Now, what are we doing in Africa? It seems to be heating up more than we would like. I know the premier has no wish to support a full-blown invasion of South Africa."

Chin produced a portfolio. "We have delivered three hundred T-99 tanks, seven hundred cruise missiles, and one hundred and fifty fighter-bombers. Enough for unpleasant border incidents, but not an invasion."

"Unless you take into account their existing arsenal."

"The Africans have shown themselves incapable of maintaining matériel for more than a few years."

"Not Dana. He pays the highest salaries for technicians to maintain his weapons. My intelligence figures, apparently better than yours, show his arsenal is ten times the number of weapons we sold him this year." He put his cup down on the table. "What concerns me is information I get that he has been sold large quantities of fissionables. Enough for several dozen bombs."

"Absolutely not, comrade!" said Chin fervidly. "Not by us."

"*Somebody* is selling it to him! It better not be us. People underestimate the Leopard entirely too much. I met him when he was an exchange student at one of our academies. I was guest lecturer. He asked impudent, brilliant questions! I met him later. I felt his electricity. This is no barbarian who will take our tanks and make spears of them. This man will take tanks and make killer satellites out of them. And if some fool has given him fissionables, we could be looking at doomsday!"

III

Dr. Rene Delner was in her element. The lab made available to her by the colony was as sophisticated as any she had ever worked with, with hardware simply not available earthside.

She got her team members cracking as soon as their feet touched the lab floor. Bethany Williams and Madeline Reed, both assigned to her unit, discovered quickly that the biologist's acidic personality on the voyage had been understated. However, she proved a remarkably effective motivator.

At her first briefing, she stood before an electric blackboard. A loose-fitting smock flapped as she talked.

"What we're doing here on the moon is preliminary work for when we're in zero g. We'll isolate proteins and amino acids that we'll later form into crystals in zero g. And analyze structures of new protein molecules by subjecting them to X rays to see how the rays form patterns on light-sensitive panels."

Madeline Reed raised her hand. "Will we be redesigning some of these proteins in space?"

"I don't know."

"Is there a particular reason why this zero-g work has to be done twenty million miles from the sun, instead of at L-5?"

"I do know that we will be exposing these proteins and other compounds to the sun's radiation. But no, I haven't been told exactly why we need to place the PH Station in that orbit."

"Well, how does our work relate overall to the project?"

"I don't know that either!" Delner shifted uncomfortably. "Each unit is working independently. We won't know how our work relates to theirs and vice versa. Only those in charge will know exactly what's going on."

"Typical Pentagon BS!" remarked one of the scientists, Dr. Harvey West, in the back of the room. He was very tall, with an aggressive black beard and arrogant manner. He had made it clear to all that he thought he was more qualified than Delner to run her section. "I thought this project is to benefit all mankind!"

"That doesn't mean we want leaks before we're done!" said Delner heatedly. "Such secrecy does discourage freewheeling speculation and theorizing. But I get the impression that Scott, Nye, Michlanski and Kane know where they're going once we're in orbit."

"Better hope to God they do!" said West. "Michlanski is the biggest dilettante I've ever met. God knows what he does with his time! I saw him on the common yesterday playing with his antigravity toy. When we're putting in sixteen-hour days!"

"Fortunately, Professor Michlanski doesn't have to account to you for his time, Dr. West!" snapped Delner. "I imagine you thought Newton was wasting his time sitting under apple trees!"

"The world doesn't have time for fumbling in the dark."

"Fumble maybe," said Delner with a tight smile. "In the dark, twenty million miles from the sun? I don't think so."

She pointed to a work-flow chart on the electric blackboard. "We'll tackle the problems with five teams, except for the first, which will be taken by all five teams. We'll compare results and methodology. I have my own idea how long this should take and what the results should be.

You'll live up to my expectations. After our first results, we'll recalibrate methods and hopefully achieve maximum efficiency of effort in a week or so.''

She dismissed all except West and Bethany Williams. The tall doctor sauntered over with an infuriating hubris all the more annoying when she saw he was chewing gum and blowing bubbles.

"West, I hear you're pretty good at what you do."

"I've been told that too," he said lazily.

"You've shown you can be an asshole and chew gum at the same time. But I think all your bubbles are filled with hot air."

He scowled. "Give a woman a little power and—" He found her dun-colored index-finger nail aimed at his hooked nose.

"Finish that sentence, West, and make my job a lot easier!"

Caught off guard, West backed away. "Wait up, now. I meant no disrespect to your sex."

"Uh-huh. I'll give you a chance to show what a hotshot you are. I'm giving you one of the teams. But if it doesn't prove to be the best, I'll find you a more suitable position."

"What if you saddle me with a bunch of zeros?"

"Won't work. Everybody on this team's a heavy hitter. So this better be your championship season, West. One more thing—"

"Yes?"

"If you ever question my authority in front of my people again, I won't wait for the results of your work to can you."

"Yes, that's very clear, Dr. Delner. Obviously you can't deal with a frank exchange of ideas."

"Yes, that's right, West. Good day."

After he stalked out the swinging door, Rene Delner regarded Bethany Williams curiously.

"You come highly recommended, Bethany. My problem is that I don't know what to do with you. I'm not even sure why you're in my group, since you're not a biologist."

"Then it's up to me to prove myself useful to you, Rene."

"That's marvelous! In the meantime we have work to do."

"I think I can help you make the entire operation work more efficiently. That's what I do—or have done."

"I'll take you up on your offer to prove yourself first, at least before I trust your judgement. You're assigned to Madeline Reed's team E. She'll tell you all you need to know."

Welcome to the doghouse, Bethany thought. Madeline was Delner's favorite goat; obviously she considered her group the least likely to be productive.

Bethany confronted Madeline with this one day at lunch in a neighborhood cafeteria. The redhead crinkled her nose with good humor. "Hey, I'm a flake. I know this. What Rene doesn't know is that while I may act like an airhead and I may like men a lot, I'm very good at what I do. Jason Scott, whose body I'd gladly lick from head to toe, doesn't hire people who aren't superqualified. So let's get to work and give Rene a kick in the fanny!"

"Sounds like a plan!" agreed Bethany. "You know, it's too bad someone as attractive as Rene is so hostile toward men." She described the confrontation between Delner and West. "Granted, West is a swine and had it coming, but Rene seems to project a barely suppressed signal against males."

"Not all," said Madeline, coyly sipping from a plastic cup of coffee.

"What! I don't believe it!"

"I never lie about something as serious as who is sleeping with who, Bethany. We must keep our priorities straight."

"Who is it?"

"Let's take an after-lunch stroll and you'll see."

Madeline led the way in a walk that took them near the Tycho City Common, crossing over a small Japanese bridge that spanned a pond that flashed and sparkled with carp, like living ingots.

The garden park was landscaped cunningly to take advantage of every inch of a small area, with trails coiling and almost meeting, like a colon, bringing walkers within inches of each other, yet out of each other's sight. The hidden nooks and glens gave the illusion of a much larger park.

The park was the hobby of several hundred Selenites, chosen by lot. Each got the honor of caring for a spot in the park. One kept the algae down in the pond. Another might be assigned cosmetics for one of the trees. The colony wasn't old enough for the many gnarled, enchanted forest trees to have aged on their own. Some colonist aged each tree and kept it pruned and healthy.

As they passed a miniature arbor, Madeline raised her finger to her lips. Bethany followed her eyes and saw Rene Delner and a dark-haired, stocky man with a weight lifter's slender waist lounging against a tree. Rene Delner's head was against his chest, playing with his curly black hair with her fingers.

Then they were past. Not knowing how much conversation carried in the little forest, they waited until they left it before they resumed their conversation.

"I don't believe it!" said Bethany. "Who was that guy?"

"Victor Ames. He's with Matt Taylor's construction crew."

"No kidding? Rene and a Neanderthal from the hardpalms?"

"Maybe she likes rough hands."

After a week the first project results were posted. West's group came in last. That was the last anybody saw of him in that team, although he surfaced later in another part of the project.

Madeline Reed's group came in first, which clearly displeased Delner, although she made the best of it.

"Very well, Madeline," she said from her usual place at the blackboard. "Explain how you achieved these results. I'm particularly interested in knowing if you sacrificed any steps or cut any corners." Her gaze roved around the room. "I want input from the rest of you, too. We are supposed to be the brightest, most talented scientists in the nation. I'd think some of you'd have ideas how Miss Reed's group did it."

Madeline raised her hand. "Actually, the credit belongs to Bethany. She saw something I'd never have noticed—"

"I don't doubt it. Bethany, please let us in on the secret."

Bethany walked to the blackboard and sketched a work-flow chart. "This is how this type of production is usually run. Usually that is correct procedure. However, in the case of the formation of protein and amino acids, Luna's lower gravity is a factor, which wasn't taken into consideration." She pointed to the antepenultimate square in the chart, and using the light pen, made it change places with a production box nearer to the beginning.

Rene Delner looked pained. "Sometimes I think genius is the capacity to see simple things in a way others do not. Congratulations! Despite your lack of experience in biology, clearly you should be running one of these teams. Meantime, during the breaks we get between our sixteen-hour shifts, I expect you to do some cramming. Or these whiz kids will murder you. You'll take Mr. West's team. Anyone else have suggestions for improving our work? Then I suggest we do some."

Chapter
* 27 *

And what rough beast, its hour come round at last,
Slouches towards Bethlehem to be born?
—William Butler Yeats, "The Second Coming"

I

Juba Aman Dana, the Leopard, Anointed One, Hammer of Allah, Mahdi, Prince, Prophet, High Chieftain of the Unified Tribes, Ruler for Life of the Union of Black Africa, celebrated his birthday with parades, fireworks, feasting and an orgy.

He was thirty-three, strong, tall, virile as a bull, with several dozen offspring from his seven years in power. As a youth he had fled his native Kenya to join the army in Nigeria. He led a revolt of army officers that swept the continent and brought every black nation into his hegemony. He absorbed the lesson that idle armies are cocked weapons aimed at the heart of the state and kept busy consolidating his power until he was master of a coalition more formidable than the old "Pan-African Alliance."

That first "union" had formed against the hated whites of South Africa. It failed because it wasn't a true nation but a loose collection of tribes who couldn't bury their prejudices to unite effectively against their common enemy. The pariah state of South Africa, allied with two other outcasts, Israel and Taiwan, stopped the offensive cold. This led to the enfeeblement of the never-solid alliance.

Twenty years later Dana stepped into the power vacuum. His ultimate aim was not merely to destroy white power, but to build an empire to equal the Great Powers. His methods resembled those of a unifier of an earlier age, Bismarck, who had used a common enemy to unify disparate elements into an unbreakable whole.

For years he had controlled the news to the foreign press, whom he encouraged to think of him as a version of the Idi Amins and Pol Pots: a despot who posed no threat to the outside world.

He smiled when his battles were reported as genocidal slaughters like the Nigerian Civil War or Cambodian Revolution. He wrote many of those reports himself. He perceived that the most civilized nations were reluctant to interfere in Africa's internal affairs. As long as his actions were not seen as a prelude to aggression, the Great Powers would even tolerate genocide.

The world press reported Dana's manufactured atrocities, but bloodshed was actually minimal and confined to loyalists of the old regimes. The horror stories suited his purposes. As long as they continued no one would investigate the growth of Black Africa's military, particularly her *nuclear* arsenal, made possible by shipments from the renegade industrialist Horatius Krebs.

His instrument was almost ready. Like a modern Alexander gazing across the Indus, or a Hitler pondering the Russian steppes, he ached to test its sharpness. To the north was Israel's client state Egypt, the priceless Nile Basin, and North Africa. Palestine was depopulated by the Epiphany except for Jewish urban centers such as Jerusalem, centered around the rebuilt Temple. At the other end of the continent was redoubtable South Africa. Its black population had self-government and coexisted with the white enclaves who controlled the region's defenses, but no black patriot would rest as long as whites ruled anywhere in Africa. To attack Israel was to attack South Africa, and to tangle with Taiwan's corporate economy in the bargain. Dana had to decide whom to concentrate against while fighting a holding action against the other. He pondered this choice, until, when the bacchanal was at its peak, he reached a decision.

From his throne of pure gold (formerly owned by the last Ethiopian emperor) he watched dancers in G-strings perform outrageously lewd dances. Girls from all over the world, of all races, all of them in his service voluntarily, even eagerly.

His attention was on a voluptuous Eurasian who danced as if a snake were inside her. Dark eyes boldly held his and every hand she ran up her thighs was a stroke of fire in his groin. She approached a frenzied climax. He spoke to his chamberlain, a dignified Watutsi. The woman would be waiting in his bed.

He gestured imperiously. The music died and the dancers evaporated. Guests who were not members of the court or military officers removed to the outer chambers of Dana's palace. Most of them wore tribal ceremonial costumes for the celebration. Dana vigorously pursued modern technology but encouraged conservatism for tribal culture. This helped erode the artificial national loyalties of the states his empire had replaced. By honoring tribe and family he elevated himself. He was of the Masai, a nomadic cattle-raising people of Kenya, but he had been adopted by every major tribe in the Union, endured their often grueling rites of manhood, and bound them together in the symbol of his person. When his generals and ministers attended his birthday in traditional garments they honored him as well as themselves.

He had elevated twelve officers from the major tribes to be warlords. They dressed and lived lavishly and appeared in the official holographs. They formed now at the foot of the throne.

"My people!" He lifted his muscular arms as if in an embrace. "Thank you from my heart of hearts for honoring me on my birthday. I am touched by your devotion. To show my favor to you I have a great announcement." The crowd stirred. Rumors had been afloat for days, but, as always, the Leopard had kept his own counsel.

"In a few weeks we begin the crusade we have prepared for for seven years." He let his gaze rove over them. They knew what his next words would be, but they wanted to hear them. "Our Holy armies will attack the hated tyrants who enslave our brothers. We will purge our land of the white disease that has kept us from our destiny. We will burst the frontiers of our enemy." He raised his arms, his hawklike gaze riveting. "With Allah's help, I will celebrate my next birthday in Capetown!"

The crowd went wild. From a detached part of his brain Juba Aman Dana marveled that they could be brought to a frenzy with a few words. He had possessed this gift since youth. It had propelled him into prominence and kept him there.

He allowed them to weary themselves with celebration. He sat back in his throne and drank sparingly from a gold cup. Later he departed, eager to enjoy the exotic Eurasian woman.

II

The silver skeletons of the three uncompleted spaceships sprouted from the lifeless gray soil of the moon and pushed into the velour black of space like macabre towers for the dead. They glinted an unbearable white where the sun caught them.

The *Euclid, Archimedes,* and *Descartes* were named for three master mathematicians. At voyage's end, when they were joined twenty million miles from the surface of Sol, they would vindicate the theories of another master mathematician, Alfred Strubeck.

Workers crawled through the unfinished ships like insects exploring partially eaten carcasses. Occasionally a vacuum welding torch gleamed as a piece was added to the structure.

Jason Scott and Matt Taylor sat in a Lunar rover a few hundred meters from the *Euclid*, which was the farthest along.

Nearby, in a cluster of blockhouses, armored space marines practiced assaulting and defending. Their colonel, Jackson Drew, had been assigned as the Sunside Project's security officer.

Lasers winked harmlessly as one squad moved forward, while their comrades provided fire support from behind the blockhouses.

Scott touched helmets with Taylor. "They haven't proved to be the pain in the rear that you predicted, Matthew."

"No, but their colonel sure as hell is!"

"Davis didn't assign him to make friends. He's supposed to protect us—from ourselves if necessary."

"Things are coming along, Matt. It might be a good time to take Philip Norrison up on his invitation to visit him at Newton Observatory. But I won't if you can't get along without me."

"Oh no, massah, I don't think we little chilluns can make it through the day without you all! The project'll just stop dead!"

"Point taken, Matt. You could probably run the whole construction site for six months if you had to."

"You feel guilty takin' off a day, an' you want me to talk you out of it. Which I won't do. Besides, the mark of a good boss is that he can leave his operation and it'll run without him."

"I'll go soon. Any problems with the *Euclid* since the last accident?"

He saw little of Taylor's face through the faceplate, but he saw a nod. Taylor still hadn't reacclimated to pressure suits; he forgot that others had difficulty seeing through polarized glass.

"We've had some accidents on that ship lately," he purred in his native Creole accent. "Reminds me of the Challenger Tap."

"I wouldn't jump to the conclusion that we have a saboteur."

"I've been workin' too long, boss, not to recognize when someone's stickin' his wrench in my gears. It's too systematic. Even Jonahs take a rest. They let you catch 'em makin' dumb mistakes. These accidents are different. Somebody slips on a 'misplaced' tool. A load of special paint is mislaid. A joint isn't welded right, collapses an' delays work on a section—"

"Those things happen on every construction job," said Scott, feeling more and more like the devil's advocate.

"You trust me or no?" Taylor's temper was starting to flare.

"Yes," said Scott wearily. "You say we have a saboteur, I'll go along. What do you suggest? Let Drew's goons run our project?"

Through the faceplate his white teeth grinned. "If I catch him, I want to work on him 'fore you give him to anyone else."

"We're not free agents here. We can't set up a vigilante court and mete out frontier justice. We have to turn anyone we catch over to the Selene authorities, or to Davis."

"I'm not talking courts! I'm talkin' about beatin' his face until he tells who put 'im up to it. Or maybe takin' him to the top of the *Euclid* and pushin' 'im off unless he spills his guts."

An intolerably brilliant light from the base cast everything in stark relief. A small warship rose on a finger of flame.

"Admiral Davis." Scott followed the flight with his eyes. "Bound for earth and some high-level conference."

"Mus' be quite a confab. He never leaves Luna. He even testifies to Congress over holocube."

"He's rendezvousing with two battleships: an escort to low earth orbit."

"Why? They tryin' to impress the Russkies?"

"The game is impress the enemy. It's a territorial squabble between orangutans. Violence is rare, but always possible. Without it the game is meaningless. They impress us with the *Aurora*; we impress them back with two battleships. Tomorrow we may impress ourselves into a space war."

"Maybe war's started on earth. Why else call back Davis?"

"Why indeed?"

Chapter

* 28 *

I

"**S**olarz is nothing. Don't worry about him." Horatius Krebs sat at his desk in his office atop Python Tower in New York City.

"He wants to deal himself into the game," said Lewis Cocker. "He asked about Dollfuss's work. Apparently there are many rumors about half-man, half-dog mutants."

"No one will believe such rumors, particularly if they're true." Krebs absentmindedly watched a fly which had evaded every defense mechanism in the building. Its whine grew higher-pitched as it circled closer around the desk.

"I'm just saying it would be a good idea to keep an eye on Solarz. He's untrustworthy, without loyalty."

"I don't trust people who are trustworthy, and I don't believe people who say they're loyal—"

"But sir, surely you don't believe—"

"Spare me!" said Krebs, holding up his hand. "The day is short. I've become a pragmatist. No matter how much I paid Jason Scott and Jacob Kane, they left when something more important to them came along. Even Emil had an agenda. On the other hand, Dollfuss stays, although he hates me, because only through me can he do the work that drives him. The lesson, Cocker, is that little men can be bought; great men can only be rented. If great men get in my way, I must obliterate them. Bribery won't work. Bribery will work with Solarz until he decides that what's in that building is worth more than what I'm paying him."

The fly's zooming arc brought it within millimeters of a red beam of light originating from a crystal ashtray on Krebs's desk.

"Solarz arranged an ambush of Hardrim in Denver. Hardrim proved more difficult than he had anticipated," said Cocker.

"Translation: Solarz screwed up by not bringing enough men."

"He's determined to bag Hardrim." Cocker moved a half-step toward his employer and linked his hands behind the back of his immaculate business suit in a contemplative pose. "It's more than a money thing. It's a blood thing. He's collecting information on the streets, while I collect it my own way." He unlocked his attaché and took a dossier from it. "The FBI has put out an advisory on Hardrim. For 'questioning.' They also want a man named Ralph Ferman. He's the reason Hardrim left the Washington police."

"I remember Ferman! During Emil's debriefing, before Kali had her way with him, didn't he talk about a man named Ferman he overheard during his sabotage of the FBI Detroit bureau?"

"I vaguely recall," said Cocker. "I can have that debriefing for you in a few minutes."

"I can have it right now!" Krebs attacked his desk keyboard. The printer began to produce plastic sheets. He grabbed each one as it emerged.

"Damn, yes! The pieces fall into place. Ferman apparently has hooked both Hardrim and an FBI man named Ferdinand into believing that the Santa Bella Blight is a man-made virus. According to Emil, Ferman told the agent interrogating him that the Blight was used to fool the government into funding the Sunside Project! Emil killed that agent, so Ferdinand knows about the man-made virus, but not of the conspiracy that snookered the president. Ferdinand was in charge of investigating the Dorian Nye assassination and the wetwork Emil was doing for me.

"Don't you see, you mental insect!" Krebs's eyes drilled his assistant.

"The key is Ferman! His information could destroy the president. He is the bait to lure Ferdinand and Hardrim, and destroy them."

"Ferman has proven extraordinary elusive, sir."

"His run of luck has ended! We'll drain him, then kill him. Then we won't have to worry about escapes." He looked up just as the fly flew through the beam of light, which instantly became a laser that disintegrated the insect. It fell like a flaming jet shot from the sky and was sucked into a small hole.

"Ferman," repeated Krebs. "It rhymes with 'vermin.'"

II

Ferman decided he must be getting used to absurd situations. His initial urge was to flee, but as the three figures stared at him, he stared back.

Strubeck should have been dead. Michlanski and Kane were too young, in their mid-teens or early twenties. Michlanski was beardless, but still obese. Kane was even more of a scarecrow.

"You're not real!" declared Ferman. "You're simulacra, ghosts from a machine! I wonder if you can even hear me."

"We hear you perfectly," said Alfred Strubeck. "The question that occurs to us is, who are you and why are you here?"

"And where is here?" said the young Michlanski.

Kane pulled a switchblade, which shone so brightly in the dim basement that it gave Ferman pause. To preserve his sanity, he began searching for the source of the projection.

"I know holographic projection has made great strides in the last decade, and that storage of personalities has been possible at least that long. In Michlanski's den, anything is possible."

"What do you mean? I remember having my memories stored." Michlanski looked at Strubeck. "You oversaw the procedure. But you're older—" He nodded. "How long has it been, old teacher?"

"Ten years by my reckoning, Sherlock."

"This house is mine?" He started up the stairs. "I built it?"

"Yes. Here you will make your greatest discoveries. Here you will become known as the greatest mind since Einstein."

Michlanski stopped halfway up the stairs. "I can't go up. Something prevents me." He looked sad. "Is that why you told me, because I can't use the knowledge? How cruel. Just as your manipulating us as children was cruel." Strubeck looked up sharply. "Yes, I figured it out," said Michlanski, with a hint of the omnipotent air he would develop in later years.

"Sherlock, I am as much a victim as you," said Strubeck. "For if this man is here under these circumstances, I must be dead."

"What about me?" Kane prowled the basement like a caged wolf. He reached out to a cabinet, and his hand disappeared into it.

"Of you three, only Strubeck has died." Ferman pitied these pseudo-life-forms. He found the holographic projector mounted on a filing cabinet. It resembled a multiple-lens planetarium projector. Different from a holocube in that it could create a three-dimensional object that became part of existing surroundings, whereas a holocube created its own environment inside a finite cube.

"Why the ten-year gap between your recording and mine, Dr. Strubeck?" asked Michlanski.

"And what has brought us out of hiding?" demanded Kane. He looked at Ferman in a threatening way. "You?"

"An electrical storm destroyed part of the house and the island's generator—"

"I have an island, too? I'm going to love my life!"

"This room has an independent power source," said Strubeck. "The immense release of energy from a lightning strike could have damaged the equipment and activated our recordings."

"That doesn't explain the elapsed time between my recording and yours," said Michlanski.

"*You* can, if you examine your work habits. You're terrible about backing up files. It's likely you have several personality recordings stored. You neglected to copy over the old ones."

"There's another explanation," said Michlanski. "Since I find the idea of talking to myself so intriguing, my older self would too. Perhaps, he —or I—preserved them to talk to them—"

"I can see that!" said Kane sarcastically. "You're always mooning around that you don't have anyone of your level to talk to. This way you could set up roundtable discussions with all your selves. You'd be in heaven."

Talk of recordings had excited Ferman. If there was evidence to be had about the Argus Society, this was the place to find it.

He opened the filing cabinet, which he concluded was for storing experiment and test results not yet transferred to the computer. It also had articles sent to Michlanski by a clipping service, including ones about the Sunside Project.

He sat at the terminal and called up the directory. It showed thousands of files in Leonardo's multiterabyte storage capacity.

"What are you doing?" demanded Kane. "Who are you?"

"Why, precisely, are you in my residence, which I haven't built yet?" said Michlanski.

Ferman covered the holographic projector with a wastepaper basket. Michlanski and Kane disappeared, but Strubeck remained.

"What the hell?" said Ferman. "Why aren't you gone?"

"A fascinating question." Strubeck looked around him. "One I am not equipped to answer." As Ferman looked for another projector, Strubeck held up his hand. "I won't disturb you."

"How do you know I'm not doing irreparable harm to Sherlock Michlanski, the Argus Society, or the Sunside Project?"

"What can I do to stop you? That is the operative query."

"Nothing, I hope." Ferman inserted a tile in the terminal and began downloading any file that seemed useful. But that was an impossible task, so he looked for names such as "Argus Society," "Noah Chambless," and "Santa Bella Blight." After an hour, he stood up.

"Young man, why are you here?" asked Strubeck softly.

"Strubeck, you know the evil the Argus Society has wrought. I hope there's a special hell for those who sell the human race!"

Clutching the clipping file and the computer tile, Ferman climbed out of the basement and closed the door behind him.

Chapter

* 29 *

An ETF commander can spread out his force in a paper-thin formation, or infiltrate enemy lines with individuals, but still retain total control, with the flexibility to perform maneuvers so complex they wouldn't ordinarily be discussed.

ETF can resist frontal attacks by armor and aircraft or react decisively against airborne drops to the rear because it doesn't experience communications breakdowns. The heavy weapons squad carries enough high explosives for use by two-man howitzer teams to reduce most strong points. If they must engage the enemy hand-to-hand, ETF troopers are trained in the Lao Tse psychodynamic method used during the Drang War.

—Brig. Gen. David Keith, introduction to
Extraordinary Tactics Manual

I

The Voortrekker FB-12 fighter-bomber flew at ten thousand feet. Below spread the vast wild-game preserve, the Kruger National Park. Beyond lay the Mozambique frontier and an unknown quantity of enemy troops, tanks and artillery.

The pilot banked to fly parallel to the border. At this height a corps could have hidden in the tangled woods. He wiped sweat from his blond mustache with a gloved hand. To pilot the Voortrekker, which could subject him to thirty g's, he was encased in webbing, held like Superman over the instrument panel.

Radar showed no enemy airplanes. He was alone, flying along a tense border, wishing he'd slept more the night before.

Blips appeared on radar: a squadron of Black Union aircraft. Probably planning to put everybody on alert. At the base they would be scrambling. It was lunchtime and they would be mighty upset at the interruption.

Out across the beautiful wilderness of the park, he saw a bright flash. A reflection on the Limpopo River? But he ought not to be able to see the river from this height.

He saw it again. A bright crimson line moved across the sky like a searchlight. The cockpit exploded as the red laser sliced into it, reducing it to its component molecules. The beam moved on relentlessly, seeking new victims in the sky.

II

President Shefferton sat at his desk, working on the draft of his rationing speech. He had agonized over it for three weeks. He wasn't planning to deliver it until summer, but he kept returning to it, again and again.

He didn't approve of speech writers. He had written his own speeches as congressman and his acceptance speech for the Progressive Nationalists. Even now he often extensively rewrote drafts produced by his writers.

This speech might be the most important he would ever give. In it he would tell the American people that they must sacrifice to fulfill a commitment to keep the world from starving, until the Sunside Project became a reality. The specter of sacrifice had always existed, but few had foreseen rationing. This generation thought about hardship the same way it thought of the Revolutionary War. The world wars, Korea, and Vietnam were chapters in dusty books. The Cuban War had been an easy victory. It was the most deadly of wars, one that promoted war's romance, without dwelling on its horrors.

He had to convince them that sacrifice was necessary. Resentment was bound to spring up against the have-not nations who had to "leech" off their neighbors. Such anger missed the point. If your neighbor's house was burning (he often borrowed metaphors from FDR) you didn't rail against his carelessness. You put out the fire to prevent its spread to your house. The famine wasn't America's fault, but America would be caught in the storm when the hungry nations went to war.

A more pressing concern was the upcoming Senate vote to repeal the Thirty-first Amendment. He wanted it brought to a vote at least two months before his speech, his "July Firecracker," as the vice president called it.

It was important to keep the two issues untangled. The House had gone his way, barely, but the big fight would be in the Senate.

He stood up and stretched. He had been working steadily for three hours. It was time for a break.

His intercom buzzed. Secretary of Defense Grover T. Wells was on the line. War had broken out in Africa.

Idiots and maniacs! It was all piling on at once! He was discovering that no one made allowances for the president being human. He set about doing what he could to avert another disaster.

III

Le Monde—During the opening hours of the attack ten South African planes were destroyed. An infantry battalion, the Capetown Highlanders, was overrun. The Prince Alfred Guard and Cape Peninsula Rifles were mauled. The Israelis lost a missile cruiser in the Red Sea. South Africa's new VTOL carrier is dead in the water off Capetown. Two Taiwanese tankers were sabotaged in port. Reuters reports that the Israeli base at Gibraltar is under continuous bombardment from Casablanca-based jets.

Fighting is not entirely one-sided. A recon battalion, the Royal Natal Lasers, has deflected a huge tank attack. The Israelis are counterattacking from Egypt against an entrenched enemy.

Sergeant Major Ransome entered General Keith's office and saluted. The general was grinning.

"Sergeant Major, we're flying to Washington."

"Is it Africa?" It was hard to hide his excitement.

"When the invasion story hit the news, I sent our situation study to the joint chiefs, just as Senator Macadew and Bertram Lambert-Healey advised. The Man saw them. He wants to see me."

He slapped Ransome's shoulder. "Lean times may be over."

They were met at Andrews Air Force Base by two White House aides and Senator Macadew. A limousine took them to a ritzy downtown hotel where they were told to wait until sent for.

Macadew spilled into the room like a bag of marbles and found the holocube, disguised as a twentieth-century mirror. "A fine, goddamn how-do-you-do! Treatin' my guests like stowaways!"

Keith loosened his tie and stretched out on his bed with his hands behind his head. He was comfortable. He could wait.

The sergeant major checked the small stocked bar and refrigerator provided to the room, but it was locked.

"What do you mean, they can't leave the room?" bellowed Macadew. "Listen!" He looked astounded. "Bastard hung up on me! You two stay here until the National Security mob sends fo' you."

And for three days they waited.

They were ordered to the NSC chamber, a high-vaulted room with a half-moon table. Around it sat the joint chiefs, the state and defense secretaries, the vice president, and the president.

As Macadew and Keith entered, the Security Council was being briefed by CIA chief Colonel Farley.

After initial gains, the Black Union had ground to a halt against the stiffening ISAFTA alliance. Mobilization was complete and South Africa expected a Taiwanese division by the weekend. An Israeli airborne brigade was en route, to be followed by four regular brigades. Meanwhile, Israel had launched an offensive to relieve Gibraltar before the Spanish entered the game.

Dana's initial advantage of ten to one in men, three to one in armor, two to one in artillery, and three to one in the air had eroded in the most important area: the air, where the ratio was now 1.5 to one.

"Dana lacks resources for prolonged war. Without quick victory, we believe he is prepared to use nuclear weapons. We have evidence that he has a delivery system to hit white cities with 'dirty' bombs," said Farley.

"Elaborate on that, Jim," said the president.

"Intelligence is sketchy. We know he has a project here"—he indicated central Nigeria—"but the delivery system is unknown. Conventional missiles could be neutralized by the ABM lasers around South African cities. He may try to swamp them with a mass cruise missile attack, using some sort of stealth technology."

"The missile doesn't exist that ABM lasers can't bring down," declared Lieutenant General Putnam, chief of staff of the Air Force.

"Dana seems to think it's viable," said Farley.

"Or wants someone to think he does," said Admiral Hanley Davis. "What better way to blackmail the South Africans?"

"Blackmail?" said Putnam. "This is a war of annihilation. They will die in the ruins of their cities before they surrender."

"That's why this is so critical," said Shefferton. "Both sides are fanatics. We could be dragged in despite ourselves."

The council divided into two camps: those who felt the South Africans deserved their fate, and those who felt the chances of the war erupting into a holocaust were too great to ignore.

Secretary of State Harmon crossed swords in a heated exchange with Senator Macadew.

"Mr. President, if I may—" said Harmon with patrician aplomb. "If we aid South Africa, we will be reviled, as we were reviled as Israel's ally. That cost us a city! Everything that I—we—have done to restore this nation's reputation will be undone."

Macadew took his boxer's stance, head almost down, shoulders forward. "This putting what other countries think ahead of what's right is buncombe. We, the world's oldest functioning republic, used to let the comic-opera countries tell us what was proper. They made a bloodier mess than we ever thought possible. We *know* it's wrong to let the Leopard slaughter millions. If it's not moral to stop him, then I'll go back to bein' a pagan!"

"Thank you, voice of reason!" said Harmon sarcastically.

"Gentlemen!" snapped Shefferton. "I want recommendations! If Dana uses nukes, millions of blacks and whites will die. We must stop him. By persuasion or, if that fails, then by force."

IV

"Another man anxious to give me advice." Shefferton handed a jigger of bourbon to Keith. "What do you think I should do?"

Shefferton, Keith, and Macadew had retired to an anteroom while the generals debated how to neutralize the nuclear site.

"That's a hard question, Mr. President."

"That's why I asked it." Shefferton's eyes probed like surgeon's fingers. Was Keith removed from command because he was too innovative, or because he couldn't follow orders?

"We don't have much time. The South Africans have pledged not to use nuclear weapons unless attacked by them. The Israelis have already lost the heavy crusier *Ben-Gurion* to a nuke, so they're harder to restrain. We must act."

"Sir, I've heard the proposals: the air strike, spaceborne drop, and amphibious landing. I don't think bombers can penetrate the laser defenses Dana probably has around his secret weapon. If they did, they couldn't guarantee destruction in one strike without using nukes, which is self-defeating.

"The spaceborne drop has merits. But the best use of the spaceborne brigade is to neutralize the five Black African geosynchronous spy stations: the Pride of the Leopard. Otherwise we lose hope of surprise whatever option we adopt.'' Keith unconsciously took the stance that he adopted in the classroom: legs spread, right hand jabbing his points home.

''The coast landing has the same drawback. Dana can move the weapon before the force can fight its way into the interior.''

''It's only a hundred miles. Our troops can move faster than that. They could take the site in two or three days.''

Keith smiled disarmingly. ''There Lambert-Healey and I differ with army doctrine. We believe today's battlefield is dominated by defense. Tanks are not obsolete, but antitank and antiaircraft lasers will slow down the best army. The Black Africans just have to delay it long enough to use their secret weapon.''

''I'm beginning to understand why you are so unpopular, General. Nobody likes to be told that his army is obsolete.''

''Not obsolete. But not tuned to modern combat.'' He pushed his hair back into place. ''I believe an amphibious landing, in conjunction with a secret landing of the Extraordinary Tactics Force farther up the coast, could gain us the installation intact.''

Shefferton exchanged looks with Macadew, who was grinning. ''Go on. Now I'm dealing with something I understand, a man trying to promote himself. You trained the Extraordinary Tactics Force, and you think it can do a job no other unit can do?''

Keith's eyes flashed. ''Sir, I'm not promoting anything! I think ETF can do the job because it's the best unit in the whole damned army!''

Shefferton chuckled. ''General, I'm going to have to bust you out of the army or else let you run it. What's your plan?''

''Sir, if the enemy is hunting for you everywhere except where you are, he is half beaten. My plan is for a force of ETF troopers to land by submarine several hundred miles up the coast, in the desert, then move to occupy the nuclear installation. Simultaneously the marines will assault the Nigerian coast.

''Dana's reserves will meet the amphibious threat, while the ETF moves commando style across the country, taking the nuclear installation from behind. The marines will push into the interior and relieve the ETF.''

''General,'' said Shefferton briskly, ''my top military men, except Admiral Davis, are against you. They say you lack respect for authority or discipline, that you contradict tactical doctrine, and that only a fool would believe Lambert-Healey's theories that the tank will be replaced as the main arm of the land army.''

Keith's face took on the look of a man who was used to being regarded as a lunatic, but who wanted to at least get the facts straight. "Mr. President, Lambert-Healey does not prophesy the end of mobile warfare. But something new besides the tank is needed to achieve a breakthrough and cause confusion in rear echelons. Something very like the Extraordinary Tactics Force."

Shefferton scowled. "I can't afford not to have options. My friend Admiral Davis disagrees with the joint chiefs and he's often right. I'm keeping my options open by giving you back the Extraordinary Tactics Force and ordering you to stay ready, in case my generals turn out to be idiots!"

PART

* 4 *

"LOOKING AT THE STARS"

Chapter
* 30 *

We are all in the gutter. But some of us are looking at the stars.

—*Oscar Wilde*

There was an eerie novelty in the absence of the huge blue-green globe that was so ubiquitous on the side of the moon where most human settlements were located, thought Jason Scott as he walked with Dr. Philip Norrison to the Newton Observatory.

Was that why Farside was so sparsely settled? Only the observatory, a training camp for space marines, a Hudson's Bay Company mine, and a Buddhist lamasery were located there.

He followed Norrison's leaps, the gait of choice of Lunar pedestrians since the day Armstrong introduced it, along a narrow trail and over a rise.

"Pretty spry for a man with a bad heart," said Scott. They stood on the spur and saw an amazing sight: a lake where no water had any business being.

It wasn't water, but a glassteel mirror, called "Hec" because it was a hectare in area, sprayed with vaporized aluminum. Newton Observatory had opened the heavens in a way comparable to the revolution wrought in 1948 by Palomar's Hale telescope.

"If I left Luna, you'd see how pathetic I am. Here I'm young. Biobots keep my arteries clean, so my ticker's weakness isn't a factor. What'll get me in the end is riotous living!"

"With whom, the monks or the marines?"

"Both are good neighbors. Hardly surprising, since they're more than a thousand klicks away."

They stood next to the mirror, the stars at their feet. It was like staring into an abyss. A crisscross skeleton of superstrong spider-silk filaments rose from the mirror's edges a thousand feet to its focal point, where the collecting mirror reflected light sideways to a cage into video cells and spectroscopes that had long ago replaced photographic plates.

"Four thousand four hundred square inches," said Norrison. "Twenty-two times the size of the 'Big Eye'! Jason, we're looking the Lord in the face."

"The next step, I guess, would be to shake hands with Him."

"Care to take an elevator ride?"

"That's what I'm here for."

The platform ascended six feet a second in absolute silence, although they felt the vibration through the soles of their boots.

"Alfred ever tell you about the night on Palomar when the White Point Probe transmission came in on laser beam?"

"Many times. It was one of the great moments in his life."

"For me also. It reaffirmed my faith in my choice of professions. I felt I had a purpose in life."

"Yes," said Scott, so softly that Norrison didn't hear.

The elevator had reached the top. They walked into the cage.

"I could show you this on video in the imaging lab, but I thought you'd appreciate seeing it as Newton and Herschel would have." He indicated an eyepiece mounted on a periscopelike device. "We don't sight manually. We move the mirror by typing in coordinates, but the eyepiece fulfills a childish desire on my part to look directly upon God's handiwork. I know, the visible spectrum doesn't show the true glory of the heavens, but I got into astronomy to look at the stars!"

He touched several dials and moved his helmet to peer into the eyepiece. He motioned Scott. "Take a look. I guess it doesn't matter if you actually put your eye to the ocular, since your prosthesis gives you eyes at the back of your head."

Scott, thoroughly sick of variations on that joke, just nodded and bent forward—and caught his breath. "Is it—?"

Norrison nodded. "Tau Ceti."

"I can make out the disk!" There was no swimming sensation to the image, as there invariably was in any seeing done in the earth's atmospheric soup. The star, seven light-years away, was accompanied by a jeweled necklace: four faint points like the Galilean moons around Jupiter as viewed through binoculars.

"This may be the first time anyone has ever seen a planet from another system."

"Which one's the earthlike planet? The one McClaren and his people kept under wraps all these years?"

"At three o'clock. I named it something you'd approve of: Prometheus."

Scott laughed.

"Just thought you'd like to see what we are fighting for. Here, let me show you this." He typed in some coordinates. Below them the mechanism moved the great mirror.

After several minutes, Scott looked in the eyepiece. He saw a cloudlike object, with a tremendously bright center. Matter and energy seemed to spin away from it like a lawn sprinkler.

Scott turned toward Norrison. The light from the eyepiece was reflected in his faceplate. "What is it?"

"Possibly light from the creation of the universe." He smiled gently. "I'm joking, but it is at a tremendous distance, millions of light-years farther than anything we've seen. It comes from a sector where we've recorded huge bursts of radio waves."

"You mean it's a quasar?"

"If it is, this tells us that this quasar could be a white hole, a place where all matter and energy that is sucked into a black hole finally emerges. Or it could be something else—"

"The galactic probability perturbation Strubeck predicted?"

"I think so," breathed Norrison. "Alfred predicted dimples in the fabric of space, where probability would be at such a primordial, postcreation stage that parts of the fabric of time that occurred microseconds after the commencement of the Big Bang might be thrust in and out of that dimple, along with every part of the space-time continuum from that moment all the way to the end of the universe.

"He predicted such perturbations near Sol, but also that huge galactic masses would produce correspondingly larger dimples. A galactic dimple might produce a fountain of energy that would broadcast across the universe, calling to us from the threshold of creation. Alfred may have explained the origin of the quasar."

"I imagine the one near the sun will be a lot less dramatic."

"You'll find more than enough drama to keep your hands full!"

Chapter

⋆ 31 ⋆

Feb. 15—*San Franciso Examiner*—President Shefferton today appealed to the warring African states to negotiate. He said America won't tolerate the use of nuclear weapons by any side. South Africa quickly denied any intent to use nuclear weapons. Black Africa declined to comment.

Feb. 16—*New York Herald*—United States forces worldwide were put on alert after the Union of Black Africa announced intentions to pursue the war to "total victory."

I

Sheridan Mayfield was drawn and ashen as he stepped out of the airlock into Tycho City. He tore his helmet off. His reception committee included the territorial governor, Jason Scott, Sherlock Michlanski, and Dorian Nye.

Mayfield pushed past the governor and grabbed Scott by the shoulder. "Where are your quarters?"

Scott led the way. They passed a grassy hill where placard-waving demonstrators were demanding statehood for the colony.

"Idiots!" Mayfield glared as they walked past. "The world is on the brink of holocaust and they're interested in statehood!"

"They are a bit self-centered here," said Scott.

"They're insular as hell! Some twit tried to reinject me with that stuff that keeps you from spreading diseases. I'd already spent a day on the shuttle puking my guts out from the stuff!"

Michlanski bounced cheerfully in the Lunar gravity like an overweight puppy. "Selenites look on earth as a bacteriological cesspool. They have the same sort of feelings for us that we have for SoHi addicts."

"Is there much of that up here?"

"Anyone caught with SoHi is put 'outside,' " said Scott.

"There's no death penalty for SoHi addiction." Mayfield looked troubled at this discrepancy.

"Nevertheless," said Scott, "they end up in the vacuum. SoHi has sinister effects in low gravity. Users go berserk—"

They arrived at Jason's quarters. Mayfield grabbed the one chair. Scott stretched out on the bed, Nye sat on the holocube in the center of the room, Michlanski squatted on the toilet in the tiny bathroom.

Mayfield began, "How's progress on the ships?"

"On schedule," said Scott. "We've had some accidents but my foreman, Matt Taylor, is a genius for keeping people working."

Mayfield's face screwed up. "Are these real accidents?"

"Taylor is convinced we have a saboteur. If so, he is a subtle one. Maybe someone has a grudge, against me or Prometheus Enterprises. Or maybe we're having some bad luck."

"Don't underestimate the human capacity for illogical, suicidal evil," growled Mayfield. "There are those who would blow up the universe to call attention to bad working conditions. A case in point is the madman Dana, who has threatened to start an atomic war rather than take charity from a hated neighbor." He looked around. "Do you know how serious things are at home?"

"W-we k-eep up with current events," said Nye, whose bald head glistened in the subdued light. "Is-is it worse than we hear?"

"Well, there's no danger of missiles falling on New York. Our ABM system still works. But war in Africa could polarize the Great Powers, wreck food distribution and the Sunside Project."

"We're all little droplets of water on the same web," said Scott softly. "When someone disturbs that web we all tremble."

"We must redouble our efforts," said Mayfield. "The project is already our last hope. We're putting all our eggs in one basket. It's worse than that because we've only got the one egg."

"You said redouble our efforts?" said Scott wearily.

"I want you to move up the completion date."

"I'm already working my people on maximum shifts."

"Put them on double shifts. If you need people, I'll get them, even if I have to shanghai them. Selene's territorial charter gives the governor almost unlimited emergency powers. Not modified by nonsense like due process. If I must draft qualified men into the militia, I'll do it."

"Governor Jackson won't agree to such a thing."

"Then we'll have ourselves another governor." Mayfield rubbed his chin. "See how easy it is? Shefferton gave me carte blanche."

"In that case, I guess we'll move up the schedule."

"You'll be Mr. Popularity on Luna!" chirped Michlanski.

"S' okay, I'm not running for anything." Mayfield stood. "I want the spaceships finished, or nearly so, in time for a special event: the first visit to outer space by a U.S. president."

"Shefferton's coming to the moon?"

"And Midway and L-5. Frankly, it's a political stunt, cooked up by me. I want the territories to gain pride as Americans." He gestured expansively. "More important, the trip will legitimize space in the eyes of the average citizen. If the president rides a GILGAMESH scramjet to the moon, that means it's safe, right? I want the average citizen to think of space flight like he thinks of riding in a jet. I want to build a ground swell of support for the Sunside Project."

"Secretary Mayfield, this is the second best idea you've ever come up with!" said Scott.

"What was the first, the Sunside Project?"

"No, that wasn't your idea. Putting me in charge of it was."

II

Michlanski was at his electric blackboard, manipulating equations and comparing them to the old results, when his beeper said to call Tycho City's central network.

"Dr. Michlanski, I've some disturbing news," said a colony official. "An accident on Wolverine Island. Authorities report lightning knocked out your generator and damaged your house."

"Zzerk! Has anyone been there?" He hoped the answer was no. He couldn't afford to have unauthorized visitors snooping.

"No. An air rescue helicopter saw smoke rising from the island and investigated. But since no one is on the island, once they ascertained there was no immediate peril, they flew away."

"Returning to inspect the damages myself is impractical. I can't interrupt my work for more than a few hours."

"We have a tactile suit you can use. We can drop a sensor robot on the island. You can inspect the damage in the suit."

"Won't work, young man." Michlanski shook his blond curls vigorously. "Time lag. If I tell my hand to pick up a rock, three seconds will elapse before it closes around it and relays the sensation to me. Better to drop a robot with a holographic recorder on the island, and interface with it from a projection room. I can control the robot, but won't have tactile contact."

"We can set that up for you in a few minutes."

Michlanski stood in the holographic projection room as technicians made the adjustments necessary to establish a three-dimensional link with a tiny island in the Great Lakes.

The room flickered as if in a thunderstorm, then it flooded with the brilliance of noonday sun. He blinked. The clear sky reflected in the gently rolling waves of the lake showed no trace of the storm that had caused so much damage a few hours ago.

"Move ahead," said Michlanski. Seconds later the robot began to move forward, climbing over a rise until he saw the house. The west end had collapsed. "Stop. Turn thirty degrees right. Move ahead one hundred meters." The robot's smooth motion told him it was riding on a hover unit.

He inspected the generator, then crossed the shattered walls of his mansion. The sitting room had been exposed to the elements. The wine and yellow carpet was swelled with moisture. A line of ants was marching over the bricks, up a wooden coffee table to an open bowl of sugar. A book lying open in a red velvet wing-back chair was soaked so that the lettering was fuzzy. A whitish splash of bird droppings decorated the matching red velvet chaise longue. Michlanski sighed.

The picture wavered and there was a sound similar to feedback noise from an amplifier.

"What was that?" demanded Michlanski.

"Power surge. Our signal must have intercepted a satellite. A multi-terabyte data burst traveled up the link for a millisecond."

"That's a fair amount of data. What happened to it?"

"We're checking. Nothing yet. Fortunately, it didn't get into the system. This happens occasionally. There's too much space junk out there to keep track of all of it."

"How comforting!" Michlanski guided the robot into the den, which looked as though a hobo or other transient had spent the night. The heater and other supplies from the utility closet were strewn on the floor, along with opened cans of food.

"Not very polite guests!" Michlanski muttered to himself.

"That is the least of your worries, Sherry."

"Old teacher!" said Michlanski, suddenly dewy-eyed as he saw the shade of Alfred Strubeck. "How? Your image emanates from the basement. You shouldn't be able to project beyond that."

"I can't explain it, Sherlock. There was a disruption of the house's electrical circuits, apparently from a lightning discharge, coinciding with the arrival of the intruder—"

"Did you recognize him?"

"No, but the security cameras may have photographed him. They are independent of the house power, I believe."

"Correct."

"He copied files relating to the Argus Society from the basement computer."

"They'll become gobbledegook without the password."

"I'm glad—" The image shimmered and flickered.

"What's going on?" Michlanski made the robot scan the room. Sparks were coming from a fuse box at the top of the stairs.

"The power system is failing." There was fear in Strubeck's voice. He started toward the basement. Suddenly he wasn't there.

Michlanski's eyes teared up. He had always had philosophical problems with recorded personalities. He didn't believe a human being could be quantified to a series of on and off commands. Life, which so far as man knew was confined to this one spot in the universe, could not be such a simple thing. He compared it to the way a synthesizer reproduces the sounds of a grand piano, except for the resonance of the key on the wire just as the note is released. The recorded personality would never contain that person's resonance, or so he believed.

Yet he *had* been talking to Strubeck. The recording had behaved like the man Michlanski had known.

Suddenly the inside of his house vanished and he was standing in the neutral white projection room.

"What now?" he muttered.

"Sorry, Doctor. We lost the signal. Another power surge. This time at our end. We'll get it reconnected in a jiffy."

"Don't . . . bother." His voice trailed off. "You weren't on earth, old teacher," he whispered. "I couldn't have talked to you. You were on the moon—there was no transmission lag. You caused the power surge, didn't you?"

"Dr. Michlanski, are you talking to me?"

"Yes indeed, young man!" said Michlanski in his professorial tone. "Have you tracked down the origin of the first information burst? And most importantly, where it went?"

"A power surge was reported in the base mainframe. No damage was reported. Maybe it bled off."

"I suggest you run a thorough diagnostic of the system."

"We're not due for another for two days. They must be paid for, you know. There's no such thing as a free lunch on Luna."

"Thanks for reminding me. I'm always in such danger of forgetting that on your charming colony."

"No problem."

"When you get around to running a diagnostic, I'd appreciate knowing if your equipment records additional files added at this specific time. Please note the time."

"Will you want a dated report?"

"Please."

"For personal or business reasons?"

"Charge it to my personal account." Michlanski smiled. It was the nature of life, even artificial life, to try to prolong itself. When the floater robot arrived, the house power had been fading. That was probably when Strubeck's persona made the try: Maybe when the robot passed in front of one of the security cameras, perhaps then he had triggered a burst of energy and was downloaded into a beam that passed into the robot's camera eye.

"Alfred, I know what you did. You rode a light train to the moon."

III

Premier Peter Brasnikov was in a foul temper. His sensuous mouth worked furiously and his aristocratic hands clenched. He pushed away a glass of vodka.

"The fool!" he raged. "The stupid, asinine, uncomprehending, infantile, vainglorious, idiotic fool!" He picked up a tea samovar and smashed it against the wall. His man-servant cringed: The samovar dated from the days of the czars, as did most of the furnishings in the premier's opulent office in the Kremlin.

Brasnikov's rages were becoming as legendary as those of the "old premier," Kurtzov. His aides watched him apprehensively, except for the defense minister, Marshal Tiomkin, and his assistant, General Wen Chin, who both seemed perfectly at ease.

Tiomkin slumped on the burgundy damask sofa, teacup balanced on crossed legs. His pale blue eyes, candid and childlike, followed his chief's movements with detachment. He finished the tea and folded his soft hands over his paunch. His face, which always seemed unshaven, even after shaving, looked expectant.

Chin sat ramrod straight, his dark eyes darting about the room, with its Fabergé eggs and Louis XIV desk sitting over a two-hundred-year-old Persian carpet, behind it an oil portrait of the premier's namesake, Peter the Great, by one of the French masters. But his eyes always returned to the figure of the premier.

Brasnikov turned to Tiomkin. "Explain why this ingrate African ignored my pleas for moderation. We gave him tanks, guns, and ammunition. We promised to aid the uprising against the South African imperialists. But this—threat to use nuclear weapons. Inconceivable! This black gnat has compromised us completely!"

"He has betrayed our trust," agreed Tiomkin. "He deserves to be squashed. But we must be cautious. We have made him almost too tough to squash."

"Too tough?"

"Almost, Comrade Premier. But perhaps not entirely."

"Elucidate, Vasily Alexandrovich."

"The Americans may be planning an expedition to stop Dana."

Brasnikov rubbed his hands thoughtfully. "They have put their forces on alert, and Shefferton, damn him, strikes me as one who doesn't rattle sabers without using them."

"Perhaps he has studied President T. Roosevelt's dictum."

" 'Tread lightly before attacking your enemy from behind with a large cudgel'?"

"The proverb says, 'Talk in low tones but carry a big club.' "

"So," said Brasnikov softly, "how will he use the stick?"

"He will tell us before he strikes. Americans feel they must play fairly with their enemies. We can use this to our advantage."

"How?" Brasnikov leaned forward expectantly.

"This is General Chin's idea, developed independently, so he will present it," said Tiomkin with a nod toward Chin.

"Chin?"

"First Secretary, we can protest the use of force against the peace-loving Africans and insist on our presence to ensure that imperialistic designs are not carried out. When the Americans have done their job, they will go home. We will stay."

"Brilliant! What forces do you propose using?"

"Our amphibious division is ready to embark. Carriers *Murmansk, Archangel*, and *Vladivostok* are within cruising range."

"Is it possible to beat them and land first?"

"Their dirigible aircraft carriers can cruise at twice our speed."

"Dirigibles!" said Brasnikov with contempt. "Sick whales! Vulnerable gasbags!" His mood had changed entirely. He clapped Tiomkin's shoulders jovially. "Get to work!" He looked about the room. "Where can a man get vodka when he's thirsty?"

Tiomkin donned a heavy overcoat and took his leave. Chin remained. He never missed the chance to be alone with the premier.

Outside it was snowing. Tiomkin looked up and let the flakes caress his rough skin. He enjoyed cold, although he didn't consider Moscow "cold." He reached peak efficiency in what others considered paralyzing temperatures. His subordinates called him "the Snow Giant" behind his back. He approved. A man needed to be brawny and durable to survive in the far north. He was both.

He had risen on ability, and survived because of his apparent lack of ambition. He always pulled other people's chestnuts from the fire, earning their trust. He was often in the right place at the right time. But he also sniffed out career-destroying assignments and avoided being in the wrong place at the wrong time. Africa had that scent. He had given Wen Chin credit for the invasion plan because Africa smelled like Afghanistan.

He pulled his collar tight to keep the snow from dripping down his neck, and trudged slowly toward the War Ministry building, leaving giant bear-like tracks in the snow.

Chapter

★ 32 ★

I

Through the window of the Oval Office, President Shefferton watched the snow fall. His face was moody and deeply lined.

He had just finished talking to President Gernais and Premier Brasnikov. He had shared his intelligence data and told them the U.S. could not tolerate the use of nuclear weapons to alter the tactical balance on the plains of the Transvaal.

Gernais had made the offer Shefferton had prayed for: troops. With even a small European contingent, the expedition gained legitimacy as an international force. Such points were important. Recent American history—the occupation of Mexico, annexation of Greenland and the Cuban War—still rankled many nations. The African police action must not be seen as that kind of war.

But he was stunned when Brasnikov gave his blessings to intervention and insisted on providing ''observers'': Soviet marines. He had obviously been looking for such an excuse. If the U.S. had the right to intervene, how could it reject Soviet aid?

That was a thorny problem, but he could afford to worry about it later. Right now he intended to exploit the public relations benefits of having both Europe and the Soviets on his side.

He ordered a link with the joint chiefs and Defense Secretary Wells and began to put in motion the machine that would launch itself upon the shores of Africa.

II

Two hours before dawn, U.S. marines landed on the coast of Nigeria, between the port cities of Lagos and Porto-Novo. There had been a delay until the European Space Command confiscated a shuttle owned by the French firm that built the Pride of the Leopard and, manning it with troops, took the satellites without firing a shot.

The satellites neutralized, submarine transports surfaced, spewing air and water like whales. Hover assault craft roared onto the beaches. By the first hour three thousand troops had poured from their bellies and dug in.

By hour two the marines were in a dozen firefights. As black changed to magenta and faded to shell blue, the thud of mortars shook the morning. The artillery began landing, but too slow to loosen the congealing enemy position, which now had support from its own big guns.

Giant dirigibles, like floating hives, became visible, spewing hundreds of darting black shapes to support the marines.

Each dirigible aircraft carrier was two thousand feet long, three hundred and thirty feet wide, and held one hundred fighter-bombers. Fusion-powered, it could cruise at a hundred and fifty mph indefinitely. It carried forty-three million cubic feet of an artificial, stable, nonflammable hydrogen isotope in hundreds of self-sealing envelopes. It was armed with super-Gatling guns and particle-beam antimissile weapons.

Fiery lances crisscrossed the sky, sending planes flaming into the ground or waving impotently as they slipped past. The fighter-bombers pounced on the laser emplacements like vengeful sparrow hawks, but as they returned home, their ranks were thinned.

III

David Keith woke with a start. His holophone was chiming. Since he slept raw it took a moment to make himself presentable.

"This better be good!" he growled. "It's two A.M.!"

"White House calling," said a prim female voice. "Just a moment for the president, please."

Shefferton's torso materialized in the cube. "Sorry to wake you, General Keith, but this is rather important."

"It's all right, sir," said Keith fuzzily.

"How soon can you be ready to fly to Washington?"

"It will take a while to arrange transportation—"

"A helicopter will pick you up in twenty minutes. Okay? You're taking the ETF into action, General."

Keith bolted upright, instantly alert. "Africa?"

"We're not fighting a war anywhere else. Have the battalion ready to move. Army dirigibles will fly them to Norfolk."

"Thank you, Mr. President. Thank you very much!"

"You may reserve your gratitude until you've heard the whole assignment, General," said the president.

"What happened, Mr. President?"

"Your reputation as a crank has undergone rehabilitation the last few days. Your predictions were accurate. What's more, the Black Africans were waiting for us when we landed! Goodbye!"

IV

Sergeant Major Terry Ransome felt a jangled, tumbling moment of free-fall, then he was jerked upright by the opening chute. He was suspended over a vast field of liquid obsidian that tossed restlessly in the moonless night. The lights of the two HSTs disappeared south. He switched on his hover saddle's impeller and his parachute went limp. He released it. It plunged like a rag into the ocean. The saddle stabilized half a meter above the water. Around him hundreds of chutes were dropping into the drink.

He ran a check of his hover saddle. Computer and command monitor were okay. The straps holding him to his mount were secure. Nothing was lost in the jump. He homed in on Keith's signal and brought his saddle next to his.

"Good jump, Sergeant Major." The screen template on Keith's command computer cast him in a pale blue glow. The screen showed him at the center of a polar projection two hundred miles in diameter—the command radius. Six hundred lights clustered around the center. He could, if he chose, focus on an individual or group and learn their status from their personal computers.

His exec was Colonel Phipson, followed by Major Britten, in charge of C3CM (command, control, and communications countermeasures), and a major and four captains who had been with him at the beginning. All had undergone strenuous training to qualify to serve under him. He spoke briefly to them and signaled the battalion to move toward the mainland.

The battalion took the form of a crescent fifty miles from horn to horn. Except for Ransome at his side, the others were ghosts in the velvet blackness, accelerating until they reached two hundred miles per hour.

Keith brought his saddle out of the spray. The crescent slowed. Scouts ranged ahead to the mainland. Radar showed nothing for a hundred miles. But many things were unknown in this equation, and the things that were known weren't encouraging: For three days the First Marine and Twelfth Armored divisions had been stuck on the beachhead. As one of the generals who scorned Keith's theories had put it: "Antitank capabilities are stronger than anticipated."

Soviet marines ten miles north of the Americans had been unable to effect a link. The Europeans were expected to begin arriving today, but there was no room on the beachhead for them. Their carriers, *Karl Der Grosse* and *Napoleon I*, would just barely replace the aircraft losses suffered so far.

Keith slowed the formation. He expected to encounter tribes that still roamed the Sahara, but it was unlikely they would have the means to contact the central authorities.

He gave the order to operate under the "bola," an aggressive reconnaissance formation. The bola was an ancient South American weapon, two stone balls connected by a rope. When cast, the balls wound around the target with great force. Under the bola the formation operated strung out, but upon encountering resistance, the flanks turned inward and struck from all sides.

The sun rose on the Sahara, as monotonous and inhospitable as it had been for centuries. Scouts reported Taureg nomads, in trousers and long indigo robes. They were given a wide berth.

By midmorning they left the desert, approaching the Niger River, which emptied in the Atlantic. They were a few miles from the ancient metropolis Timbuktu, which Keith also intended to avoid.

They dosed each village with sleep gas. Even tall mud huts with roofs like grass skirts had radios. They left behind a wide swatch of slumbering natives.

Major Britten's C3CM specialists ranged wide, jamming broadcasts within a hundred-mile radius. They planted units that suppressed land-to-air communication and scattered decoys with electronic signatures similar to command units, to deceive the Africans about their whereabouts. One "ghost command" decoy gave the impression that a battalion-sized column was descending on a city hundreds of miles north. Another group sabotaged the Kainiji Dam power plant, creating a brownout over much of Nigeria.

The rest of Britten's men were deployed to see that the Africans didn't do the same thing to the ETF.

Shortly after noon Keith's navigational template showed them to be in the outlying area of the nuclear site in the savannah grasslands of Nigeria. Natives they questioned called it Site Shaka, after the bloodthirsty, brilliant Zulu king who caused the British so much grief in the nineteenth century.

Keith waited until C3CM sniffed out the spy equipment guarding the approaches to the base before deploying the battalion in a circle. Keith studied the base through his spynoculars, which combined high magnification, ultraviolet and infrared and was linked with the radar in the master computer. The computer fed data back into the spynoculars, letting it construct an accurate picture of what it was looking at, rather than what camouflagers intended it to see. The contrast between the untouched and enhanced views showed the pains that the Black Africans had taken to hide their site. Keith saw places of ambush and hidden artillery and many laser sites. He felt cold contemplating what they would have done to incoming bombers or paratroops.

He spoke into his communicator. "Colonel Phipson, I count ten laser sites. What about you?"

"Twelve, General."

"Computer estimates twelve hundred troops in this area, based on the barracks size and the number of artillery pieces."

Site Shaka was a large, enclosed area divided into two sections. Keith guessed that the first was where radioactive materials were stored and perhaps made into bombs. Here a large central dome was surrounded by five smaller domes. Spy satellites had shown the most heat emanations from the big dome.

Keith gave the orders to launch the attack.

Chapter
33

Mar. 5—*Washington Post*—The Pentagon has revealed that an elite commando force has penetrated a hundred miles into Black Africa and occupied a plant for building atomic bombs to use against South African cities. Called the Extraordinary Tactics Force, it is commanded by an obscure general, David Ian Keith, who graduated from West Point six years ago.

Mar. 10—Reuters—Black African forces are collapsing before the combined attack of Soviet, American, and European expeditionary forces. With the capture of Site Shaka, by the Extraordinary Tactics Force, the government of Juba Aman Dana, known to many as the Leopard, has fallen. Elements of the Twelfth Armored Division have punched through to Site Shaka, relieving the ETF.

I

Newsweek—We found General David Keith taking a few hours to relax at a hotel in Washington, D.C., before he was due to appear at a dinner in his honor at the White House. The general consented to an exclusive interview. We found Keith to be a strange combination of scholar and fighting man, at turns humble and sometimes almost arrogant, always articulate:

Q: General, there have been conflicting reports about the battle at Site Shaka and about whether or not Juba Aman Dana actually died. There are reports that the man they call the Leopard was so overcome by his defeat at your hands that he committed suicide. Could you give us your opinion?

A: The idea that Dana was so "overcome" by defeat that he contemplated ending his life is ludicrous. Throughout his career, he has shown himself to be resourceful, daring and totally without fear. He is the kind of soldier to whom defeat acts as a tonic. It makes him fiercer, more brilliant. When I study Dana's work, I'm reminded of Rommel, Robert E. Lee, Julius Caesar, even Napoleon; all became more formidable when they were at bay.

Q: What exactly happened at Site Shaka?

A: We caught the brigade assigned to guard the facility completely by surprise. One of the most important capabilities of the ETF is the ability to infiltrate an enemy position and still remain in contact with the commander. Our commandos are trained in the Lao Tse psychodynamic school of personal combat. Most of the vital positions—lasers and artillery sites, and most important, the nuclear containment facility on the base—were secured before the alarm sounded. Half of Dana's forces were trapped in the cafeteria. The other six hundred were dealt with piecemeal.

Q: What happened to the men in the cafeteria?

A: They fought us, I'm sorry to say. They were Dana's handpicked men. Not the kind who give up without a fight. Since we were outnumbered, we couldn't wait them out, particularly since we didn't know if reinforcements were on the way. We reduced the building with our portable artillery, and the artillery that we had captured. It became an inferno. Few survived.

Q: And Dana?

A: During the worst of the fighting a helicopter took off. We shot it down because we didn't want the Black African high command learning of our raid. The chopper was piloted by an extremely skillful pilot and we almost didn't bag it. When it went down, the fight went out of the men around the reactor. We later learned that Dana had been at Site Shaka on an inspection. We just happened to catch him there.

Q: Was his body identified?

A: We found the helicopter, charred, with several unidentifiable bodies in it. No one saw Dana die, but news of his demise spread rapidly, and his warlords took advantage of it to mount a coup and make peace with the allies. Well for them, since none of them had Dana's magic touch. They were just vessels that the Leopard filled with his genius.

Q: Do you think he's alive?

A: Like most cats, he probably has nine lives. In a way, I hope he survived. I don't have a quarrel with him personally. We achieved our military objectives. I hold no animosity. And I remind your readers that frequently our enemies have later become our friends. I rather hope he's alive, and if he is, I salute him.

Q: Regarding military objectives, several right-wing members of the Progressive Nationalist party have criticized the Soviet army for allegedly dragging its feet about pulling out of its occupation zone of Black Africa. Any comments?

A: No, except that may be an example of what I was talking about.

Q: You mean that once the Soviets were our adversaries; were in fact our adversaries several times in the last century, yet we are friends today, cooperating to keep peace and feed the world?

A: Something like that.

Q: Thank you, General Keith.

II

Kirsten Fale stepped lightly from the two-man helicopter as soon as it touched down in front of Michlanski's mansion.

She wore khaki slacks and a baseball cap over her red hair. A mainland cop with a belly that spilled over his belt ran up holding his cap to keep the chopper rotors from blowing it away.

"Deputy Inspector Fale, FBI." She flashed her shield.

"I can't imagine what the FBI would find interesting about this burglary. If you don't mind my saying so."

"I don't mind!" She sauntered past him toward the mansion. "Imagination probably isn't a requirement for your job."

"There's a state trooper and a news reporter up there."

She whipped around. "A news reporter?"

"The trooper said it was okay."

She burst through the first door she found. "Mel Hardrim and Kirsten Fale together again!"

Hardrim and Perle Gracie looked down from a holotape camera they were detaching from the ceiling in the sitting room. Hardrim was at the top step of a ladder.

"What a coincidence," said Hardrim.

"You'll have to do better than that, big man." She put hands on her hips. "You look good. The Smokey the Bear hat isn't you, though. How did an out-of-work cop get the tip that Ralph Ferman burgled Michlanski's house?"

"Lenny told me," he lied, and wished he hadn't. If Kirsten reserved the slightest bit of jealousy for Lenore Lippman . . . He had actually received word from Michlanski, through Chambless.

"Roger'd be pissed! Lippman's been giving him all sorts of information on you. I figured she was stiffing you. I was about to fly to D.C. and rip her cute little interface out of her neck—"

"Lenny's okay, Kirsten."

She switched her attention to Gracie, who blushed under her appraisal. "What's a famous news personality doing on the case?"

"I gave him a story in return for using the resources of the Science Network, such as doing quick analyses on holotapes."

"Well, I never supposed that you would tell me the truth—"

"Considering who you work for." He got the camera detached and climbed down to the floor.

"We can trust each other. We both want Ferman. *Verdad?*"

"Your boss Roger Ferdinand is also after *me*, Kirsten." Hardrim handed the camera to Gracie, who examined it with professional skill.

"We both want Ferman *and* we have limited resources."

"The FBI got a tight budget, Kirsten?"

"Tight as my breeches—" She gave him an evil grin. "Rog is running a rogue operation. Like Mexico. His ops calendar lists me as on assignment in Alberta. He's cooking the books to keep a small army looking for you and Ferman and trying to connect it all to Krebs."

"Got to admire the man his enemies. Why's he want Ferman?"

"You must have heard Ralphie's story about how the Santa Bella blight was a designer virus manufactured to cause a global famine. Roger thinks Ferman is not so crazy. He wants to interrogate him—give him a 'mental enema' is his charming term—and see if there's a connection between the alleged traitors on the South American team and Europe or Krebs. That could give him the leverage to off Director Houston Pollux.''

"How did Ferdinand know Ferman would still be in this area?"

"He has a list of people who know Ferman. He sent each a letter asking Ferman's whereabouts, saying Mel Hardrim was trying to contact him.''

"That bastard!"

"Each person he sent that letter to, he gave a different return address, all post office boxes used by the Bureau.''

Hardrim closed his eyes. "Then what?''

"We figured Ferman had to be in contact with someone. What we knew of him said he could never stay so incognito that he wouldn't occasionally call, say, his older sister, Denise, in Spokane.''

"You monitored all the phone calls?" He shook his head. "No, of course you didn't.''

"With our limited budget? After we sent the letters, we waited until someone inquired about who owned one of the post office boxes. Ferman thought he was being clever by finding out who sent the letter. We knew which return addresses went with which letter, so we knew who Ferman was contacting. We monitored her holophone, and when Ralph called, we traced the call to a pay phone in Charlevoix.''

Hardrim groaned. "I can't believe he fell for that old chestnut!''

"We both need Ferman. Let's work together, for a while.''

"She makes a persuasive case, Mel," said Gracie quietly.

"We have a common problem, but not a common goal. I won't give Ferman to Ferdinand.''

"From your perspective worse things can happen. And from my viewpoint worse things can happen than if you get to him.''

Hardrim folded his arms. "Yeah? Like what?''

"Horatius Krebs could beat us both.''

III

Ralph Ferman came close to death a second time in twenty-four hours after he launched one of Michlanski's ro-boats and was caught by the currents and almost dashed against the rocks. It was hard steering with one good arm, but he managed to get the ro-boat into deep water.

He landed on a rocky, deserted beach glazed with oily slime. With sludge up to his ankles he abandoned the boat and took a sandy trail away from the dunes, wincing as his arm reminded him he had not had it properly attended to.

The trail led to a dirt road, which led to a highway, with a strip of small businesses, mostly related to fishing or boating.

He needed a doctor, but first he found a software store and bought a disposable computer, to see what he had liberated from Michlanski's files.

In a block-sized park he sat under an oak tree. He carefully inserted the tile in the flimsy tile reader. He adjusted the angle of the electric paper screen until he could read the directory.

He called up the file: ARGUS SOCIETY. It was nothing but nonsense symbols. He called up SHERLOCK MICHLANSKI. Gibberish.

He grimaced. The files were completely worthless. Or else copy-protected. He had suffered a broken arm for nothing.

One file was readable: an article by Frank Silverado, publisher of *The Conspiracy Weekly Reader*, a sensationalist magazine for readers who saw conspiracies under every rock. In his current frame of mind Ferman didn't find it that outrageous. The article was about the Sunside Project, which Silverado called a government hoax.

Michlanski had found Silverado's theories interesting enough to record. Maybe Silverado was the man to tell his story to. He touched the print button for a hard copy. About that time the cellulose molecule bubble memory began to degrade and in seconds the computer became as useful as the package a hamburger comes in.

That was okay. He knew where to find Silverado. The magazine had said it was published in one of the most famous landmarks in Los Angeles: the old City Hall. Just like the *Daily Planet*! thought Ferman as he set off on foot for the Golden West.

IV

Mar. 4—*Micronesia Times*—The government of New Hong Kong has been overthrown in a bloody coup d'état that left most of the governing council dead or captured.

The intensely developed man-made island is one of the "pocket republics," populated by refugees from old Hong Kong.

The coup was engineered by a thousand mercenaries led by a notorious general known only by his nom de guerre: Bamboo.

Tsunamis of panic are coursing through the financial world. The Bank of New Hong Kong caters to venture capitalists and holds some of the fabulous Duce holdings of the Tectonics Corporation.

"Whitechapel is almost ready—to come alive," said Dr. Dollfuss from the holocube in Lewis Cocker's office in the Python Tower. "My work with him will soon be finished."

"Come now, Doctor, it couldn't have been that bad."

"Try living inside the brain of a madman sometime." Dollfuss lifted a sardonic eyebrow. "I mean, instead of just down the hall from one."

"Biting the hand that feeds you, Doctor? How would your warped theories of recombinant DNA play to the audience of *The Conspiracy Weekly Reader?*"

Dollfuss sneered. "Silverado's another one of Krebs's goons, just like you, just like me. And just like Emil—"

"Whitechapel!"

"Call him Frodo if you want! He's your baby and I want him off my doorstep—before I feed him into a garbage disposal!"

"Temper, Doctor."

His face was so close to the cube that he seemed to be emerging from it. "You don't understand! I can alter his memories. I can't change his basic nature. You've cut off the Hydra's head. But he'll grow more."

"Hydras and Pythons get along famously."

Dollfuss sighed. "Fine. Do you know that Solarz's men are here constantly now, to 'protect' us from the Crips and the Bloods? You better beef up security. I'm not joking."

"Noted. I have a group of mercenaries in mind to send there to cool Solarz's passions a bit. Would that make you feel safer?"

"Not safer, but hurry up anyway."

"I am your servant, Doctor." He ended the connection and went down the hall to Krebs's office, where he told him the news.

"Good!" said Krebs. "We may use Whitechapel against Solarz but we'll first use his tracking skills to find Ferman."

"Have you read the report of the seizure of New Hong Kong?"

Krebs rested his hands on his desk. His strawberry nose twitched. "That may be fatal to Mrs. Duce's Sunside Project consortium. She had a lot of gold in the New Hong Kong Bank."

"Since most money is really credit, how can we know we've actually trapped a real amount of her capital?"

"We've got the head of the bank. Granted, it has limbs throughout the world, so Rita's credit lines are intact. However, she had bullion there. That's unrecoverable. 'Bamboo' can use it to finance his national defense fund. He'll recruit enough mercenaries that she'll never retake New Hong Kong.''

''What about the Europeans? Or even the United States?''

''I have enough influence in Europe to keep that from happening. Shefferton's too busy with Africa to interfere in the affairs of a little island. It's not being taken over by Genetic Communists, just drug dealers, pimps, hoodlums and murderers. We send ambassadors to such people every day.''

''So Duce must dig deeper into her own pockets to fund the Sunside Project. Just when it needs a lot of new supplies.''

V

''What is the self-defense force of the Pocket State Alliance doing about New Hong Kong?'' Rita Duce asked its commander, General Pietro Poldark, who sat glumly at the conference table.

Also at the table were Duce's remaining partners in the Sunside Project, venture capitalists from the pocket republics, an Alaskan timber magnate, and a Mexican hovercar mogul thrown in.

Poldark answered, ''Mrs. Duce, I am here as a courtesy. I report to the alliance's defense ministers' council.''

''Half of those ministers are sitting here! Surely you can say if you intend to get New Hong Kong back?''

''Ma'am, I'm using my troops to prevent a coup in Thebes, Sparta, and Hamilton, which are hours away from New Hong Kong. My problem, which I don't mean as criticism, is that our governments have been comfortable with my command not being much larger than a metropolitan police force. I have two thousand men to cover the three most obvious targets of an attack, not to mention the rest of the republics. Bamboo has a thousand men, but he's only got to defend one island, which he can do and still strike one of the islands we would have to uncover to mount an assault.''

''So the best defense is a good sitting posture?''

''I won't go into theory and practice of modern warfare with a civilian.''

''So we do nothing. I notice that when you mention republics that you must defend, you never speak of Hellas.''

Poldark looked scornful. ''Of course not. Everyone knows that Hellas has a thermonuclear capacity.''

''Well, dammit, Hellas is part of the alliance! Why don't we use their bomb to force Bamboo to pull off New Hong Kong?''

"He knows we won't destroy the prize we want back. The beauty of the Hellas bomb is that it is rigged to blow up Hellas if anyone tries to capture it. Who wants a radioactive cinder?"

The president of the Bank of Hamilton cleared his throat. "Which brings us to something I'd rather not bring up. But I have a duty to our stockholders. I'm beginning to think this investment in Prometheus Enterprises may not be safe. Horatius Krebs"—he said the name they had avoided —"is obviously behind this takeover. If we continue to back Scott, he won't stop. With your gold in his hands, that mercenary army will get a lot larger."

"We have money, too!" said Duce with exasperation. "I'll buy the troops, if you let us use your islands as staging areas."

"Too risky!" said the bank president.

"Our stockholders would never allow it."

"And you don't have as much liquid capital as all that, Mrs. Duce. A lot of it is in the hands of your bitterest enemy."

"*Our* bitterest enemy! And I want it back!"

"We could always protest to the United Nations."

"Does anyone have an actual suggestion?" asked Duce. "If not, I guess the only thing is try to get the U.S. to intervene."

Poldark cleared his throat. "I don't want to rub it in, Mrs. Duce, but to quote you: Do you have an actual suggestion?"

Chapter

* 34 *

I

Senators Macadew and Manners were playing poker in the Senate Cloak-room while Idaho's senior senator belabored an empty chamber on the subject of improving tourist travel.

"How we gonna handle this debate on th' Thirty-first Amendment, Percy?"

"What do you mean? I'll take two cards."

"One to the dealer. What are the ground rules? How personal do I get? How far into my bag of tricks do you want me to reach?"

"Sounds like a threat, Senator. I'll bet two red chips."

"No, no, no! But I notice you don't hesitate to stack the rules o' debate against yours truly. I jus' wonder if you intend to add personal attacks? I see your two red chips and raise you."

"I think Senator Dreyfuss may see his way clear to vote my way, since

I have photos of him in a very compromising position with a Senate page. Call, two kings.''

"Three ladies." Chips crossed the table. "I thought Joe was straight, or at least confined his malfeasances to dogs and sheep. Wal, you know, Senator Jerome's brother-in-law is in hock to the Arabian Mafia. Cut-off-the-hand type of thing. He snookered ol' Jerome for defense contracts for his Arab friends. Your deal."

"I've learned a lot from you, Charles. You're still the man I admire most in the Senate—"

" 'Sides Number One?'' Manners simply shrugged eloquently.

"I want you on my side. It would make things a lot easier. We might even be able to avoid embarrassment to the president."

"Actually, I was hopin' to avoid embarrassing him by kicking your ass, Percy. I'll keep these cards, and bet ten red ones."

Manners looked at his cards again. "Call. I'll take one."

"Drawin' to an inside straight? Well, like the desert said to the donkey, I got a lot more gopher holes than you got legs."

"Rather than waste time with trivialities, what've you got?"

"Here's a list newsmen would give their left eyeballs to get a peek at!" He spread a handwritten sheet out on the table.

"Here's mine." Each man looked at the other's list.

"If we publicize these, lots of our colleagues will be sharing a cell with SoHi dealers, smugglers, thieves, pederasts, and con men, and they won't have to get to know anybody new."

"We'd have trouble getting a quorum," agreed Manners. "I suggest that everyone on my list agree to sit this vote out, in return for everyone on your list doing the same."

"Son, that's kind of balanced in your favor a brown hair."

"I agree not to press a vote to close debate, no matter how long things go."

"Agreed. Now, I want to see your cards. I bet twenty reds."

"Call."

"I got a flush."

"Full house."

"Shit."

II

The elevator arrived at the top floor. It opened and Lewis Cocker found himself facing Dr. Dollfuss and two armed guards—and Ivor Solarz, who limped into view, favoring his bad leg, light gleaming off the soft silver hook handle of his cane.

Dollfuss looked unhappy. "I dislike you, Cocker, but I'd never—"

"Shut up!" commanded Solarz. His sharp teeth overfilled his small mouth, perhaps accounting for his peculiar speech pattern that cut off each syllable almost before it was past his lips. His face was lumpier than when Cocker had seen him last, with his piggy eyes like blackheads surrounded by sphincter muscles.

"What happened to Mr. Krebs's people?" asked Cocker.

"All twenty are being made comfortable in an old dressing room. This place is impressive. You ever seen the auditorium?"

"There were thirty men here."

"Yeah."

"I'm a prisoner, of course. What are your demands?"

"Le's take a little walk." They walked to the steel door behind which Jack Whitechapel, once known as Emil, had spent his entire existence, from a cloned cell to what Dr. Dollfuss euphemistically referred to as a human being.

They entered through the twisting light trap into the eerie blue of Whitechapel's womb. They heard a rhythmic pumping and the regular sounds of breathing.

"Lights up, I wanna see my investment!" ordered Solarz.

"His eyes are still very sensitive."

"Do it, kraut."

At first they saw a hulking shadow that sat on a contraption of wheels, handles, pulleys and weights that suggested an exercise machine. The figure more resembled a piston-driven engine than a man. Heavily muscled legs pumped with an inhuman power and unchanging rhythm. His skin was as pale as a trout's belly.

He did not relax his pumping, but slowly turned his closely shaven skull and regarded them with eyes that seemed huge. The pupils shrank into points as the illumination increased.

"He's buff," said Solarz admiringly. "How'd he grow up to be so strong in such a short time?"

"Designer steroids, mated with Serum T for 'terminus.' We haven't done enough experiments to know all the ramifications. I suspect one is a truncated life span. Having his cells constantly bathed by accelerated growth medium may have permanently implanted a tendency toward hyper-rapid growth. I also expect he'll be highly susceptible to Rogue Cancer."

"Hello, investment," said Solarz. "I understand you're the perfect killing machine. We'll have to turn you loose on the streets. Teach the Crips and Bloods something.'' Whitechapel didn't move, except for his relentless pumping, but his tiny pupils fixed on Solarz and clung there.

Solarz looked at Dollfuss. ''When will he be ready?''

''He's ready now.''

He looked at the pale, Promethean figure. ''We'll talk again.''

Solarz led the way out of the lab. ''It's this way, Cocker. I couldn't allow your boss, who I respect very much, to operate such a lucrative operation in my range, not without taking a cut. With the Crips and Bloods crowdin' me, I need an edge. I need what Dr. Dollfuss has been working on. I need an infusion of capital. I think Mr. Krebs and I can reach a position of mutual respect.''

Cocker didn't have a kernel of courage from which to grow even the scrawniest crop of bravado, but he had dealt enough with powerful men to know that if they knew you had no leverage, they would crush you. He had to pretend he had leverage.

''You seem to get a lot out of this deal, Mr. Solarz.'' Cocker calmly pushed away the barrel of the machine gun pointed at him. ''Whereas Mr. Krebs gets very little.''

''That's a reflection of how the infrastructure has shifted in my direction.'' Cocker hated ignorant people who used jargon.

''A shift more apparent than real. Krebs could arm your rivals and you'd have Beirut on your hands. Or use mercenaries. Perhaps you read about the overthrow of New Hong Kong. Those men are available to work elsewhere.'' That was a lie, but he was betting his life that Solarz didn't know it. ''You could lose everything.''

''I'm more interested in gaining everything. We can cut a deal. Don't worry, I won't rough you up or anything. I know Krebs wants to get his hands on Mel Hardrim and Ralph Ferman—''

''You messed up getting Hardrim in Denver.''

''All right!'' Cocker thought it expedient not to press the matter. ''Here's the deal: Ferman is headed this way. Hardrim has to be followin' him.'' Cocker wondered who had told Solarz that.

''Ferman will end up contactin' Frank Silverado in L.A. When he does, we open the bag and in he goes.'' Solarz's piggy eyes glittered with a special hate. ''We also nab the former pig. He might not survive the trip, but I give my personal guarantee Ferman will. That should be worth something.''

''There's no guarantee that Ferman will do anything right away. You could be waiting for months.''

"I got plenty of time."

"My employer wants Hardrim as much as he wants Ferman."

"That's negotiable. That's why man invented gold."

"I'll gladly carry your proposal to Mr. Krebs in New York."

"Oh no, Cocker." Solarz chuckled without mirth. "You're a bargaining chip, too. You stay."

"I assure you I possess no bargaining value."

"Little brownnoses like you are hard to replace." Solarz reached over and roughly took hold of Cocker's soft left hand and examined it. "He'll cough up a little extra to ensure I don't send him one of your fingers."

Cocker hoped to God it didn't come to that. When he closed his eyes he saw ten fingers, lined up on the polished mahogany of Krebs's desk, like so many pale, pink, fat worms.

III

It was hot on the dirt road in Michigan's Upper Peninsula. Hardrim, Fale and Gracie were shaded from the worst by a stand of sugar maples that rose like pillars of an arboreal temple.

Kirsten Fale stood next to a twenty-five-foot staghorn sumac that grew by the road. She broke off a cluster of the dark red fruit and popped one into her mouth, frowned, and spit it out.

After weeks of following every possible lead on Ralph Ferman, the three of them had met to admit that they were stumped.

Hardrim leaned against the night-black Ford Mustang. "If the FBI's best computers and the Argus Society net can't find Ferman from the data we've fed it, it's time to try a long shot.

"We know the only legible data file Ferman got from Michlanski's mansion contained articles by and about Frank Silverado and *The Conspiracy Weekly Reader*. We should work under the assumption that eventually he'll turn up at the *Reader*'s headquarters in L.A. I propose driving there to stake it out."

"You don't mean all of us at once. You mean we take turns, so the others can keeping chasing leads, however chimerical?"

"Yes, Perle, that's what I mean."

Kirsten Fale carefully walked around the Mustang. "These rubber wheels are real, aren't they? They're not for show."

Hardrim smiled with pleasure, like any man having a beautiful woman pay attention to his car. "In *this* car, the driver is the driver, not some computer."

"That sounds dangerous and impractical." She found herself enchanted in spite of herself.

Gracie looked at his reflection in the high-gloss hood and pushed a red lock back into place. "Do you know how many died annually during the years when cars were manually driven?" He took his computer from its holster and started to key in an inquiry.

"No, Perle, and please don't tell me," said Hardrim firmly.

"Look at these primitive seat belts! You might as well make out your will if you get in an accident."

Hardrim fumbled to open the trunk. "You want primitive? You want minimum survivability? Look!" He pulled out a dull metal helix-shaped device. It reflected sunlight like a metallic snake. He held up his .45 Colt pistol with the other hand. With a flick of his thumb he ejected the old magazine.

"This French Cobra autoloader extended clip is from the last war." He took out a magazine that mated with the helix-shaped tubing, then wrapped the metallic snake around his arm. "Compressed gas feeds up to fifty extra shells into my Colt."

"Gee, big man, if you can't hit your target with six shots, why not give up?" Fale took out her Dan Wesson "Mamba" .45 automatic laser/slug combo with fifteen slugs in the clip and one in the pipe. "If this doesn't bring down your target, you need to call in an air strike."

"I presume from the tenor of this conversation that you two expect to run into resistance once we find Ralph Ferman."

"We'll be operating in the playground of the biggest mob kingpin in California, who already tried once to collect a bounty for me from Horatius Krebs. You make up your own mind."

Gracie looked thoughtful. "Should I purchase a handgun?"

"I doubt that would be a good idea."

"Do you have a spare?"

"No!" said Hardrim, a bit louder than he had wanted to.

"I do." Fale produced a small .22 automatic. Gracie checked to see if a shell was in the chamber and stowed it in his bag.

"That should serve." He caught the extra clip Kirsten tossed him and packed it next to the gun.

"You've used one of those before?" asked Hardrim.

"I'm proficient in several areas that you might at first glance not consider, Mel. Versatility runs in my family."

Chapter
* 35 *

I

The president's visit to the moon had been a nightmare to his Secret Service detail.

They were happy only once: at Newton Observatory, where he talked to Philip Norrison before returning to Tycho City. After that everything, from a security standpoint, went downhill.

There were no autos on the moon, so Shefferton walked everywhere. The Secret Service wanted to bring a bulletproof limousine from earth for the occasion, but he vetoed it. His instincts told him he had nothing to fear from the colonists.

The first day, Shefferton visited the construction site, where the three Sunside Project ships were nearly complete. Jason Scott and Jacob Kane were too busy to give a guided tour and said so. Sheridan Mayfield was horrified, but when Shefferton reacted positively, he felt a grudging admiration for Scott and Kane.

"They're right," said Shefferton as they entered Tycho City. "I'm a tourist, and they're on a deadly timetable."

"They're working eighteen-hour shifts," said Mayfield. "But what you're doing is important. It's vital that these colonists know they're part of America."

Shefferton put his arm around Mayfield. "I know your fears about the colonies seceding. But that won't happen for years. By then predictions based on today's situations will be worthless. Let's take care of today and leave next week for my successor—if it's a real shit train let's hope Percy's sitting in my office when it hits!"

Shefferton toured the colony with its leading citizens, with Mayfield at his side, wearing a communicator to keep updated on the Senate vote on the repeal of the Thirty-first Amendment.

Also in the group, at Shefferton's request, was General Keith. It had been impressed upon the general by the White House chief of staff that his was a singular honor.

He couldn't think how to be useful, so Keith decided to enjoy himself. He had heard that the Pentagon was contemplating deactivating half of the ETF. After his success in Africa, he had half expected his enemies to be confounded. But aside from a public pat on the back, he was as much a pariah as ever.

He assumed that his presence in the entourage was a sop before he was given a really limp assignment, until, between items on his itinerary, the president took him aside to speak privately.

"I didn't bring you along for the ride, General." He kneaded Keith's shoulder with his big hands. "I want you to stay and report to me on the military readiness of the Lunar base."

"I'm not really an expert on naval warfare, sir."

"I'm talking about land warfare, son."

"I didn't know anyone else had troops on Luna."

"Colonel Farley tells me that may not be true any longer."

"Won't Admiral Davis mind me nosing about his turf, asking questions and maybe writing a report critical of his operations?"

"Don't worry about Davis! Kick his ass if he gets in your way and tell him I said you could do it!" He gave Keith a parting squeeze and his entourage started moving again.

Keith looked after him, doubt written on his face.

The tour started at the huge fusion plant, the famous "fusion lake" built several levels under the surface.

Grasping handrails over the lake, Shefferton donned sunglasses and looked into the depths to the benevolent golden glow of the reactor's ignition plasma point, looking like a sunken sun. The liquid around the glow was of the family of stable elements above 152 on the periodic table. It was incredibly dense and transparent. It absorbed the deadly rays of the thermonuclear reaction while allowing the energy to be siphoned off.

The glow was beautiful, like life and power and love and peace and the future rolled into something almost like a life-form. He shook his head, reminding himself there is nothing benevolent about nature, whose single-minded determination to kill is the one pervasive truth of the universe.

Mayfield, who was at his side, suddenly frowned and tapped the mechanism of the communications unit. "What the hell?"

Others in the group looked at their watches or wrist computers with concern. The five Secret Service agents in the building simultaneously began tapping and shaking their headsets.

One of the reactor techs consulted a control board.

"Mr. President, you better leave. We're getting electromagnetic pulses from the reactor. They're harmless in small doses, but we like to play it safe. I'm afraid they've already messed up your electronics. We should've warned you not to bring any devices with computer components or molecule bubbles into the enclosure."

"That would've meant leaving behind almost everything but our underwear, I fear," said Shefferton. "Let's get to the surface."

Once out of the "lake" room, most electronic devices began functioning. The electromagnetic pulse had disabled two headsets belonging to Shefferton's guards, but they had spares.

When Mayfield's com unit was functioning again he listened a moment, then turned to Shefferton. "They're starting the roll call in the Senate, Mr. President." He had gotten out of the habit of calling him "Mr. President," but he was so caught up by the drama that he couldn't help himself.

"Let's get moving! I want to get to the square and give my speech on time. Governor Jackson tells me two thirds of the population will be there." He grinned. "Too bad they can't vote!"

"Perhaps you can do something about that, Mr. President," said Selene's Governor Merle Jackson with a sly smile.

Shefferton donned an earphone to hear the roll call. He mounted the podium in the central square's crescent-shaped amphitheater. He grasped the lectern and looked out across thirty thousand people, packed as deep as an audience for a pop star, so dense that several small structures, like a fountain and a rest room facility, seemed to grow from a soil of human faces.

He didn't know why he felt so excited. It was like his first speech. A man who had talked to five hundred million holovision watchers felt intimidated by a mere thirty thousand.

Alexander the Great conquered the world with this many men, thought Shefferton. What will they conquer?

The audience grew quiet. He wondered how many of them had watched old clips of the first President Kennedy. How long before a clever newsman made the connection on what he was about to say?

"My fellow Americans, today I *am* a citizen of Tycho City. Today all Americans are citizens of the moon. I share your aspirations for the future. Luna is just the first step, as Neil Armstrong noted so many years ago, on a leap that will eventually take us beyond the solar system."

On his earphone he heard: "Senator Aynsworth"—"Aye!"; "Senator Buckram"—"No!"

"The day will come when the average American will think no more about taking a shuttle to the moon than about taking a hypersonic transport from New York City to San Francisco."

Shefferton felt the crowd grow excited. He saw a woman with a child about three years old, pressing against the security officers. She hoisted the boy up over the heads of the adults.

He had an inspiration. "Let her through." The Secret Service detail chief looked at him like he was crazy, then shrugged fatalistically and politely asked the young woman for a look in her purse and side pouch. Then he examined the child as if he expected to find his diapers packed with explosives.

The mother advanced hesitantly, then with confidence as the president smiled widely. He wrapped her small hand in his huge one and asked her name and occupation. She was a hydroponics farm shift supervisor when she wasn't caring for the child.

"How old is your boy? What's his name?" he asked.

"Two and a half. His first name's Galileo." She giggled nervously and added, "If I had it to do over again, it'd be Jeffrey. Jeffrey Armstrong Pike."

Shefferton laughed hugely. This woman and her child were a gift from God as a reward for living right, he decided. He gently took the toddler and held him up to the crowd.

"This boy, Galileo Armstrong Pike, is a special child, citizens of

Luna.'' He paused. ''This child, born so recently, will *live to see the stars!*''

The crowd went wild, except for those near the edge who were waving signs demanding statehood. The president seemed to notice them for the first time. He gave the child back to his mother.

''You folks in the back, I can't blame you for wanting to be citizens of an American state on the moon. My advisers tell me that's inadvisable. That it will cause many problems.'' He looked over the crowd. ''I disagree!'' A huge roar of applause broke out. Down in the front row, where the dignitaries were seated, Mayfield was steaming. Statehood for Selene was his least favorite subject.

''As president I can't promise statehood. I can pledge to work for it. First, we have many challenges ahead. Most of you are involved, in one way or another, with building the Sunside Project spacecraft, so you know my administration's first priority. But let me reiterate that I intend to be the president of progress. Technology has been a nasty word in the last few decades. But it tastes sweet on my lips.

''I pledge myself and my nation to progress. To challenges conquered, to climbing higher mountains, to achieving the impossible. You citizens of Luna typify America's greatness. You dream with your eyes open. To you lies open the road to the future. Thank you for making me welcome!''

''Senator Waverly.''

''Aye!''

''Mr. President, the ayes have it and the motion carries,'' said the distant voice.

Shefferton left the podium, and before his bodyguards could intervene, waded into a sea of outstretched hands.

II

June 23—*Washington Post*—President Shefferton's announcement of support for statehood for the Territory of Selene, following on the heels of the narrow passage of the repeal resolution in the Senate, has caused considerable political ripples in the Capitol.

Senator Charles Ellsworth Macadew was quick to call the proposal ''incredibly visionary. The very thought of a U.S. state in space sends tingles up my spine.''

Senate Majority Leader Percy Shelley Manners, stung by yesterday's vote, was cautious. "We always seriously consider administration proposals. This has such ramifications that we may be studying it for months."

Washington Times—Pundits have had a field day on the fact that half of the U.S. Senate sat out the vote to repeal the Thirty-first Amendment. Nobody is answering why the president of the Senate didn't order a quorum call. . . .

Sherlock Michlanski left his tiny shower stall, where he had stood for two minutes before he realized the water had stopped. He turned sideways to get his heroically proportioned bulk out of the stall. In front of the tiny mirror he studied his blond beard and realized he hadn't rinsed the soap off.

He swore in Polish. This was the third time this week that he had started to dry off when he was still covered with soap.

Rather than go back inside and get another snotty memo from the bookkeepers of Selene's There Ain't No Such Thing as a Free Lunch paradise, he toweled the soap off his body and returned to his study where the electric blackboard waited, like an idol that needs hourly sacrifices.

The search for Strubeck's secret was becoming all-consuming. For the first time in his life he had to be reminded to eat!

Michlanski had begun the project with his usual lighthearted jocularity. The universe was a wonderful puzzle. It was fun. But unlocking Strubeck's equations wasn't fun. Would a surgeon call the most challenging operation of his career "fun"?

It wasn't fun to awake sweating in cold rooms. To have waking nightmares; to roam the common, looking for patterns in leaves and grass, to try to stare past the artificial sky into the mind of God. More than once he had conquered his distaste for space suits, which were not made with big men in mind, and gone onto the surface, to stare at Tau Ceti and try to read the mind of Strubeck, who, in his last days, had achieved a clarity of thought that was—no other word for it—beautiful.

He was so close—the basics he knew by heart: Create a dimple of probability, using forces created by the sun twenty million miles from its surface. Duplicate that dimple by creating a "bottle" of magnetic forces to confine a genie of antimatter to concentrate on one point in space-time and alter probability so radically that particles would begin to phase out of existence and reappear elsewhere in the universe.

Easy to say. Hard to do.

He stared at the blackboard's crabbed cuneiforms borrowed from dead languages. Something was missing. But what?

His brow furrowed. One symbol was wrong, out of place, not even his handwriting. He replaced it with the old symbol.

It reappeared. "Zerrk! What is this, a short?" He started to erase it again, when in a corner of the blackboard, the white pixels that imitated chalk began to form a pattern: a crude drawing, but undoubtedly a human figure. He dropped the stylus.

It was a child's caricature of Alfred Strubeck. It stayed on the board for a moment, and then it vanished.

"This is like getting tips from a Ouija board!" He studied the equation, with its unwanted and unasked-for symbol. That one alteration completely changed the direction from which he had been approaching the problem. It was impossible. And yet—

"Thank you, old teacher."

III

The voyage from Luna, and the Midway transfer, were uneventful. After the transfer, Mayfield sat by himself to study. After an hour he looked up to see the president.

They made small talk. Shefferton's doctor had ordered him to get his biobots serviced immediately upon return to earth. Electromagnetic radiation at the fusion lake had caused a malfunction. The doctor also worried about the radiation effects.

Mayfield decided to ask a question that had bothered him for days. "When did you decide you were for statehood for Selene?"

"It was a sudden inspiration when I was giving the speech." His smile was so childlike that Mayfield couldn't stay annoyed.

"You did yourself a lot of good with the Selenites. A poll I saw gave you a ninety percent approval rating among colonists."

"Why do you think I did it, Sheridan? I need the votes!" He slapped Mayfield on the thigh. "Tell me why you're against it."

"I am no longer against it, sir, now that you're for it."

"I make it hard for you sometimes," said Shefferton quietly. "I know the *Aurora* incident was hard. You and Charley are my greatest friends. You're the only ones who tell me when you think I'm wrong."

"Statehood isn't wrong. It's just badly timed, until we get an infrastructure in place to ensure control over these people."

"You keep people loyal by giving them a piece of the pie." Shefferton looked out the porthole at the white half-moon poised over the earth's horizon and thought how apt the analogy was.

"I also worry that if Selene gets statehood, the outer colonies will demand it. When it takes people ten minutes to receive a radio message, it's hard to get them to obey a manufacturing regulation."

"My old bureaucrat! I don't care about regulations. I want them on the road to freedom. If we throw enough seeds and fertilizer, things'll be all right. We don't need to do their farming for them."

Mayfield didn't believe it. "If you say so, Jeffrey."

"You know, one of my main pleasures is trying to find ways to help people do what they want with their lives. I know I'm impractical; that's why I've got practical men like you around!"

"This is the captain, Mr. President," said a soft male voice. "We'll enter the atmosphere shortly. For several minutes there will be no communication possible with earth."

"The government can do without me for a few minutes."

"Thank you, Mr. President."

Shefferton looked out the quartz window again. The blue and white arc of the earth was, for most purposes, man's universe. Time was when a single comet could change the destiny of life. But no longer. Give us a few years and we'll be living around two suns. We've removed fate from the equation, he thought.

The cabin began to vibrate. Both men were strapped in, but the computer Mayfield was working on went flying away to crash into the bulkhead. A Secret Service agent stumbled into the cabin, lost his balance, and hit his head on a padded armrest. He got up.

"Mr. President, are you all right?"

"Yes," said Shefferton. "Captain, what's the problem?"

"We've lost some heat shield tiles. We can't abort reentry without creating an equally dangerous situation. There is danger. If you like, you and your staff can get into the emergency pod."

"Well, how safe is the pod? Didn't that fellow who stole the GIL-GAMESH a few months ago escape in one? How did he get along?"

"No one actually knows that he got the pod operating," interjected Mayfield. "There's been plenty of tests on the survival pod. It's as safe as we can make it."

"That's comforting. Well, once a Texas oilman went to the dentist, who told him he didn't have any cavities. The oilman said, 'Drill anyway, Doc, I feel lucky!' "

Mayfield smiled tightly. The Secret Service detail chief, who had joined them, didn't smile at all. "What does that mean?"

"That I trust the captain to get us through."

"I advise against it," said the Secret Service detail chief.

"I know you do, Max. But that's the way it is today. Captain, we'll stick with you, this trip."

"I'm honored, sir. In that case, we'll get you there."

During reentry Mayfield clung to the armrests like an owl on his perch. The Secret Service men, and Shefferton's aides, looked like zombies. The president read the latest edition of the *New York Hourly News* while the scramjet felt as if it were breaking up.

After a two-hour ordeal, the GILGAMESH landed smoothly at Andrews Air Force Base, just outside Washington.

As they left the shuttle, Mayfield stopped the detail chief.

"Max," said Mayfield, putting on his fiercest expression, which had been known to send his underlings at the SED office to the rest room, "if word of this gets out, and I find out it came from any of your people, I'll be eating raw brains for breakfast."

"I believe you. But why pick on us? Nobody's ever accused the Secret Service of being a kiss-and-tell bunch of guys."

"I'm not saying anything to you I didn't just tell everybody else. And I mean it. I'm not going to have Jeffrey's successful trip marred by bullshit about the GILGAMESH being unsafe!"

"You've got my word, Mr. Secretary."

Chapter
* 36 *

I

Jeffrey Shefferton put the finishing touches on his speech. In five hours he would appear before the nation to announce rationing.

The Senate vote to repeal the Thirty-first Amendment over, he was entering a new crisis, prepared to spend some of the popular coin minted by his tremendously successful tour of Tycho City. It was as good a time as any to announce rationing. Although he would have preferred not to do it right before the July Fourth weekend.

He would lose seats in November, but he had delayed rationing as long as possible. He reread the speech. . . .

Percy Manners offered his distinguished visitor a glass of brandy. "I'm pleased you accepted my invitation, Mr. Secretary!"

Secretary of State Randolph Harmon shifted uneasily on the sofa. "I wrestled with my conscience, communed with the deity, and concluded that duty to my country lies before loyalty to the administration. Besides, I'm not compromised by merely talking to you. I'm obliged to consult members of Congress on national policy." His rich, vibrant voice flavored everything he said with importance. Manners, no slouch at speechmaking, thought Harmon could read a menu and get an ovation. The Harmon of twenty years ago, who had worked the Progressive Nationalist convention into a frenzy with his "You won't break our children on a rack of poverty!" speech, had been a man to follow into hell. Now he was a shade of his former self. Still pompous, still drunk on himself, still useful to the administration of the first president of his party; and at this historic moment, still useful as the silver bullet to shoot that administration dead.

"Duty, sir? You practically invented the word."

"That's very generous of you," beamed Harmon.

"You're one of the greatest men our country has produced. Everyone knows you were never president because your dedication kept you from devoting the time necessary to win. Such an irony of history!" He folded his hands. "The president was wise to appoint you secretary of state, but foolish to ignore your counsel."

"He *is* the president," said Harmon. "I am merely his tool."

Manners caught the plaintive note. "A pity, that a man such as yourself is nothing more than a tool."

Harmon drank from the snifter. A slender, translucent finger flicked toward his collar to loosen it. He sighed.

"I dislike complainers, but you don't know how trying it is."

Manners murmured sympathetically.

"I have the highest regard for the president, but I find him incomprehensible. Particularly since he has repeatedly stated his intentions to raise America's prestige among the less advantaged nations. For instance, this adventure in Africa—"

"Deplorable!" intoned Manners piously. "Gunboat diplomacy."

"I don't disapprove of the force, so much as the nation it was directed against. We shed the blood of blacks in defense of whites! Any hopes we had of persuading the emerging nations of our sincerity has been wiped out. The damage is irreparable, I fear."

Manners nodded. "You're right. Perhaps we can retrieve much of what we have lost through the food distribution program."

"Thank God for that! But even there we show poor judgment. We should concentrate on food production at home instead of pinning our hopes on the outlandish theories of Thomas Furbeck."

"Alfred Strubeck, Mr. Secretary."

"Quite so!" snapped Harmon. "My point is we should funnel resources into increased productivity and cut waste. At least Shefferton is taking the first step with the rationing program."

Manner's eyebrows shot up like skyrockets. "Rationing?"

"I forgot you didn't know about that. I suppose it doesn't matter since the speech is to be given in less than an hour."

Manners was sorry he hadn't had more warning. He might have used it to his advantage. "Seems like an excellent idea."

"It doesn't go far enough. We must reintroduce income tax. We must sacrifice for a better world. America's standard of living must fall so it will rise elsewhere. We must quit wasting money for space research. Earth's problems come first."

"I can almost see that as the slogan of a future great president!" Manners said with admiration. "Earth comes first!"

"I'm not running for anything!" snapped Harmon, preening. "We are talking about common sense, after all. What is in space that should siphon off so much of our resources?"

"I heard rumors years ago after the White Point Probe signals were received that habitable worlds were found orbiting Tau Ceti."

"Hardly rumor," sniffed Harmon. "I was on the Senate committee that voted to classify that information. We judged it would arouse public passions and create demands to colonize these worlds. Some self-serving person leaked the data, but no one took it seriously."

"That accounts for the tenacity of some champions of the space program, like Senator Macadew and Speaker Saratoga."

"Macadew and that presumptuous pip-squeak Mayfield set the president on this treacherous course. They planted the seed in his mind to visit the moon. That infected the public with an unhealthy interest in space." He gulped down his brandy. "Macadew was on the committee. He voted against classifying the information. I suspect he leaked it. If I'd stayed in the Senate I'd have seen him prosecuted for that!"

"It's a pity the voters of Minnesota didn't reelect you."

"Sometimes I wonder if democracy is a good thing," mused the secretary of state.

"You can't allow them to dominate the president!"

"I owe it to the country to try to make him see the light."

"But if you can't—"

"Then . . . I—" Harmon faltered.

"You must see that right is done. Distasteful it may be to displace the president, but you must not be deterred. Great leaders allow lesser considerations to fall by the wayside."

"I hope it doesn't come to that."

"I know you'll do what is right. You can count on my unswerving support!" He escorted him to the door.

They said goodbye. Manners returned to the sofa, satisfaction playing on his handsome features. The trap was set. The old fool believed he would support him for president. He lived in a dream world. The party would never nominate him again. But while Harmon might not be presidential timber anymore, he was influential enough to help bring down the biggest tree in the forest, especially if the tree was rotten with disease. With Krebs's backing, Manners could make those circumstances a reality. And if Krebs began making noises like a master, Manners had plans for him too. He settled back on the couch. It was all very satisfying.

II

The aurora borealis shone through the frost-encrusted window and danced on the thick, braided rug that kept the paralyzing cold from creeping up past the clapboard floor.

In his home, a few miles outside the far-north city of Archangel, Marshal Tiomkin nursed a cup of tea in his favorite hand-carved chair. Only the fireplace glow competed with the Northern Lights, a spectacle he had loved since he was a child. A huge, woolly Alsatian curled around his boots kept his feet toasty. He stroked its head. Being at home was a luxury these days.

He swirled the tea, a strong brew that looked like dark wood stain, and took another sip.

Soviet arms had not shone brightly in Africa. The Black Africans had proven tough opponents. The Americans had also discovered this, but their daring desert attack had made their humiliation less stinging.

But there were lessons to be learned. A quick resolution of differences by conventional means was becoming unfeasible. On earth all was stalemate. Tiomkin had long believed this, but Africa had proved it. The arena of decision was space. Only there did skill and strength count.

The tide was running toward America again, but if she was isolated, deprived of her space colonies, she would wither. The Unified Soviet State was almost ready to challenge her in that arena. The third battleship was due to launch in days.

Tiomkin had been impressed by the American Extraordinary Tactics Force. It had made him rethink his ideas about warfare and had set him rereading the Englishman Bertram Lambert-Healey. He had ordered every word written about the ETF and its General Keith passed on to the commander of the CosMarine Division, Pavel Orlov.

It seemed to Tiomkin that Keith's tactics would be even more pronounced on a playing field such as Luna. If a battalion trained in these tactics had proven decisive in Africa, three Soviet brigades ought to prove invincible on Luna.

The premier might be hard to convince. He saw the need for a space fleet but didn't comprehend that earth was destined to be a sideshow.

Tiomkin's immediate problems were his deputy, Wen Chin, and the bleeding ulcer of Black Africa. That ulcer was Chin's doing but Brasnikov had supported the adventure. Tiomkin had divorced himself as much as possible from it, keeping in mind that it was often dangerous not to share Brasnikov's enthusiasms.

After the collapse of Dana's armies, the Soviets had sliced deep into the interior. But the incision had festered. Commandos daily harassed them, led by one claiming to be Dana, whom everyone had thought dead. The guerrillas had given the Soviets an excuse to expand their pale to "preserve order."

Tiomkin had allowed Chin to maneuver himself to be put in charge of Africa. But to make the plan bear fruit required that Tiomkin become ill, almost unto death, so he had to retire to his home, to recover. He had decided to time his "illness" right after he ordered funding for Orlov's new special troops, whom he was calling the "Space Sharks." He would then recommend that Wen Chin fill his chair as minister of defense, and continue to command in Africa.

It was a dangerous move. If it worked, it would checkmate the nasty little Tatar. If it didn't, Tiomkin might find himself in operational command of his reading chair for good.

Which might not be so bad, he thought as his wife, Anya, poured his cup full again. She was a matronly woman with deep wrinkles and callused hands who had never been even pretty. But she gave him something plainness could not dim, nor physical beauty enhance. He loved her deeply. She rested her head on his shoulder and they held hands and together watched the Northern Lights.

III

Vice President Teresa Evangeline St. Clair climbed out of her indoor swimming pool and dried herself. She had just finished twenty laps and tingled all over from the exertion.

She examined her slim but robust body in the mirror: a body to cause envy in women twenty years her junior. She donned a robe and trailed water into her den. She fell into a leather chair.

She hadn't relaxed long when the holocube chimed. She masked the camera so she could see her caller without revealing herself.

"Teresa?" It was the Speaker of the House, Melvyn Fitzgerald Saratoga. He peered uncertainly from the holocube. "Aren't you decent?" He put on a satyrlike leer.

"Melvyn! I'm dripping on my rug and getting a chill!"

"All right!" said the Speaker with mock alarm. "I just got Jeff's speech, which he's delivering in an hour. Seen it?"

"I'm familiar with the contents."

"Did you ask him to wait until after the midterms?"

"Yes, I did. He didn't cotton to the notion."

"Lord, you're beginning to sound like Charley Macadew. Listen, I called to see if you thought a last-minute appeal by both of us might sway Jeffrey into postponing this atrocity?"

"He'll deliver it, and damn the consequences. If you want to know the truth, I'm glad!"

"What? You hot to be the first woman president?" He instantly regretted saying that. "Sorry, but you know I didn't mean it."

"You're forgiven. What I mean is, if we have rationing, it must be soon. Jeffrey would be wrong to postpone it. He is putting the nation above himself. I admire that, even though I tried to argue him out of it."

"I suppose you'd do the same in his place?"

"Absolutely."

"Maybe you and the president know something I don't. I can't see torpedoing your own presidency over a few weeks. But then, I'm a venal politician concerned only with winning elections."

"Why don't we both face the fact that Jeffrey's doing what's right, and that we're proud of him?"

"I guess that's probably best," he conceded. "His popularity is pretty high. It might survive this kind of blow."

"People will wait to see if things get worse before they look for someone to lynch."

"Jeff's a fighter. I hope we can save him. I had doubts about him, but in all my years in politics, he's the best, with apologies to your Uncle Bill. It took guts to send troops to Africa but it took more to ask the country to pin its future on a little satellite orbiting the sun!"

It was early evening. In a few minutes the President would deliver the speech. Already the tech people were clambering to get at him. He opened the door to the Rose Garden and stepped out. Summer odors were tangy and rich. A fat moon hung benevolently over the city, like a well-fed tabby digesting a bowl of milk.

The moon, where the last hope of mankind rested prior to making the leap across the void to the sun.

The three ships were now completed. The dedicated scientists were prepared to man them to their destination, dismantle them, and construct a space station from their bones. They were due to launch in two days. After that, the world was in their hands.

All I have to do, he thought, is keep things from falling apart until they succeed, or—he didn't let himself consider the alternative. If the Sunside Project failed, there was no future worth contemplating.

Chapter

* 37 *

I

That night they celebrated the completion of the *Euclid*, the last of the three spaceships.

Project members and their Selenite hosts gathered at the communal swimming pool. The colonists were nude bathers. Some Terrans balked at shedding their clothes; but most gleefully joined their hosts in the hot tubs or frolicked in the big pool.

The colonists had prepared a buffet of foods adapted to Luna, and examples of such cultural fads as *cucina dell'arte*. One table was devoted to the strange, compelling Martian "tech cuisine."

Typified by astringent plants that grew in greenhouses under pink skies, tech cuisine was dominated by Martian garlic, with bulbs the size of peaches. Hot as a jalapeño, its insidious heat intensified the more water you drank. Trace chemicals in Mars's soil made the garlic a benign addiction. Authorities had tried to outlaw its export but former Martians refused to do without it. That was why ninety-five percent of them ended up on the moon. The proper mate to tech cuisine was Martian wine, which tasted like vinegar.

The younger colonists gave a demonstration of rod dueling. Duelists were armed with metal rods with slightly electrified tips. They were amazingly graceful and agile, like ballet dancers. In the past the sport had been outlawed because of the practice of clandestine duels with high voltage to settle quarrels.

After the bout ended, Jacob Kane lifted a tall frosted glass. "Ladies and gentlemen, I give you Jason Scott. Congratulations upon completing the first rung!"

Scott looked uncomfortable. He was still in his fatigues.

"This may be the last opportunity we have to drag Jason from work. So implant this moment in your memories."

"Thank you," said Scott. "Despite an increased work load, we finished ahead of time. You all deserve every bit of relaxation you can get before lift-off. I'm sorry, but I can't stay. I have some more work to attend to—"

"Not tonight, Jason," said Kane. Several burly construction navvies, led by Matt Taylor, rushed Scott, stripped him, and dumped him in the deep end, where he made languid, slow-moving, low-gravity waves. He surfaced, sputtering, and made for the side.

"I guess I'll stay, after all," he said.

Madeline Reed and Rene Delner lazed at poolside. Madeline was nude and golden brown, and mischievously aware of her effect, stretched out invitingly, red hair marvelously unkempt, falling on round shoulders. Delner wore a one-piece suit, but her severe expression fended off most suitors.

"Where is your young man this evening?"

"You mean Michael? He can't make it tonight. Extra duty."

"You don't seem to be pining away, do you, dear?"

"Michael's nice," said Madeline. "But I don't love him."

"You like sleeping with him, but don't want a permanent relationship."

"That's right, Rene. We're compatible, natural, uninhibited lovers. But I can't imagine him as a life companion."

"Well, that's honest." A slight, condescending smile tugged at Rene's thin lips. "Do I take that to mean you don't want such a companion, or that Michael is just not the one?"

"Both." Madeline looked at her toes and wriggled them. "I'm still young." She looked at Rene Delner archly. "You're one to talk about casual relationships. What about Victor Ames?" She glanced at the heavily muscled man swimming with powerful strokes.

"He's just someone I see." Red spots blotched her cheeks.

"You *do* sleep with him!"

"I never said that."

She touched a bruise on Rene's shoulder. "Victor's violent. Jason almost fired him for brawling." She lowered her voice. "Is that why you wore the one-piece suit? To hide the bruises?"

"Mind your own business, Madeline!"

"Okay, your private life is your own. But you're walking on a tightrope. He's mean. A lady with your class deserves better."

"Has it occurred to you I might encourage his behavior?"

Madeline's eyes widened. Rene returned the look calmly. Madeline let her breath out. "No, that didn't occur to me."

"Things aren't always as they seem. I take care of myself."

Madeline, who considered herself a sophisticate, had to work hard to keep her voice level. The nonchalant way Rene Delner had revealed a dark part of her soul was both frightening and sickening. She decided to change the subject.

Jason Scott climbed from the pool, slipped into a robe, and ambled over to the buffet table.

Madeline's eyes followed him. "If I wanted a permanent relationship, it would be with him. He's drop-dead gorgeous. Too bad Bethany Williams has that field to herself."

"She's wasting her time. He's a professional bachelor, too involved with his work to get involved with a woman."

"Perhaps he hasn't found the right one."

"Many have tried, my dear."

"I admire him enormously! He's a great man. I've never met anyone less hypocritical, who lives life according to strict ethics. It's refreshing to find a person at peace with himself."

"Fascinating! I hadn't thought you held such deep thoughts."

"That's because you never bothered to find out."

Sherlock Michlanski bobbed like a cork with a tray of delicacies beside him.

"Cowardice is the most valuable human instinct," he said, stuffing a sandwich in his mouth. Next to him was a voluptuous blonde Selenite.

Dorian Nye sat self-consciously at the pool's edge, stirring water with his skinny legs.

"I th-think you underrate humanity, Sherry," said Nye slowly. "Altruism is the instinct that separates us from the beasts."

"I agree." The girl turned her body such that Michlanski almost went under. He marveled at the miracle of Lunar gravity.

"Sorry." He recovered his composure. "I missed that."

She grinned archly. "I said altruism motivates us to care for our sick, lame, or old people. We feel pity and sorrow upon the death of loved ones, or even beloved pets."

Michlanski waved aside that argument imperiously. "Apes feel grief," he said. "Porpoises help wounded comrades stay afloat at risk to themselves. Perhaps altruism is a suicidal trait. No other species preserves its unfit to perpetuate weak genes. I say cowardice helps the species. We cowards tend to survive, while our braver, stupider fellows die."

"Are you a coward?"

"Certainly! The Greeks commanded us to know ourselves. No one knows better than I that the man who floats before you quakes at the thought of risking his fat limbs in any dangerous undertaking. I'm a quivering mass of self-preservation."

"Y-yet you ride in space shuttles and you'll soon be living on a space station," Nye pointed out. "That's risky."

"I can calculate that. Spacecraft are statistically safer than aircars. But ask me to take an uncalculated risk, to enter unknown territory, and I will quail. Ask Kane."

Kane stood at the edge of the pool. "Yes, Sherlock, you are a disgusting specimen of selfish timidity and a gelatinous mass of quivering flab ready to collapse at the slightest pressure."

"Put that in your pipe and smoke it, Dr. Nye!" Michlanski looked placidly at Kane. "The psychiatric profession lost a man of rare compassion when you became an engineer, Jacob."

"What sort of discussion have I intruded upon?"

"We were debating what is the most important characteristic of man. That which separates him from animals."

"Dr. Nye and I maintain it is altruism. Sherlock says it's cowardice," said the woman.

"You're both wrong," said Kane. "Mankind is the only race that wastes time on philosophical discussions when a desirable woman without clothes on is within reach."

She laughed. "Surely you have an opinion, Mr. Kane."

Light glittered off his coal-black eyes. "I believe man's most important characteristic is will. To ruthlessly cut away impedimenta and do what needs to be done, no matter whom it hurts, or what it costs."

"Are you a student of Friedrich Nietzsche, Mr. Kane?"

"I have no time for philosophy. I formulated my creed from observations, and from what little I know of history and society."

"Jacob is being uncharacteristically modest, so you'd better watch out," said Michlanski. "He did a master's thesis entitled 'The Meaning of the Universe.' It was laboriously researched and annotated. He's read Nietzsche, Hume, Kant, Hegel, Schopenhauer, Kierkegaard, all the Germans. He remembers *everything* he reads." He smiled sweetly. "Don't you, Jacob?"

"My chapter on human history was small," said Kane tightly.

"Still, it's an interesting view of life." She regarded Kane with obvious interest. She climbed out of the pool. "Predatory. Ruthless. The vitality of life and struggle."

"We should discuss it further. Besides, it's unwise to be in the vicinity when Michlanski goes into a feeding frenzy."

"I'm Sandra." She dried herself, slipped into a diaphanous garment that veiled enough so she could be in public, yet hid less than would be covered by an airbrush in a men's magazine.

They linked arms and wandered away from the pool.

"Zerrk!" said Michlanski to Nye, who was rubbing his bald pate absentmindedly. "Another nifty philosophical discussion down the tubes!" He sighed and chewed on another sandwich.

II

"I'm afraid I've been stealing beautiful women from Sherlock for most of our lives." They took a path that led through a park toward what passed for "nightlife," a short block of pubs, cafés, and Luna's version of four-star cuisine.

"You sound like all you do is prey upon women, Mr. Kane."

"It does take up a significant part of my life. I have old-fashioned ideas about women, which have nothing to do with opening doors for them or spreading my cloak upon a mud hole."

"I had guessed that you have a singular philosophy."

"I believe women are like grapes that produce a superior vintage. The more thoroughly the grapes are crushed, the more pleasing the final product."

"Mr. Kane, you make a Neanderthal look progressive."

"I accept as a compliment what others would take as an insult. Buy you a drink?" They had come to the Crescent Moon, a bar where a band of Selenites played regressive jazz.

"Wine."

They sat at the bar and while Sandra discussed the obscure points of a sexual philosopher of the Arabian Malibu School, Kane's eyes were drawn to another woman, which surprised even Kane, since she was completely clothed.

She was in her early twenties, with an unconscious dignity, without arrogance or egotism, but with simple, natural grace, as uncommon as it was attractive. It was beauty without adornment, nor needing it. She wore no makeup, no jewelry, no special contact lenses, no hands painted to identify with a cause.

She was not a Lunar colonist. The way she held herself suggested familiarity with a much lower gravity, like one of the Jovian moons. She was drinking what smelled like hazelnut liquor from a crescent-shaped cocktail glass.

"Jacob Kane!" said Sandra sharply.

"What?" He didn't hide the fact he was admiring another woman.

"This particular wine does not wear well left alone. It needs to be decanted almost immediately."

"Then I suggest that you put a cork in it!" He wasn't about to give her the upper hand. "Wines are best stored horizontally."

He caught the eye of the mystery woman and stared, unabashed, expecting her to give in. They looked at each other for several moments, as if sharing a private joke.

When he looked back, Sandra was gone.

"Your friend left," said the bartender, freshening his drink.

"She's outside the bar. She wants me to think she left."

"I think she's gone," said the mystery woman, who put a tiny gold piece on the bar. She walked by and the dim lights caught her just so. She was slimmer than he had thought, with long legs. Auburn hair cascaded around her shoulders like a dreamy waterfall caught by a late afternoon sun and turned into molten metal.

"If I hadn't been staring at you, she would never have gone."

"Where I come from, women don't put up with your kind of behavior. They'd open you up with their mining drills."

"Charming. Where do you come from, a colony of bees?"

"No, of self-reliant, independent people. I live on an asteroid."

"Really? Can I buy you a drink?"

"No."

"Buy me one, then?"

"Sorry. I'm afraid I must go to bed early tonight—"

"I can fit that into my plans."

"No thank you." She pushed him away firmly. Kane guessed she could have done a lot more if he had resisted.

"When will I see you again?"

"You won't." She paused at the door. "And don't bother looking for me outside, because I won't be waiting."

"I'll bet you won't," he said, raising his glass in salute. Nevertheless he half expected that she would be, and he was doubly disappointed to discover that Sandra had gone too.

He shrugged. There were still plenty of nude Selenites back at the party.

III

Victor Ames catapulted himself from the pool, performed a somersault, and landed on his feet. He rubbed his chest, matted with thick black hair, and shook himself like a dog. He sauntered over to where Madeline Reed and Rene Delner were relaxing and stood with one foot on Madeline's beach towel. His muscular arms bowed away from his torso while water pooled at his feet.

"Very nice, Victor." Madeline didn't hide her distaste.

Ames boldly caressed her with his eyes, until she looked away with a jerk of her head. He chuckled and turned to Rene.

"I'll be back." He leaned over and kissed her roughly, letting his thick hands fall on her shoulders. When he pulled away she was breathing hard. She watched him leave, ropy muscles knotting and relaxing with each stride.

Jacob Kane met Matt Taylor, who acted like a man with a purpose. "Seen Scott?" he demanded in his rich Louisiana drawl.

"Not in the last half hour. Why?"

"I have to talk to him."

"You can tell me." He sensed that Taylor was hiding something.

"I don't know. I guess it's okay. I'm not too keen on telling you this, Kane, but somebody's got to know."

"Your trust in me is touching."

"Truth be told, Scott's the only man I truly trust. We been discussing the accidents we've been having. I've had suspicions, but nothing I could prove. But I had a couple of people watched.''

"Without telling Jason? Naughty! What'd you find out?''

"Victor Ames has left the party and suited up to go out to the construction site.''

"He's a subforeman, isn't he?''

"Work's completed. He has no business out there.''

"You think he's the saboteur?''

"I'll find out.'' He rubbed his hands together. "If he is—''

"Jason won't let you. Why don't we see if you're right?''

"Mr. Scott won't like it.''

"If you're wrong, he won't know. But if you're right—''

"He likes doin' things lawful. He won't thank us for roughin' up Ames, even if we get him to talk.''

"Do you want to catch Ames in the act or not?''

"You're a sly one. We'll try it. Maybe we can get him to talk before we give him over to Colonel Drew.'' He grinned.

The Lunar tractor scuttled across the boneyard plain toward squatting shapes that reared out of the gray dust into the black sky. The trio of spaceships, half in darkness at the close of the long Lunar day, threw shadows behind them like daggers.

The tractor's driver did not look back and didn't see a second tractor leave the colony for the construction site.

He showed his credentials to the guard at the gate to the site and said he was making a final inspection.

Ames took an elevator halfway up the *Euclid* to scaffolding that still encircled the ship. He was not challenged. He carried a small bomb with a time fuse, which he intended to place at the crucial joint of one of the three wide legs supporting the ship. When the bomb detonated, the leg would be weakened enough to collapse under the ship's weight.

Ames had no illusions of maintaining anonymity. Too many had seen him leave the party. Too many had seen him on the site. But he would be gone long before the explosion. He had several days of air in the tractor. A spaceship waited a hundred miles away. He could lose himself in the barren lunarscape before a search began.

To reach the critical joint, Ames had to climb off the catwalk encircling the ship, down to a platform built to support welders. On earth he might have experienced vertigo, but on the moon it was like playing on a large jungle gym.

He reached the joint and began attaching the package. He didn't see two figures creep down the ladder onto the platform. He felt the vibration through his boots and turned.

Trapped! They blocked his only escape route, unless he chose to jump to the Lunar floor, a hundred meters below.

One of them motioned Ames away from the bomb with a laser handgun. The other examined the package and disarmed it. The man with the laser made a sign for Ames to turn on his radio.

"Well, Victor," said Kane, "we have you, don't you think?"

"Kane?" He couldn't make out features through the faceplate.

Kane bowed. "Your servant! Don't waste time. It's obvious what you're doing. Whom do you work for, Victor?"

"What are you talking about? I came up here on a last-minute inspection and found this. I was going to disarm it—"

"Talk quickly, or you won't be able to talk at all."

Ames laughed harshly. "I've nothing to say. You have no proof. You must turn me over to the authorities."

"A faulty assumption. We're going to chat before the colonial authorities hear anything. Go over to the edge and look down. It's a long way, even for the moon. Like falling fifty feet or more on earth. Would you survive? It's an interesting problem."

Ames was no coward, but the cool way Kane discussed his death made him shudder. He forced himself to sound confident. "You won't make me jump. You need my information."

"True." Kane fired a beam that singed Ames's suit above his collarbone. Ames stifled a scream and reached for the spot, where mist was escaping through the blackened fabric into the vacuum.

Kane directed another shot at his right leg. Ames howled with rage and pain and clasped his leg to stop the escaping air. But his blood did that, freezing in the vacuum to make a painful sealant. "Make it easy on yourself, Victor. Talk!" said Kane reasonably. "I can keep this up for hours. I doubt that you can."

Ames's hands worked and he started for Kane, who aimed the gun at his chest. Something between a whine and growl escaped the burly man's agonized lips and he stopped, swaying.

"Back up, Victor. Unless you like death better than life."

"I'm saying nothing," said Ames through torn lips.

"Such a stubborn man." Kane fired again. Ames convulsed until he was covered with a dozen burns, each slowly leaking oxygen.

"I've watched this long enough!" said Taylor.

"Shut up, Matt! I'm not doing anything different from what you'd do if he was in your power. Except you'd use your fists."

"That's different! This is—torture."

"I know men who could reduce you to putty in five minutes with fists. Pain is the universal persuader. This is a simple way to apply it without killing him. It's *supposed* to hurt, idiot!"

Taylor pointed toward the plain to where three vehicles were approaching. "You'll have to stop now!"

"Damn!" Kane whirled on Ames. "Talk, or before they get here I'll burn you so bad you'll be sorry you didn't die."

"Go to hell!" Ames swayed dizzily. Kane came toward him, laser leveled at his chest. The big man retreated, sobered through his haze of pain by what he sensed as a murderous intent.

"Stop it, we want him alive!" shouted Taylor.

"Want—him—alive," Kane repeated tonelessly. He stopped. Ames was at the edge of the platform. He took a deep breath and let it out. "Thanks, Matt. I almost went too far."

Ames sprang at Kane, shrieking. Instinctively Kane used the laser butt to shatter his faceplate. Ames staggered back, his mouth working soundlessly. He fell off the platform.

Every nightmare Kane had had about falling struck him in that instant. He felt himself twisting, twisting, dangling—falling from an airplane— or, most terrifying, into an abyss. Ames's plunge seemed to take forever. It was bad enough to watch someone fall to his death. Quite another level of horror to watch it stretch out into a long moment. To see Ames twist and writhe in every imaginable configuration, all, of course, to no avail.

His grotesquely twisting body struck the dark gray ground.

"That's unfortunate," Kane said in a normal voice.

"I thought *I* was cold. This is murder, pure and simple," said Taylor. "You tortured him until he was insane with pain."

"Don't waste your pity. Hundreds could've died if he'd gotten away with it. And don't think you'll pin murder on me. Anything I did, you did. We came here without telling Jason. We share the responsibility for Ames's death. That's what you'll tell them."

"You ain't human, Kane."

"Of course I am," he said as if talking to a child. "I operate under different ethics. By my ethics it's no crime to torture or kill someone who is trying to disrupt our project, which will ultimately benefit mankind in incalculable ways.''

"God help you.''

"I stand before my mythical creator, without shame.''

The tractors arrived and Kane went down to meet them.

Chapter
* **38** *

Jason Scott looked up from his desk. He had circles under his eyes. He motioned Kane to sit and regarded him sadly.

"Why did you do it? Why did you torture him?"

"To find out who was behind the sabotage."

"You didn't feel that was the job of the authorities?"

Kane's lip curled. "Ames was hard as steel. Special persuasion was needed. He reacted unpredictably. But he killed himself as surely as if he jumped."

"Is that how you rationalize it to yourself?"

"I don't nurture self-doubts or worry about the death of scum like Ames. I'm sorry he's dead because we may never find out who is behind the sabotage. But his life was meaningless."

"You expect me to save you, don't you?"

Kane smiled grimly. "That wouldn't fit in with your morals. You couldn't cover up for 'murder,' even to protect the project."

"Then you understand." He sounded agonized.

"I'd no more expect you to abandon your ethics than I would expect an eagle to feed on vegetables. Yet after all these years you still judge me by *your* standards. You insist on thinking me part of *your* civilization, when I stand above it. I live, I work, and when threatened, I kill."

"Alfred once told me there was great good in you, Jacob. Sometimes I see it glimmering, but today it's very hard to see."

Kane sneered, and for a moment Scott saw the little boy who put rocks in snowballs. "Nobody ever said being a little tin god was easy."

"I won't intercede." Scott fought back an angry reply, made his voice neutral. "The project can survive without you."

"Wrong!" Kane pointed his finger at Scott. "I'm one who counts, and you know it. You can't do without me any more than Hammer's Spike could do without Hammer!"

Kane stalked out of the office. Scott knew he was right. He hadn't felt so miserable in ages. He had anguished on how to respond to Kane's vile (necessary?) act every since he had gotten the report. Scott, who prided himself on keeping situations under control, had lost control. He was confused and angry. The last time he had felt this bad was the month he left college. Kane, damn him, had recalled all that with his reference to the man he knew was Scott's hero: Jonathan Hammer.

For three days he had driven up the coast of California. A fever burned in his mind. Four weeks ago it became so unbearable he dropped out of college, without a word to anyone.

Since then he and the motorcycle had been one, like a centaur. He drove all day, lashed by wind, sun, and sometimes rain, taking hairpin curves by throwing his machine almost parallel to the road, so its gyroscopes whined. At the end of the day he dashed himself to the ground to sleep, beastlike.

He was tired of hypocrisy, easy answers, facile motivations. He was an engineer! He wanted to learn an art, a craft, not a con. He wasn't taught to carve new worlds from the wilderness, to blaze trails, but to please the masses and plutocrats.

The end came when his comfortable, superior professor attacked the acknowledged greatest engineer of the age: Hammer.

He ridiculed Hammer's great statue *Triumph* and his bridge that spanned an estuary near Oregon's northern border, the incomparable Hammer's Spike. Built of Osirium, the new metal of a new age, the Spike stretched engineering, with gossamer trusses and towers that seemed to end in the heavens. Yet it was as stable as a mountain. It was the Sistine Chapel of bridges. An altar to the Mind of Man.

But Jonathan Hammer died a pauper. *Triumph* was finished just before the terrorists bombed San Diego, making it a macabre joke. He tried to rebuild his career with the most impressive engineering project of the age, but his genius was condemned as eccentricity, his originality hooted as grotesque and incomprehensible to the common man.

The professor called Hammer a failure. "He is a model—of what to avoid. The Spike was really the last nail in his coffin.

"When we consider the travails technology has brought us—whole species destroyed by science—I don't think we as a nation or race have anything to feel 'triumphant' about.

"It is unfortunate Osirium was invented. At this time in history, we don't need visionaries. We need serious plodders. Engineers to build functional structures—not fanatics who don't realize that too much knowledge can be a dangerous thing."

Jason stalked from the classroom to avoid smashing the professor into the floor. The professor, of course, didn't know that he was the son of the infamous Adam Scott, whose scientific genius and philosophy he was indirectly attacking.

Since he had whipped onto Highway 101 Scott hadn't had a coherent thought. If the road that snaked between rocky cliffs had suddenly vanished, he would have driven into the Pacific without a blink.

The warm beaches of the decadent south gave way to cold, rocky cliffs that were more starkly beautiful the farther north of San Francisco he drove. The salty spray was freezing as it blew into his face, pasting his bright red hair to his forehead in greasy tendrils.

Late in the afternoon he rounded a long curve of a cliff and saw it. Hammer's Spike.

He crossed the span. Blood pounded in his head. On the other side he took a left turn that led to a spit of land under the bridge. He got off the cycle and walked to a rock seawall that overlooked the sound that passed under the bridge. Through the supports he saw a dirty, faded town that made its living from the sea, built into the side of a hill with a bay thrust into it.

The arches and weblike trusses of the Spike soared over his left shoulder. To the right the seawall merged into a tongue of man-made land that extended half a mile into the ocean before curving inland to shelter the bay. This rock mole took the full brunt of waves born in the wild Arctic.

Two couples strolled along the seawall, admiring the view until the spray chased them to their cars and they drove away.

He was alone. Calm gradually descended, like a soft blanket draped on his shoulders. He felt totally receptive. His body was transparent, like crystal. His mind was a tuning fork, ready to vibrate at a touch.

He became conscious of the richness his senses brought him. The sun was starting down. Twilight had always been an almost mystical part of the day to him. He felt, rather than saw, light draining from the air, sinking into the sand.

As it soaked into the sand, it absorbed all pain, all doubts. The water under the bridge passed up and under the waves, up and under, in a rhythm attuned to the flow of his blood. The glassy water changed from milky blue, to gray, ashen gray, purple, and finally ink. All the colors of the world mixed and swirled in that ink, and danced on it, and flashed.

Far away the ocean splintered against the seawall, sending a million white shards into the air. As it became darker, he heard only the pounding, more and more distant until it was a feeble touch on his consciousness.

The lights of the town came on. Magically, all the dinginess and commonness of the place was replaced, as if a clay town had been painted with light and dark into a chiaroscuro masterpiece.

His attention focused on minute details. On wave interference patterns stroking the nearest leg of the bridge, or caressing the sand directly below the seawall he leaned against.

A pattern of lights resolved into a returning fishing boat, its low-voiced chugging, its bow shouldering aside the water.

The craft was a quarter mile away, but a strange quality of sound over water brought him the life of the boat as if he were standing on it. He thought he could make sense out of the quiet voices. He imagined he smelled fresh coffee, shared in comradeship, the smell of the day's catch, oil and gasoline from the engine.

It was dark. There were no stars, except lights lining the bridge that arched over him. He swallowed convulsively, and realized he hadn't had a drop of moisture since he climbed on the motorcycle that morning.

He felt more alive than ever before. He was fulfilled. He had purpose. He felt peace.

He looked up at the bridge and tears welled. It didn't matter that Hammer died without honors or riches. His life had transcended such artificial measurements of worth. He did what no one else had ever done before. In the doing he had fed his own soul, and perhaps neglected his body. But he guaranteed that no kindred soul, seeing his work, ever needed to hunger.

Jason Scott nourished himself, and cleansed himself, and girded himself for the struggle ahead. If he never again experienced such a moment, it was enough. . . .

Jason Scott's face was wet from the memory. He knew he was going to have to do something for Kane. But what?

Chapter
* 39 *

I

As the shuttle left the LEO station for reentry over North America, Jacob Kane felt deadly gravity beginning to have its way with him as he was strapped to his flight couch.

"Ames is getting his revenge!" he muttered, thrashing in discomfort, smelling his own sweat, mixed with the antiseptic, rubbery scent of the shuttle. A smell that crawled into the essence of his being, clung to his tongue, contaminated even the distilled water of his flight suit.

No, he decided. It wasn't Ames. It was Jason.

He fought the pain in his chest by sleeping, helped by illegal SoHi drugs. He didn't relax, he just had bad dreams. . . .

Jacob awoke to a buzzing, as if a large angry insect in cotton wadding were packed between his ears. The room was dark. A blanket hung from the curtain rod to block out daylight.

The woman in bed with him sighed in her sleep and flung a brown arm across his hairless chest. He regarded it with distaste. At close quarters, without rosy glasses of alcohol and lust, Kane found her ordinary.

He remembered she had a fine body and lifted the sheets to confirm it. Her face lacked distinction, but beauty was subordinate to Kane's need to sate his passions regularly.

He squinted at the clock. Eleven. The party had gone on until dawn, celebrating his earning a bachelor's degree in under three years. Many people had showed up, not because they liked him, but because he was a lavish host, who always had interesting guests.

Two of the most interesting were his old schoolmates Jason and Sherlock. But, strangely, neither had done much for the party.

Jason had drifted with his head in the clouds, his habit since he had left college. Kane considered that a poor move. The paper chase was a crock, but the diploma unlocked many doors. More important, it gave a financial leg up. Jason had put principles over money. That was just plain stupid.

Jason had obviously been working hard. His shoulders were broad, his waist slim. He had a deep tan and callused hands. He left early, pleading that he had to rise at dawn. Kane was not sorry. Scott's air of crusader, prophet, and madman and his laborer's appearance did not mix well with the kind of people Kane wanted to cultivate.

Sherlock, usually the yeast that lifted any party, was, this time, too damned eccentric. He hadn't learned to tone down his intellect to fit the audience. Sometimes, influenced by alcohol or a pretty girl, in a burst of youthful hubris, he would launch a pyrotechnical display that was part brilliant philosopher, part poet, part cosmologist. Some people could read a phone book and be entertaining. This time, Sherlock was not one of those people. His intellect was arresting, but after a while he lost it. It was like James Joyce reading to a class of second graders. One or two might respond to the cadences of a master of language, without understanding. The rest would twist in their seats.

Kane had wandered past a slightly inebriated Sherlock whose audience had shrunk to an unattractive young woman. When he passed again, Michlanski was alone, precariously propped against the wall. He muttered something. Kane leaned closer.

"She lay spread before me like an open-faced sandwich!"

Kane decided to call a taxi. The party went downhill from there. The only bit of light in the gloom was when he finally got the girl he had lusted after all night into his bedroom.

He decided she would sleep until awakened, so he drew back the sheet and gave her bottom a resounding slap. His rule was never to sleep twice in a row with the same woman.

The woman dressed, threw him a poisonous glare, and slammed the door behind her. Kane winced and locked the door.

After half a pot of coffee he began to feel human. He looked in the mirror. Aside from bloodshot eyes he was presentable. He had just enough time to make his appointment.

II

Strubeck leaned against a tree. He chewed on a grass spring and watched a towering cumulus driven before high-altitude winds.

His face was deeply lined. White hair blew in downy tufts. He was in his fifties, but looked fifteen years older. He moved like an old man too, measuring each step. Is that a price he pays for brilliance? Kane thought. Does nature demand debits for her gifts?

"I'm happy to see you, Jacob!"

"Not as much as I, Dr. Strubeck." Kane felt a twinge. He was such an emotionless creature that he didn't recognize his affection for the aging man. "Did you attend the graduation?"

"Do you need to ask that, Jacob?" The old man shook his head with disbelief. "To miss your graduation would be like ignoring a son, if I had one. I'm sorry I didn't speak to you, but you swept off so quickly with your friends—

"I'm glad we could meet. I'm curious about your plans. I know what Jason and Sherlock are doing, but not you." He looked at him artlessly. "I'm really interested, you know."

"I know. I'm already at work on my master's. I've even decided the theme for my thesis: 'The Meaning of the Universe.' "

"Isn't that a bit overambitious?" said Strubeck gently.

"Comprehensive." Kane found himself somewhat impatient at his former teacher's chiding, Socratic approach. It was, Kane felt, condescending to someone of his demonstrable intellectual gifts. "It will," he said, "integrate all previous theories on the origin, formation, and ultimate destiny of the universe and reach conclusions about the ultimate meaning of cosmology. I think you'll find it revolutionary. I intend to publish it later."

"When will you finish?"

"A year."

"It took God five hundred years to do his, and he was dictating."

"You're not taking me seriously!"

He chuckled. "You're making it hard on yourself. The review board will automatically be prejudiced by your hubris in explaining the universe to them."

Kane smiled a crafty smile. "Suppose I do a superlative job, and open new roads of thought, new routes of speculation?"

"Then you'll really be in trouble," said Strubeck with a wry grin. "Of course, I expect no less from you."

"That's what I wanted to hear."

"What will you do when you get your master's?"

"I have a job offer, from Python. From Krebs himself."

"Krebs is a ruthless man," said Strubeck, frowning. "A criminal."

"He is a shrewd businessman who doesn't mind breaking a few idiot laws when they stand in his way."

"I stand corrected."

"You, of all people, should understand!" snapped Kane. "Or are you ashamed because you stood by while Adam Scott defied government decrees? Krebs was Scott's right hand."

"Aren't you suspicious how Krebs profited from Scott's death? How he ended up with exclusive rights to Osirium?"

"He outsmarted McClaren! Krebs is on the cutting edge of new ideas. He backed Jonathan Hammer's bridge—"

"Yes, and Hammer died a pauper."

"I *know* Krebs will use me, and throw me away, if I let him. But I won't. Python will be the perfect growth medium. It will be the hot fire I require to remove the impurities in my makeup. I'll emerge like a steel blade, keen and strong."

"And what end will you wield yourself to?"

"You must know that your goals are mine," said Kane earnestly. "To be at the forefront of man's expansion. Man must go to the stars, but men are lemmings. Without men like you and me, they'll tumble mindlessly into the ocean for eternity. A few geniuses with the will to act will lead mankind to its destiny."

Strubeck shook his head sternly. "Jacob, don't make that mistake. You're not some superman, or elite mind. Sometimes people must be led. In my way I'm guilty of your arrogance. But it's too easy for an intellectual to set himself up as a tin god. Too easy to confuse prejudices with facts. Resist the temptation. Be ruthless if you must, but don't enjoy it. That's fatal."

Jacob laughed. "I can't help being me. Do you object if your goals are achieved by my means? Does it matter if God or Satan is responsible for creation? It's there, we may as well enjoy it.''

As they parted, Kane saw Strubeck was disturbed. But that didn't alter his mind. He loved Strubeck as a father, but the scientist was impractical. His was a dream world of nice women and chivalrous gentlemen, who fought for honor and beauty. That world had never existed. King Arthur's knights had sweaty armpits and rode their horses over peasants. It was foolish to think otherwise.

Chapter

* 40 *

I

It would be wrong to say that Sherlock Michlanski had ever looked gaunt, but he had lost enough weight that he actually had cheekbones; for him, that was like he had been at death's door.

"We're leaving without Jacob?"

"I announced that at several staff meetings. What more do you need?" snapped Jason Scott, wearing his panorama eye prosthesis and absorbing input from a dozen screens that ringed his desk.

"Too much data can shut you off from the world, Jason."

"When did you discover that, Sherry? You've been cooped up in that lab of yours for weeks, with no contact with anyone."

A momentary smile of childlike gentleness passed Michlanski's lips. "It's beautiful, Jason. Strubeck's equations are beautiful. They're gorgeous! I've never had so much fun in my life—ever!"

"This is deadly serious!" said Scott furiously. "If we don't start moving people off planet in a couple of years, earth will destroy itself. If people find out we're gambling with their lives, they'll tear us to pieces. If we don't produce the drive, we have to explain why Strubeck's equations only feed a few thousand people.''

"I am very serious," said Michlanski with dignity. "But I wonder about you. Letting Jacob go just when we need him. You owe him more than that. Or at least so it seems to me."

"*You* don't know about us. You weren't there when we worked together." Scott was livid, something Michlanski couldn't recall ever seeing. "What makes you think you know? Who told you?"

"You did. And Jacob did."

"The stories coincided?" Scott sneered. "That surprises me."

"It doesn't me. Jacob is a remarkably transparent man, for those who know how to arrange the stage lighting. . . .''

"I suppose you expect me to hire you because I was your father's friend?" boomed Horatius Krebs.

The stocky young man with flaming unruly hair bisected by a white streak made him uneasy. He didn't like that, or the young man, but he hadn't ordered him thrown out of the tent . . . yet.

From his camp chair he studied Jason Scott. He saw the father in the son. Not that anyone but Adam Scott would have bedded that cold bitch, thought Krebs, who each day manufactured new reasons to hate the man and woman who had helped make him a success.

"So you're an engineer," he said sarcastically when Scott ignored his first question.

"Yes sir, I am."

"Self-taught? Huh? Supposed to impress me, because that's like me. Well, it doesn't." He grabbed his hands and turned them palms up. He was disappointed to see they were heavily callused.

"You want something to match your talents and experience? Perhaps project manager for our Tubeway tunnel here. I'm sure you could take over immediately, don't you?" His strawberry nose turned red from all that sarcasm.

"Would you like to skip the crap, Mr. Krebs?"

"Let's do that." Krebs bared his teeth in an imitation smile. "You expect an easy job because of Daddy. I'm supposed to get all weepy about the tragic rich kid. Well, if I hire you, you'll sweat every dime. I don't have little princes in my organization, and don't even think of telling me what I 'owe' you because of Adam. I built what's mine." He stopped pacing. "Still want a job?"

"It depends on your offer—and whether I have to listen to a lecture from you every morning before breakfast."

"Why you—" Krebs laughed harshly. "Okay, let's see what you're made of, other than smart-ass mouth. There's a crew at the south end of the tunnel—which runs under the Mojave Desert. They break rocks, with dynamite and jackhammers, but mainly with their insides. It's not pleasant work and I doubt you'll be able to stick it out for more than a day."

"Would that be the crew Mr. Brandon bosses?"

"Yeah, you know Brandon? Well, it won't do you any good—"

"Call and ask him about a man named Protho, Donald Protho."

"I don't like games, Scott—"

"It's no game, Mr. Krebs. Go ahead, call him."

Krebs dialed with quick punches of his stubby finger.

"Brandon? Krebs. What do you know about Donald Protho? Yeah? Your best man? How long has he worked for you? Six months?" Comprehension dawned. "Describe him. Yeah, okay." He hung up. "No, I don't guess you have a twin." He sat and chewed on a piece of bacon. "Cute trick. Brandon says you've increased efficiency at his end by fifty percent. You may be foreman material—"

"I'm an engineer. I've proved I know my job in the pits. If you won't give me an engineer's job, I'll go elsewhere."

"I'll give a man enough rope to hang himself. Matter of fact I'll pair you with another young smart-ass. Maybe you'll wear the rough edges off each other. Or kill each other. Either way I'm minus a smart-ass or two." The entrance darkened as a figure bent to enter. "Speak of the devil." He smiled unpleasantly at the lean, dark young man. "Jacob Kane, meet your Gemini twin."

II

"You finessed Krebs, but I'm damned if he didn't find us nastier jobs than breaking rocks." Kane's face was streaked with black as he and Scott inched along the steel latticework that held up the Banker Tunnel. A false step would plummet them seventy-five feet into darkness. "He hates you. He'll destroy you any way he can."

"Why did he send you along?"

Kane grunted as he crossed between two girders. "He and I are alike.

322 ✳

He's throwing this at me to make me tougher. But you—I think he'll throw things at you to kill you.''

'' 'That which does not kill me makes me stronger.' ''

"Quoting Nietzsche? He's not your type. He's more my type.''

Scott focused his hard-hat lamp on a girder. "Look at this—it's supposed to be laser-fused. Examine it closely.''

Balancing precariously, Kane brought his sharp face close to the girder. He used a laser cutting tool to slice green Osirium shavings from the seam between the two girders. After several passes with the laser rounded shapes were exposed.

"It's riveted and covered with a layer of solder! Somebody's fudging safety standards to save hours. Let's see how far this goes. This could get us in good with Krebs. Congratulations.''

"What if he doesn't like what we find?''

"He will. Krebs is a lot of things, but he's not unscrupulous enough to save money ignoring safety standards.''

"What if he is?''

"Look, Jason, I'll go head-to-head with Krebs on this with you if I have to. Does that make you happy?''

"No. I wouldn't expect anything less.''

III

"You two may be useful, after all,'' said Krebs, seated at his tent desk. "If the feds catch us riveting girders instead of fusing them for a Tubeway they'd hang us out to dry.''

"What about Ganning?'' said Kane softly.

"Ganning's gone. Only an idiot tries a trick that can be linked to him if it goes wrong. He fed me a story that Osirium requires such high temperature to fuse that it's impractical to use anything but rivets on some sections. You'll take his place.''

"Thank you.''

"Make sure this sort of thing doesn't happen again. I'm hard to please when it comes to safety.'' His expression became foxy. "However, I don't expect you to be a fanatic.''

"What do you mean?''

"Certain sections of the project you won't need to monitor. That means less work for you. Also, when you see something that isn't kosher, bring it to me first, understand?''

Kane's eyes gleamed. "You mean a safety violation that can't be traced to you is preferable to one that can."

"One that can't be traced to either of us is even better."

"Definitely."

"What you don't know about, you don't have to worry about. Your new salary will reflect your added value to me."

"I appreciate it. You going to have a similar conversation with Jason?"

"He isn't as practical as you. I'm going to remove him from the temptation to be a fanatic. I'm sure he'll be pleased I'm finally putting him to work on plans for a new project."

"I'm glad to hear it." Kane turned to leave.

"Your friendship with Scott has been noted. Friendships can stand in the way of a career, if you're not careful."

"I'm always careful."

"Excellent. Now get to work. You've got a lot of catching up to do to make up for Ganning's ineptitude."

IV

The tower puncturing the New York sky looked like a half-eaten corpse. Its naked girder skeleton of greenish Osirium pushed out of the skin and muscle of glassteel that already covered its bottom third. Half completed, the tower was taller than any other in the city. Finished, it would be taller than any in the world.

Scott boarded an elevator. The streets and people sank and the brownish atmosphere faded as he rode out of the layer of smog.

The metal was molded into rounded curves that coiled around the building. Completed, it would bear more than a passing resemblance to a serpent coiled around a pillar. (The *New York Hourly News* art critic had called the tower "the Darth Vader Memorial." He no longer worked at the *News*.)

The tower was a monument to the growing prominence of Horatius Krebs.

During the past few years Scott had proven himself by designing, and sometimes directing, construction of domes beneath the sea, a tunnel between Hawaii's big islands, and an extension of a Lunar dome. He had begun work on plans for a self-contained city in Alaska's far north to utilize cheap energy from fusion and core taps. Alaska and her natural allies, the new states of old Canada, were set to exploit their natural resources, freed from paralyzing cold, and become economic giants as the

Sun Belt once exploited air-conditioning to break free of a semitropical climate.

He was interrupted by Krebs's imperious summons to fly immediately to New York from Anchorage.

The sun was sandwiched between ground haze and low clouds that threatened a summer thunderstorm. It created a hellish red light that suffused the tower.

Krebs was waiting on the most recently completed floor. He was hatless. Kinky hair curled around his skull like a Roman crown. The red light from below added to the unpleasant effect.

"Amazing view, isn't it?" said Krebs without preamble.

"Yes."

"They told me New York is a dying city. That the age of skyscrapers has passed. Had a hell of a time getting the city to approve my design. These boys demand bribes far out of proportion to their power. Well, they'll learn—

"It's filthy down there. They look like insects, swimming in muck, while we breathe fresh air." He walked to the edge. "Long as you stay with me, all that"—he gave a careless wave at the world below—"is yours for the asking. But I know that really doesn't appeal to a man like you. Right?"

"What do you want, Horatius?"

Krebs stretched his right palm up toward the boiling thunderheads. "That's what *you* want. We're going to get it, you and me." His hand closed as if grasping something. "Ever heard of the Midway Project?"

"The new space station."

"It will make L-5 obsolete as Skylab. I'm going after it—"

"If I do plans for Midway, there'll be a different arrangement between us."

Krebs frowned. "I've already said I'll pay whatever you ask. I know a valuable commodity when I own it."

"You don't own me," said Scott. "Or my ideas. If I design Midway, my new conditions will have to be met, otherwise I walk."

"Go to hell, Scott!"

"I wouldn't have to go very far."

"Get out of my sight! Leave before I have you thrown off—" Scott started to leave. "Wait! What are your conditions?"

"Approval of changes to my plans and total freedom once you approve the concept. I want to supervise the construction in space."

"You and God, huh? What kind of fortune will I shell out for this plan you're going to engrave on a sheet of gold?"

"Pay whatever you want. I don't care."

"You want this bad," said Krebs with satisfaction. "That's your weakness. You'll do anything to do the plans."

"Wrong. I'll only do them my way."

"Then be damned. I'll get someone else."

"Fine. I'll sell my plans to someone who will meet my terms, and you won't win the bid."

"I'll assign a dozen men to beat you to it. Even you aren't that good, Scott."

"The plans are done, Horatius."

Krebs's voice was almost unintelligible. "What?"

"I've been working on them two years, since I heard the government was considering building the station. They're done."

"You did this on my time?"

"On mine. The plans are in my computer. I worked on weekends, on holidays, between jobs. They belong to me. If you want to buy them you have to pay my price."

"Biting the hand that feeds you, eh?"

"At least I'm not biting the hand of my best friend."

Krebs chuckled. "I always wondered why you never mentioned that. All right, but I won't agree to your conditions until I see the blueprints."

"That's acceptable."

"So now we enter a new relationship, Scott. A relationship between equals. I wonder how long it will last. . . ."

V

When Jason Scott woke up his eyelids felt nailed shut. His head throbbed like a steel drum. Immediately he knew he had been drugged. He opened his eyes and focused on Jacob Kane.

"What did you give me?"

"Unimportant." Kane knelt by the sofa. "What's important is that you're alive."

"Why?"

"Because I like you."

Scott closed his eyes to block out the painful glare. "How much of this are you involved in?"

"Most of it. I altered the plans and put Python's logo on them. I'm not the one who burglarized your flat to destroy evidence that you developed the blueprints independently. I figured you'd try something violent. I've seen you reading *The Fountainhead*. I saved you from yourself. Otherwise, Krebs would've had you murdered in the act."

"In what act?"

"Breaking and entering the office. I presume you meant to retrieve the original blueprints. They've been destroyed."

"How can it be breaking and entering if I have a key?"

"You no longer work for Python. The records will support Krebs's claim that you were a former employee wanting revenge for being sacked."

"I see." Scott forced himself to sit up.

"Knowing his plans, I hired a couple of hood friends of mine to give you a sedative."

"I feel like all my teeth were extracted. Nice friends!"

"Nicer than Krebs. Sorry they had to mug you, but that was part of the deal." He gave Scott a glass of water. "You're alive."

"Won't Krebs be angry?"

"Another street crime." Kane shrugged. "He can't connect me to it. Besides, I helped him rip you off." He looked at Scott. "You're upset. I can tell. This is for the best, my friend. You aren't in his league yet. You weren't prepared to match wits with him. You didn't think he'd give over complete control to a project like Midway, did you? You're so upright and stubborn about concessions that must be made to practicality—you'd have cut profits ten percent. If I were you I'd shrug it off as a lesson and start over. Later you can get even."

"I'm not worried. A man like Krebs destroys himself finally. I do intend to go to the police and charge him with theft."

"Hard to prove. I'd take the money and keep quiet."

"Money?"

"Check your bank account. Krebs transferred ten thousand ounces of gold there yesterday, when his plan to kill you fell through. He's ruthless, but not stupid. He doesn't want you dropping out of the sky on him like a kamikaze someday. And you might, if he hurt you badly enough. Take it. Enjoy yourself."

"I'm an engineer. That money will give me a fine start."

"Make yourself competition and he'll try to destroy you."

"I don't intend to let hatred of Krebs eat my soul and color my life. He's in the past. He has nothing to fear from me."

"You're in a war. You walked out on Krebs. When he saw your plans for Midway he knew you could take them to Gigatex, Rockwell, or Transnational. You're good. Not as good a designer as me, but you had two years to perfect your designs. You're a hell of a project manager. The combination is a red flag, particularly if you have your own company. There's not room enough in space for two engineering firms. That's the battleground.''

"There will be no battle,'' said Scott firmly. He stood, swaying, but refused to sit back down. "If Krebs strikes at me, I'll move out of his reach. Sooner or later he'll trip himself up. His hate is based on jealousy, not any real threat. As space opens up there will be work for a hundred companies.''

"You're a fool. Don't put me in the position of choosing between you and Krebs. I'll choose self-interest. It's my nature.''

"You already made that decision. You chose to save my life. Even at the risk of displeasing your master.''

"Don't count on me making that choice a second time.''

"I can't help counting on it. It's my nature.''

Chapter
* 41 *

I

Kane's attorney was Whitney Bates Urbine, senior partner of the Anchorage law firm Urbine, Feldman, Roget & Talbot, the second largest in the country. They were in Urbine's office.

Urbine was in his sixties, short and dapper, unwrinkled except for deep creases on his face when he smiled, which was a wise, bemused, sophisticated expression. Parchmentlike skin enclosed a hook nose and birdlike eyes. In some light his ruff of hair made him look like an Indian chief. A dogsleg vein on his temple throbbed when he was agitated, which he was now.

"Mr. Kane," he said in a deep, gravelly voice, "I've cut a deal to allow you to escape with your freedom, but not much more. Do you want to hear it?"

Kane clung to the chair with feeble claws, felled by earth's gravity. He had refused a hospital, figuring that such a surrender to weakness might get him condemned to prison in absentia.

"What's the deal?"

"We're up against extreme odds. The prosecutor is a partner in the richest law firm in the country. How he was appointed to this case I don't know, but he is a longtime friend and occasional attorney for Krebs. I'm not positing undue influence here. I merely note the coincidence."

"Can't we get him removed?"

"I can't prove a thing. Denny—his name is Anderson Nobel Denny—hasn't worked for Kane for years. But I have the feeling that once you work for Mr. Krebs, you always do."

"I'm beginning to think so too. Krebs told me he would destroy me, the day I left his employ."

Urbine's vein twitched. "Did he say that in front of anyone? No? Too bad." He continued. "Regarding your wife's divorce suit."

She was making legal what had long been a fact. Kane had even forgotten to call her when he arrived on earth. "She wants half of your estate."

"She won't get it."

"She is represented by the nation's third largest law firm."

"What a coincidence."

"Yes. It also turns out that Victor Ames had a wife on earth, and she is suing you for wrongful death."

"Let me guess: She is being represented by an attorney from the fourth largest law firm in the country."

"Your powers of divination are admirable."

Kane stood painfully. He regretted not buying a wheelchair.

"You look terrible. You really shouldn't exert yourself."

"No? When everybody is exerting themselves to punch my ticket?" He looked at Urbine. "Since Horatius can buy the best attorneys in the country, how is it he didn't hire you?"

"Well, he tried but I said no."

"Why? His gold's as good as anybody's."

"No . . . it isn't. You don't know the history of our firm."

"I know you were the only firm willing to take my case."

"Our first big customer was Adam Scott. We've been with the Scotts since then. So you see, Krebs's gold isn't as good as anybody's."

"Jason Scott, you big hypocrite!" said Kane with a laugh.

"I hardly see—" said Urbine a bit huffily.

"What's the deal?"

"Selene won't prosecute. That makes Ames's death a federal matter. The deal is this: Earth law applies only on earth. If you leave, you won't be prosecuted as long as you don't return. You must abandon your property to be divided up by your wife and Ames's widow. But you'll be free."

Gravity clawed Kane's insides. It took a moment to decide.

II

The man was tall and sallow, with dark glasses, immaculate in pinstripes. He opened the leather briefcase on the conference table. It was full of gold ingots.

"The first payment from Mr. Krebs."

Lewis Cocker, seated, with Solarz's goon a constant presence at his elbow, tried not to breathe too loud a sigh of relief.

Solarz licked around the edge of his small mouth.

"Gold is nice, but I want the Crips and Bloods called off."

"Krebs doesn't control the activities of the city's lawless elements. Any more than he controls you," said Dark Glasses.

"Cut the bullshit!" Solarz limped over to the window, one of the few on Symphony Towers not boarded up. Ragged machine-gun fire came from hundreds of feet down. "For the first time since anybody can remember, these hoodlums are working together against a common enemy: me! They'll joyfully jump in front of a bullet. I wish I could command that kind of loyalty. But wait, I almost forgot!" he said as if he had just made a discovery. "Maybe I do!"

The door opened and Dr. Dollfuss and Jack Whitechapel came inside, in front of three of Solarz's men.

Cocker had never seen Whitechapel dressed. His "ancestor" Emil had never looked so good. Whitechapel was a pale angel of death, like an albino cobra Cocker once saw in a zoo. Wide of shoulder and tiny of waist, he was reptile cold and when he moved, he slid. A black tunic and corduroy slacks contrasted with his complexion.

Solarz looked at him. "You'll do whatever I say, right?"

Whitechapel nodded, and a thin whisper escaped: "Yes."

"Prepare to go outside and attack the bad men who want to take this big tower away from me. They are very bad brown and black people. They are not like us. I want you to kill them all."

"Kill them all," repeated Whitechapel.

"Perhaps they are trying to do that because you stole money from Mr.

Krebs," said Cocker softly. It seemed to him that Whitechapel cocked his head slightly at that.

"Cocker, I've had it with your mouth." Solarz's face reddened and he turned on Dark Glasses. "*You!* Tell Krebs I want those niggers and greasers off my back. I'll destroy everything the kraut has done, unless I get equal access to it *and* have it explained so I know what to do with it. I'll have Whitechapel strangle the life out of Cocker, then send him out to fight the Crips and Bloods. Which should be entertaining, no matter how it turns out. I spit on his gold!" He picked up an ingot and threw it with all his force against the tinted window. It crashed through and plummeted twenty-five stories where it either made the day or ended the life of one of Solarz's men.

III

Lenore Lippman returned to storm's eye of the *Animus* and Sergei was not long in coming. His ship was still in earth orbit.

"Where is the *other*?" asked Sergei with a child's petulance.

"He's gone. I may never see him again."

"Are you sad?"

"Not today, Sergei. I am happy to be with you."

"I am glad, too."

"Sergei, are there many of you who serve the ship?"

"Many of us serve the state and serve the ship, for the ultimate fulfillment of Genetic Communism." He said it as if by rote, and there was an element of fear too. Lenore Lippman wondered what could be so terrifying to such a young mind.

"You have time when you don't do your job on the ship?"

"Yes. I do not mind having time away from the ship. I input from the data banks."

"Are you allowed to read, then?"

"Oh yes! Without reading technical manuals I would not know how to do my job. I also input many factors of the ship. *And*"—a special note of pride entered his projected voice—"I am allowed to input *Genetic Communist Manifesto.*"

"Would you like to read some other things?"

"What other things? If it does not serve the state and ship it is not necessary or allowed."

"Some history? To know how things came to be?"

"There can be no harm in that," he said.
"Good. Next time we meet, I will bring you input, Sergei."

IV

Cocker had a very comfortable room; even a balcony to remind him that freedom was just a thirty-story drop away.

He was on his bed, his arms behind his head, when he heard the door open to his suite. He felt a catch in his chest and had an almost irresistible urge to leap off his bed and try to run.

But he stayed on the bed, although he clenched his jaw so tightly that it made his whole face ache.

Heavy footsteps in the next room. His bedroom door opened.

Whitechapel looked made up like a savage, an Indian or a headhunter. The red paint was all over his face.

Blood. He was drenched in it. It soaked his black tunic and slacks and made them darker. His hands were dipped in gore. His face was streaked in it. It caked in his white hair.

Whitechapel looked at Cocker for a long time. Cocker's heart stopped. He found himself gasping for breath, but he couldn't even move, couldn't move the arms under his head.

Then Whitechapel was gone.

Cocker forced himself to stand. His mouth hurt like hell and when he reached into it, he found a ragged edge of a tooth he had broken by clenching his jaw. For the first time in his life, Cocker laughed at pain. The more it throbbed, the happier he became. He cackled to himself and cautiously walked out his door.

The first body was crumpled by the elevator. He turned the corpse over and was sorry. The face did not exist. Just bone and cartilage splinters amidst a bloody, pink mass that had once been a human face.

He took the elevator down to the twenty-fifth floor. He found three more bodies. One's neck was broken. Another's abdomen was ripped open and he had choked to death on his own viscera. The third was just dead. No marks. No blood. Probably died of fright.

He entered the office Solarz had taken over. He put his hand over his mouth. Blood literally covered every available inch on what had once been an off-white wall. How could so much exist outside a body? Unspeakable atrocities had been performed on each body. He had read about some of them, but others showed great originality, or else Whitechapel was just better read.

There had been ten people in that room. Only two had time to draw weapons. Not that it had done them any good.

There was no sign of Solarz. Even if that muscular hulk had been torn to pieces there would have been a clue—if nothing but his silver-headed cane. But there was not. He had escaped.

Dollfuss was cowering in his lab. There were the ubiquitous corpses, artfully mutilated with medical instruments. The lab was unscathed. It was touching, the reverence the creature felt for his "mother."

"He's killed everyone in the building!" He was so agitated that his native Austrian accent made him almost unintelligible.

"I think you're right. When did Solarz leave?"

"A few minutes before Emil—Whitechapel started. I don't know how it happened. I heard shots. Then he came into my lab and looked around and . . . left."

"You did your work of imprinting loyalty to Mr. Krebs. You should be proud." Cocker went to the corpse in front of the lab door and turned him over with his foot. It was fascinating how quickly one became accustomed to the sight of death, he thought. He might even grow to like Whitechapel, given half the chance. "Mr. Krebs will reward you handsomely."

"To hell with you, Cocker! Have you no eyes?"

Cocker ignored him. "Do you think he'll come back?" Dollfuss didn't answer. "I said, do you think he'll come back?"

"He's already here."

Cocker faced the blood-soaked figure, who looked like an evil elemental vomited out of the stomach of a righteous god.

"What do you want me to do, Mr. Cocker?" said Whitechapel.

Chapter

* 42 *

I

"**G**eneral, it's a pleasure," said Admiral Hanley Davis as Keith sat at the booth in the small Lunar restaurant. "The food's good. We have a reservoir of seawater under the city. It produces some monster lobsters. It may take two of us to finish off one of the suckers! Try the caviar, too."

"Caviar? I read that Russia so polluted the Caspian Sea that sturgeon caviar's worth its weight in radium."

"True. The caviar is ersatz. Like your career at the moment." He raised a small glass of water. "Cheers."

Keith flushed. Davis must have heard that the army had "temporarily" deactivated the ETF.

"General, is there a reason why you remain in the army?"

"I know many civilian companies would hire me. Just as you could be pulling down ten thousand ounces a year. Word has it that Grumman Aerospace offered to make you CEO on your terms."

Davis gulped half his water as a plate of tomato-sized vegetables, the famous Martian garlic, arrived. "A vice acquired when I was supervising construction of our Martian base. Yes, Grumman offered me a job. Perhaps we answer to a higher authority. Which may be as voluntary as my craving for this shit. Want some?"

"No sir."

"Good. Stuff'll eat your insides." He wrapped his mouth around a forkful. He ate with large bites. Obviously he hadn't gone to West Point, where they taught cadets to eat in small bites, in case they were asked a question at dinner. "I don't mean why you don't work for civilians. I mean, why not work for me?" He regarded Keith. "Don't answer now. Think about it. You're loyal to the army. I was loyal to the navy. But I'm running a new service. We aren't inbred. We don't have stupid prejudices, or ridiculous rules, except ones derived from my own considerable biases."

"Why do you want me?"

Davis pushed away the plate, refraining from chasing it with water, which would have ignited a five-alarm fire in his mouth.

"I want you to train an extraordinary tactics force for Luna. Don't tell me that the thought hasn't crossed your mind."

"I'll say it has! It's the ultimate challenge for ETF technology. I can't do it, of course. The army's in my blood."

"Spare me that! You've run aground. Those ironbutts have long memories. With mandatory retirement age moving up to eighty-four, you'll be shaking hands with Jean Luc Picard before you get a good assignment again."

The waiter brought the lobster on a dish that could have accommodated a roast pig. Davis attacked it with pliers and the enthusiasm of a besieging army cracking open a fortress.

"The president wants you to join us. He feels he owes you for pulling his nuts out of the fire in Africa. He thinks there may be occasion for you to do so again."

"I'm not sure I understand."

"The Russians have formed a David Keith fan club. The CosMarine Division's General Orlov smuggled copies of your service manual into the country. They are studying your Site Shaka maneuvers. Even Marshal Tiomkin is interested in your theories."

"Naturally they are interested in tactics that worked against the Leopard, since they appear to be fighting him again."

"Tiomkin's a big cheerleader for space. He's the father of the railgun battleship. You should read his book. He is ready for war in space. He's figured out the logistics and tactics.''

"I read it. Maybe if we traded autographed copies, we could avoid war. We could weigh them and the heaviest wins.''

Davis stuffed his mouth with lobster. "The Russians must eventually decide they can win the whole ball game on Luna. Tiomkin already believes that. If he's half the leader I think he is, he's already training a Red extraordinary tactics force.''

"You know something, Admiral? I met Tiomkin . . . at the president's New Year's Eve bash. Quite impressive.''

"The party or the marshal?''

Keith chuckled. "You've met him. You know what I mean. Talking to him was like watching a hurricane storm front. I didn't know exactly whether to run for my life or admire the power.''

Davis smiled. "But you think you can take him, don't you?''

"Don't misunderstand. I have no—''

"Sure. I don't have a desire to turn the *Aurora* into slag.''

"I'll still have to think about it, Admiral,'' said Keith firmly. "That means I need to return to earth to think about it.''

"You'll have carte blanche. I have budgetary constraints, but by God, I know how to squeeze whiskey from moon rocks. If I must, I'll melt down a battleship to get what you need!

"Shefferton will sign an order saying you can raid any of the services. You could transfer the entire ETF into the Space Corps.'' He put the pliers down. "This is the greatest opportunity since President Lincoln offered the Union Army to Robert E. Lee.''

"I still need time. Thanks for lunch.'' But as Keith left the restaurant, he knew what his decision would be. Marshal Tiomkin had already thrown down the gauntlet and Keith had picked it up.

II

"I don't think this is the best idea in the world, us teaming up.'' Mel Hardrim's hands were wrapped around the leather steering wheel of the Mustang, which vibrated like a purring jungle cat.

It was dark and he saw his own and Kirsten Fale's reflections in the windshield. Gracie was sleeping quietly in the backseat.

This was their last time together before they split up to pursue separate threads they hoped would lead to Ferman.

"Why not, Mel? Don't you trust me?''

"As far as I can, but, ultimately, your boss is Roger Ferdinand. I mean, what do you work for? Ultimately?"

"Same as everyone—money, power, advancement. Roger's a shitheel, but he's a stepping-stone to rank that will set me up."

"I didn't think FBI perks were so great, unless you're the director."

"That's where he's aiming. I'll be right up there with him."

"Have you considered how Ferdinand will feel about those who knew him when, if he does get the power he craves?"

"Roger's a rat, but not a double-crosser. Betrayal of loyalty violates everything he believes." She punched him playfully. "Enough, big man. Tell me what motivates you. You could patch things up with your lady, instead you're trying to save some flea-bitten friend. Or is there more to it than that?"

"I have a job to do; a cold, cruel job. The only thing that lends it dignity is that maybe I can save my friend. So it's stupid for us to work together. Because I'll kill anyone who tries to take Ferman away from me."

"Even me?"

"Yes."

"Let's stop. I'll drive." They changed places. Kirsten accelerated to one hundred forty, effortlessly shifting gears.

"That's another thing that pisses me off. You drive better than I do!" He folded his jacket for a pillow. As he dozed, he saw Lenny as she was before the operation. She was so beautiful, and he loved her so much.

He woke up, startled, because the girl in the dream, Lenore Lippman, had had the face of Kirsten Fale.

III

July 15—*Denver Star*—The International Weather Bureau announced today that three previously unexplained bursts of energy in the Himalayas were caused by launches of kilometer-long warships into orbit by the Unified Soviet State. The U.S. has the ability to detect such launches, but chose not to report them.

Reaction on Capitol Hill has been a mix of stunned disbelief and calls for an investigation. Today Secretary of Space Sheridan Mayfield was summoned before the Senate Space Services Committee and cross-examined by Senator Iowa Thurgood.

Senators Macadew and Manners paused at the bar outside the handball court. Macadew was panting like a hound, covered with sweat; Manners was fresh, not a black hair out of place.

Macadew swallowed half the contents of a tall, dew-covered glass. "Some sonofabitch put iced tea in my iced tea."

"That's unhealthy for a man of your girth and age."

"Mind your own damn business, son." Macadew patted his forehead with a towel. "You're a hell of a handball player, Percy. Your son's gonna be a bodacious young Adonis and super athlete rolled into one. A double threat."

"Triple threat. He plays hardball as well as I do, too."

"You don't play hardball all that well, son." Macadew caught the bartender and had him replace the iced tea with "Tennessee Tea." "Reminds me! If you don't get that horse's petootie Thurgood to leave off bullyraggin' Jeff for lettin' the Russian battleships go by, I'll send videos of Randy Harmon's 'let's bend over' speech to the press. You did know Harmon was the big noise in the National Security Council for lettin' Russia get away with it?"

"I don't see the connection. I'm not Harmon's protector."

"Mebbe, but I get the impression you're allies." He smiled his "killer" smile. "Prove me wrong, son. Oh, I know you couldn't care less what happens to him. Old fool's your stalkin' horse, isn't he? One o' these days Jeff'll get a bellyful of that old fart. I'm trying to talk him into making that day real soon."

Manners put his arm around the older man. "Another game?"

"If you can't beat me, kill me, huh? Sure! Why not?"

PART

* 5 *

"THE MEANING OF THE UNIVERSE"

Chapter
* 43 *

July 5—*Boston Globe*—The Sunside Project expedition left Tycho Brahe Base today on a seventy-million-plus mile voyage to an orbit within the orbit of the planet Mercury.

When the *Euclid, Archimedes,* and *Descartes* arrive in eight weeks, their crews will begin joining the three ships into the PH Station. More materials and personnel will follow and work will begin on the real purpose of the Sunside Project: the realization of the Strubeck equations, i.e., artificial photosynthesis.

July 17—*New York Hourly News*—Rationing cards were distributed nationwide today. Rationing begins in two weeks, and protesters gathered at the old United Nations building. . . .

July 20—Editorial, *Christian Science Monitor*—However onerous rationing may be, it is our obligation to comply. There is no nobler motive than saving the human race from starvation. The famine-ridden nations have a right to expect that we will obey the rules and resist the urge to hoard. Sacrifices today will stand us in good stead with our neighbors in the future. . . .

Aug. 23—Moscow, *The New Man*—Distinguished Hero of the Second Revolution Marshal A. Tiomkin, defense minister of the motherland, has been forced by ill health to take an indefinite leave to his modest home outside Archangel.

First Secretary P. Brasnikov expressed hope that the marshal will soon return to state service. In the interim, he has appointed Tiomkin's deputy, W. Chin, acting defense minister.

Sept. 29—*Los Angeles Times*—Frank Silverado, publisher of *The Conspiracy Weekly Reader*, has stirred up readers by writing that the Sunside Project is a government hoax.

Silverado, who served ten months in a federal penitentiary for document forgery two years ago, claims to have documented proof from experts that the Strubeck equations could not produce more than a fraction of the food substances claimed.

His charges are discounted by the physics departments of California Institute of Technology and Columbia University. The U.S. attorney for Los Angeles has announced she may charge Silverado under provisions of the Emergency Technology Act, a law unused since the days of Senator Archer McClaren. . . .

Oct. 12—Johannesburg, *The Citizen*—The U.S. Third Marine Division today left Africa, leaving the Seventy-eighth Brigade to raze the Site Shaka nuclear installation as was agreed by America, Unified Soviet State, United Europe, Israel, Taiwan, South Africa, and the Union of Black Africa.

The Sixteenth French Airborne Battalion will occupy Lagos until the agreement is executed. The Kremlin has announced that fighting with guerrillas will prevent Soviet forces from evacuating on schedule. The Black African junta has denied giving the Soviets permission to expand anti-insurgency activities. . . .

I

Jacob Kane stood on the observation deck of the E class fusion freighter *Clarion Call*, outbound from Terra.

It wasn't a true "observation deck," but a Surroundee projection room. He seemed to float in space, the Milky Way a band of ice particles, the individual stars cold, hard points; brighter objects that were planets. The illusion vanished when he faced the immeasurably bright sphere that was Sol. It dimmed, allowing him to view it directly. He felt almost omnipotent.

The months since Ames's death had not worn well. Kane was even more gaunt, his dark jumpsuit limp as he stood, arms folded, gazing at the sun: boiling, restless, throwing great streamers of matter, and dragging them back to its fiery bosom.

Shortly before Kane's deadline to leave earth, Jason had sent word to take charge of supplies bound for the PH Station and arrange transport for new construction workers.

He entered into the task with gusto. Working in a white heat against gravity was constant agony, but he had no time to brood during his last days on earth. He bought a shuttle, cut red tape with bribes, and found a skipper who would lift on short notice.

And so, after surviving the launch, Kane had transferred to the *Clarion Call*, where he fell into a twenty-four-hour stupor.

On the observation deck, the brightest planet was earth, followed by Venus. He saw the slim needle of the escorting federal corvette. Sunward was Mercury's dim crescent. Off the bow was an object that changed intensity. It was an asteroid; an unusual one, to be found between the orbits of Mercury and Venus.

"Mr. Kane, kindly come to the bridge." The captain's voice came on the intercom, a soft baritone with an Irish brogue.

The bridge was operating with quiet efficiency as Kane entered. Captain Stephen Finn was relaxed in front of a holocube playing an old 2-D movie musical. A cowboy astride a horse crooned: "The corn is as high as an elephant's eye!"

Finn was a handsome man, compact, with a smooth baby face, hamlike hands, and muscles as tight as a spring. He had no legs. He had been available on short notice. Paraplegic skippers were not in demand earthside, although that prejudice was nonexistent in space, where legs weren't all that useful.

Finn was a math wizard of astonishing clarity of thought and speed of calculation. He had lost his legs as a fighter pilot for the Republic of Eire against an invasion by the Red British.

The cowboy finished his song, and Finn killed the cube.

"There's a distress signal from the colony on Icarus, the asteroid there in the navigational cube. They've requested assistance of any ship with a space botanist, and Dr. Gilbert is aboard. It's customary to give aid in this situation."

"How desperate are they?"

"Not desperate, but a colony like Icarus can't let any problem get that far along." Finn shrugged. "I'm obliged to consult you since this involves a course change and loss of time."

"How much?"

"Bein' a clever fellow, I figured you'd ask. Icarus is a strange piece of flyin' junk. His orbit takes him beyond Mars then brings him back to kiss the cheek of the sun—seventeen million miles. We can change course this much"—he displayed the figures—"and match courses in two hours. Icarus has nearly the same trajectory as us. We can get back on course, providing we do our business in twelve hours. We'll lose about ten hours. There it is. Do we help them?"

"Yes."

"I was hoping you'd say that!" Finn beamed. "Now I won't have to reprogram the course after all that work."

"I thought I had detected a slight change of course."

"Why, man! That's a change so small you could pass it between a grasshopper's legs!"

"I can read a navigational program," said Kane coldly. "What would you have done if I had refused permission?"

"I'd have done it anyway! You may be the owner's agent, but in space there's one ship's master. Of course, you could have fired me when we landed on Mercury." He looked serene.

"Good thing I agreed with you, isn't it, Captain Finn?"

"A very good thing," he agreed.

II

They called it the Place Where Dreams Come to Die and the Graveyard of Lost Souls, the Freak Show, the Combat Zone. The men of the Special Contamination District called it Ground Zero.

Twenty-five years later, experts estimated that the plutonium bomb had gone off near the Fightertown U.S.A. barracks at Miramar Naval Air Station. The base had disappeared. The posh high rises of the Golden Triangle had survived as grisly skeletons. Much of La Jolla was destroyed. The fireball travelled through the canyons and incinerated Del Mar Racetrack, where a hundred thousand people were attending the county fair.

San Diego's downtown office buildings remained intact save for shattered windows, which had fallen on the streets like deadly rain. It was rush hour. Half a million had died on the highways.

Responsibility was claimed by the Unified Liberation Front, which fused the Irish Republican Army, Black September, and a dozen like interests. U.S. commandos had retaliated, simultaneously hitting every international terrorist headquarters, and, for good measure, rubbed out any heads of state known to sponsor terrorism.

Condemned in the United Nations, America withdrew from it and kicked it out of New York. The bombing, more than any other cause, led to the adoption of the Thirty-first Amendment. Before the attack, San Diego was America's fastest-growing city. After, tourism died and the no-growthers got their wish: Nobody wanted to move to San Diego. Except in neighboring Tijuana, where conditions were so bad that nuclear fallout was an improvement. TJ's citizens were also attracted by cheap land. Others came too: junkies and dealers, every variety of outlaw. Balboa Park became a gang battleground; San Diego a place to vanish, a district authorities rarely entered, except in force.

A few blocks away from Balboa Park, on India Street, figures were walking quickly and trying not to call attention to themselves in the darkness. The bearded man was no exception. He negotiated the shadows in spurts, followed by intervals of watching. He wore his overcoat collar upturned.

A teeth-vibrating rumble drove him behind a pile of rubble as three hover tanks from Pendleton turned up the street, turrets revolving. Some kids opened fire and grenades popped harmlessly on Collapsium armor. The tanks ignored them. The kids were too young to be in the gangs, although they wore the light blue of aspiring Crips. The tanks continued their patrol. They traveled in threes. One wouldn't have made it out of the contaminated zone.

After the children finished howling epithets and went looking for easier prey, the bearded man emerged from hiding. The time was ripe for a sweep through the district by the marines. The last time, they had suffered embarrassing losses, so they'd be out for blood. They were still smarting from a painful raid by the Bloods on the San Onofre nuclear power plant two weeks before.

Pendleton's commandant had pledged to "restore law and order," so things were going to get unhealthy since marines were good for two things: killing people and occupying property.

He followed Interstate 5 north toward the Contaminated District boundary, which ran between the beach towns of Encinitas and Carlsbad. It would take hours to get there, but he could see Oceanside's holographic floating billboards advertising a musical on the life of Jack the Ripper, called *RIP!*

He knew places near the checkpoints where he could slip through. He had been slipping in and out for weeks.

The bearded man, Ralph Ferman, arrived in Encinitas at dawn, and nested in a condemned housing project until dark. Here buildings were in better shape and maintained tenuous contact with the Contaminated District. Churches and charitable organizations had missions and breadlines.

Across the street, in an old bank, light shone through the stained glass of the Church of the Holy Aggressor. The glass was the type used in warplane canopies. Martial organ music emerged through steel doors. Above the doors, in red, was the motto "Vengeance Is Mine, Saith the Lord."

He listened to the music and watched darkness descend and shadows emerge. Then he began working toward his crossing point.

The electronic devices the authorities used to stop traffic in and out of the zone were daily sabotaged by street urchins. There were too few human guards to be effective. Ferman had found a chink in the armor: a section of old underground sewer. When sewers were sealed off owing to the home disposal unit, this section was overlooked.

The sewer began a hundred feet short of the boundary, its manhole hidden by rubble. It ended under an abandoned hotel a thousand feet away. He always crossed right before dawn.

He heard thunder. The sky was overcast, but the thunder was not of nature. He peered down the street and saw marines and tanks filing past. To the north a dozen gunships skimmed low on their way to Pendleton. The marines were going to move soon and in far greater force than ever before. The question was, exactly when?

Ferman turned up his collar and began walking toward the Amtrak station where he could catch a train to Los Angeles.

III

In the *Animus*, as nowhere else, Lenny Lippman felt peace. The cyclone of thought and transmission let her focus her own energy.

"Sergei!" she called silently. She had come three times now and Sergei had not been there. She assumed that his ship was no longer where its transmissions could become part of the *Animus*, although she had begun to get glimmerings of a larger, more tenuous *Animus* that existed beyond the earth's.

"*I am here!*" Sergei, for all his mental powers, was still a child, with a childish sense of humor. Playing hide-and-go-seek was still a big thing for him. That, or surprising his friend by not announcing himself right away. The sad truth for Sergei was that his body would always be a child's, no matter how his brain matured.

"I've more books. Did you read what I sent you before?"

"I finished *Wealth of Nations* and have begun *Capital* by Marx, who interests me as he founded our economic system. Are these representative samplings? All people are interested in economies and conditions of workers?"

"Grammar school kids cut their teeth on such books."

"Then I have much to read. What else have you for me?"

"*History of the Molly Maguires, Chávez and the Farm Workers, The Story of the UAW, Rise of Solidarity, The Anarchist Cook Book*, and Marcuse's *Counterrevolution and Revolt*. That'll give you a broad overview of history."

"I must be careful about my reading. Careful that no one knows. There have been two bad things aboard the ship." The child faltered, but Lenny felt a great outpouring of emotion.

"What is it, Sergei?" She tried to project a comforting, maternal warmth. And found that what she was trying to fake was in fact a real feeling deep inside her.

"Two of my mind partners have gone away. I saw them through the cameras that the captain installed inside airlock twenty. They were terminated by the Steel Bloom."

He projected a mind picture. Lenny tried to escape the picture, tried to rotate away from the transmission, but Sergei's mental power was tremendous. It was like trying to shut out the sunlight by closing transparent eyelids. She saw the pinkish, writhing shape brutally sucked by the vacuum through a dilating diaphragm; torn to fleshy shreds in a moment. The silent scream of the victims of the captain's special hatred of Dough Children. God, it was awful!

"He said it was to encourage us to work harder," said Sergei's whispering voice, its normally powerful transmission barely amplified. "He wants us to be more creative in our programming. To achieve more for the good of the state, of the ship."

" 'Necessity is the mother of invention,' " said Lenny with murderous bitterness.

"What is a mother?"

"Someone who loves—someone who protects."

"Dough Children do not have—mothers."

"You do," she said firmly. "Now."

Chapter
* 44 *

I

Icarus was called an "earth grazer" because its elongated orbit periodically brought it within four million miles of earth.

Once when it was that close, a small colony of miners and scientists had been planted by a Hamilton-based company to exploit its minerals, many of which were now scarce on earth. That made Icarus the only privately owned, independent space colony. But the backers lacked the resources to move Icarus to a more congenial orbit; every four hundred days brought it so close to the sun that it glowed cherry red. At such times the colonists erected great sheets of sun-reflecting foil and took refuge in the core. Icarus was several months away from the next perihelion.

As *Clarion Call* approached, Icarus was a flying mountain-sized peach pit tumbling end over end. The ship's lifeboat, containing Dr. Gilbert and Kane, landed on a flat area the size of a parking lot. The negligible gravity wouldn't counteract the centrifugal force that tended to set the lifeboat adrift, so it attached to the rock via grappling equipment.

Icarus was honeycombed by shafts. Older ones provided living quarters; the new ones were active mines. They entered through one of the old shafts. They were met by Icarus's leader, Samuel Davenport, two of his lieutenants, and his daughter. It seemed to Kane that he had seen the slim, leggy beauty with long, auburn hair previously. But he couldn't place when.

Davenport was a cheerfully authoritative, self-assured figure. His thick, whitish-yellow hair was in a pigtail. His pale, smooth skin gave him a peculiar, ageless look.

He led the way to the hydroponics farm, where Dr. Gilbert tested the specimens and talked animatedly with Davenport.

Kane realized where he had seen the daughter: in the bar in Tycho City, the night he killed Taylor. She saw him staring and held his eyes for a moment, without looking away, and then, just as suddenly, severed the link and returned her attention to Dr. Gilbert.

Kane wandered into the catacombs. As an engineer, he had always held that fabricated space colonies were preferable to hollowed-out asteroids. This was his first chance to examine such a miniature world.

He ended back at the hydroponics farm, where Gilbert had finished and was waiting to return to the ship.

"Simple problem," he said cheerfully. "Used to see it on zero-g space stations. Bacteria that break down recycled wastes become less energetic after several hundred thousand generations—several years. I introduced fresh earth bacteria into the system. They will crowd the others out, restoring things for a while."

"You coming back down, then?"

"I can send a canister of it down. They can do the rest."

"Dr. Gilbert," said Davenport, "let me offer my heartfelt thanks." He turned to Kane. "Mr. Kane, did you enjoy your tour?"

"Impressive. If you get a decent orbit, you'll become rich. I understand fighting radiation at perihelion wastes a lot of man-hours."

"True," said Davenport. "Our sponsors barely make a profit. Unless we convince them that a new orbit will dramatically up profits, they won't give us the rands. But if I can get the word out that an asteroid home is viable, I can raise the money."

"Until you do, I have a suggestion," said Kane. "As you know, the PH Station must operate within twenty million miles of the sun. We've come up with some effective shielding."

"Isn't that a government patent?"

"Jason Scott's Prometheus Enterprises developed the patent, a variation of the laser-reflective 'goop' used on warships. I think he'd license you to use it. I'll ask, if you like."

"What do you get out of it?" Davenport arched his eyebrows.

"A hefty finder's fee, I trust."

"Mr. Kane, I like you."

Kane rather hoped that sentiment might run in the family.

"I understand you want no help from national governments, even the United States," said Kane.

"Particularly the U.S., which has been trying to take us over. That's why every colonist renounces Terran citizenship. We are freemen, without taxes, conscription, or interference."

"Don't you and your men constitute a ruling council?"

"We are anarchists, in the finest sense," said Davenport proudly. "We cooperate voluntarily on projects that benefit all, but we each own and work for profit a portion of the asteroid."

"Someday you'll need protection."

"Little Icarus?" Davenport laughed. "We aren't worth it. Besides, we're under the protection of the U.N. Peace Force."

"Both ships?"

"It's symbolic." Davenport's eloquent shrug seemed to say that he thought the universe was crazy. "America won't touch us while the battle rages in the World Court and she won't let other powers intervene. We're safe because we're insignificant."

"When the big bull elephants start trampling the fields with no thought to the little people, you'll get flattened."

"You have a cynical view of the universe."

"You're not the first to make that observation."

"Let me ask another favor." Davenport touched Kane in the easy physical familiarity that seemed to develop on such closed habitats. "Your next stop is Mercury. Would you allow my daughter to go with you? I would pay, of course."

"I have no objections." Kane gloated inwardly at his good fortune. "We must leave shortly. If she could be ready—"

"I'm ready now, Mr. Kane," called Elena Davenport, who floated toward them with a duffel bag in tow.

"No other bags?"

"Three changes of clothing. I sew if I want more variety."

"Come with us on the lifeboat." Kane was beginning to think the remainder of the trip was going to be interesting.

II

Captain Finn pretended indignation at a passenger being added without consulting him. Kane saw through his act: Finn wanted the crew to see that he took guff off no one, including his employer.

"Finn, when you see the young lady you'll agree she's a welcome addition and sure to raise the morale of the crew."

"Sure, and all I need is to have my lads mooning over some pretty lass like lovesick schoolboys!"

"To make amends, let me invite you to my cabin. I've been saving some Bushmill's I bought earthside for a proper occasion."

Finn licked his lips. "Bushmill's is it? I'll be by when I have a spare moment."

Kane went to his cabin to lay out glasses and fetch the four-cornered bottle. The ship was under a one-quarter-g acceleration, so he felt safe placing the bottle on the table near his bunk.

He programmed the holocube for a game of three-dimensional Go. Finn had high tastes in literature and art, and a passion for the mentally taxing hybrid of an ancient oriental game. That he loved Broadway musicals almost to the exclusion of other music was another facet to a complex, somewhat contradictory character.

There was a knock on the hatch.

"Come in, Captain," said Kane without looking up.

The hatch opened. "Drinking already, Mr. Kane?" Elena Davenport was smiling mischievously from the hatchway.

"I'm waiting for the captain, but I'm happy to see you." He waved her inside. "I wasn't expecting this honor just yet."

"You're the only one I know on the ship. Why shouldn't I visit you?" She spoke so ingenuously that Kane believed she didn't know she was encouraging him. "I live on an asteroid, with a few hundred familiar faces. I'm a little leery of strangers."

"You seemed at ease in that bar in Tycho City."

"It took a great force of will."

"It's not a bad thing, your fear of people. Trust has gotten more people into trouble than almost any human foible."

"You consider trust a character flaw?" she said, her eyes widening. "When you say trust no one, does that include yourself?"

"Yes!" said Kane with exasperation. "That's my last warning. You're on your own now. You learn about fire by getting burned."

"Without trust we wouldn't get along a day on Icarus. That and affection, honesty and honor."

"I know isolation causes societies to regress, but I'd never guess you could fall back to the Middle Ages in five years!"

She looked at him intently. "You use mockery to cover your fear that someone may exploit a weakness. You allow no one close and you run from trust and love, emotions you consider naïve."

"You think you know a lot?" He rubbed his hands nervously.

"I perceive some things from your behavior. Others I can guess. I know your wife just divorced you after three years of marriage, most of which you spent away from her.

"I read the newstapes about the murder charge. I was curious when I learned you killed the man the same night we met."

"Curious behavior."

"I'm mature enough to find out all I can about something, or someone, that interests me. I find you interesting—"

"That's a very good start—"

"But not attractive." She said this in a matter-of-fact way.

"Why the hell are you making this trip?" Kane was furious for allowing himself to be irritated by this surprising woman.

"To buy electronic equipment and try to interest people in settling on Icarus."

"I thought perhaps you were making the trip to study me!"

At that moment the captain entered, a tune dying on his lips as he paused in the hatchway, supporting his legless torso with one hand while he took in the scene at a glance.

"Hello, children, having a spat?"

"You ever heard of knocking, Finn?" snarled Kane.

"You left the hatch ajar, boyo. And it's 'Captain' to you! Where's the spirits?" He spied the glasses and whiskey and pounced. He sat, opened the bottle, and poured, in one motion.

"Why don't you sit down?" said Kane sarcastically.

"I'm already sat." He drained the glass and smacked his lips. "Don't you let me interrupt you two. I never stand on ceremony."

"Actually," said Kane nastily, "it was my impression that you never stood on anything."

Elena Davenport was shocked, but Finn merely raised his eyebrows slightly and poured another drink.

"I'm going to enjoy beating you." He looked at Elena. "Don't be offended, lady. Beneath that gruff exterior lies a rotten human being. Shall I move first, or will you?"

"I'm not in the mood," grated Kane.

"Ah, well, perhaps I've come at an inconvenient time. Miss Davenport, do you play three-dimensional Go?"

"No, I'm sorry." She smiled brilliantly. "Could you teach me?"

"Ah, that'd be pure joy!" He beamed. "Go's a fine game. A wonderful cultural study too. It reflects the oriental mind. You surround your opponent, rather than attacking frontally. You strike me as a lass who knows a thing or two about cutting your quarry off from retreat."

"Why, you've lost me, Captain."

"Sure I have." He inclined his head. "I'll be on my way." He recapped the bottle. "I trust the invitation stands, Kane?"

"Yes!" he hissed.

"Well, then, 'I go to forge in the smithy of my soul the uncreated conscience of my race'!"

"I'll go with you, Captain."

"My pleasure, Miss Davenport."

They exited and Kane fastened the hatch. He sat on his bunk a long time, clenching and unclenching his fists, wishing passionately that he'd never met either Finn or Elena Davenport.

III

Clarion Call and her escort approached Mercury, which looked remarkably like earth's moon, although it was denser, with a core of metals that were scarce on earth. It had proven more valuable than Venus, or rather, the Venusian S.S.R., certainly more valuable than Mars, which was of little use to anyone.

Mercury's ports and intracolony traffic were administered by the United Nations, whose garrison kept local squabbles from boiling over. More than once ideological strife had forced the U.N. administrator to walk the line to avoid provoking one of the Great Powers into overt defiance.

America cooperated with the U.N. although it denied its authority, and maintained the fiction that its colonies were administered under duress. Even so, the American colonies always took care to bring their grievances before the U.N. administrator.

As the *Clarion Call* prepared to land, a U.N. patrol ship approached.

The American corvette would remain in orbit because warships were forbidden to land on the supposedly neutral world.

Kane went into the observation deck, where Mercury, a dark, unlit presence from this approach, blocked the sun, although its silvery corona was like some sort of ghostly aura around the dark disk. The ship was in Mercury's shadow at the moment. Elena Davenport was there, enjoying a last view before planetfall. He turned to leave, not wanting to repeat their unpleasant scene.

"Mr. Kane, please don't go," she said softly.

"I don't wish to cause you discomfort." With a shock he realized that was the absolute truth, despite the irritation she had caused him. He didn't want to hurt her.

"We both behaved badly. I had no business poking into your private life; and you overreacted, because I wrecked your plans to seduce me when I turned out to be different than you supposed."

"Oh, you guessed that, did you?"

"It was fairly obvious."

"I haven't abandoned those plans."

"You won't have the opportunity. We land in an hour."

"Perfect!" He moved closer.

She put her hand out. "You misread me. I'm interested, but I'm not panting to be swept up in your arms. There's more to it. You'd know that if you'd ever known more than one kind of woman."

"A woman who prizes her virtue. How charming! But you're wrong, I have associated with more than one kind of woman. In fact, I married one of the other kind. She prized her virtue."

"Once again you misinterpret me. If you think I don't glory in life and enjoy its pleasures to the fullest, then you're wrong. But I *do* pick and choose whom I enjoy them with."

"*Touché!* Do you suppose that if I eat my vegetables, I might someday qualify to be included in that exclusive sect?"

"The possibility exists," she said primly.

"If you enjoy life so much, why haven't you fled that little rock before now? I can't imagine anything more stifling!"

"I've lived on earth. I prefer Icarus. Life is hard but we work for ourselves, not a government. You can have your open air and green hills that hide the chains that enslave you. I prefer corridors of rock and freedom!" Her eyes shined guilelessly.

"Perhaps it's having a choice that's the charm," murmured Kane. "If

I ever see blue skies again, it will be shortly before they give me a lethal injection. I must content myself from now on with falling in love with caverns of igneous rock. My sky will always be black, but at least it will have stars in it.''

''You're a dreamer too, Mr. Kane.''

''My dear, you're not a dreamer, you're a fool.''

She laughed. ''You're trying to provoke me! You use that tactic when you wish to avoid a subject. But I know you well enough now to know that you are as much a dreamer as I am.''

''Yes, but I try to confine them to the sleeping period.''

Behind Elena, the sun, its apparent size many times larger than on earth, thrust a fiery sliver above Mercury's disk as the *Clarion Call* moved toward the north pole. The perfect black disk was squeezed into an ovoid. The terminator seemed to move south as the ship moved north. The Surroundee equipment dimmed the sun, but it still caused a breathtaking halo effect on Elena's auburn hair.

''You don't fool me!'' She shook her molten tresses. ''You're a leader of the Sunside Project, the most outrageous dream brought to life. I know about Jason Scott, and that quote of Lawrence of Arabia's he has on the door of his corporate headquarters.''

''Dreamers of the Day?'' said Kane. '' 'All men dream, but not equally. Those who dream by night in the dusty recesses of their minds wake in the day to find that it was vanity; but the dreamers of the day are dangerous men, for they may act their dreams with open eyes, to make it possible.' Strubeck's favorite quote.''

''Now you're bringing the biggest and most outrageous dream of mankind to life, freedom from want.''

Kane shook his head. ''If that was the ultimate freedom, America would have made a paradise long ago. Freedom from want is nothing if the individual isn't free.''

''Yet you are so contemptuous of common people.''

''People don't know what to do with freedom. Half of them hook into Surroundees. The others will sell themselves and everyone else down the river for an increase in comfort or security.''

The ship was directly over the north pole. Mercury was evenly divided between light and dark. Above it the sun was still a churning, ominous presence.

''That's a paradox,'' said Elena. ''You want freedom for the individual, but you don't trust him to exercise it.''

''The answer is to give man unlimited room to expand. Only then can ultimate freedom coexist without the violence that results when man can give his desires free rein. Ultimate freedom is the ability to travel to the stars, for Everyman to exercise if he chooses. That's the only way man will truly be free.''

Elena frowned in wonder. ''If you don't believe the Sunside Project will cure mankind's problems, why are you working on it?''

''When we pull the great masses of society away from the brink of starvation, then we can work on getting to the stars.''

''Do you think the Strubeck equations will work?''

''I know so.'' Kane turned away from the sun. His eyes were tired from so much light. ''I knew Strubeck. And I know Sherlock Michlanski, the man who will make the equations work.''

''I hope you're right.''

''Why? Icarus is safe. Why concern yourself?''

''Aside from purely humanitarian reasons, I'd think my interest would be obvious. Think of the benefits of producing food from sunlight. We could increase our living and working space and ultimately our production.''

''You are your father's daughter.''

''More. I'm his right hand, and ultimately, his successor.''

Kane laughed. ''Is there no doubt that you will succeed him?''

''I'm the most qualified.''

''Your people are anarchists!''

''Rational anarchists. They follow those whose judgment is most likely to be correct. A wrong decision could cost our lives. So they will follow me.''

''You're pretty sure of yourself.''

''I was brought up to be sure of myself.''

The intercom spoke. ''Landing will commence in five minutes.''

Chapter

* 45 *

Johannesburg, *The Citizen*—Unconfirmed reports from Uganda, Union of Black Africa, say that a brigade-sized Soviet unit has been surrounded and forced to surrender by irregulars in revolt against the army junta in Lagos.

The last Soviet unit reported in that area was the Twenty-second Guards Light Laser Infantry Brigade.

I

Little of Mercury's North Polar was visible aboveground. Extreme temperatures, ranging from hundreds of degrees below zero to over four hundred degrees Fahrenheit, able to crumble the toughest building materials, dictated that the colony be built below the surface, where man had transplanted his environment to a hostile place, and made it pleasant and livable.

He had transplanted his inconveniences too: With the crew of the *Clarion Call* transferred underground, an inspection team from the U.N. Port Authority inspected the ship in detail.

Finn and Kane were questioned in a large office by a young captain of the garrison's Swedish contingent. A little man, he disguised inexperience with brashness, strutting with his hands clasped behind him, posing questions like a schoolmaster.

"What is your ultimate destination?"

Finn sat with his hands behind his neck, his prosthetic legs crossed. He cocked an eye languidly at the officer.

"Our destination is the PH Station."

"Do you carry contraband of any kind?"

"Define contraband." Finn absently scratched his dead leg.

"Surely you know what contraband is?"

"It's been a while since I was here. I'm not sure what you call contraband. I wouldn't want to give inaccurate information."

"Contraband," he said with exaggerated politeness, "is any nuclear device, or fissionables used to construct such a device, or any drugs of the sodium-hydrogen quadride group."

"I could check—" Finn pulled up his pants leg and started to unfasten the straps that bound the prosthesis to his stump.

The captain watched, horrified. "Enough! Your attitude constitutes contempt for proper authority. That is serious."

"Captain Norge!" The voice snapped like a rifle shot.

A tall, slim officer, Caucasian, but very dark, with a white turban, had entered. Black, piercing eyes roamed restlessly. He puffed on an aromatic cigarette in an elegant holder. He returned Norge's salute.

"Do we have a problem?"

"Just a misunderstanding on the subject of contraband."

"Let me get the documentation on this cargo." The turbaned officer went to a larger desk in the far corner of the office.

Kane walked over to Norge, who was a full head shorter. Smiling with brilliant white teeth, Kane looked Norge in the eyes. To the casual observer, he was making amiable conversation.

"You're another one of these little short bastards," he said. "I bet the rest of you is short too. Probably doesn't stick out past your pubic hairs. Probably can't get it up, either."

Norge's anger boiled over. He cursed in Swedish, backhanded Kane, and drew his weapon.

"Norge!" roared the turbaned officer from across the room. "Are you insane? That will be all, I think, Captain Norge!"

Norge looked like he wanted to dispute the colonel, but he slunk away. The colonel turned to Finn and Kane. He put the cigarette holder squarely between his lips, above an inky spade beard, and took a drag. Eyelids closed, he exhaled.

"I am Colonel Kemel, of the Pakistani army contingent, commandant of the United Nations Peace Force."

"Happy to meet you, Colonel." Finn put his leg back on.

"Are you in the habit of removing your prosthetic limb in public, Captain Finn?"

"Just checking for contraband, Your Excellency!"

"Are you people in the habit of assaulting civilians?" demanded Kane.

"I apologize for Norge's extreme exuberance." He said "exuberance" like it was a new part of his vocabulary. "I hope you won't make it a habit to make our jobs harder than neccessary."

"We won't be here that long, Colonel," said Kane. "I hope I don't have to report this incident to the U.S. commissioner."

"That won't be necessary," he said coolly, clearly not intimidated. "Exuberant relations are more desirable than the antithesis, you agree? Mercury is the Sunside Project's nearest neighbor. All traffic to that point must be certified by the Peace Force as nonlethal."

"Your authority does not extend within the orbit of Mercury!"

"We contend otherwise, as I told Mr. Scott the other day."

"America doesn't recognize U.N. authority in space."

"I bow in the face of superior firepower," said Kemel. "Your Mr. Scott was more subtle. You exuberant Americans place an inordinate faith in your ability to bully whomever you like."

"We're trying to save the world. Tends to make us myopic."

"You have our best wishes for your endeavor." He lifted his gloved hand to his cap. "Now, please excuse me. Good day."

II

"How long will you remain on Mercury?" asked Kane.

"Two months. This is not only a mission for Icarus. It's a vacation, a fling, even a sabbatical," said Elena Davenport.

They stood near the airlock that led to the surface where the ship waited.

"You actually crave change from that rocky tomb? I could pick a better place than this! 'See the rocky beaches of Mercury, where it's always sunny, and get the best tan in the solar system.' "

"Icarus is home, but that doesn't mean I shouldn't know other places. If I am to succeed my father, an understanding of other points of view is a prime requisite of statecraft."

"I can see you're going to have a real wild vacation."

"You never change, do you, Jacob?" she said, laughing.

"It's a bad sign to say that when you've known me a few days."

"I'm not sure if it's a bad sign or not."

"When you're sure, let me know." He donned his helmet.

"Will you be returning to Mercury soon, Jacob?"

"Depends. Jason's last message had a queer note to it, as if he thought it was being monitored. He seemed worried. 'Doubt' has never been part of his vocabulary. I don't know how long before I see you again. But I will see you again. Count on it."

She held out her hand. Kane took it awkwardly with his gloved hand.

"It's an unusual form of leave-taking for a man and a woman, Elena. But we are an unusual pair. Goodbye!" He entered the airlock, and as it closed, he raised his hand in a final wave.

III

The PH Station looked like a shining, fragile toy floating beside the sun, whose stormy orb appeared larger than earth does over the lunarscape. But the difference between the serene, blue and green home of man and the restless, dangerous star that both threatened and sustained life couldn't have been greater.

The ships *Archimedes, Euclid,* and *Descartes* had been joined at the nose to form spokes of an incomplete wheel. Built to be cannibalized, they were no longer recognizable as ships. Great sheets of reflective foil hung between the space station and the sun, protecting working zones. Completed sections were covered with sun cells. They gleamed like individual facets of a jewel.

"It's a truly lovely thing, Mr. Kane," said Captain Finn softly. "You must be very proud."

"I've little to be proud of yet. They used my plans, but without me. From now on, things will be different." He turned away from the viewing cube, a thin but triumphant smile on his lips.

Finn turned to the navigational computer, where a series of equations glowed briefly. His hand played across the keyboard. He whistled softly through his teeth.

"All set. A well-nigh perfect set of equations. We'll lightly kiss the cheek of that lovely jewel in nine minutes."

"Mixed metaphors, Captain Finn?"

"I was carried away by my muse."

The ship maneuvered until her nose synchronized with the slowly revolving station hub. As a wisp of lint alights on a wool blanket, she touched the hub. They were joined. In a few minutes they were able to go from spaceship to space station without a pressurized suit.

A third of the station was complete, and half of that was under pressure. Kane took an elevator from the hub to the wheel.

Jason Scott awaited Kane in one of the wheel's pressurized chambers. He wore airtight fatigues; blowouts were a constant possibility during construction. Helmets hung in every compartment, so everyone aboard could be airtight within moments.

"Good to see you again, Jacob." Scott offered his hand.

"Is it?" said Kane, taking Jason's hand and eyeing him skeptically. "You're reconciled to having a murderer working for you as long as it's for the good of the project?"

"That judgment was not mine to make. I don't relish your style of morality. You are out of joint with your own time, Jacob. It's not your fault you were born in a time when we don't casually eliminate those who stand in our path."

"And you need me. That has something to do with it, too."

"Yes, it does. What have you been doing with yourself?"

"I always like to keep occupied. I've been writing a book."

"Really! I remember *The Meaning of the Universe* quite well."

"This goes from the general to the specific. I call it 'The Interplanetary Agenda.' "

"That's a rather innocuous title. Hardly like you, Jacob."

"It's subtitled 'A Guide to Freeing Earth's Colonies from Economic and Political Domination.' "

"My faith is restored." They walked along the wheel, which was large enough that the illusion that they were in the bowl of a valley climbing up was almost unnoticeable. They passed several space marines, in gold and black, conspicuously armed.

"What's this? Admiral Davis got his way, after all?"

"I requested them. We have twenty marine security officers throughout the wheel. We'll also be getting the corvette *Crazy Horse* coming on station in about a week.''

''What's going on?''

''I'll get into that later.''

Coming from the opposite direction was Rene Delner. First the top of her head was visible and then the rest of her. When they met, she extended her hand to Kane.

''Welcome back. You're a valuable member of the team.''

''Thank you,'' said Kane serenely. ''So are you.''

She turned to Scott. ''I'll get the report on mutated proteins to you in a couple of days. I've assigned Bethany. She's the best person working for me. I'm sure you're not sorry to hear that.''

''Rather pleased, actually,'' said Scott, smothering a grin.

''Goodbye, Mr. Kane,'' she said coldly.

She passed Kane, who speculatively contemplated her backside. ''Under the right circumstances—'' he murmured.

''Amazing!'' said Scott.

''I have a weakness for women who idolize me.'' Kane smirked.

''You killed her lover! Don't you think she remembers that?''

''She didn't seem too broken up about it.''

''Well, actually, she never seemed particularly devastated by Ames's death,'' said Scott. ''Bethany remarked on it at the time.''

''That's because Ames was an asshole.''

''So are you, Jacob. That doesn't mean some of us wouldn't be hurt by your death.''

''Never happen.''

''That tells me you think about it at least twice a day. I bet you also think about it every time you're with a woman.''

''That could put a crimp in a man's sex life,'' said Kane soberly. ''What about you and Bethany? Is the romance finally taking off, or have you done everything to kill it?''

''I've decided to let nature take its course. I was attracted to Bethany from the start. She appeals to my heart and my head.''

''Yeah, have you jumped her bones yet?''

''That's not any of your business!'' Scott flushed angrily.

''Did you try the zero-gravity chamber yet?''

Scott charged through: ''I'll bring you up to date. I want you to go to work immediately. There's little leisure time here.''

''Except for hosing young systems engineers in the zero-gravity chamber. Is she engineering your system?''

"I said there's no time. We steal moments together for lunch. If you're serious, Jacob, you'll put in the same kind of schedule!"

"That's what I want. Work to take my mind off other things."

Scott led him through the finished compartments where Dorian Nye and his staff were busy installing equipment.

"And Michlanski's work area?"

"It's done. Sherlock has been working like a dog. He locks himself up and spends days at a time poring over equations. I've never seen him work this hard. He's lost thirty pounds."

They came to a compartment with a sign over the entrance that read "Security." Kane noted it with raised eyebrows.

"The security precautions are my idea, but the man in charge is cut from the same cloth as Admiral Davis. He came on board at Tycho City. I don't believe you two ever met."

"Does some immutable law say I must make his acquaintance?"

"Eventually. Might as well be when I'm around."

The cabin was stark compared to the bright colors of the station. White and chromium dominated. The only sound was the clicking of fingers on a keyboard. The officer turned as they entered. He wore the black and gold of the Space Corps, and the insigne of a bird colonel.

He made a slight gesture of respect to Scott. He was black, with hair like steel wool and a bristly mustache. Kane guessed he was a frequent visitor to the exercise centrifuge.

"Jacob Kane, let me present Colonel Jackson Drew."

"A pleasure, Colonel," said Kane suavely.

"Mr. Kane." He acknowledged the introduction with a slight incline of his chin. "I've wanted to meet you. I'm glad you saved me the trouble of looking for you."

"How can I serve you?" said Kane with a mock obsequiousness that Drew didn't catch.

"I've read your dossier and reviewed the facts of Victor Ames's death. But I want to question you to satisfy myself that you meet security requirements. Naturally, you'll be without clearance until then."

"That won't be necessary," said Scott. "Jacob was certified before we left earth. His certification has never been revoked."

"Sir, he has been absent from the project for six months—"

"It's okay. I can vouch for him." Scott smiled slightly. "But please don't relax your zeal, Colonel. You're doing a good job."

"Thank you." Drew was almost visibly seething.

"Any luck on the source of the mysterious transmission?"

"Two telecommunications experts are working on it, sir. We'll find it."

"I understand you had a ruckus with Professor Michlanski."

"He wouldn't let my men into his lab. They did everything but draw a gun on him."

"I'm glad they didn't! A gun is no match for a man for whom the universe is a toy! I'll speak to Sherlock, if you'd like."

"That would expedite things, sir."

"Very good. Well, good day, Colonel."

Scott led Kane from the compartment. "Drew's very competent, but he's not used to working with civilians."

"Seems like an ambitious type."

"Drew is considered a hot article on Luna. He's one of Davis's bright young men. But I'm glad he brought Sergeant Drake along. He's the one we deal with day to day. But we should probably consider ourselves lucky to have them on our side.

"Drew's collected a bucket full of medals. Very brave man. Tough as they come. He's no more worried about the situation than I am. Although he's letting it get to him."

Kane stopped and looked at Scott. "What's worrying you?"

"I'm glad you're back, Jacob! Did you meet Colonel Kemel?"

"Yes! These U.N. people act like we're the enemy."

They reached Scott's office and cabin combination. Scott closed and locked the cubicle's hatch and sat behind his desk.

"You're right," said Scott. "When we first arrived, the U.N. command was the epitome of cordiality. Kemel gave us every courtesy. Lately, ships from earth have been detained, sometimes for days, at North Polar."

"Why the change?" Kane, ever restless, stayed on his feet, and ran his fingers over every corner of Scott's small office.

"I was hoping you could tell me. You've been on earth recently. I watch the holocasts and sense tension. Am I paranoid?"

"Hard to say." Kane folded his arms. "How do you gauge tension? The tone of the news reports and announcements changed. The world, at least our countrymen—or rather, yours, since I am now the modern equivalent of the *Man Without a Country*—were euphoric after Shefferton's first speech about the Strubeck equations. They thought their problems were over. Then came the African war and bad harvests, now rationing. There's a lot of antagonism toward rationing. By some weird alchemy, the antagonism was transferred to the Sunside Project. But that doesn't explain the coolness of the U.N. Peace Force toward us."

"You're feeding my fears. I told Drew to bring his people on board

because we've had more accidents. A navvy was found floating outside with a smashed faceplate. His head was like an eggplant Par-
mesan. I've delayed leaves because I didn't want word of our problems
spreading.''

''What's the significance of that remark you made to the colonel about
finding the unauthorized transmission source?''

''A few days ago, when Michlanski and I were in a mini-shuttle, we
accidentally intercepted a laser message to earth.''

''What did it say?''

''We only interrupted the signal for a microsecond. It was unauthorized.
Drew's going crazy trying to find the source of that transmission. If Sherry
and I hadn't been out in the shuttle, we wouldn't have that clue—''

''What were you doing?''

''Sherry's located the Strubeck anomaly, the 'Lagrange' probability
point. We were getting close-up readings. He's returned several times.
He's even conducted experiments using antimatter, held together by a
'bottle' created by a highly powered magnetic field. He's ready to start
on the prototype.''

''We're that close?'' His chest constricted. They had gone far without
him. ''I thought Sherry needed the complete station to create a magnetic
'lens' to focus the sun's energy.''

''He's found a way to create the effect before construction is finished.''

''But the idea is to make the PH Station into a starship that can transport
several hundred people to Tau Ceti in one jump.''

''But if we don't have time to do that, we might have to put the device
aboard a smaller ship. Maybe even a shuttle.''

''And he's that close?''

''Possibly days away. We need one more antimatter shipment.''

''No wonder he's lost thirty pounds. Do you think someone on board
the station is transmitting this information to earth?''

''Have you heard of this man in Los Angeles, Frank Silverado?''

''*Conspiracy Weekly Reader?* No one takes him seriously.''

''I take him seriously.'' Scott was grim.

''You're joking!''

''Every issue makes new charges about the Strubeck equations. The
scientific arguments are written for infants. But behind them is knowledge available to only a few. If this person goes public, it may be too
late to undo the damage. You can bet that the Great Powers monitor such
reports. That probably accounts for the U.N.'s coolness toward us. The

General Secretariat will watch the situation and decide which way to jump.''

"This is serious."

"That someone is secretly fighting the implementation of the Strubeck equations suggests something very unpleasant. Someone has discovered the true purpose of the PH Station."

Chapter
* **46** *

I

The place announced itself a long way off. Holographic signs flashed garish enticements: "The Hoax Revealed—Strubeck Was a Fraud—Silverado Speaks Tonite—Tickets Available." Carnival-like music beat on his eardrums, brassy and badly played. Ferman suspected it was supposed to be, to maximize the irritation. Disgust, in its way, is more attractive than beauty, witness the success of freak shows throughout the ages. Revulsion brings in the busloads; beauty is just—another pretty face.

He rounded the corner. It sprang at him like an alley cat with a Roman candle tied to its tail: an old two-dimensional movie theater front, a marquee for decoration, but obsolete because of sky holograms. The building was the old Los Angeles City Hall, in its day the city's tallest building; still a dominating phallic presence. Marrying it to movie house decor was a stroke of breathtaking tastelessness that tickled the gag reflex and forced an involuntary gasp of admiration at the audacity of the thing. This was headquarters of the Worldwide Conspiracy Society, publishers of *The Conspiracy Weekly Reader*, whose editor and prophet was Frank Silverado.

Ferman idly fingered his pocketful of gold coins; his last reserve. His chances of getting work in the city were nonexistent. Still, this was the magnet that had drawn him across the continent. Whatever the cost to get in, he would pay it.

He bought a ticket and went looking for a bite to eat.

He hadn't had a hot meal in weeks. The way he was dressed he wouldn't be served in a decent restaurant, so he found an open-air café, whose faded candy-stripe awnings had enough holes to let in either sunlight or rain. The day was warm and the café was busy. He waited until a seat near the counter was free.

He sniffed at the prices. Ersatz coffee was expensive, but honest-to-God coffee was priced up past Mars. Somebody was making money off the famine, he thought. Maybe Chambless. Or Michlanski.

A greasy, overfed man with bulging bloodshot eyes, who looked like a onetime overseer of a Cambodian home for the aged, watched Ferman unblinkingly, anxious to take the order.

"I'll have a plate of scrambled eggs, two toasts, orange juice, ham, and a cup of real coffee." The cook mumbled something and held out a hand that might once have belonged to a cadaver.

"What?"

"Hand or yer rashion card," he repeated more distinctly.

For a frozen moment, Ferman panicked. "What?" he croaked.

"What, are ye deaf or sumpin'? Rashion card! Yer know, the thing yer gots to have to get grub." He spoke as if to a child.

Ferman relaxed. He had lived for so long on food from the black market, or stolen, that rationing laws had escaped his mind. Fortunately, he had picked up a few counterfeit ration cards the last time he had dealt with the black market. They were issued without names, so anyone could use them.

"Sorry," he said with a sheepish grin. "I was preoccupied."

The cook ran the ticket through his computer, which added a few invisibly tiny indentations. "Do yer thinkin' elsewhere!" he snapped, and threw the card back. "People here eats!"

The food was greasy and unappetizing, but compared to what he had eaten lately, it was four-star. He wolfed it down, taking his time over the expensive coffee. He lingered over a second cup until the cook began to eye him impatiently. He finished the coffee and put the exact change on the counter.

He spent the rest of the day finding a place to stay. There was no shortage of abandoned buildings, but the law was highly visible, so it wasn't safe to camp. Better to find a legitimate boardinghouse, the more run-down the better. Such places asked few questions and took a minimum amount of gold. They weren't the safest places in the world to sleep, but Ferman could take care of himself. Strange, a few months ago, the prospect of such an experience would have turned his bowels into water.

He found a dump a rat would have shunned, although it did have dead cockroaches. The landlady's interest in her boarders didn't extend beyond collecting the rent. It was perfect.

II

"The ship will be moving soon, and then I shall not see you for a long time," said the voice of Sergei, which seemed to emanate this time from the very center of the *Animus*.

The child savant and Lenore Lippman had spent many minutes together in the *Animus* this time. That translated into days in terms of communication and sharing, although Sergei's ship would probably not even notice that he was gone. In recent weeks, the bright young interface had discovered a way to do much of his duties at a distance, to transmit a phantom Sergei that the ship's operating system could not distinguish from the actual entity.

He was learning quickly, this young, tragic genius, doomed to always live his life in the mind.

"You promised to tell me about your country." He had found many references to the United States in the reading material Lenore Lippman had provided. Not all of it positive. Since his ship and its mission were diametrically opposed to everything America stood for, Lenore felt it vital that he understood at least how she felt about her homeland. Particularly if he was headed in the direction she thought he was.

"I sense intense emotion on your part when you think about your country. This I find alien. I do not know the Unified Soviet State. Only that I, my comrades and I, serve it, and sometimes die for it."

"My country is, and has always been, a place of great contradictions, Sergei. A land that guaranteed freedom to all men, and yet kept millions of black people slaves; a land of laws and justice that stole the land from the Indians without regard to law or justice. A land where people wept at slaying animals to provide food or wrappings, yet killed unborn children without emotion. My ancestors were an emotional, illogical race, who demanded clean air and water, yet refused to use the nuclear technology that would guarantee these things. It has a mad passion for its geniuses and creators, yet insists on punishing them when they become too great. My nation is far from perfect. It is a crazy quilt of silliness, and yet quite noble in its way. It is worth preserving, I think, at least for a while."

"You would make an admirable propagandist, Lenore." She was quite shocked. It was an extremely mature observation from what she continued to regard as a childlike mind.

"I'm sorry. I was trying to distill a lifetime's worth of experience down into a few moments. My imperfect observations should not influence you as much as the reading material I brought." She had, of course, brought the Declaration of Independence and the Constitution, but also examples of some of the best American novelists such as Twain and Steinbeck, and philosophers such as Thoreau. No, she didn't have a hidden agenda. Not her!

"I hope that we speak again, Lenore."

"We will," she said fiercely. "My son."

III

Ferman arrived for the lecture forty-five minutes early.

Entering the building, he felt uncomfortable. So distinct was the feeling of being watched that he almost fled. But he resisted the urge and continued up the stairs.

The brilliance almost blinded him. In a corner of the auditorium a poor but enthusiastic band played diluted popular hits. The atmosphere was a cross between a carnival and a revival, with a pinch of political convention thrown in. A large display told the story of the Worldwide Conspiracy Society, and the cases on which it had built its reputation. Another exhibit carried dramatic reenactments of famous conspiracy cases of the past: the Lincoln, Kennedy, and King assassinations, the Watergate conspiracy, the Great Clone Hoax, the Alf Nadir perjury case, the Cardiff Giant and Piltdown man hoaxes, and most recently the Perryville UFO scare. What the exhibit didn't say was that the Worldwide Conspiracy Society, so recently established, couldn't have solved any of these old cases. Yet concentrating these cases in one place was enough to make the most trusting soul paranoid. Ferman didn't need a lot of pushing in that direction anyway.

Another exhibit showed, in vivid, bloody color, stories *The Conspiracy Weekly Reader* had exposed in recent months, with emphasis on the bizarre and perverted: like the coven of mothers who ate their own children.

After seeing the exhibition, Ferman grabbed an aisle seat as far forward as he could get, ready for a fast exit.

He studied the individuals who began to straggle in. The types of people, their clothes and affluence, or lack of it, provided an interesting barometer of the *Reader*'s audience. A young woman sat across the aisle, fashionably attired in an ankle-length neo-Puritan dress. When she stood to let someone slip past, she revealed a slit up the length of the dress, which exposed a shapely thigh and glimpses of a small but exquisite breast. In front of him sat a dignified man in his early sixties, scrupulously dressed like a member of the diplomatic corps. A few seats away, just far enough to keep Ferman from swooning at the smell, was a garishly painted young man with shaved furrows crossing from the back of the neck to the temple and tiny silver bells dangling from his eyelashes. His ripe odor resulted from a carcass of a small dog, several days dead, worn as a decoration on his chest. He was plugged into intravenous music, a candy-striped syringe clinging leech-like to his bare forearm, feeding blue liquid into his blood. He jerked spastically to a beat only he could hear.

For the most part the auditorium was filled with normal citizens, who were alternately awed and delighted, shocked and repulsed by the eccentrics also waiting to hear the word from Silverado. They were middle class, with a slice of the poor, but no trace of the burned-out souls who lived in this part of town.

Ferman saw why when an obvious SoHi addict stumbled into the building. His eyes were swollen and milky, his skin had a bluish cast, and a string of green saliva trailed from his lips. He was in an advanced state of addiction: approaching the crisis, when the addiction would end forever or he would die. The chances of the latter were better than two to one.

Before he could create a scene, the creature was seized by two burly men and borne bodily from the theater.

The program was introduced by a person Ferman vaguely recognized as either a radical political figure or a show business personality who performed bizarre sexual acts on a cable network. His speech gave no clue which it was. He bestowed fulsome praise upon the evening's speaker. Ferman might almost have believed he was seeing a parody, except for the fanatical gleam in the man's eyes.

He finished and the stage dimmed. A circle of light appeared on the speaker's rostrum. A man walked purposefully onto the stage, and briefly surveyed the audience while applause boomed like the surf, then strode to the lectern and stood behind it.

"Good evening, ladies and gentlemen," he said. "I come tonight to bring you the truth."

The applause surged and he drank it in. He was tall, with an immense frame, and an immense load of flesh hanging from it. His egg-shaped head had as much hair on top as an egg. What hair he had was black, long, and stringy. He was swarthy with a shadow where he shaved. His outrageously flamboyant mustache was waxed stiff as a stand of cacti.

His black, almond-shaped eyes had true magic. They sparkled and shimmered, searched and explored every inch of the auditorium, locking onto every face in an ocean of faces. When he looked at Ferman, he felt the eyes drilling him, plumbing every secret. He shifted uncomfortably. A thin smile appeared on Silverado's lips and his gaze swept on.

A born rabble-rouser, his Latin accent was caressing, like dark syrup flowing over smooth rocks—and fiery and stinging, like a whip. He evoked every emotion, made his listeners feel he was a sincere, empathic friend. He was—the voice of truth.

Sometimes he spoke so low that he was whispering. Then he would lean forward, searching for a lower octave, and every member of the audience leaned with him. At other times he thundered his message to the vaulted ceiling like a prophet of old.

Later Ferman couldn't recall memorable phrases or sentences from his lecture. Yet there was no mistaking the message:

The great crutch America leaned on was cut from a rotted tree. The hope for a better world was false. The Strubeck equations were fake, conjured up by unscrupulous officials when they discovered that the real equations were the senile dreams of an old man desiring a last illumination of glory. The government wanted to quiet the people, to keep them from finding out the truth, that their plight was desperate beyond measuring. Greedy government minions were stockpiling food in a redoubt in the Alaskan wilderness, where they would retreat when starvation consumed the world. That was the message Silverado brought them.

"I have proof!" he roared. "Scientific proof corrupt Washington cannot refute. They feed lies to the people, but the people believe them not! The president trembles at this evidence, soon to be released in *The Conspiracy Weekly Reader*. He trembles because his seat of power is cracking! We will bring him *down!*"

The roaring tide from the crowd washed over Silverado as he held his hands aloft, his fingers writhing like the Medusa.

"Where will we bring the conspirators?" he demanded.

"Down!"

"Where will the lying scientists go?"

"Down!"

"Where will the traitors who brought Armageddon be sent?"

"Down!" They began to chant: *"Down! Down! Down! Down! Down!"*

The sound merged in Ferman's tortured ears and he thought he heard the words *Doom! Doom! Doom!* taking their place.

"Friends," Silverado said in a cracked whisper, "you know our needs. Our evidence will be published soon. It would be already, but the conspirators have labored to prevent the *truth* from reaching the people. We are persecuted by the corrupt Justice Department, which seeks new illegal ways to restrain our publication. We need money!

"I know you paid to attend this lecture. But what is money compared to *truth*? I ask your help in our fight. My associates will pass among you. Give what you can. Remember, we seek the truth!"

His teeth gleamed like porcelain, and with a deep bow he left the stage. No screaming applause, no stamping of feet, was sufficient to make him reappear.

Chapter

* 47 *

Seattle Star Herald—Yukon's state assembly today voted 45–20 to ratify the constitutional amendment repealing the Thirty-first Amendment, becoming the fortieth state to do so. Three fourths of the sixty-one states are required to amend. California and Prince Edward Island have scheduled votes this week.

Johannesburg, *The Citizen*—A daring daylight attack on the Soviet compound in the Black African capital of Lagos today briefly threatened to capture the Soviet ambassador.
The attack was carried out by commandos whose leader claims to be Juba Aman Dana, former dictator of the Black Union. . . .

I

Marshal Antonine Tiomkin had lost forty pounds since General Pavel Orlov last saw him. He sat in a wheelchair on a grassy knoll overlooking a plain in Central Mongolia where Orlov's brigade of "Space Sharks" maneuvered against a mechanized infantry regiment, a tank brigade, a light laser regiment, and an engineering company, who were trying to cross a river.

On the knoll was the headquarters of the Space Sharks. The unit was meant to travel light. So headquarters was essentially in the "saddle," which Soviet technicians had copied from plans stolen from the American army.

Tiomkin had been invited from his sickbed to visit the maneuvers, the first time he had been seen in public in months.

"Outnumbered three to one, Pavel?" said Tiomkin weakly.

"I wanted daunting odds," replied Orlov. "I don't want someone claiming we loaded the dice in favor of the Space Sharks. I even asked for one of Wen Chin's protégés to command the opposing force. Wen was happy to oblige. He'd love to make me eat dirt on this."

"Poor move on Wen Chin's part," said Tiomkin with a smile. "He gains nothing if his man beats your force, which he outnumbers. If you win, he loses face." He chuckled thinly. "Chin's judgment hasn't improved. I'm told that the Young Premier had Wen up all last night trying to explain how African guerrillas got past our finest troops and almost captured our ambassador."

Orlov bent over the tactical screen with intense concentration as his troopers on hover saddles exploited a gap in their opponents' formation and swiftly cut off and enveloped a company of mechanized infantry.

"Excellent maneuver, Pavel."

"Harder perhaps when the enemy is firing real bullets." He looked at Tiomkin. "Speaking of realism, don't you think you've taken it a bit too far with this weight loss of yours?"

"It had to be convincing," said the older man. "My physician, Dantes, gave me injections to cut my appetite and speed up my metabolism. I didn't exercise, to lose muscle instead of fat, giving me a wasted look. I'm told Brasnikov is worried. He's lost faith in Wen Chin, and it looks like I'm at death's door—"

"What you've been doing is incredibly dangerous. Not only the risk of discovery—if some ambitious member of the 'K' interrogates Dantes—but also the terrific strain on the body of a man your age."

"Something tells me I may make a miraculous recovery soon."

The Space Sharks had, by this time, effected a double envelopment, that looked like an elongated infinity symbol.

"You'll need entirely different equipment on the moon." Tiomkin was so absorbed by the exercise that he forgot how weak he was. He did some calculations in his head. "There will be the considerable logistical problem of transporting matériel to Luna without discovery by the Americans."

"I work with what I'm given. Chin has done his best to hamstring this unit. He didn't dare contravene your orders. But if you remain out of action much longer, he might try it."

"Chin is already destroyed symbolically." Tiomkin slapped his knee for emphasis. "Smitten by his own hand. It remains for him to acknowledge it. If I paid somebody to bring him down, I couldn't come up with a better scheme than attacking our compound in Lagos. It makes us look like donkeys."

"It will be good to have you back, Comrade Marshal."

"After a decent interval." He looked into the sky. "Let the Leopard have Africa. The fate of nations and worlds will be decided on a lump of gray clay. The Marathon of modern history will be upon the plains of Luna, my son."

II

Autumn waned, giving way to the second winter of the Shefferton presidency, where all thoughts were now focused on the results of the midterm congressional elections.

Representatives and senators had maneuvered endlessly for moments on the holocube, or given speeches to empty galleries to justify their existence to the voters. The political waters of the Potomac churned with the thrashing of sharks.

But the end result was that the Progressive Nationalists had retained a healthy control of both houses of Congress.

President Shefferton looked out his bedroom window. He had just risen. It took more effort than usual and he was convinced he had a virus. he decided to schedule a quick exam by his doctor, who had been virtually foaming at the mouth to give a new injection of biobots. It was the law, after all.

He loved this time of year, made all the sweeter by the sweeping victory, which owed much to his vigorous campaigning.

There had been rumblings over rationing. Nothing serious enough for the opposition to use as a campaign issue. Ironically, with their majorities guaranteed, some members of his party had begun to nip at the White House to increase their prestige. Shefferton found this depressing. he hadn't expected the honeymoon to last forever, but he thought it was a bit early for head-hunting season.

On his way to his shower, he paused at the holocube to call up the headlines on the major dailies and hourlies. He grunted:

Committees were investigating the food distribution program, some senators were attacking the space program, others delved into the conduct of the African campaign, hoping to find an abuse of authority. He was still catching flak for not publicizing the fact that the Russians had put three superbattleships into space. Now seven—

Percy Shelley Manners had kept a low profile since Charley Macadew had, in his own words, "cleaned his possum." Manners was not obviously behind any of the new efforts against the administration. But Shefferton suspected that Manners, backed by Horatius Krebs, was not about to go quietly into that good night.

The Sunside Project was about the only administration policy not under attack at home, although it was souring overseas. Europe and Russia had sent communiqués to Secretary Harmon, expressing fears that the PH Station might house deadly weapons. They had obliquely suggested that an international commission should tour the facility and establish that its purpose was peaceful.

Shefferton had squelched that idea. A project to build a faster-than-light space drive might not be a weapon, but it was not a development he wanted the Great Powers to know America had, until it actually had it. Harmon was miffed by the decision. Since he was not privileged to know about the Sunside Project, he couldn't understand why foreign delegations couldn't tour the jewel of America's space program.

That had finally convinced Shefferton that Harmon's usefulness was at an end. He couldn't ignore Harmon's latest intrigues with Manners. Worse, Harmon was not the man to handle a possible diplomatic crisis.

He spent longer in the shower than usual. The hot water pulsating against his athletic, still-youthful body, combined with sonic massage, was usually enough to rocket him through the most grueling of mornings. Today it wasn't working. Well, a flu shot would take care of that, he thought.

He stepped out of the shower, dripping, and toweled himself vigorously. Something at the back of his mind bothered him. Something about the

Sunside Project. What was it? He shook his head. Damn, he was having trouble concentrating on just a simple thing like—like what?

He blinked rapidly. What was wrong, for God's sake? He looked around the bathroom. What was he doing? What time was it? Would someone just answer his question? What was wrong with him?

He seemed to be looking at the world through the wrong end of a telescope. No sound. No feeling. The only thing he could see was blue tiles, like a ceiling. He wanted to move his head. Don't do this to me! It's not fair!

III

"Can you hear me, Mr. President?"

"Yes, perfectly, Dr. Knust."

"Sir, you know you're in a hospital?"

Shefferton nodded, an effort that seemed on the level of doing a hundred pull-ups. He focused on the navy surgeon, a lieutenant commander, with a white beard.

"Sir, you passed out in your bathroom. We're trying to find out what's wrong. I wish to God I'd insisted that you replace your biological monitoring robots when they were damaged." Knust saw his career going into the dump. Shefferton found the strength to grasp his white coat.

"Doctor, I want all records pertaining to the destruction of my biobots destroyed. . . . Do you . . . understand?"

"Frankly, sir, I do not understand!"

"Doctor, what does he want done?" asked the president's wife, who was standing between Sheridan Mayfield and Charles Macadew, who, with the White House chief of staff and the head of the Secret Service detail, were the only ones in the room.

"To destroy the data relating to the fact that his biobots were disabled on Luna by an electromagnetic pulse while he was visiting the 'lake' fusion plant," said the doctor.

"It's important that you understand before everyone else arrives. There is data of a national security nature regarding his visit to the fusion lake," said Mayfield.

"But it's common knowledge that he went there."

"Aspects of that visit are classified. For national security reasons we are going to order you to classify all data relating to the visit. That means you are under orders not to reveal the cause of the president's illness, just the illness itself."

"I don't know—"

Mayfield put an edge on his voice. "I'll get it in writing from the secretary of defense, if you want, Commander."

Knust saw he was outgunned, and he wasn't anxious for it to come out that Shefferton had contracted Rogue Cancer on the moon because his doctor failed to insist on a new injection of biobots. Of course, now he would have to come up with a new explanation.

"I presume I'll have White House support on the explanation that I'm to be forced to manufacture."

Mayfield turned to the chief of staff, who looked at the president, who held his eyes a moment. The chief of staff chewed on his lip and nodded. "You'll have our cooperation, Commander."

"Very well, then."

Shefferton closed his eyes. "Sheridan, Charley, come closer." They obeyed.

"I want the two of you to look at a video I made a few months ago. I want the vice president to see it too."

"Why the rush? You'll be back on my ranch shooting, or rather, missin' ducks in a week. You're just tired," said Macadew.

Shefferton shook his head weakly. "Don't try to shit a shitter, Charley. Just promise you'll see the video. It's a recording I made about the Sunside Project. It will explain what has gone on. I hope you'll understand and forgive me."

"Nuthin' to forgive, Jeff."

Macadew glanced at Mayfield as if he was annoyed at him for not adding his voice to that sentiment. But Mayfield wasn't about to grant absolution without knowing the sin. And he had a sneaking suspicion about that—

IV

Teresa St. Clair entered the room in Walter Reed Naval Hospital. When she first glimpsed the president she was struck by the ridiculousness of it. He had so many tubes and attachments running from his body that he looked like a human still.

It's strange the stupid things that run through your mind at a time like this, she thought. She had noticed, walking down the hall, how loudly her heels clacked on the floor, and she had the thought that someone might shush her for walking too loud.

She turned at the voice, a bit too quickly. "Uh, yes?"

Randolph Harmon looked every bit his age. He was shaky. "Madam

Vice President, the president has suffered a seizure. Are you prepared, under provisions of the Twenty-fifth Amendment, to discharge the office until the president can resume his duties?''

"I am.'' The room was filled with Secret Service agents, the White House chief of staff, and several cabinet officers. Mayfield was off in a corner, looking stonily at the bed. Macadew was quietly weeping. The only person in control was Shefferton's wife, who was bent over the bed, talking normally, as if he were sick with a cold.

St. Clair saw the doctor. "Commander, what's wrong with him?''

"Rogue Cancer. Brought on complications that led to a stroke. That made him fall in the bathroom. It's not a catastrophic stroke in that he's not paralyzed. But it is serious.''

"How long before he's able to resume his duties?''

Knust held out his hands helplessly.

"I see.'' The vice president turned to Shefferton. "Don't worry, Jeffrey. I won't mess things up. Everything will be in place when you want it back.''

"Teresa, I'm sorry I haven't kept you more informed. I want you to look at the recording. . . . I left instructions . . . that you—'' He looked as though he was trying to sit up.

"It's all right, Mr. President. I'll watch your recording. Don't worry. Lie down. Everything will be all right.''

"Thank you.'' Shefferton's smile looked beatific, relaxed, as if meditating. The air-conditioning came on, stirring his close-cropped hair. It occurred to St. Clair that he was dead.

Chapter
✻ 48 ✻

I

The president was dead.

Teresa Evangeline St. Clair didn't remember much of the past twelve hours.

The first time she sat at his—her—desk in the Oval Office, she felt like an interloper. The president's wife, through her own grief, had sensed her discomfiture, and insisted that she conduct business there. That she sit in his chair, even as his belongings were packed away.

She had much to ponder. There was a speech to prepare, reassuring the people and grieving with them for a fallen chief. Part of the nation was cheering because a woman had reached the presidency; others viewed it with alarm. She hoped America had matured enough that the former far outnumbered the latter.

St. Clair had asked her cabinet members to remain at their posts after it became clear that she wasn't going to be allowed even a brief honeymoon before being confronted by a crisis.

The national security adviser delivered a message from Premier Brasnikov, demanding that an inspection team be allowed aboard the PH Station. It was followed by similar messages from Greater Asia and Black Africa, obviously prearranged. Fortunately, Europe's President Gernais, although under pressure to join the coalition, was sitting on the sidelines.

A short time later she was given a coded message from Admiral Davis, confirming the presence of Soviet ground troops near the New Moskow colony and on the move, probably toward Tycho City.

If the Soviet battleship had been stopped at the outset, this wouldn't have happened, she knew. The Lunar fleet could have covered Tycho from orbit, and simultaneously threatened New Moskow. Now it was forced to uncover Tycho to meet the Soviet move.

And then there was Shefferton's video, his political last will and testament. After viewing the video, which revealed every secret he had kept about the Sunside Project and the Strubeck equations, she had been emotionally and spiritually numbed.

She had thought he was exaggerating a few months before when he had said he might be impeached for his actions regarding the Sunside Project. Impeached! That was an understatement!

Her intercom beeped.

"Madam President, you have several appointments in the next few hours. Are you ready for them?"

She started to reply and caught herself. This was history with a capital *H*. If she answered with weakness, History would record that she was afraid. If she was snappish, hesitant, or flippant, History would note it. She made her voice as firm as when she had ordered the National Guard to fire on the rioters who threatened the fusion power plant on the Columbia River.

"Send the first gentleman in."

Speaker Melvyn Fitzgerald Saratoga held her hand a long time, like a father comforting a daughter. He looked like hell. He had loved Shefferton.

He sat down heavily. "Well, Teresa, all the women in the country are watching you today."

"Melvyn, I don't have time for you to ruminate about how the republic's going to hell because a woman is in charge."

He sat up straight. "Now look here! I came over here . . ."

"To comfort a woman! I'm the president now, and a potential coup d'état is brewing. I must know who's on my side!"

"What are you talking about?" he asked sharply.

St. Clair walked in front of her desk and stood on the carpet emblazoned with the president's seal. She folded her arms, almost belligerently. "Harmon and Manners urgently requested an audience. Requested is not the word: They demanded I see them."

Fitzgerald chewed on his little finger. "What's brewing?"

"Percy will ressurect his scheme for government by cabinet and suggest himself or Harmon for what will be, practically, prime minister." She supported her right elbow with her left hand and cupped her jaw with her right hand. "They figure I'd make a photogenic figurehead."

"Well, you would!"

"Up yours, Melvyn!" She paced across the Oval Office purposefully and leaned against an ancient teak cabinet facing Saratoga. "What's your feeling about this maneuver by the Boy Wonder and his senile partner in crime?"

"Percy's got a loose flywheel! A few weeks ago he came in my office and said I'd better find a graceful way to exit my job. He said I'd opposed him once too many times. What a look in his eyes when he said, 'It's up to you, Melvyn. Leave gracefully. The clock is ticking.' Jesus!" He shuddered. "There's no doubt in my mind who's senior partner in any coalition formed by those two."

"So what's your advice?"

"I don't *have* any. The combined fleets of Asia, Russia, and Black Africa are about to attack our space station. God knows if we'll have a Lunar colony in a week. We're all relying on you. If you don't have something up your sleeve, we're cooked!"

"Don't worry, Melvyn. I have a plan."

"You do? Thank God!"

"I need for you to start glad-handing and reassuring all the faint-hearts in the House. I'll have my hands full with the prince of the World's Oldest Debating Society."

Fitzgerald slapped his knees and stood. "What time tomorrow do you want to address the joint houses?"

She shook her head impatiently. "I'm going to be too busy being president of the United States to talk about it for a while."

When the Speaker left, she had Randolph Harmon and Percy Manners escorted in. They acted miffed that she had seen Fitzgerald before she saw them. She pretended she didn't notice.

"Madam President, you have our deepest regards, and, I'm sure, the prayers and meditations of all right-thinking Americans as you contemplate history's verdict," said Harmon.

"Thank you."

"In a time like this," added Manners, "it helps to know that people are ready to stand beside you—to give you a helping hand with what must be an almost intolerable burden."

"Well, yes, you're right. I need all the help I can get."

Harmon leaned forward. He was impressive! "It's vital to decide whom you'll name vice president. I—" Manners coughed, not so discreetly. "Eh, we've taken the liberty of preparing a list of people we regard as top candidates. I hope you don't mind?"

"No. Not at all." Harmon slid the list across the desk and St. Clair read it. "Neither of you gentlemen is on the list."

"Many fine public servants share our worldview," said Manners smoothly. "Any of these will make an outstanding vice president. My personal favorite is Senator Iowa Thurgood. Although you could not go wrong naming one of our nation's finest government eminences. I speak of the man who sits next to me."

Harmon started, and looked at Manners, not sure whether to be puzzled, angry, or flattered. "I thought we agreed—"

"Yes, but I sense that Mrs. St. Clair needs a good right arm. The republic has called you many times. I don't think we should let petty political preferences stand in the way of the greater good."

"Ah, true," said Harmon doubtfully. "I wonder, ma'am, have you given thought to the concept of the Executive Cabinet that we presented to the president a few weeks ago?"

"He gave it to a top-level committee of aides to look at and report back." Jeffrey had told her he intended to have them report back on the plan sometime after he left office.

Manners was familiar with the president's committees from his White House spies. He put a hard edge to his smooth voice. "I really think you should look it over, ma'am. I think you should do so very soon. You should regard it with the utmost seriousness."

"I regard everything you say with the utmost seriousness."

"We're at a desperate crossroads," said Harmon. "If we don't let the Soviets inspect the PH Station, we may cause a world war! They already regard the fact that Shefferton moved the fleet to block them as an intolerable provocation."

"Randolph," said the president, "one unique contribution you make as secretary of state is your unerring ability to put yourself in the place of our enemies and think like them. It's almost like having the first secretary here with us.''

Harmon forgot for a moment how much he detested having his first name used and preened at what he perceived as a compliment of the highest order. ''Thank you, ma'am.''

Manners's eyes hardened, in that frightening way Melvyn Saratoga had described. ''I think you should retrieve the Executive Cabinet proposal from the committee, and go over it personally.''

''You would like a decision on it from me posthaste?''

''Yes, although I think you'll agree there can be only one conclusion,'' said Manners. ''Once you weigh the alternatives.''

''Would tomorrow morning be soon enough?''

''At your convenience. We need to formulate a policy to deal with this crisis. And if you do implement the Executive Cabinet proposal, we will need to convene it and decide what to do next.''

''I do have a plan.''

''I'm sure the Executive Cabinet will give it a fair hearing, ma'am.'' They rose to leave.

''One thing more,'' said Harmon. ''I think it wise to summon this Jason Scott home to justify his conduct before an inquiry. It would not be good to sully the good name of President Shefferton when we can lay the blame for this fiasco at Scott's feet.''

''Good day, Madam President,'' said Manners.

St. Clair leaned on the massive desk for a moment after they left, took a deep breath, and touched the intercom button. ''Send in Mr. Mayfield and Senator Macadew.''

Mayfield still looked stunned. Macadew's wrinkles looked deeper and his white hair was more askew than usual, but he was as combative as always, or, more accurately, defiant.

She put on her sternest face. ''I believe you passed Senator Manners and Secretary Harmon on your way in.''

Macadew snorted. ''They looked like dogs given the run of the chicken coop.''

''You were Jeffrey's advisers, so I'll do you the courtesy of being frank. Harmon and Manners favor implementing the Executive Cabinet proposal given to my predecessor a few weeks ago.''

''Predecessor? He was President of the United States.''

''And now I am the president,'' said St. Clair, with steel in her voice that Mayfield found encouraging. "The reality of politics necessitates that I give close consideration to their proposal. I'm from the party's conservative wing, which has never had a strong voice in policy making. My position is weak."

"Wal, ma'am, whether you decide to sit back and be a figurehead, while some damned committee runs the country, is your decision. It'll probably be the last decision you make. I, for one, object to turning our republic into a parliamentary form of government without so much as a constitutional amendment."

"But you don't have the decision-making authority, do you?"

"No, ma'am, but I have a voice. I'll use it in the Senate."

"You'd defy Manners, and act against my explicit wishes?"

"I would act as my conscience directs, Madam President."

"Pity your conscience didn't direct you to give more forceful advice to the president. I know that you both opposed his inaction when the Russian battleship was just a hulk."

Macadew lifted his face, moist with tears. "Madam, I did not see you at that Security Council meeting. I respect your reasons for not attending, if you respect mine for not stabbing my friend in the back—even for the good of the country."

She rested her chin on her clenched fist. "*Touché!* Since we're not friends, perhaps you'll give me the benefit of your advice. This situation was brought on partially by Jeffrey's naïveté, and because he was ill. He tended to keep his eye upon the zero yard line, and often forgot that many people wanted not only to sack him, but to make sure he never got up again.

"The situation is that we must put our nation's prestige, power and destiny behind the Sunside Project, which is nothing like what President Shefferton told anyone."

"What're you saying?" The color drained from Mayfield's face.

The president explained what Shefferton had said in the videotape. "Not since Truman was kept in the dark about the atom bomb has a vice president been so uninformed about a major area of national policy. I know he wanted to protect us from the fire storm if it came out prematurely. That doesn't make me feel any better."

"My God." For months Mayfield had suspected something like this. He was torn by anger that Shefferton had kept him in the dark and admiration for the project, whose aim—faster-than-light travel—he had cherished for years.

"Harmon and Manners want to let the Russians on the PH Station and set up Jason Scott as the patsy, so we won't soil Jeffrey's name. Which makes them look like loyal party members—"

"Adam Scott's son will fight to keep from being a scapegoat!" said Mayfield. "They don't know whom they're dealing with!"

St. Clair continued as if she had not been interrupted. "Then we have the problem of a possible attack by Soviet CosMarines on Tycho Base. No one has given me advice on that yet. Want to give it a try?"

Macadew stood. The roly-poly comic figure was gone, replaced by the man of the Senate, who had crossed swords with every major politician of his day. "Ma'am, I won't offer advice until you promise to scrap the Executive Cabinet. Until I know you are your own woman, I won't dirty my hands on your administration. I'd rather sink with honor than stay afloat as a puppet. Percy knows that if he comes into my den, he'd better come packing a lunch!"

"And you, Secretary Mayfield?"

"I agree with Charley. I won't work for someone who's having her strings pulled. My advice is to do what you think is best. If you do, you won't lack for people to carry out your orders."

"You've already given me your resignation, along with everyone else in the Cabinet," she reminded him softly.

"Yes, but this time I mean it." Mayfield stood up and both he and Macadew turned to leave the Oval Office.

"Gentlemen!" Her voice had a new ring of authority. "Come back and sit down. We have work to do. I have a plan."

"Well!" exploded Mayfield. "I'm glad somebody does!"

II

Her last visitor was Rita Holcombe Duce, who walked into the Oval Office and gravely offered her hand.

"My congratulations, Madam President. And my sympathy. I have nothing but high hopes for your administration. If you can survive all those who will seek to give you advice."

The president smiled her first sincere smile of the day. "You're not one of them? I did ask you here for your assessment of the PH Station situation. And I wanted to ask you something."

Duce sat in front of the president's desk and rested her hands in her lap. "I'm at your disposal. Although Jason Scott is probably the best person to ask anything about that subject."

The president leaned forward. "You trust him that much."

"I trust him with my life. I am trusting him with my fortune, which is entwined with the success or failure of the project."

"Mrs. Duce," said St. Clair gently, "has he ever told you the full details of the project?"

"You're going to tell me Jason has not told me everything about the Sunside Project, even left out a vital element. Right?"

St. Clair felt disarmed. "Well, yes."

"It doesn't matter," said Duce, her face suddenly glowing. "I love Jason; not like a lover, like a mother. Even that's inaccurate. I love him for what he is: a doer, in a world almost entirely made up of followers. He is a creator, in a world that leeches off creators. Jason is working on something spectacular, I know that. I know he will give it to the world, no questions asked. If I can reap a small gain from that gift, fine. If I must go down to ruin, I'll do it—not for the world, not for the hands grasping at me, but for Jason. He's worth impoverishing myself for. He's going to give us something wonderful."

"He's going to give us the stars," said St. Clair. "If we let him."

"A star drive!" breathed Duce. "Yes, I'll give my fortune for that. In fact, I have given half of it."

"You're speaking of your gold that was at New Hong Kong when it was taken over by those pirates?"

"Horatius Krebs's private army. And it's still there, to help finance Krebs's takeover of the pocket republics. And to keep me from sending vital supplies to the PH Station."

"What vital supplies?" St. Clair leaned forward in her seat.

"Antimatter. The vital ingredient of Michlanski's experiment. I assume his experiment is the real purpose behind the project."

"According to a tape I viewed recently, that is correct. What keeps the pocket republics' defense force from acting?"

"A lack of resources. The defense force is really a joke. Only Hellas, which has a hydrogen bomb rigged to explode if anyone invades it, has any kind of effective deterrent."

St. Clair called up the New Hong Kong file. "According to this, Shef-ferton rejected taking action on the advice of the secretary of state, who said it was an internal affair."

"And how do you feel about it?"

"It's going to be my policy for a while to follow the course set by the previous administration. In this case, I think, that course was to do every-thing to advance the Sunside Project."

She touched her intercom. "Put me through to the secretary of defense." The pink dial tone pulsated as the connection was made.

"Grover, hello! Sorry to interrupt you at dinner. I know you're really busy, but I was wondering: Do you have a marine division that you're not using right now?"

After a short conversation with Secretary of Defense Grover T. Wells, the president looked pleased. "I think we can take care of your problem, Ms. Duce. Now, all you have to do is spend all of your money to help save the world."

"What are you going to do?"

"Don't worry, I have a plan. Now, if you'll excuse me." She quickly ushered Rita Duce out the door.

She didn't have a plan yet. But she had all night to think of one.

Chapter

* 49 *

Dec. 3—*Washington Times*—President St. Clair today announced the resignation of Secretary of State Randolph Harmon. He will be replaced by Senator Charles Macadew, who will leave the Senate to serve in the Cabinet. In a surprise move, the president said she will nominate Space Secretary Sheridan Mayfield for vice president. Mayfield will continue to hold his portfolio as SED secretary.

The president's bold actions stunned the capital, where observers had predicted she would name a vice president acceptable to the party's liberal wing. This is seen as clearing the decks for the impending international crisis over the PH Station.

Dec. 4—*Micronesia Times*—Elements of the U.S. First Marine Division captured the island of New Hong Kong shortly after dawn. Marines rode helicopter gunships from the amphibious carrier *Iwo Jima* and after a short battle forced the surrender of the mercenary forces of self-styled Colonel "Bamboo," who was killed, possibly by his own men. Brigadier General Art Crawford told newsmen he will hand over the island to Pocket Republics Defense Commander Poldark within the week.

Deseret Gantry—*Clarion Call's* Captain Stephen Finn, recently returned from Mercury, told reporters on Midway he plans to break a speed record established two years ago for the earth to Mercury run. The U.N. has protested that the ship should not be allowed to transport "contraband" to the PH Station.

Dec. 15—*New York Times*—An armada of four of the Unified Soviet State's seven *Aurora*-class battleships, and support craft, commanded by Admiral Novo Arbatov, plus the Asian self-defense squadron of battlecruisers *Musashi, Akagi,* and *Atari* and the Black African fleet, with its flagship *Battle of Ladysmith,* escorted by light cruisers *Qaddafi* and *Shaka,* are en route to Mercury. Most of the U.S. Lunar fleet, including battleships *Thunderer, Republic, Constitution,* and *Liberty,* commanded by Rear Admiral Bevel Hawkings, is waiting to intercept.

How did I do it? I used up all my fuel on one fabulous
mother of a burn—that's how I did it!
—Stephen Finn's reply to a query from the
U.S. space frigate Jamway

I

"She'll back down, I hope!" said Lieutenant Commander Mark Park (permanent rank Second Lieutenant) aboard the heavy cruiser *Patton.* The short, monkey-faced man had gone through a dozen cigarettes in an hour, while the ship rendezvoused with the cruiser *Inchon* in Mercury orbit and took on a contingent of fleet officers. Watching the *Inchon* as it left orbit to join the fleet, Park worried the fingernail on his left little finger. He was standing next to Captain Erskine Collins (permanent rank Lieutenant Commander) in the *Patton's* tiny bridge.

Collins looked up from the holocube and frowned. "Marcus, I thought I broke you of that crap. Be as big a coward as you want when we are the *Hyperion* but I'm damned if I'll put up with it when we're about to fight the first space battle in history."

"We won't if St. Clair throws in the towel." Park lit another cigarette. His wizened face twisted as he sucked out the nicotine.

"If you read anything besides racing news and book reviews, or did anything in your spare time but guzzle beer and fantasize about oriental women, you'd know that our commander in chief was the only man in Shefferton's Cabinet. She won't let the Russians on the PH Station without a fight."

"Fight! It'll be a massacre! It'll be like two sitting ducks shooting at each other. We're a fleet of eggs chasing another fleet of eggs, armed with hammers. They'll name a new constellation for us: the Omelet!"

"Don't let the kids hear that stuff, Marcus," said Collins. "Battles get fought because old guys like us convince young kids they have a chance of surviving in one piece. Speaking of which—" He turned to the intercom. "Attention, all hands, we're going to make this into a fighting navy ship. I'd like to welcome back Ensign Andrew Thumb, and welcome new fleet ensigns Veronica Van Dyke, Elizabeth Neeld and fleet Lieutenant Amerigo Trask. Ladies and gentlemen, report to the bridge in ten minutes!"

"So what's the plan, Commodore Collins?"

"Task Force Four, that's us and the *Crazy Horse, Jeb Stuart, Geronimo, Grierson, Puller, C. J. Johnston, Ticonderoga* and *Tycho City*; we stay behind the main fleet, cover the enemy, and plant proximity mines along its probable trajectory."

"Forcing them to plot new trajectories. By then we can put ourselves in front of that new course. They must either give us a wide berth and swing around the other side of the sun, adding two weeks to their trip, or cut velocity and go straight through us."

"Marcus!" Collins was geniuinely astounded. "You've been reading the tactical manual!"

"It's wonderful bedtime reading. Puts you to sleep, then scares the hell out of you in your dreams. The rotten thing about our role is that we can never get up much speed. Which makes us an easy target."

"My instructions are not to sacrifice ourselves, but to slow them down.

If I feel I'm endangering my force, I'm to fall back." Collins didn't look as though he bought it entirely either.

Park screwed up his face. "There must be some logic to this."

"There is," said Collins. "Hawkings is outnumbered one and a half to one. The enemy is traveling in a close-order spherical convoy. Hawkings thinks that's because the Russians are unsure their allies will follow orders once battle begins. Also because in sheer firepower, they have the advantage.

"However, we have the advantage in ship-to-ship combat. We had the only space navy for a long time. Our ships spend three quarters of their time in space, one quarter being refitted. Russian ships spend a third of their time in space, two thirds in Cosmograd. It's also the old story of inferior Soviet quality. We've got the experience, we've got better ships, except for battleships, and we've got professionalism."

"Preach to the converted, Captain. No one's ever fought a ship-to-ship battle before," said Park bitterly.

"That's a handicap for both sides. Hawkings's strategy goes back to Nelson at Trafalgar—"

"Who?"

"Sorry! Horatio Nelson didn't write great literature, or run any memorable races. He did kick the crap out of Napoleon's navy by breaking up the French line, forcing them to fight ship-to-ship, where the British had the advantage. Hawkings wants to use the mines to break up the Russian fleet—"

There was a knock on the hatch and the young officers entered. The bridge was too small for extended parties. Collins handed out assignments to take the crew's minds off the upcoming battle, and make the ship ready for combat. The most practical assignment was painting a new coat of "goop" on the hull. The last coat was showing signs of pitting. He saved his favorite assignment for the lieutenant, a chunky, capable-looking man in his early twenties who spoke with a deep Texas accent, which Collins found droll coming from a man named Amerigo.

"Lieutenant, this ship's civilian role is as a water tanker. When we take up station we put our tanks in orbit. This time I decided to keep 'em on. They have water in them. I want you to prepare a plan to spray the water to form ice crystals as a defense against laser attack."

"Interesting problem, Commodore, sir," drawled Trask. "I did a term paper on that very thing in my sophomore year at Annapolis." (Space navy cadets were sent to Annapolis and Colorado Springs until it built its own academy.)

"I know you did, son. That's why I gave you the problem."

"Uh, sir, I'd think the tanks would, well, make excellent defenses too. It doesn't matter if they get hit."

"Only to my pocketbook, son. But that's good thinking! Carry on." When he left, Collins looked at Park. "What do you think?"

"Nice kids. I'll be sorry to see them dead."

Collins ignored him. "Ensign Thumb's more cheerful than the last time. Like somebody removed the pole that was up his behind."

"Maybe he got his ashes hauled."

"Or anticipates getting them hauled with the young ensigns."

"They'll never look at him as long as I'm around," said Park with a high-pitched cackle that made Collins wince.

"I intend to keep those youngsters busy for the next couple of days, and then we'll evacuate the air out of the ship. It'll take a mighty determined Romeo to overcome that difficulty!"

Park made an entry into the navigational computer, frowned, and repeated the calculation. He cursed under his breath.

"What is it?"

"Look! That's Icarus, the one inhabited by the mining colony. Its orbit will take it right into the middle of our battle!"

II

At five in the morning Marshal Antonine Tiomkin was piped aboard the flagship *Lenin*, in Lunar orbit with its sister ships *Aurora* and *Kirov*.

The marshal, looking remarkably fit for a man who had been nearly visited by the hag, walked between two black and red lines of impeccably uniformed CosMarines, nodding with approval. If any man had ever made a triumphal return, it was he. If any man was ever totally in command of the situation, it was he.

He stayed in command for all of five minutes, until, entering the fleet command center, he found First Secretary Peter Brasnikov in the seat normally reserved for the admiral, sipping from a plastic bulb a clear white liquid that some people called the senior member of his Cabinet: vodka.

"Ah, Antonine Mikhailovich, I'm so happy you are well!" He launched himself at Tiomkin, and in the one-third gravity of the ship, almost overshot the mark. Tiomkin caught him.

"Careful, First Secretary!"

"It is I who should look out for you, old friend," said the premier in that sentimental sloppy drunk manner that could change into treachery and murder with the swiftness of a cobra strike.

"You have. You brought me back from retirement to serve the motherland. You saved an old warrior from dying of boredom. That made me well. Knowing that you, that the state, needed me."

"Well said."

Tiomkin spoke carefully. "I am most pleasantly surprised to find you here. No one told me of your coming."

The premier leaned over in a conspiratorial manner. "It was—a surprise. I came over from the *Admiral Danilo* in a lifeboat when you were flying up from the Baikonur Cosmodrome. Ever since that bungling Mongolian, I've trusted no one. Most military men are fools. You're the only one I know with vision. You're the only one who knew that the decision must be made in space. But even you can use help, from a practical man, a man of the people. And here I am!" Even in low gravity he swayed. "Kindly explain the tactical dispositions. I can't give advice if I don't know your plans."

"Of course, First Secretary!" Gods, how he wanted to push that sensuous, weak face up the hairy ass of some little dray pony back home in Archangel!

Tiomkin activated the globular tactical display of the earth, moon, and the space between. It highlighted Midway and Cosmograd, the American bases L-5 and L-4, the ever-changing pattern of U.S. ABM satellites, the Soviet satellites circling the earth and moon, the three Soviet battleships and escorts, against the American fleet of one battleship, *Terrible Swift Sword*, and her escorts.

New Moskow, the large colony near the crater Archimedes in the Lunar northern hemisphere, was shown in red (naturally). Three brigades of Space Sharks were indicated by rectangular symbols.

"The American colonies stretch like a necklace north to south, with Clavius and Tycho near each other, and Copernicus isolated." Tiomkin traced this line with a thick finger. "This is not lost on the Americans. They once started a direct Tubeway tunnel between the colonies. The European colony Atlantia is in the Sea of Tranquility, near the *Apollo 11* landing. Since Europe has chosen neutrality, its colony's location becomes moot. However, the White Chrysanthemum Colony at Pytheas crater is in our line of march. It can provide us a base close to Copernicus. We can also, in a stroke, retake our rebellious comrades at Plato, which calls itself the Lunar Free State. That will come later. I choose to concentrate

our forces in a line of march down the necklace, taking first Copernicus,
then Tycho, the most important, because of its shipyards; and finally
Clavius.''

"And the American fleet, Antonine Mikhailovich?''

"We have three battleships against one. Although their fleet stands
between us and Luna, we ought to be able to dominate the skies over the
moon and force the issue shortly.''

Brasnikov studied the display with considerable seriousness. "And what
American ground troops are there?''

"Keith's Extraordinary Tactics Force defends the city. It is a third the
size of ours, which is commanded by General Orlov. We don't underestimate Keith, but the odds are against him.''

"And what about the PH Station?''

"A great battle will be fought between the orbits of Venus and Mercury.
If the PH Station houses a secret weapon, we have struck at an opportune
moment. It will not be completed for several weeks. Once we deal with
the American fleet, we can take the station, and whatever technological
marvel it contains.''

"Intact?''

"Yes, because *we* have a secret weapon on the PH Station. Someone
above suspicion. A spy, who, at our signal, will neutralize the station and
allow us to take it without a fight.''

"What will the signal be?''

"A call to surrender, broadcast by Admiral Arbatov.''

III

The first shots of the war were "fired" when laser cannons on board
the *Terrible Swift Sword* took out the Soviet spy satellites orbiting the
moon. This stunned the Soviets, who had been counting on making a
surprise attack.

It wouldn't have surprised them if they had known that Admiral Hanley
Davis had taken command of the fleet and left the surface defense to Keith's
ETF and space marines. Davis had written admiringly about the Japanese
attack on Pearl Harbor and the Israeli preemptive strike of the Six-Day
War.

On earth, the belligerents signed an agreement not to fight on earth or
in earth's orbit. Where once the concept of importing man's favorite pas-
time, war, into outer space had seemed horrible, it now seemed a pretty

good idea to confine it to the vacuum, where only a few thousand people, and inestimable millions of ounces of gold, were at risk.

The Soviet satellites winked out in little flares of nuclear fire, and with them hopes of orbital intelligence regarding the movements of Keith's troops. Nevertheless, General Orlov was confident as he moved the three Space Shark brigades to invest the small U.S. colony at Copernicus. Isolated and abandoned by the space marines, Copernicus surrendered.

"Several factors are working for us," David Keith told his staff. "One is that General Orlov has adopted a predictable line of march. It's a logical strategy, taking the plums one by one. But one that allows us to meet it without uncertainty."

Virtually every officer who had served with Keith in Africa had transferred when the Extraordinary Tactics Force was recommissioned in the Space Corps. They sat at a circular table while Keith stood in front of an electric blackboard overlaid by a Lunar map. Terry Ransome, now Captain Ransome, sat next to Keith.

"Once Orlov's army reaches Tycho City, it will be at the end of a lengthy supply line, while we will be in front of our base."

Governor Merle Jackson, who had requested to sit in on strategy sessions, frowned. "Aren't we going to try to keep them from reaching Tycho City?"

"No, I withdrew the marines from Copernicus, and ordered them not to harass the Russians on the march because I want to have as much of the Soviet army in front of Tycho City as I can."

The rear admiral left in charge of Tycho Brahe Base raised his hand. "General, would you explain your people's activities in our hangars. What are you going to do with those ships?"

"Well, they can't fly. Correct?" asked Keith.

"They're being refitted, but I doubt we can ready any of them for combat in time to make a difference in this fracas."

"We agree they can't fly. We disagree about their usefulness." Keith smiled disarmingly. "Can they be mounted on the tractors within the time I specified? And be given coats of antilaser paint?"

"Everything as you instructed. The tractors already transport ships from the port to the hangars. It's just a matter of making the attachment more sturdy," said the admiral slowly, still totally baffled. "But why?"

"Admiral, no one has ever built a tank for use on the moon. Those ships were built to fight. They just can't fly right now. I propose to use them for the purpose for which they were built.''

"But I thought you were the general who hated tanks!''

Keith smiled disarmingly. "I hate conventional thinking. I love tanks, particularly when I'm the only one who's got 'em!''

PART

* 6 *

"THE
EIGHTH
RANK"

Chapter

* 50 *

I

"This is Admiral Novo Arbatov of the United Nations Humanitarian Fleet calling the PH Station." The Soviet flag officer was obviously cut out for imminent retirement. He was grandfatherly, white-haired, bluff, and wide, with hanging jowls. His English was atrocious.

"We broadcast in the hope that reason will prevail." He leaned forward, pudgy white hands folded on his desk. "People of the PH Station, we are *not* aggressors. We will not attack, no matter what your leaders tell you. We will defend ourselves against the powerful weapon aboard your station. We are a U.N. sanctioned relief force, authorized to occupy the station until it can be determined how to deal with the offensive weapon you carry.

"Do not let your misguided leaders start a war. Do not let them fire on our peaceful force. We implore you to allow us, your friends, to board you in peace. We plead, in the name of mankind."

Colonel Jackson Drew floated nearest to the auditorium holocube, so he shut off the image. He and the twenty or so top people of the project were gathered in the station's zero-gravity meeting room at the hub, for a "council of war." Absent were Jacob Kane and Matt Taylor, who were outside working on the wheel, and Sherlock Michlanski, who hadn't left his lab in weeks.

"It's broadcasting every five minutes," said the colonel, who managed to remain stiff and tense, even weightless. "A powerful transmission. If not for the sun's interference, it would bleed onto every terminal. However, we're surrounded by materials that reflect radiation or convert it into power. The Soviets are providing us with a few nanowatts of electricity." He smiled slightly at his microscopic joke.

"What do they mean?" asked Bethany Williams. "We don't have a secret weapon aboard the station."

"Or even artificial photosynthesis yet," added Rene Delner.

"Typical Soviet disinformation," said Drew, "and incompetence. Anyone who served in Africa and met the Genetic Communists knows how capable they are of stupidity. Like sending a message no one will ever receive." He kicked off the deck to the center of the auditorium. His "audience" above and below him were strewn about like fruit on a tree. "Or *is* it incompetence? What if the broadcast is a blind to hide another message?"

"H-have you discovered an embedded message hidden in th-that broadcast?" asked Dorian Nye.

"I'm operating under that assumption, but in the time we have left, we can't identify and decipher a code. We've detected a transmission emanating from this station, directed toward the 'U.N.' fleet. We have a traitor aboard."

Rene Delner raised her hand. "The traitor knows what this is about. Apparently so do the Soviets. Why not let the rest of us in on it? I've suspected for some time that the Sunside Project isn't what it seems to be. If you expect us to risk our lives, we deserve trust in return." She looked at Jason Scott.

"Rene, I think you're right," he said.

II

The wing where Sherlock Michlanski worked was called the Leslie Groves wing: a whimsical joke on the part of Jason Scott, naming it for the general who had run the Manhattan Project. It was separated from the

rest of the wheel, which was divided into wings for the construction crew
and the scientists supposedly working on artificial photosynthesis.

Some actually were working on photosynthesis, in hydroponics labs.
Others were subjecting inert crystals to high-intensity sun rays. These
experiments were not intended to bear fruit, only to provide a highly visible
blind for the station's real purpose.

Most of the other scientists were working on projects bearing on Michlanski's work, although in most cases they didn't know it. They worked
alone, fed the results into their computers, and never knew what was done
with their work.

If things had gone as planned, much of the work of making the PH
Station a functioning star ship would have been done by the construction
crew, which included a high percentage of former engineers and crew-
men from space navy shipyards. But things were not going according
to plan.

Michlanski called the lab where he worked "the Eighth Rank." Only
Scott and Kane knew the significance of that.

Inside, things looked much as they had in his lab on Wolverine Island,
except he couldn't be quite as sloppy when gravity might cease suddenly.

Michlanski had finished twisting the screws on a device that resembled
an interplanetary probe. But as far as that went, it also looked like a five-
foot-tall cocktail mixer.

"Done!" He touched a key that sent a summons to Jason Scott.

He sat wearily next to his table, and for the first time in weeks, thought
seriously about food. Specifically, a leg of lamb, cooked in red wine and
raisins, smothered in onions and garlic—

There was a quiet knock on his lab door and Scott entered.

"You're done?"

"Without a doubt." He indicated the chromium shape.

"None too soon!" Scott examined it, running his hand along its cold
surface. "We've gotta figure out how this'll help us."

"Correction: We have to find out if this even works. We need to train
a pilot and install this—" His cherubic face frowned. "Wait! What will
we install this on? We've only got the two-seat mini-shuttles. This will
take the space of one of those seats."

"I can't say when a larger ship will be here." He was facing away from
Michlanski, although still looking at him with his vision prosthesis. "How
long to train someone to use the device?"

"I'm the only one who knows the instrumentation, which is eccentric,
to say the least. It'll take two weeks." He held up two fingers. Scott's

new habit of talking to people while facing away from them didn't faze Michlanski. He had always invented his own social rules as he went along.

"We don't have that kind of time," said Scott.

"It takes time to teach a new technology. Calculating the first return trip will be an enormous undertaking. The instrumentality will calibrate with each trip, helped by the pilot. The first jump, the ship will appear somewhere. Don't know where. Don't know when. But we'll meet again someday!" He picked up his antigravity ball and flew it around the lab, doing curlicues and loop-the-loops. "It'll take several jumps, with bearings taken at each jump, to see how it works. I have to teach somebody how to do that."

"What if the student is not as proficient as his teacher?" Scott saw the ball coming at the back of his head and grabbed it.

Michlanski nodded admiringly and jumped down from the table. "He or she'll have to be. Because if he doesn't catch on quickly, the chances go up that he will land inside a sun."

"But you know how to do it."

"Sure, but I'm not going."

"Why not?"

"I'm a coward, Jason," said Michlanski. "We've discussed this. I'm willing to travel on any form of transportation where I can figure out fairly accurately what my odds of survival are."

"That's impossible in this case. And somebody has to go."

"Remember the words that most accurately describe me are 'craven,' 'yellow,' 'sniveling'—"

"You'll have to give me a crash course and hope for the best. I understand you better than anyone. I have the best chance—"

"Stop! You made your point!" Michlanski looked unhappy. "I'm the indispensable man, and once in a lifetime being indispensable brings responsibility. Like your father, who made the right decision. All my life, you and Alfred said this could happen. Now I either turn my back on everything I've worked for to save my life—or risk it on a cosmic die throw whose odds I can't even calculate!" He closed his eyes. "Jason, it scares me."

"Sherlock—"

"Okay, let's get some of your strong backs and weak minds in here and move this thing to the mini-shuttle on Deck C."

" 'This thing' is hardly a proper name for what may be one of the watershed inventions in history, Sherry. We owe it to succeeding generations to come up with something better."

"I'm already doing my part for succeeding generations! But if you insist, let's call it the Strubeck Motivator."

"The Motivator it is. Before we install it, let's come clean with the people who have worked with us for six months."

III

"The Strubeck Motivator!" said Sherlock Michlanski with a dramatic sweep of his right arm. "And you are all about to become midwives to the birth of the human race from the womb of Sol."

"I don't understand," said Drew, puzzlement lines creasing his dark skin, "why the Soviets would attack us over—this. It's not a weapon. How can this be significant? It's not large enough to threaten anyone."

While they were discussing it, the Motivator drifted from the center of the spherical room and settled against the deck, as did the people in the audience.

"It's just a faster-than-light drive. That's all!" said Michlanski. "Not much different in size from the original atomic bomb. Except that for once, good things come in small packages."

"It's a weapon all right," said Rene Delner. "If you can't see that, Colonel, that demonstrates why you're not a general."

Drew didn't respond, but his eyes broadcast the message that he would like to have his hands around Rene Delner's throat.

"How did you produce such a wonder by yourself, Dr. Michlanski?" she asked. "We have hundreds here and thousands on Luna. Yet you seem to have built an FTL drive by yourself in the Eighth Rank lab. Have all of us been a blind for your experiments? I'd like to think my work wasn't an entire waste!"

"You must realize that the equations see the universe in a radically different way." Michlanski slipped into his professor persona. "To use a transportation metaphor, instead of building new forms of ground transportation, evolving from the horse to the auto, we're looking at flying. The technology doesn't require vast labs. It's fundamentally simple.

"Essentially, we were looking at a wall beyond which humans couldn't pass. The challenge was establishing that there was a passage. Once we did, the instrumentality to use that knowledge is almost child's play to build, relatively speaking. However, for one person, even one of stunning genius, such as myself, it was a nearly killing task." He smiled modestly.

"You were all unwittingly working on the problem. That's why the project was compartmentalized. If you could've compared notes with Dr. Hanson or Fredrika Parker, you'd have gotten suspicious.''

"How does examining the structure of molecules to create food from sunlight relate to FTL?'' asked Delner.

"You did experiments at the molecular level, on transference of energy to matter, and vice versa. Strubeck's equations are about taking matter and changing its phase so it exists elsewhere. See?''

A strange smile formed on Rene Delner's sharp, yet attractive features. "I'm beginning to.''

"The PH Station was meant to be the instrumentality.'' Michlanski formed a circle with the thumbs and forefingers of both hands. "To focus energy with a magnetic 'lens' to enlarge a hole punched in space-time by antimatter and reproduce the 'dimple' in the fabric of space-time that occurs near any sufficiently large mass, such as our sun. However, it turns out we don't need to finish the PH Station to make the device.'' He indicated the Motivator with a sweep of his right arm. "It stands before you.''

"Does it work?'' asked Drew.

"That is what I'm about to find out,'' said Michlanski.

"Such a simple device would have inevitably been discovered,'' mused Rene Delner. "It's sheer luck we will have it first.''

"You could look at it that way,'' said Michlanski. "Although ultimately it's lucky for humanity. Travel to the stars will become as cheap as taking an SST from Los Angeles to New York. International rivalry, even governments, may become irrelevant. If people can pick up and leave, governments will have to better things to keep them there, or be forced out of business.''

"You're predicting the fall of national states?''

"I'm not a political scientist, but it seems plausible.''

"It's good someone figured out how to stop you,'' she said.

By now, everyone was sitting on the globular deck. They all realized simultaneously that there was now gravity where before there had been almost zero gravity. The spin was accelerating.

Chapter

* 51 *

I

Ferman lingered until the auditorium was almost empty, then slipped into a rest room and out through the window. Always assume you're being watched, was a motto that was second nature now.

On the dark streets his mind was an agglomerate of mismatched notions. The speech had excited him, but his gut reaction was that Silverado was a dangerous con man. He distrusted anyone who could manipulate crowds. Yet he was telling the truth: The Strubeck equations were not what they seemed. A conspiracy involved scientists like Dorian Nye, Noah Chambless, and Sherlock Michlanski, who had evidently helped spread the Santa Bella blight. The unavoidable conclusion was that the Argus Society was part of the same conspiracy. With what aim?

He couldn't begin to guess. Perhaps they wanted to make the world dependent upon synthetic foodstuffs from the PH Station. But Silverado said the equations were fake. If so, then the PH Station had another purpose. What?

How did Silverado know the equations were fake? Had he made a wild guess, or did he have a valid source of information?

Ferman walked until it was late. Storm clouds that had threatened the city all day opened up and washed the filth from the streets. He let the water drip off his face. When the rain ceased, he had decided. The time had come to take a chance. He had walked across half a continent. It was time to abandon anonymity.

He returned to his hovel-like room and slept until dawn. It was grim and gray. The rain hadn't finished with the city, and Ferman knew fate hadn't finished with him yet either. He donned his raincoat and went to see Silverado.

II

"I think I've got our man." From the hotel room that overlooked the entrance to the old City Hall Perle Gracie sighted along a device that resembled a telescope, but was actually a highly sophisticated spy video.

Before he made the call that summoned Mel Hardrim and Kirsten Fale to Los Angeles he wanted to be certain.

The device's optical lasers measured the subject's height and breadth and recorded his profile, particularly the ears. Ears are almost as individual as fingerprints. Ultrasonic probes determined weight. This was fed into the computer during the instant the subject was in the viewer, and matched against recorded descriptions. Gracie had used the instrument before on an exposé of a politician. Chances were excellent that this was Ferman.

He signaled his operatives, borrowed from the Science Network, to cover all of the building's exits. But they didn't see Ferman come out again. Fortunately they did see him come out early the next morning.

III

Frank Silverado kept a sumptuous suite atop the old L.A. City Hall. The rent came from the organization's coffers, although "creative book-keeping," as Silverado termed it, spread it over many budgetary items. Silverado treated the organization as an extension of his ego. This sort of behavior had earned him a prison term some years back for selling forged artworks. But it had not affected his meteoric rise after he hit upon the idea to cash in on the public's belief in almost anything fantastic, as long as it was couched in terms of conspiracy.

Vast numbers had believed, at various times, in a government plot to hide the existence of UFOs, that the CIA planned to overthrow civilian rule, that the assassinations in the last century were carried out by a vast, all-powerful network of Reds, Nazis, the Illuminati, or Texas oilmen.

So it was no great feat to convince them of new conspiracies. Silverado did it without qualms for the credulous suckers he seduced. His con was harmless. It used wild fantasies to excite the imagination, and asked for nothing more than a pittance in return. It was hardly Silverado's fault that he stumbled onto a real conspiracy—

Warren Badger was Silverado's lieutenant. His official title was vice president in charge of operations. In reality, he ran the organization's national activities and finances, while writing most of the copy for *The Conspiracy Weekly Reader* except for the inflammatory editorials and most lurid "investigative" pieces. He also screened the people who came to see Silverado. He pronounced his name *Bay-jer*. Silverado pronounced it *Bad-jer*, like the animal.

Badger was a small man, with skin like yellow parchment. His breath whistled as he puffed on the cigarette never absent from his lips. It was his shout of defiance at God, for he was under sentence of death, a sentence stayed by medicine, but never lifted. He was ravaged by a slow form of Rogue Cancer. The only weapon against it was the most fearful: the knife, or more accurately, the laser scalpel. He had been gutted, his digestive tract removed, along with most of his organs. A machine attached to his chest and powered by a radium pellet did the work of each unit he had lost. Plastic sacks collected his wastes. His sexual organs were long gone. His lungs worked, barely, and still the cancer devoured him. What passions remained were directed to his work. He was thirty-five and looked seventy-five.

He hated Silverado, but saw him as necessary. He hated his shams and bogus plots that filled the *Reader* weekly, but he believed real ones existed, particularly the Strubeck conspiracy. He worked for the cause, not the man.

He held Silverado's fate in his hands. He balanced his books, and at any time he could expose the crookedness. But he preserved Silverado, whose charisma attracted people to the organization. No one would pay to see a palsied, yellow, wheezing machine-man. Silverado had to stay. But sometimes Badger used his influence for worthwhile purposes. Like now.

He brought his skeletal hand to knock loudly on Silverado's door. He heard a muffled curse from within, followed by a liquid female laugh, then heavy steps before the door was flung open.

Silverado glowered. Silk pajamas hung from him like laundry thrown on a rock. His sparse hair was in disarray, his eyes bleary, his cheeks dark with stubble, and his breath inflammatory.

"You're early, Warren," he growled.

Badger looked at his watch, a purely ritual gesture, for he knew he was perfectly punctual. "It's ten o'clock."

Silverado opened the door and indicated the woman in bed in the next room. She was redheaded and busty and was amused when Badger refused to acknowledge her presence. "You can lose track of time sometimes, Warren. You ought to try it."

Badger's feelings were so encased in carapace by now that the brutal reference to his enforced celibacy produced no reaction.

"How much longer will you be, Frank?"

"Give me thirty minutes. Then you can help me get dressed."

"Your friend can do that. I'm not your damned man-servant."

"But you know what looks good."

"I know what looks bad. Practically your entire wardrobe."

"What's so important it can't wait, Warren?"

"I want you to meet a man. It's very important. I'll see you in thirty minutes."

IV

An hour later Silverado sauntered into his office, a man metamorphosed: scrubbed, coiffed, and pampered by his outrageously expensive revitalizer. His mustache points were cocked at a jaunty angle; his eyes gleamed clear, dark and deadly.

"Okay, Warren, here I am!"

"Good," said Badger drily.

"Who is this—fellow?" Silverado indicated Ralph Ferman with a wave of his jeweled hand.

"Let us say he is a man with important information for us, even invaluable information," said Badger carefully.

"Let us say his name, shall we?" snapped Silverado. "Who in hell do you think is paying your salary, Badger?"

"The same idealistic people paying you to live like a rajah, if only they knew it." His voice was soft, almost inaudible.

"Somebody's going to bump you off someday, Warren."

"Somebody has. Let's stop fencing. I know about your syndicate friends. You know about my file buried in the central computer network, waiting for news of my untimely death to send it on its way."

"Untimely death! You're going to croak any day now, you little mummified bastard! If you die of natural causes, what am I supposed to do about that?"

"I'd donate some gold to the American Cancer Society."

"Hilarious! Okay, your friend remains anonymous. For now."

"He remains so for as long as I wish it, Frank."

"Have it your way!"

Badger was satisfied. "Tell him your story."

Each time Ferman told his story, it took longer. This time it took an hour, even the bare bones. He began haltingly. He didn't trust Silverado, but he didn't question the sincerity of the pathetic doomed creature who drew smoke into his wrecked body, eyes closed, blotched features relaxed as he listened.

When Ferman finished he looked at Silverado, whose hooded eyes hid whatever thoughts passed inside that egglike head.

"Let's see if I understand," he said. "The Argus Society, including Sherlock Michlanski, Dorian Nye and Noah Chambless, engineered the famine, after planning it for thirty years. If you're telling the truth, this is linked with the PH Station, which probably is not doing anything to alleviate world hunger. My God! A real conspiracy! I never believed it before."

Badger looked disgusted. "He should talk to Sten. He'll know if what he says is theoretically possible."

"Sten, yes, Sten! I never believed him either. But he must be right! This is too much of a coincidence, isn't it?"

"I don't believe in coincidence," said Badger.

Silverado twisted in his chair and touched a key on his holocube terminal. "Have Tinzel Sten come up. What? I don't care what orders he gave! Let the molecule collapse! Get him here!"

Five minutes later the door opened and a painfully thin man in his fifties entered. He had iron-gray hair and a spadelike beard. He wore corduroy pants and a cream-colored wool sweater, and he looked as rough as a rusted iron spike.

"What now?" He spoke with a blunt Scandinavian accent.

"Manners, Tinzel! You astonish me!" said Silverado with mock outrage. "I'd like you to meet this gentleman, whose name, unfortunately,

I'm not at liberty to reveal. May I present Professor Tinzel Sten, formerly of the University of Copenhagen.''

Ferman, who read *Scientific American* and other journals, had seen that name on articles on matter conversion and unified fields. Sten had made no major discoveries, but he was a respected voice. This was the intellect behind Silverado's screeds.

Sten observed Ferman studying him and was annoyed. "Are you going to tell me what this is about?''

"First, let me ask *you* something," Ferman said.

"What?''

"Do you know that the Strubeck equations are a fake?'' He asked it with an intensity he thought he had lost.

"Now hold on!'' Silverado jumped up. "You don't ask the questions. You only talk about what I tell you to talk about—''

"Shut up, Frank!'' said Sten.

He shut up.

"I don't know that they are fake,'' he said in a contemplative voice, as if all things besides him and Ferman had ceased to exist. "I know they are not what they are represented to be.''

"Hardly novel," said Ferman. "Governments hide things from the public all the time.''

Sten frowned impatiently. "That's not what I mean. Some reticence is to be expected in a state-financed science endeavor. I am speaking of inconsistencies in the facts fed the public. They say the PH Station must be located within twenty million miles of the sun to get enough energy to manufacture elementary carbohydrate molecules. Nonsense. If the equations work, they'll work nearly as well in earth orbit. If they must locate within twenty million miles, it's for other reasons.''

"Why, do you think?''

"I never guess. I know its purpose is not to manufacture food. I've answered you, it's time for you to talk to me.''

Ferman cut several minutes off the narrative this time. Sten listened impassively, delicate hands caressing his beard, piercing blue eyes staring straight ahead, as if in another room. When Ferman finished, he nodded.

"Well," demanded Silverado, "is he telling the truth?''

"His story sounds plausible, although it doesn't fit in with what I know of the Argus Society. That has always been an innocuous philanthropic and education fraternity.''

"That's what they want the public to believe," said Ferman.

"I never much liked the people connected with it. I belonged for a short

time. I quit after I realized how boring everyone connected with it was."
He frowned. "Could I have been so wrong? Why wasn't I considered
worthy enough for their inner circle?"

"Can we skip your ego problems?" said Silverado. "The first thing on
my agenda is to find out just who the hell this man is!"

"No problem, Frank," said a voice. The doorway was filled with the
hulking figure of Ivor Solarz. He smiled with sharp teeth. "This is Ralph
Ferman, a very important man."

Chapter

* 52 *

I

The Space Sharks had been pounding Tycho City's gates for a week. Although outnumbered three to one, General David Ian Keith had countered every move by his opposite number, General Pavel Orlov, and had administered a severe setback to each attack.

The Russians had arrived full of their bloodless triumph over Copernicus colony. They anticipated the same with Tycho City, although Orlov was under no such illusion. Their hopes were shattered by a counterattack while they were still deploying.

Then ice chunks, bigger than houses, began hailing their positions from space. Their origin was the satellites L-5 and L-4, where ice from Jupiter was stockpiled. The first "hail attack" achieved the most damage by nailing a supply train the Soviets had dragged from New Moskow.

Orlov had to keep his head down until he deployed the heavy laser cannons used as antiaircraft weapons on earth. It was impossible to achieve surprise with the ice bombs, since they could be seen coming for thousands of klicks, giving the lasers time to turn them into vapor, which refroze and fell on the moon as harmless ice crystals. Almost like snow back home.

The cruisers *Aleksandr Nevsky* and *Kursk* silenced L-5 and L-4, but not before the mass drivers got off a disorganized volley of ice that fell randomly over a million square miles between Copernicus and Tycho.

Orlov's first assault on the American position suffered a setback when Keith uncovered his secret weapon: jerry-built "tanks," actually the hulks of small warships, mounted on tracks, coated with "goop" to make them laser-resistant. The tanks broke through the Russian lines, but instead of inflicting casualties, they trashed the nearest supply dump, then retreated when the Soviets moved up their railguns.

Orlov began to get tetchy about his stores of oxygen, food, high-energy storage batteries, and ammunition, which had been hit twice. He pulled them back and assigned large guard details, cutting the number of combat troops.

The battle harkened to the oldest battles of mankind. There was little artillery bombardment. In a vacuum anything but a direct hit was a miss. So, like besiegers and besieged of a walled medieval city, the two sides flung rocks at each other.

Unlike a medieval siege, the besiegers made no attempt to bombard their goal. A Tycho City that was smashed, its citizens suffocated, was as worthless a prize as an empty crater.

Orlov had read Keith's book and thought he understood him. Yet each time he found the chink in Keith's defenses and sent in his Space Sharks to exploit it, Keith was there with a superior force or a column of his makeshift tanks.

Orlov decided to exploit superior numbers by extending the lines until even Keith couldn't cover them. The lines grew, first as a horn-shaped sliver, finally a great crescent, like the old symbol of Islam, with Tycho City between its horns.

As the sun set, Orlov was confident that when it rose in two weeks, the largest city on the moon would be his.

"We've got them where we want them!" said David Ian Keith, watching the computer simulation of the battle. He was using Tycho City Hall as his headquarters and had been tremendously amused when he got his first bill from Selene for the electricity and air consumed by his army. The bill didn't stick. The city had finally realized that a war was on.

"Would you explain that one, General?" said Governor Merle Jackson.

"Their army faces us in a great semicircle. Their supply line snakes thousands of kilometers from New Moskow, around craters and mountains and down into the crater Tycho. I compliment Orlov: Getting his army here ranks as a great military achievement. I hope to tell him that in person someday."

"Let's hope we don't all meet him in a POW camp, General Keith. Let me ask you this: What's the bad news?"

Keith smiled. "For them, a tremendously vulnerable supply line, most vulnerable at its origin, New Moskow. If we interrupt supplies anywhere along the line, it'll cause Orlov discomfort, but he'll stay supplied. Only by striking at New Moskow can we do crippling damage."

"Orlov's army is three times as large as ours, yet he hasn't been able to break our lines. How can we dream of damaging or capturing New Moskow, or get near it without being detected?"

"I intend to use the smallest possible force," said Keith. "Fifty men. I never said I intend to capture New Moskow—not in the sense you mean." He touched a button and a broken black line appeared on the map, running from Tycho City to Tycho Brahe Base and north across the crater, ending thirty miles outside Tycho's rim. "Governor, how familiar are you with the old Tubeway tunnel?"

"Just that it was a great waste of the taxpayers' money."

"Maybe they'll get back some of it. At this moment, Captain Terry Ransome and forty-nine ETF troopers are emerging at the other end of the tunnel. They have one tracked vehicle and two weeks to cross to New Moskow, hidden by night. If we hadn't destroyed the spy satellites, even night wouldn't protect them."

"What's the point? Fifty troopers against a city of twenty thousand and at least a few hundred CosMarines."

"Should be about an even match, Governor."

II

"What is this, Frank?" said Warren Badger, frowning at the figure of the most notorious capo of Southern California.

"You've been double-crossed," supplied Ivor Solarz, who limped slowly into the room, followed by five of his hired men.

Ferman looked around, confused, but sure he didn't like what was going on. Two of Solarz's men positioned themselves on both sides of him.

Tinzel Sten frowned and stroked his mustache.

Warren Badger stuck his face in Silverado's windpipe. "You'll pay for this, you skink!" He was so worked up that his artificial lungs failed him and he broke into a fit of coughing. He caught his breath. "Don't you remember that I have every illegal, immoral, and stupid act you ever committed on file?"

"That's right, Ivor!" said Silverado. "He's got things set to blow up in my face if I betray him."

"S'okay, Frank," said Solarz. "You got me to take care of you. You owe me this. But since you were kind enough to call me when Ferman walked into your office, we'll square it between us."

"But what about Warren?" Silverado asked.

Solarz lashed out with his cane's silver hook and caught Badger a glancing blow on the temple. He fell and Solarz was on him in an instant, beating him. He stood over the half-dead man, breathing heavily. "I got a blood-crazed maniac after me. He's killed half my people. He throws their intestines on the chandeliers and stuffs their tongues down their throats. The only way I can stop him is to have something his boss wants. So believe me when I say *nothing* will stand in my way." He rested his cane on Badger's throat, which convulsed as he tried to breathe. "Release your information on Frank if you want. You don't have much to live for. I wouldn't blame you for committing suicide—"

"Now, Ivor, just hold on!" protested Silverado feebly.

Solarz ignored him. "Maybe you got six months. Maybe a week. Any time you wanna know exactly how much you got left, screw with me." He got off Badger's body and ordered his men to bring Ferman.

"On second thought, bring the kraut, too."

"I'm Danish," said Sten.

Solarz ignored him. "Nice doin' business with you, Frank."

III

As the elevator carrying Ivor Solarz, Ferman, Sten and Solarz's men went down to the ground, it passed an elevator that carried Mel Hardrim, Perle Gracie, and Kirsten Fale.

Solarz's men had taken care of security on ground level, so Hardrim, Gracie, and Fale were not challenged when they stepped into the elevator or when they got out.

They found Silverado, cradling the head of Warren Badger, alternately cursing him and pleading with him not to die.

"Where's Ralph Ferman?" said Hardrim, while Kirsten Fale checked the curtains and adjoining rooms.

"I—I don't know what you're talking about."

"Don't believe him!" Badger's breaths came in gasps.

"I don't have much time, so subtlety is ruled out." Hardrim dragged Silverado over to a heavy wooden door between his office and his secretary's. He held the middle finger of Silverado's right hand against the jamb and slammed the door.

Silverado's howl was hair-raising and he rolled around on the rug, holding his hand away from him and panting.

"Where's Ferman?"

Silverado groaned and whimpered. Hardrim grabbed his wrist and put his thumb in the jamb. He slammed the door again.

Silverado clawed the carpet like a run-over cat.

Next it was his little finger. By now his screams were making Hardrim's ears ring.

"Solarz took Ferman to San Diego," Badger whispered.

"Why didn't you tell me before now?"

"I was enjoying myself." He was convulsed by a deep cough.

Gracie knelt beside him. "We need to get him to a doctor."

"In a moment," said Hardrim. "Where in San Diego?"

"I don't know—precisely where."

Hardrim started for Silverado.

"Horton Plaza, the old shopping mall!" Silverado said quickly. He scuttled to a corner and shielded his broken fingers.

"Mel, call an ambulance, then we can leave," said Gracie.

"No! No ambulance," said Badger. "I want you to let me die."

"Don't listen to him. He's nuts!" said Silverado.

"Whatever you say," said Hardrim. "We'll lock Silverado in the service closet. I'll leave a phone receiver by you and you can call, or not call. It's entirely your wish."

"You murderers!" howled Silverado as they dragged him down the hall and closed the door in his face.

On ground level they climbed into the Mustang and Hardrim gunned it onto the San Diego Freeway.

IV

Jacob Kane and Matt Taylor and twenty navvies floated in the safe zone between the PH Station and a two-acre sheet of reflective foil that shaded the wing they were working on. It had been detached and pulled out fifty yards from the spinning wheel.

The foil protected them from being fried by the sun. More than two minutes of exposure, and even the heavy-duty space suits' refrigeration units would lose the battle.

Kane was pushing himself and everyone around him as though he was possessed by a demon. No one could remember the last time they had seen him go to his cabin to sleep.

Taylor had felt uncomfortable around Kane since Victor Ames's death, although he had always been leery of him. Kane reminded him of the strange loners who eked out a living in the bayou swamps.

Kane was maneuvering a roll of insulation into position to be unrolled and attached to a hull section. He had grown impatient with the progress a navvy named Millard was making and sent him to another task with blunt words.

Taylor shot over to Kane with his backpack jet. He touched helmets for privacy. "Millard's got two broken ribs from when he got hisself between two girders yesterday,"

"We're not running an infirmary. If he can't work, he should stay in sick bay. If he can, then I'm not cutting him any slack. We've got to get this completed before the Russians get here."

"I guess. You want a job done fast, hire an asshole."

Kane glared. Taylor expected him to lash out, and was prepared. So he was astounded when the explosion didn't occur.

"Perhaps," said Kane tightly, "you're right. Give Millard the rest of the shift off."

"No can do, much as I'd like to. We need every man if we want to get this mother done and reattached to the wheel. He's one of my best, even with a couple of crosspieces cracked."

"Do it anyway, Matt. You can pick up the slack—or I will." He laughed, his nasty, metal file rasp of a laugh.

Taylor shot away from Kane and muttered French swear words.

Kane returned to his task. Taylor was right, he was being driven by a hunger he couldn't feed. He thought he was suffering from a virus, or more likely, the effects of abstention from sex.

He had never made a decision not to bed other women. He never told Elena he would be faithful. It was against his nature and she should understand that, if she understood him at all. Women were like air or water—to do without them was to defy nature. Yet he had found excuse after excuse. He didn't lack opportunity. Women had always been fascinated by him. The more he treated them like dirt, the more they lined up. He guessed they liked it. At least the ones he knew did. Elena was different. Whenever he started opening moves on one of the willing women aboard the PH Station, he visualized Elena and recoiled. He was ashamed of himself. He needed to talk to the doctor. He didn't know it, because he had never experienced it before, but at age thirty-seven, Kane was in love.

He shook his head. He had been daydreaming, staring at the huge revolving wheel, the seams of its skin passing like seams in a road. Unconsciously he had been counting the seconds to complete a revolution.

It wasn't right. With his tongue he flicked on a chronometer display inside his helmet. He counted off the time once again. It was going too fast, and if he had counted correctly the first time, it was accelerating.

He turned on his helmet radio and began calling the station.

Chapter
* 53 *

I

Three days after the tractor emerged from the unfinished Tubeway tunnel, they came to the field of ice crystals.

An acre of ice glittered under the earthlight, where one of the projectiles thrown by the Lagrange satellites had ''missed'' the Russian position and landed hundreds of miles away.

Ransome halted the tractor and the men stretched their legs as much as was possible in the space suits.

''Sutton! Take five men and find the supplies. Martin! Gold! Shovel ilmenite in the oxygen processor.'' They were using it faster than they could make it, but they would have enough when they got to New Moskow. If they kept up the pace.

Ransome ordered the water tanks of the hydrogen processor filled to keep the batteries charged. He looked at the horizon. The sun was still days away. They could charge the batteries endlessly once it rose. But if that happened before they reached New Moskow, they could kiss surprise goodbye.

But they wouldn't have any surprise at all if General Keith hadn't cooked up the idea of dropping ice and supplies along the route to Archimedes.

If this worked, Keith would go in the history books next to Napoleon. Whatever happened, Ransome figured he'd be in the books. Leader of a band of doomed, heroic men. Or commander of a daring, brilliant raid.

Tasks finished, the men boarded the tractor, which lurched into gear.

II

The Soviet/Asian/African armada and U.S. Space Navy Task Force Four faced each other across half a million cubic miles of space sowed with proximity mines.

Both fleets were at a dead stop, which accomplished one of the objectives of Task Force Four: delay. But it was obvious the enemy intended to creep through the minefield, putting Collins in the position of fleeing a superior enemy or fighting.

Complicating things was Icarus, whose eccentric orbit would put it in the middle of the minefield within hours.

Commodore Erskine Collins looked at the face of his opposite number, Admiral Novo Arbatov, in the holocube.

"Admiral, an asteroid mining colony of neutral civilians is headed into the quadrant where we sowed proximity mines. They are also in the field of fire, if either of us takes hostile action."

"I am familiar with the capitalist mining colony at Icarus. They are U.S. puppets but I agree they are civilians." Arbatov smiled, a cagey old fisherman smile. "What do you propose?"

"First, a cease-fire while each fleet holds its current position vis-à-vis each other and the minefield."

The admiral spoke in Russian to someone offscreen and then looked back at Collins. "That is acceptable. What else?"

"We must calculate Icarus's exact trajectory, so we can detonate the mines in its path."

Arbatov smiled his fisherman smile again. "Why not detonate them all while you are at it, and save us a lot of mischief?"

"Admiral, are you an angler?"

"I do not know this term."

"Do you like to catch fish?"

"How did you know? Yes!"

"Do you ever talk to the fish? Try to, ah, sweet-talk them into biting the baited hook?"

Arbatov chuckled a deep, chocolatey chuckle. "Are we talking about fish still, Commodore?"

"Perhaps both. Admiral, I do not wish to fight you any more than you wish to fight me. But I can't accede to your request."

"I agree to your proposal, with the knowledge that your main fleet, under Rear Admiral Hawkings, is under full thrust toward this position. However, it will not arrive in time. One caveat—"

"Yes?"

"Any sign of treachery and we will not hesitate to open fire, civilians or no civilians."

"Thank you, Admiral. Collins out."

Collins established contact with Icarus. He couldn't help but stare at the beautiful young woman with auburn hair and ethereal dignity. He was torn from his daydream by her all-business voice.

"Commodore, this is Elena Davenport. I speak for my father, who is in the interior. We've had an accident. A badly timed explosion. Several miners died."

"You couldn't have chosen a worse time for it, young lady."

"We didn't ask for your war! Icarus has followed this orbit since the birth of time. You and the Russians have an interplanetary food fight and bitch when someone gets hit!"

"You're an articulate young lady. I wasn't decrying the timing of your orbit, but the unfortunate timing of the accident."

"I see." Her voice was still cold, but she made Collins wish he was twenty-five years younger. "What do you suggest?"

Collins explained the agreement with Arbatov, and it seemed the tense lines on her face relaxed. "Yes, that could work."

"Thank you," he said with irony. "The *Chesty Puller* will go to the edge of the minefield and electronically detonate the mines in your path."

"Once we're through, you can resume killing each other."

"Yes, ma'am." He terminated the picture and contacted the cruiser-minesweeper *Puller*, which in happier days had been a smaller version of Collins's water freighter, plying the space lanes between Mars, Luna, and

Jupiter. It was skippered by a man Collins had once worked for, Captain Elihu Rake.

"Collins to *Puller*, you're cleared to approach the minefield, Elihu."

III

Everyone in the globular auditorium talked at once until Colonel Drew silenced them. He advanced menacingly on Rene Delner, who regarded him with the serenity of a Zen master.

"What have you *done*?" he roared.

"I'll tell you," said Bethany Williams. "I saw her near the hub control room. She sabotaged the spin controls."

"What about the officer in the control room?" said Jason Scott. "Or the alarms that should have sounded when the rotation changed? Why isn't the rest of the station trying to reach us?"

"You have a lot of questions," said Delner. "We have plenty of time to explore them, since none of you are leaving." She pulled a plastic slug-thrower from her coveralls.

Drew, who looked like he contemplated attacking her, reacted as if someone had dropped a sidewinder on the deck next to him.

"Explosive bullets," said Delner calmly. "I don't have to hit you, just get off a few shots. Why not sit and be comfortable? I killed the guard in the hub control room, locked the spin controls, and disabled the alarms and communications between decks, plus the escalators and elevators. I also planted a bomb in case you try to enter the control room. Anything else?"

"Who do you work for?" demanded Drew.

"You security types are so predictable," she sneered. "Why does it matter? A dozen nations or people as powerful as nations stand to gain from an impotent America. I work for the same people Victor Ames worked for. I fooled you into thinking I was his 'victim.' " She looked at Madeline Reed with contempt. "Particularly you, you vacuous little nit. Remember I told you I enjoyed Victor's rough play? You thought I was lying. But there's no pleasure without pain. I loved it when he hit me!" She was breathing rapidly, red spots on her cheeks in a startling transformation from the icy-cold doctor. "But he was just a tool. I sent him on an act of sabotage I knew would get him caught, if not killed. Victor was a fool, but he loved me. He died for me."

"Do you plan to die too?" asked Scott.

"Certainly," she said serenely. "The station will achieve a rotation that will tear it to pieces, sending parts into the sun, or out past the birthplace of comets."

"You don't talk like an ideologue," said Scott. "Or like someone willing to kill hundreds of people for some ism."

"I do have a philosophy. This nonsense about governments withering away, and people becoming free through technology, is a crock. But that's not why I joined up. I expect to be well paid."

"Excuse me," said Michlanski. "You'll be dead."

"Have you ever heard of recorded personalities, Professor?"

"Seems I have."

"Mine was recorded months ago. It's a tremendously expensive procedure. In return for this job, my personality will be placed in a younger version of myself. One thousand ounces of gold will be deposited in an account in the Lunar Free State."

"Excuse me, but there's a possibility of a double-cross. What guarantee have you that they'll bring you back?"

"Well—" She looked genuinely puzzled and alarmed. Even disoriented. Drew, sensing an opportunity, took a step toward her, intending to take a bullet if he had to, to wrest the gun from her. But his muscles didn't respond.

The last thing anyone saw was everyone collapsing on the deck.

IV

"Mine Baker Jacob—detonate!"

The mine, set to explode if any object, including an asteroid, came within a certain distance, exploded harmlessly.

Collins watched, fascinated, as the *Puller* set off the mines one by one. Icarus was well into the minefield—an irregular pebble, thrown into a dark pool, tumbling through white bubbles, any one of which could destroy it.

He thought ruefully how the Americans and Russians could cooperate to save a few hundred civilians, but couldn't cooperate enough to avoid firing at each other once Icarus reached safety.

"We have a problem," said Captain Rake. "Mine Malcolm Dexter is not responding to the electronic self-destruct order."

This was why *Puller* had approached the minefield as close as it did. So it could explode any errant mines manually.

"Targeting our laser battery on Malcom Dexter," said Rake.

"Wait! I'd better inform our Russian friends—"

"Too late. I have to fire now or never!"

It happened too quickly. No one was prepared for battle, when suddenly they were in the middle of one. *Puller*'s lasers disintegrated the mine, but due to a malfunction, targeted a mine at the edge of the field, near the African warship *Qaddafi*.

Qaddafi, thinking itself attacked, opened fire with lasers and smart missiles. It wasn't close enough to launch black paint at the enemy ship's reflective surface, but it released a cloud of sand to defend from a similar attack. That prevented it from firing its lasers again until the cloud dissipated.

Puller's lasers destroyed the incoming smart missiles and lanced out with its own. Because the African had prematurely surrounded itself with sand, its lasers were useless against the incoming missiles, which exploded astern, splitting open its fusion reactor like a can of beans.

The African ships and the battleship *Zhukov* fired on the *Puller*, which survived the lasers, but was slagged by a flock of homing missiles. *Zhukov*'s heat-bleeding antennae were not up; she overheated and abruptly stopped firing. Then everybody stopped.

Collins, horrified, watched and heard the accidental tragedy unfold. He quickly ordered *Patton*'s laser battery ready to fire.

He listened while Admiral Arbatov angrily harangued the ships' commanders who had fired without permission.

"God no!" said Park, who was monitoring the navigational globe. Collins looked: Icarus was headed for several mines.

"Try to detonate them from here!" said Collins quickly.

Park's hands flew over the keyboard. Some of the mines responded, but only the *Puller* had all the codes. The only way to ensure that the mines didn't hit Icarus was to use the fail-safe device that could order all the mines to self-destruct—

One of the mines that hadn't responded went off in front of the asteroid, and the end facing the explosion melted, flowed, and hardened again, like plastic exposed to an acetylene torch.

Park's reaction was instinctive: He flipped open the cover to the switch that controlled the mines and exploded them all.

Collins watched, horrified and relieved, as the minefield disappeared in a galaxy of tiny explosions, like the climax to a fireworks display back home.

Park, shocked at his action, looked at Collins and shrugged. "Oops!"

V

"Jason, wake up! Wake up, I don't have all day."

Scott's head throbbed as he climbed out of the dark pool. He felt a sharp pain on his cheek and came fully awake to the fact that Jacob Kane, in a space suit, was astride him, slapping him.

Scott sat up and Kane tumbled off him. He shook his head to clear the mist. Sergeant Drake and Matt Taylor were also in suits. Everyone else was unconscious or waking up. "What happened?"

Kane stood. "I noticed the spin increasing. We came in through the hub port. I assumed someone had gotten to the control room. I X-rayed it. Guy's dead in there. The entrance is booby-trapped. We figured things out and pumped gas into the vents."

"What the hell we doing with riot gas aboard this station?"

Drake shrugged toward the supine figure of Colonel Drew.

"Bastard!" said Scott without heat. He looked at Kane. "We can get into the hub control by drilling through the walls."

"The booby trap has a light sensor. Any movement will set it off. That mother will take a while to deactivate."

"No time. We can reach the auxiliary controls by climbing to the wheel on one of the ladders that follow the spokes. We're at one earth gravity here. Must be two or three gravities wheelward."

"Who knows how to get to the auxiliary controls?"

"Everybody who knows is here," said Scott. "I'm going."

"You can't!" Drew stumbled erect, fighting the urge to vomit.

"No time to argue. I'm gone."

"Jason, I'm going with you," said Bethany Williams.

He hugged her, feeling physical pain in his chest at the thought of her being in danger. "That's a really stupid idea, Bethany. I— know how you feel—but there's no practical good two of us can accomplish."

"I know where the auxiliary controls are. I know the combination. If you can't make it, maybe I can."

He considered. "The only way to the wheel is by ladder. If we go in tandem one of us could fall, and take out the other. If you go, go up one of the other shafts."

"Okay!" She looked as if he had given her a reason to live.

"Dammit, you don't have anything to prove!" he said under his breath as he took his vision prosthesis from his belt and attached it like a headband.

When they left, Kane turned to Drew. "Colonel, can you handle Rene Delner now?"

"Yes," said the colonel between clenched teeth.

"Jacob, you can take your helmet off now," said Michlanski.

"Sherlock, just the man I want to talk to. I didn't tell Jason this, because he would have tried to stop me. But I'm taking the experimental ship out on its maiden voyage."

"Nonsense! I've already decided to do it. I'm more likely to return alive, because I know the contraption. Of course, I'm not thrilled to be going. . . ."

"Sherlock," said Kane in a low voice, "remember how, when we were kids, I used to beat the shit out of you when Jason wasn't around?"

"Yes." This subject brought back some unpleasant memories.

"If you don't do as I say, you'll discover just how vivid remembrance of things past can be."

"To hell with you! I may be a coward, but I'm no fool. There's more to this than meets the eye. Quit with your threats. I, Sherlock Michlanski, am only moved by logic. Talk to me."

"Listen, you blob, Icarus has been hit by a bomb. Most of the colony is dead. We picked up a distress signal from Elena Davenport when I came in through the hub. Icarus is traveling perpendicular to the two fleets; falling into the sun. There's no way any of them can accelerate fast enough to rescue anyone. The only way to get to Icarus is with the FTL device."

Michlanski sat down on the deck. The increased gravity was getting to him. "Actually, we call it the Strubeck Motivator now."

"I don't give a shit what you call it. How do you use it?"

"It will only carry one person, the pilot."

"If I can get there, I can stabilize the situation and rig up something to alter the orbit so Icarus doesn't fall into the sun."

Michlanski struggled to his feet. "Let's go while I can still walk. Have somebody bring the Motivator. Fortunately, we're not far from the shuttle." He looked at Kane. "Before you go to Icarus, you've got to test the device, to calibrate it. Otherwise, if you try as fine a maneuver as phasing in next to an asteroid, you might appear inside it."

"All right! I'll test-drive it." Kane glared at the people sprawled on the deck. "On your feet! I need help with the Motivator."

"You have a very poor chance of succeeding. You could die, Jacob. Very, very easily," said Michlanski quietly.

Kane smiled his death-mask grin. "The secret is not caring."

Chapter
* 54 *

I

The marine corporal held his palm up in the universal sign language of traffic cops. The checkpoint was the old immigration checkpoint on Interstate 5, just outside San Onofre Nuclear Power Plant, whose structures were outlined in the lights like twin aroused female breasts.

Hardrim stopped the Mustang. "We'd like to go into the contaminated zone," he told the corporal.

"Sorry, sir. Even in normal times you'd need a special pass. But we're moving in force into the zone in a few hours."

Kirsten Fale leaped out of the car. The marine and his men admired the best-looking woman they had seen in months. She displayed her FBI badge. "That should cut the red tape, right?"

"Wrong, ma'am. This entire area, from San Onofre down the coast, is under martial law. Civilian authority doesn't extend there. You might as well have a badge out of a Cracker Jack box."

"How about this?" said Perle Gracie.

"And what is that, sir?"

"A press pass, signed by Pacific Supreme Commander Lieutenant General Albert Terry, USMC. Issued to the Science News Network, with an expiration date of two years from now. How about that?"

The corporal examined it. "Happy to oblige the press, Mr. Gracie." He put on a sycophantic grin. "You know, you look just like you do on the cube!"

"You look just like you do on the cube!" mimicked Hardrim as they drove onto the deserted highway. "How much time left?"

Gracie consulted his watch. "Dad's contact on Terry's staff said the sea bombardment will start at midnight. The *Farragut* and an amphibious force are already off the coast. They're not fooling around."

"You're sure about where the first few rounds will go?"

"Sure. Sailors have got to eat, too."

"How confident are you in the utilities floor plans you have of Horton Plaza?" The lights of the city of Oceanside became visible.

"We're pretty sure this is the last floor plan. It's really a map. It was literally possible to get lost."

"I just hope you've memorized your route well enough that you don't need to keep consulting the screen."

"Thank you for your confidence in me."

Hardrim drove as fast as the potholes allowed. Above La Jolla, amidst the dead skyscrapers once called the Golden Triangle, he stopped and let Gracie drive while he loaded his Cobra fifty-round autoloader. Kirsten Fale checked her weapon.

"Know something, Kirsten? We're going to have to make a decision real soon as to who gets Ferman."

She snuggled up to him. "True, big man. I have a feeling things'll work out for the best if we let things happen without worrying too much."

"That won't work."

"I'm not trying to 'work' anything. Just trying to be comfortable. You make a nice cushion."

"Why don't you kiss the girl, Hardrim?" said Gracie. "You know how to do that: Just put your lips together and smooch."

"Why don't you put yours together and smooch my backside?"

"Righto, Mr. Bogart."

The highway went into the downtown area of San Diego, a few blocks from Horton Plaza, Ivor Solarz's headquarters.

Gracie slowed. The Mustang growled like a caged lion as it cruised the dark streets. In the distance, they heard machine-gun fire and the occasional burp of a mortar.

Suddenly, six black men, wearing red colors of the Bloods, leaped from the darkness, hoping to bag a valuable car. Hardrim and Fale opened fire without pity or remorse. Fale's Mamba sounded like a cannon in Hardrim's ears. His .45 leaped in his hand again and again. Then there were no more targets, just dead men wearing surprised looks.

"This is where we ditch the car," said Hardrim with more than a hint of regret—for the car, not the dead hoodlums. He looked at Gracie. "I hope your newsie buddy is on time."

"*You* worry about being on time. Johnny Ocarina is the network's best helicopter pilot. He'll land on the parking lot's top floor in thirty minutes, and stay there as long as he can."

"You aren't the only ones who watch those silly old movies," said Kirsten Fale. "I think I know where you got your idea for this scheme, big man. Ever see a movie about an Indian uprising in Canada? Where one of the Mounties rides alone into the Indian camp and overawes them with the force of his personality?"

"Yes!" snapped Hardrim. "It's not silly. It's bold and totally unexpected."

"Also likely to get you killed. I know, you want Lenny to be sorry she got wired. Well, somebody standing next to you is totally flesh and blood and likes it that way." She put her hand behind his head and kissed him. "You think about that."

"Okay." Hardrim reloaded his autoloader clip, cocked the Colt, and nodded. "Let's go."

II

New Moskow gleamed a half a kilometer away under the rays of a sun just beginning to peak over the Lunar horizon.

"I call that good timing!" said Terry Ransome. The men unlimbered their weapons after the ride across Luna. No one had anything with more firepower than a laser rifle and grenades.

Ransome established laser contact with the small force of U.S. space marines who had abandoned Copernicus before its surrender. They too had lived off supplies dropped by the Lagrange satellites. Those supplies would now be destroyed by the rising sun. The marines were two hundred yards to the south.

The point platoon gleefully reported that the force guarding the approaches to New Moskow consisted of five CosMarines, inside a covered tractor, with their helmets off, drinking hot tea and playing cards. A battalion of CosMarines was inside the colony.

"Remember," Ransome repeated, "three broadcast dishes are outside the dome, which has four entrances, including an underground tunnel that opens up two thirds of a mile northeast of it. It's vital to secure the dishes simultaneously, before they can send any messages."

Ransome's "army" moved out, looking like fleas attacking a huge, sleeping dog, as they bounced along in the low gravity.

The sentries were taken without a fight. As each broadcast dish and entrance was secured, the troopers reported in.

The situation was simple. The colonists of New Moskow could not leave without blowing open the doors and exposing the colony to the vacuum, and they couldn't radio out.

Ransome entered one of the radio shacks, removed his helmet, and established contact with the dome interior. He asked to speak to the military governor, who answered in a gruff, surprised voice.

"Who is this?"

"Captain Terry Ransome. Excellency, you are surrounded by a brigade of troops of the United States of America. I have the honor to inform you that you are all my prisoners."

III

Scott was sweating profusely. Halfway between the hub and the wheel, gravity was increasing steadily. It was now at least two g's. He regularly exercised in the high-gravity centrifuge, but this steady climb was rough going. It didn't help that he was climbing down, toward the pull. That just strained muscles unaccustomed to such exercise.

He had eyes all around his head, but not on top, so he didn't see the fire extinguisher that broke loose above him and plummeted "down" toward the wheel.

It hit a rung above his head, bounced off the shaft walls, and smashed the knuckles of his right hand, before continuing its plunge, turning and twisting until it clanged onto the deck below. Scott willed himself not to feel the pain yet, but the hand was useless, broken in as many places as there were bones.

His other grip did not slip, but his palm was sweating; his body was encased in perspiration. He continued down, much slower, and slower still as the gravity increased. Each individual part of his body became a point of pain. He could tell one point or maybe even two, to shut down, but he couldn't shut them all down. His lungs hurt, as if he had been holding his breath for a long time. His heart hurt, as if he had been pedaling for hours in a bike race. His head was a bronze gong of pain—his hand was a steak being barbecued, prodded, then torn by chewing teeth.

Suddenly, his knees hurt too: He had reached the bottom. He was standing, or trying to, in what must have been four gravities.

He couldn't stand. Only crawl. It seemed as if he had been crawling forever. He reached the panel where the hub controls were located. But Bethany had reached them first. She had opened the locker, then blacked out and fell backward. In normal gravity, hitting her head on the deck would have caused a bump. In this case, it was like falling from twenty feet.

Reaching those controls was the hardest thing Scott had ever done. Concentrating to turn the spin controls to reverse acceleration took more concentration than he thought he had.

When he collapsed onto the deck, it was a sweet surrender. He managed to get to Bethany and cradle her crushed head in his lap.

When he held her head a certain way, he couldn't see the blood. She looked as if she was merely resting. That she would open her eyes, and he would be able to tell her he loved her, as he had never done. He hadn't actually realized he loved her until this very moment. She had entered his life briefly, touched it, and reached out her hand for him to take in return. But men like him were not meant to put one woman above all things. And Scott had never learned how to divide his passion between his work and a woman. Now it was too late. He would carry the knowledge that they could have shared love, however briefly, but he had not acted. That knowledge would dwell in his heart like a poisonous dart.

He rocked back and forth. "It's all right, sweetheart. You made it first. You don't have to prove anything to anyone ever again. I love you."

IV

Kane examined the two-man shuttle after Michlanski installed the Strubeck Motivator. Gravity had been decreasing until it was just below earth normal.

"How much of a load will it carry?" asked Kane.

"Give it up!" said Michlanski. "A pilot, that's all. You won't be able to bring Elena Davenport back with you."

"What about that little cargo bay? That would hold a few boxes, or maybe some stasis canisters of antimatter."

"Aren't the odds against you bad enough to suit you?"

"I have a plan, since Admiral Hawkings has screwed things up so the Russians will be breathing down our necks in a day or two. Can you figure out how long Elena can survive on Icarus before the sun kills her?"

"Easily. What about everyone else on the asteroid?"

"Screw them."

"You're not a nice man, Jacob," said Michlanski without an ounce of levity. He entered figures in his holster computer. "She'll be okay for at least twelve hours. But you must allow time to get there and set off an explosion or in some way create enough reaction to change the asteroid's orbit so that it grazes the sun." He looked up. "Not that I believe you can do it."

"Trust me." Kane looked inside the cockpit at a counter that blazed red. "Why's the radiation counter showing that this ship has gotten a deadly dose of radiation?"

"When I examined the probability dimple, I sent the shuttle by remote control. It was quite hot there. It's cooled off since then. Broke the counter, though. I haven't replaced it."

"No time now." Kane climbed into the cockpit.

V

Ralph Ferman was imprisoned again, in a storeroom of what had been a Banana Republic store years ago when Horton Plaza was the newest, boldest, wackiest example of Post Modern architecture.

Ivor Solarz had turned the many-leveled former shopping mall into a fortress, honeycombed with as many traps as the Japanese had dug on Iwo Jima during World War II. He didn't have as many men as he had once had, but whoever attacked his stronghold would pay dearly. Ferman had no way of knowing, but this was all in honor of Whitechapel, the killing machine who had terrorized Solarz and his men for weeks now.

They hadn't tied Ferman up. They had frisked him, taken his knife, wallet, backpack, but left him what looked like protein concentrate. It was actually the harmonic plaster bar he had carried since he visited the Transient Artists Colony.

Many times he had almost tossed it. But something had always stopped him. He looked about the room and thought about how he had seen harmonic plaster used. He looked at the door where his captors would come in again. He looked above the door. He looked in the corner of the room and saw a can of paint. He looked above the door. At the can of paint. At the sink with water in it.

He started mixing the plaster with water. Through the door he heard voices.

VI

Ivor Solarz was nervous. He sat in the old store, in a camel's-hair overcoat and wide, floppy camel's-hair hat, and downed cups of espresso. Ten of his men were in the building, and another score on the rooftops, rifles trained on the store.

The phone rang. Solarz answered it and afterward looked less nervous. "That's Georgio at the entrance. Cocker's here with two of his people. He's gonna talk to Ferman. Looks like we can strike a deal!" He smiled thinly.

After a few more cups of espresso, they arrived. Solarz's eyes widened when Cocker entered, followed by a tall man he didn't recognize and— Horatius Krebs.

Krebs's nose was redder than usual from walking. His kinky gray hair was askew. He didn't look even slightly uncomfortable walking into the den of a gangster where a dozen weapons were trained on him. He sniffed the air.

"Ah! Espresso."

"I'm surprised to see you, Mr. Krebs." Solarz, to his annoyance, felt intimidated by Krebs. He had always known, deep down, that he was really small potatoes compared with someone like Krebs. God, he even smelled rich.

"Why is that, Ivor? You think maybe I was afraid to come here? I thought I owed you for when you visited Symphony Towers."

Solarz recognized the other man with Krebs. Whitechapel. Solarz was afraid of few things in his life, but in the presence of that inhuman monster his guts felt as if they would slide out his anus and lie steaming on the cement floor. He stood, slowly.

"You realize that in addition to the ten men in this room, another twenty are outside. They will shoot on my command."

"Very loyal, I'm sure." Krebs made himself a demitasse of espresso. "One luxury I allow myself." He looked at Solarz with burning coals. "I thought you were loyal, Ivor. I thought we had a deal. You deliver

Ferman and Hardrim to me, in return for very generous considerations on my part.''

"Prices are subject to fluctuations on the market." Solarz was feeling a little more chipper. Even Whitechapel couldn't take thirty men. "You'll get what you want. Ferman's in the next room."

"And Hardrim?"

"I expect him soon. While my pal Frank Silverado was bawling on the phone he told me Hardrim was on his way here. He wanted my help. The police were knocking at his door."

The phone rang. Solarz picked it up and smiled his sharp-toothed grin. "Hardrim is here." He spoke into the phone again. "All units, allow Hardrim and his guards to come through."

"Your men have disarmed him?" said Krebs sharply.

"He gave himself up. Fool! And I wanted him to work for me!"

"That would've been a bad career move for me, Solarz," said a voice from the doorway, which suddenly framed the tall, hulking figure of Mel Hardrim. He leaned insolently against the frame. He moved and let two men enter the store. They looked badly used. One had a darkening bruise on his cheekbone. The other dabbed a bleeding lip. They looked at Hardrim and at Solarz.

Solarz laughed. "I still like your moves, Hardrim."

Hardrim threw two laser pistols on the table with the espresso machine. "Your boys aren't feeling well today. Maybe you should keep them home from school tomorrow."

One of the men Hardrim had disarmed doubled over in pain and hurriedly bent over a trash can to throw up.

"See what I mean about not feeling well?"

"I took your advice, Hardrim. I've got a lot more men."

"Yes, I noticed that. Not very good ones, I'm afraid."

"On that point we both agree, Mr. Hardrim," said Krebs. Hardrim shifted his gaze, taking in the billionaire, Lewis Cocker, and Jack Whitechapel, he of the milky hair and leaden eyes.

Unblinking, unsparkling eyes watched Hardrim, and remembered.

"Welcome, Mr. Hardrim, to Philippi," said Krebs. "To an extent I admire you. I've learned a lot about you since we met in the hot, wet Quintana Roo. I've met only two or three other men like you. Men who can't be bought. You must, unfortunately, be killed. Fortunately for the affairs of the world, most people are not as loyal. As Ivor was reminding me."

Krebs stood up. "I've altered my opinion about loyalty." From his overcoat he pulled out a handful of gold coins. "Loyalty, Solarz, is measured in grams and troy ounces." He let the coins fall musically to the floor. "You deal in cigar boxes of gold, and I in rooms of it. You're outclassed. I brought Whitechapel to rub your nose in it. I don't need Jack for this." He chuckled gratingly. "Your personnel department needs a shakedown. Not a single man refused my money. That must be very disappointing."

Solarz propelled himself clumsily to his feet with his silver-handled cane. "Shoot them all!" he barked.

Silence. Solarz looked around him like a trapped animal.

"He names his own punishment." Krebs nodded to Whitechapel.

The first bullet caught Solarz in the thigh and twisted him around. He dropped the cane and grabbed the table as another hit him in the chest. The slugs came faster, splashing against Solarz until he lost his balance and pulled the table over. Dark, pungent espresso pouring from the stainless-steel machine diluted blood that pumped from a dozen gaping holes and pooled on the floor.

Hardrim's Colt was out, pointing at Krebs's heart. Things were not working out as Hardrim had planned. He noted that Whitechapel now had his gun pointed at him.

"Not the same as the last time, Hardrim," said Krebs. "To shoot or not to shoot! Let's up the stakes. Somebody get Ferman."

Chapter

* 55 *

I

The PH Station ejected the mini-shuttle like a whale calving, with a spume of atmosphere dissipating into the nothingness. Kane circled the station, which looked undamaged, although only a structural analysis would determine that for sure.

Michlanski had said the first jump was the most dangerous. It was impossible to predict even approximately what his chances were of reappearing inside a star, or so far from recognizable constellations that he could never plot a return.

Would his atoms be ripped apart and moved a billion miles? Or would it become more probable that he was a billion miles away rather than twenty million miles from the sun?

He didn't have time to waste on trivialities like time and space. Elena Davenport was in danger of dying.

He jumped.

II

Supreme excellence consists in breaking the enemy's resistance without fighting.

Thus the highest form of generalship is to baulk the enemy's plans; the next best is to prevent the juncture of the enemy's forces; the next in order is to attack the enemy's army in the field; the worst policy of all is to besiege walled cities.

—Sun Tzu, The Art of War

Two generals met on gray lifeless soil between their lines.

"I'm an admirer of yours," said Pavel Orlov, extending a gloved hand to David Keith. He spoke perfect English. "So it is with great reluctance that I offer to accept your surrender."

"Let's see if we can't reduce your chagrin, General. I admire you too. I admire any man who puts in as much study of my writings as you. But reading my book isn't the same as writing it."

Orlov felt a twinge. He tried to gauge Keith's face through the space suit's faceplate. Had he overestimated his advantage? He had almost cut off Tycho City from Tycho Brahe Base. A thin corridor connected them. It was only a matter of time—

"You don't have time for a proper siege," said Keith. "Do you wonder why you haven't heard from New Moskow or why your supplies haven't arrived? The answer to both questions is the same."

"You're bluffing!" Orlov smiled with big, white, Viking's teeth. "You haven't the manpower. We'd have detected an attack. Where could it have come from?"

"Allow me some professional secrets! Try to contact New Moskow. When you can't, I'll be happy to discuss terms of your surrender. You can't fight without supplies. You don't need to read my book to know that!"

III

Jacob Kane saw nothing through the cockpit window of the mini-shuttle. Absolutely nothing.

One moment he was next to the PH Station, the next he was here. But where was here? Instruments registered no gravitons within their range, which was fifty thousand light-years. No planets. No stars. Nothing.

He cursed. The first jump had put him where he couldn't even see a star. He couldn't calculate a return without a reference.

Then he saw it. The shuttle had been slowly revolving. First it was a few stars, then clouds of them, and then, so bright it hurt to look at, a lens shape that encompassed tens of thousands of fiercely burning suns.

It floated with two smaller galaxies recognizable as the Magellanic clouds. His heart pounded savagely. He was hundreds of thousands of light-years away. But he knew which way to go.

He jumped again.

IV

Ferman finished fastening the five-gallon paint can above the door with the harmonic plaster. If he could whistle E-sharp, he would bring down a headache on the next person through the door.

So he was much surprised to see a hand remove a ceiling panel over his head, exposing a rectangular hole.

A beautiful red-haired woman dropped lightly to the floor, followed by a red-haired man. They looked as surprised to see him as he was to see them.

"You're Ralph Ferman, right?" whispered Perle Gracie.

"R-right." He didn't know who they were, but they were a lot more friendly then the people outside the door.

"This floor plan is all wrong!" said Gracie. "We're supposed to come out two buildings away!"

"Be quiet, Perle! Let's just take him out of here," she said.

"Mel will walk into the Banana Republic store any minute."

"And it's ten minutes to midnight!"

"I hear Mel's voice right now!" said Ferman.

They heard a scream and several gunshots and a body crashing heavily to the floor.

Fale and Gracie looked at each other, unsure. Fale whipped out her huge Mamba, then hesitated. Ferman thought about crawling up through the hole in the ceiling.

Heavy footfalls, coming toward the door. It opened. A burly, ugly man with a broken nose and milky right eye stood in the doorway, astonished to see three people. His good eye lit onto Kirsten Fale's figure. He whistled. It was a perfect E-sharp.

The five-gallon paint can missed the top of his head, but broke his nose for him again, and laid him out cold.

Kirsten, dragging Ferman, followed by Gracie, who also had his gun out, burst out of the storeroom. "Hands up! FBI!"

The time was now 11:53 P.M.

"Funny, you don't look like the FBI." Krebs didn't raise his hands. He recognized Kirsten.

Hardrim was surprised. He had been expecting Gracie and Fale, but not in the way he had gotten them.

"We seem to be at an impasse." Hardrim moved out of the doorway, putting a wall between him and the men outside.

"Not really," said Krebs. "I have you. I have Ferman. I have ten men in here and twenty men outside. What more could I want?"

"Your life," said Hardrim. "I got fifty rounds aimed at you. Don't billionaires have stooges to do their dirty work? That was a mistake, leaving New York."

"Maybe." Krebs looked at Whitechapel. "What're you going to do?"

"Whatever you say, Mr. Krebs," whispered Whitechapel.

Lewis Cocker pulled his coat tight around him. He didn't like this. He might catch a random shot. He looked out the window—he saw ten sets of helicopter lights hundreds of feet in the air, approaching fast. Moments later everyone heard them.

Krebs's men fired raggedly at the descending helicopters before fleeing. The gunships didn't have clear landing spots: Horton Plaza was built like a medieval city, with many levels and twisting, narrow thoroughfares. So they hovered while fifty armed men rappelled down with ropes and deployed outside the store.

Gracie looked at Fale. Both shrugged. Even Hardrim muttered to himself: "Who the hell are these people?"

If it was possible for a man to wear camouflage and paint and still be the height of fashion, Roger Ferdinand was that man. He ambled across the mall toward the Banana Republic store like a model for a spread for *Soldier of Fortune* magazine shot by a photographer from *GQ*.

He smiled with the nasty, superior air of a parochial school teacher telling a student that he would spend a thousand years in hell. He rubbed his hands together. "I think a lot of people are under arrest!"

V

Kane saw a great stellar object that spewed energy and light in a whirling gyre as if forced under extreme pressure from another part of the universe.

It was huge, beyond the range of his instruments. It filled the viewport.

It was a quasar—Kane was either at the end of the universe or at its creation. Was he moving in time as well as space? Would he be able to return to his own time?

The quasar, if such it was, was fascinating and beautiful, like an attractive way to die. For that reason Kane didn't stay. If he lingered, he had the feeling he would stay forever.

He jumped again.

He was in the center of a galaxy, probably the Milky Way. His instruments said he was also in the middle of a radiation field so intense that if he stayed long he would die.

In the very thickest of the star field, the enormous black hole predicted by astronomers gnawed at the heart of the galaxy, a gaping maw that would, sometime before the end of time, devour the Milky Way. It was hidden from humanity by a veil of dust clouds.

Were the matter and energy the singularity was sucking up reappearing a universe away at the quasar he had just seen? If so, he had experienced yin and yang on a grand cosmic scale.

He let the instruments record coordinates before jumping. Without a working radiation counter he was flying blind, but he felt like he had been cooked good in that last stop.

He jumped again.

He was in the Tau Ceti system. The constellations seen from Tau Ceti, seven light-years from Sol, were almost the same as from earth. He had little trouble determining his location. He was a few million miles from the planet Philip Norrison had dubbed "Prometheus," 112 million miles from Tau Ceti. Surface gravity was .88 that of earth. It had more oxygen. The surface was half covered by water. He detected no sign of life.

Kane tried his first substellar jump and found himself ten thousand miles above Prometheus. The recorders worked furiously, soaking up as much data as they could in the short time.

He located Sol in the navigational cube. Strange, he thought, the unimaginable distances he had been traveling hadn't begun to register. It was like being in shock from an accident but continuing to function. Interstellar shock.

He jumped.

VI

"What's going on, Roger?" demanded Kirsten Fale.

Ferdinand nonchalantly stepped into the Banana Republic store. He noted who had guns and at whom they were pointed. "I've been tracing you, my dear. When you let Hardrim escape, it occurred to me that you had stopped thinking with your head and had started taking orders from a different part of your anatomy."

"You prick!"

"I'm the one who should be sore," said Ferdinand. "You, my most loyal, faithful arm, have gone native, discarded your future. And with a has-been, a failure who never got anything right." He casually turned and saw Krebs. "Mr. Krebs, you can't possibly imagine how happy I am to meet you."

Cocker jumped up. "If you're from the FBI, you know this area is under martial law. You have no jurisdiction here. You can take no evidence, make no arrests. You might as well be in Mexico."

"Oh, you're wrong. If I was in Mexico I could at least get some good suits made for me." His eyes fell on Whitechapel and widened with disbelief. "I thought you were dead."

"I was. Now I'm in hell."

Ferdinand shuddered. "He's your ticket to the federal pen, Krebs. Maybe you didn't personally break the law, but your hired assassin has. I'm sure if I arrest everybody and confiscate everything, we can provide the courts meat to chew on for years."

"With an uncertain dénouement," said Krebs. "But if you make the smart decision that you're not in your jurisdiction—"

"Don't start," snapped Ferdinand. "All your money couldn't buy what I'll get for proving that you spent twenty-five years murdering everyone who could link you to the death of Adam Scott and that you hired saboteurs to cripple U.S. aerospace industry and that your monster planted a nuclear bomb on a GILGAMESH scramjet and stole a scramjet. And we have new evidence that Python was the main supplier of plutonium to Black Africa. Have I left out anything, Hardrim?"

"You're on a roll, Ferdinand."

"I'm going to roll right over you, Hardrim. And you, Kirsten, my dear. How someone who makes such perfect fashion statements could be so stupid!"

"Maybe not so stupid, Roger." For someone caught red-handed, she was remarkably calm. "I just haven't been working for you."

"Where does working for Hardrim get you?"

"I don't work for Mel." Not moving her Mamba .45 a hair from its target, she reached into a pouch and removed a plastic document. "I work for internal affairs, specifically Director Pollux. This authorizes me to gather evidence that you, Special Deputy Director Roger Ferdinand, abused your position by conducting a private investigation, using Bureau resources, without orders, with the plan to undermine the authority of the director and the President of the U.S.''

"You traitorous little bitch!''

"I must add one more thing.'' She glanced at her watch. It was thirty seconds to midnight. "Committed acts that caused extensive destruction of FBI property and yet to be determined injuries and deaths of FBI personnel by willfully entering territory not under jurisdiction of civilian authorities.''

"What are you talking about?'' said Ferdinand tightly.

Survivors of bombardments by heavy naval guns, such as the sixteen-inch guns of the battleship *New Jersey* or the twenty-two-inch guns of the battleship carrier *Farragut*, have described the sound of the shell as it approaches as being like the roar of a locomotive. The people in the Banana Republic store who lived were to have similar recollections.

The first shell from the *Farragut* landed in the midst of a tall, block-shaped building that was once a Sears store. It exploded with a mighty noise, showering the hovering helicopters with debris. Three of the choppers immediately crashed.

Inside the Banana Republic store, by comparison, all hell broke loose.

Chapter

* 56 *

I

Aboard the battleship *Lenin* Marshal Antonine Tiomkin listened over a laser transmission to General Pavel Orlov explain his predicament. For the first time Tiomkin felt his age. And felt the futility of old men trying to tell young men how to fight wars.

"I've lost communication with New Moskow. Keith claims he has captured it."

"We can't raise New Moskow either, Pavel. We've detected movement outside of the dome, but no large formations. The enemy may be inside. They may wish to prevent us from bombarding them. In effect, they hold the colonists hostage to our good behavior."

"Without supplies I can operate a few days. We can fight on and possibly take Tycho City, but considering my opponent, that is not a bright possibility. If I march back to Archimedes, I'll be harassed by an enemy who is in supply, and I will run out of air."

"We can drop supplies to you."

"My father, we know you can't drop enough supplies to maintain my army. Unless I wish to be responsible for the deaths of four thousand men, I must surrender."

"Never!" shrieked Peter Brasnikov, who listened with growing fury. "We have enough bombs on this ship to destroy Tycho City."

"If we destroy the city, what have we gained?" asked Tiomkin. "Plus, we must fight past Admiral Davis to get close enough to ensure the accuracy we need to keep from hitting our own men."

"Give the orders! Remember what the Spartans told their sons when they went off to battle? Return with your shield or upon it!"

"Did you hear that, Pavel?" asked Tiomkin.

"Yes, Comrade Marshal. We are prepared to fight as long as there is a reasonable alternative to surrender. If you think you can bombard the American position in time, I applaud the effort."

"It shall be done." Tiomkin began giving orders. He looked at Brasnikov. "I can't guarantee your safety aboard *Lenin*, First Secretary. Nor is there time to transfer you."

Brasnikov bit his lip. "We are all warriors today, Marshal."

Tiomkin cursed. "Controls are not responding! Something's wrong. What's wrong with the Dough Children?"

He was answered by several voices over the communications system. Finally he was called by the computer officer.

"What's going on, Sasha?"

"I can't believe this! Absurd! Unbelievable! Ridiculous!"

"What is?"

"The Dough Children are on strike."

II

The mini-shuttle phased into being a dozen yards from the battleship *Kurtzov*. Kane launched a canister the size of a vacuum bottle. It contained, in stasis, enough antimatter to interact with the battleship and produce the largest explosion ever witnessed as positive molecules reacted with antimatter molecules in a pure example of matter transformed into energy.

The canister attached itself to the greater mass of the battleship like lint falling into a jar of honey.

Before *Kurtzov*'s defenses could focus on the insect that had buzzed it, Kane phased across the void a few hundred miles and placed another canister next to the battleship *Aurora*.

In quick succession, he emptied the shuttle bay and planted twenty canisters on the largest warships in the Soviet fleet.

He had finished his official business, now it was time for personal business. He jumped to the asteroid Icarus.

III

When the first shell landed on the Sears building, Kirsten Fale, Perle Gracie, and Hardrim were expecting it. They dove for cover, with Fale and Gracie pulling Ferman down with them.

The storefront window blew in from the blast. Lewis Cocker, standing near it, was nearly decapitated by a flying shard of glass. Whitechapel was showered with splinters. One pierced an eye. Another buried itself in his throat, but missed a major vein. His white hair sprouted red, but he still stood.

Krebs had leaped under a counter and was unhurt. Ferdinand was picked up by the blast and thrown on his back. Five of Solarz's-turned-Krebs's henchmen took the brunt of the blast.

Hardrim had launched himself away from the storefront in a low dive toward the storeroom. Landing on his palms, he dissipated the force of the jump by rolling into a ball that hit, but was not stopped by, the storeroom door, which tore from its hinges.

Whitechapel shook blood from his good eye and spied a stunned Ferdinand on the floor. He lunged toward the FBI man, who fired his gun point-blank. The back of Whitechapel's head exploded, but he came on, collapsing on top of Ferdinand, who screamed and screamed.

"Let's go!" bellowed Hardrim. Ferman, Gracie, and Fale scrambled to their feet and followed him into the storeroom. He saw the ceiling with the panel removed, jumped up, and hoisted himself into the crawl space. The rest followed him.

"How do we get out of here?" yelled Hardrim. "I forgot!"

"Follow me," said Kirsten Fale. "I'm sure you won't mind." She crawled past, and wiggling her perfect rear end in his face, proceeded crablike out of the crawl space into a place where they could stand up. They took a ladder down the side of the building.

They ducked instinctively as another shell fell on the mall. By now all the helicopters had either been destroyed or scattered.

Across the mall, in the old parking lot, the Science Network helicopter sat, unscathed, rotors turning slowly.

"Thank God for navy marksmanship!" whooped Hardrim.

"Let's just hope they stay on schedule," said Gracie.

"Does that have enough room for us four?" asked Hardrim.

"It only needs three," said Kirsten Fale. "I'm staying, to make sure Roger doesn't pull one of his famous acrobatic acts."

"But I thought—" Hardrim blushed. "You lied to me. Or at least misrepresented—"

"I didn't lie to you, big man," she said, squeezing his arm fondly. "I didn't misrepresent my feelings. I think you're a hell of a man. But there's no place for you with a woman who'll someday be the first female director of the FBI." She stood on tiptoes and kissed him. "Get lost before I arrest you!"

Another shell landed, this time much too close for comfort.

They ran across the parking lot and piled into the chopper. Hardrim paused in the hatch and caught a glimpse of Kirsten Fale, who waved her Mamba .45 over her cascade of red hair.

"Move your ass!" yelled the pilot, who, as Hardrim squeezed in the hatch, shot into the night air, screaming across the tops of buildings that lay east of Horton Plaza, away from the ocean.

IV

Icarus's low gravity forced Kane to grapple the mini-shuttle to its surface, near the northern axis, farthest from the blast that melted half the asteroid. It was also as close as he could get to Elena Davenport's weak distress signal. As near as he could tell, it came from an enclosure used to process ore.

He found the most efficient locomotion was pulling himself along the surface like a swimmer pulls along the bottom of a pool.

His arms were crying out in their sockets when he found the blockhouse of pulverized rock. It didn't have an airlock. Inside, a space-suited figure was slumped in a crude rock chair. The figure didn't appear to be breathing.

He rushed over and the figure raised itself up. It was Elena. Her face was totally disbelieving.

"I'm hallucinating! You can't be here. It's not possible."

"Not only possible, but inescapable," snapped Kane. "Come on, we don't have a lot of time."

"For what? The radiation won't kill us for hours yet."

"We're getting you off here, you little idiot! Now move!"

Elena Davenport, who had been shaken up but not hurt in the explosion that killed her father and most of the colonists, was strong enough to beat Kane swimming across the surface of Icarus.

"How did you get here? I thought it was impossible for any ship to match velocities with us in time."

"Don't worry about it."

"Damn you, Jacob! This is me, not some airhead bimbo. How the hell did you get here when it's plainly impossible?"

"The same way you're getting out: faster-than-light travel."

They reached the mini-shuttle. She shook her head. "Doesn't look like much."

Kane chuckled. "You're looking at the greatest explorer in history. She's just broken every record in human history. She's a friggin' *Apollo 11*, *Beagle*, *Golden Hind*, *Voyager*, *Niña*, *Pinta* and *Santa Maria* rolled into one!"

"But there's only room for one person."

"That's right, Elena. Room for one. The pilot. You. And it will never carry a more precious cargo."

"That doesn't sound like you, Jacob."

"You're right." He turned away so she couldn't see his face. "I hate to hear me talk this way, too. So I wish to hell you'd get in the goddamned ship."

"All right. But how do I pilot it?"

"I'll set it to take you to the PH Station."

"And then we send it back for you?"

"Negative. The ship will not fly without someone inside."

"Jacob, what does this mean?" She placed herself where he couldn't avoid looking at her. "Are you sacrificing yourself to save me? Think again! I won't let anyone buy my life with his."

"Elena." Kane's voice was gentle for once. "There's something called survivor's guilt. People who live through disasters get it. After the big L.A. quake, people committed suicide: They felt guilty that they weren't crushed by tons of debris. Right now you feel guilt because you survived the explosion. You want to make up for it by not taking a chance to survive."

"This is ridiculous, Jacob. I won't let you die to save me."

"I'm not, Elena. I love you, but I'm not stupid! Look at the radiation counter in the cockpit. It's way over maximum. I got enough radiation out there to breed a race of Mothras. I'm fried meat. I'll be dead in days or weeks, even if they connect me to a machine to breathe and piss for me.''

"Jacob, I—I don't know what to say to you.''

"Well, whatever it is, I don't have time. Because I have one more thing to do. I must do it before the asteroid gets too close to the sun.'' He laughed. "What a funeral pyre I'm going to have!''

"You know something, Jacob? You are an insensitive bastard!''

"Yeah, I know. Aren't you glad you didn't marry me?''

Elena realized she had to play out the game Kane's way. He could muster the will to continue only by playing the bastard to the end. He couldn't see the tears, and she kept her voice strong.

"Jacob Kane, I wouldn't have married you if you had been the last man in the universe.''

V

"Admiral Arbatov, I presume?'' Kane watched the admiral in the tiny holocube in the refining building. "I'm the man who planted the bombs on your ships an hour ago.''

"Hello, Yankee,'' said the admiral coldly. "What do you want? I am not of a mind to deal with pirates, outlaws, and terrorists.''

"Sorry I'm not part of your social register. You've gathered by now that if you mess with the bombs they'll give spectacular demonstrations of Einstein's $E = mc^2$ equation. They are antimatter canisters. If I detonate, you'll be left with just enough ships for Admiral Hawkings to have a short, nasty turkey shoot.''

"Why don't you get it over with?''

"I'm a compassionate guy. I don't want you lousy, stinking commies to die. I want you to live, to see the error of your ways and become good capitalists. I'm giving you the chance to evacuate your ships, and allow Hawkings to put prize crews on them.''

Arbatov was livid. "I'm tempted to put a torpedo into that little dungheap rock you are on and save the sun the trouble—''

"You've made my argument for me, Admiral. I've nothing to lose. But I don't have a lot of time. I won't set a time limit for you to accept my offer. But if you haven't done what I ask by the time I start puking and feeling rotten, Moskow's bright sons will shortly thereafter become Moskow's bright suns.''

He realized from the admiral's puzzled look that his pun was too obscure and was probably untranslatable.

"You'll all be dead, Admiral," he supplied. Actually, he felt just fine. He didn't have a fatal case of radiation sickness. At least he didn't think he did, but, come to think of it, it was certainly possible. Kane knit his brows. Had he received a fatal dose when he was at the core of the galaxy? It was bittersweet irony not to know for certain. What was certain was that he had a fatal case of lovesickness, and to his dying day (any minute now) Kane would hate himself for sacrificing himself for Elena. Oh well, she was almost worth it, after all. Almost.

He waited for the Russians to give up.

VI

"On strike!" bellowed Brasnikov. His eyes bulged and he was swaying. "Break into the cabin that houses the traitors and wipe them out!"

"Impossible, First Secretary," said Tiomkin. "They run the ship. They have sealed off the deck. We'd have to mount an assault with CosMarines to blow it open. If they think they're being attacked, they could scuttle the *Lenin*. Besides, they are on strike on the *Kirov* and the *Aurora*."

"I won't let them beat me!" Brasnikov pointed a claw at Tiomkin. "You want them to beat me! You wanted the Africans to beat me! You've always hated my genius! I'll show you! I know that our warheads can be manually launched, overriding the computer fire controls. I order you to destroy Tycho City and New Moskow."

During Brasnikov's tirade, Tiomkin had pushed a button that summoned a squad of CosMarines, under a trusted lieutenant and sergeant. When they appeared, Tiomkin pulled out his laser pistol and pointed it at the First Secretary.

"First Secretary, you are under arrest. The charge is—insanity, I guess. Lieutenant, put the premier in a comfortable cabin. One that has lots of soft things and few sharp edges."

Brasnikov broke down, crying and alternately blustering and threatening.

Tiomkin leaned against the console. He felt like a commander of the Roman Praetorian Guard who had overthrown a tyrant. What now? Would the feared "Committee," the "K" in Moskow, accept him? Would the other armed forces?

Well, why not? If they didn't, he could always drop rocks on them. But first, there was a strike to settle.

VII

When, in the full flower of their victory, Gracie and Hardrim returned to Argus Society headquarters with Ralph Ferman, Hardrim couldn't wait to hit the holocube to tell Lenny he was safe.

First he had to reintroduce Ferman and Dr. Noah Chambless, and referee the first few bouts between them. He couldn't blame Ferman for wanting to pop Chambless. Nor did he expect Ferman to believe a word from anyone about the Argus Society or the Santa Bella blight . . . or anything.

But explanations could come later. The important thing was that Ferman was out of circulation, and so was his damaging data.

Hardrim chortled to himself, thinking how stupid he had been to almost fall for Kirsten Fale. A beautiful body, a brain to match. But scruples like an alley cat.

The computer would not connect him with Lenny. "There is an incoming message for Mel Hardrim from Lenore Lippman," it said.

The message had been recorded when she was connected to the interface. It was, as Hardrim would have put it, the Big Kiss-off.

"Mel, you were right," said Lenny, her voice stripped of feeling. "We cannot continue to be separated by the fact that one of us is an interface and the other isn't. Such a relationship has no future. So I am ending our relationship." She smiled a frigid, almost nonhuman smile. "I did do you one favor. I have continued to maintain a relationship with our little friend Sergei in the *Animus*. He and I have much in common. I've come to realize that he is the love relationship no longer possible for me in the flat world. He is my son.

"I gave him some books to read. I think once the news comes out about what has been going on in space, Sergei's new reading habits will have contributed to the good guys/girls winning." She paused again, gathering her thoughts. "I can't say I love you. That is a fading memory. I *can* say, farewell."

Hardrim felt like throwing a vase into the holocube, or better yet, shooting the damned thing. He cursed fluently for five minutes. It was enough to drive a man to drink, or in Hardrim's case, to go on the wagon so he could then start drinking again.

He laughed. Maybe it was time to start thinking what he was going to do with his life. His work with the Argus Society was near complete. He could never return to the Washington police. He wasn't even sure he wanted to be in police work anymore. He went outside and looked up in the sky. Maybe they needed cops up there. Someday. Meantime, he would need something to do. Maybe he'd give Wilford Butter a call. Try a little southwestern law enforcement.

He lit a cigarette and drew in the nicotine and thought about Lenore Lippman and Kirsten Fale. How do you like that? he asked himself. Thrown over. Given the goodbye by two career girls.

Oh well, he'd never had much luck with women.

Chapter
* 57 *

There is more poetry in the railway that crosses the Continent than in all the history of the Trojan War.
—Joaquin Miller, upon the completion of the Transcontinental
                                                                    Railroad

If it be romance, if it be contrast, if it be heroism we require, what was Troy to this?
                    —Robert Louis Stevenson, Across the Plains

Mar. 18—*Deseret Gantry*—"The Opinion Factory," by Jack Laffco—In the four months since the first voyage by the late Jacob Kane, faster-than-light has grown almost overnight into a multimillion-ounce industry that has knocked down and abolished national boundaries and restrictions.

People don't realize it yet, but this is the biggest thing since the end of the Cold War. Even my son, Darrell, has heard about it. He's hounding me to take him to Alpha Centauri . . . so he can fight the Green Toroids or something—

So I called Prometheus Enterprises, which manufactures FTL units. Their construction is supervised by the universally famous Sherlock Michlanski, apparently so cheaply that anyone who can afford a car can afford an FTL unit. I asked a sales rep about an extended payment plan. He was very nice, but you can't extend credit to someone who may be a thousand light-years away next week. Cash, he said, is required for delivery.

Tens of thousands of people a month are ponying up the money. I saw them camped out front of the Prometheus Enterprises factory in Los Angeles. This factory has an interesting history. It's where, more than a quarter century ago, Jason Scott's father died making a point about tyranny and the freedom to create.

Today, people sleep in front of the factory, waiting for a number to make their own points. And vouchers in hand, they proceed to Deseret Space Center to become part of the largest mass exodus in the history of mankind.

Once other space centers are licensed to carry the cheap Strubeck Motivator, the exodus, now a stream, will become a flood. The only people staying at home will be me, my son, Darrell, and my wife. Maybe we can get her to go too. . . .

The Motivator's workings are the most closely guarded secret in the world. Only Michlanski knows for sure what goes into one. The only thing limiting their manufacture is the restriction that he must oversee the final installation of each Motivator.

The technology is so new that many pioneers are dying trying to land on hospitable worlds. Some are flying blind. To date, no one knows exactly how many have flown FTL units successfully and how many latter-day Wrong-Way Corrigans have ended up inside a neutron star. Nor will we know unless they return to tell us, or send a message by courier, or until somebody devises a faster-than-light radio transmitter. Dr. Michlanski says he's working on one. I'm looking forward to that. That means sooner or later, we'll have radio matter transmission. So when Darrell misbehaves, all I'll have to do is change the channel. . . .

"How can you be working on one when all you do is install Strubeck Motivators?" said Jason Scott, who was with Michlanski in the tower overlooking the space port, watching thousands of people lining up for a trip to the stars. They didn't care which star. Any one would do. They just wanted a fresh start.

Outside the main gate, workmen were changing the sign that read "Deseret Space Center" to read "Jeffrey Shefferton Space Center." That was the result of a recent congressional action, taken at the behest of President St. Clair, who was expected to be there for the christening ceremony next month.

"A good question," said Michlanski, who was starting to show the strain. But Scott didn't look so hot either. After he buried Bethany, and spent months in therapy to restore ligaments and muscles he had almost destroyed, he looked ten years older. His hair was completely white now.

"I guess I'll have to get a good assistant."

"Sherry, you can't fool me," said Scott. "I know there's more than meets the eye to the Motivators. The technical explanations you've given are full of beans. I know it and you know it. If what you say is correct, there's no reason why any reasonably well trained aerospace engineer couldn't build one. No reason why you have to do it, unless you're holding back something. What is it?"

Michlanski pointed over his shoulder. "There's one in the next room. Go look under the hood. Open it up and peer inside. But before you do, consider this thought puzzle. What if man is as much the creator as the participant in this universe? What if the observer does alter what he observes by the very fact of observation? What if that's what the Strubeck equations are about?

"Look under the hood, you may find nothing there. That, in fact, it works because everyone expects it to. Or, contrarily, you may find that it's a very simple device—so simple that if I let anybody look at it for more than five minutes, every subscriber to the Edmund Scientific catalogue will build Motivators, and we'll never make any money." Michlanski smirked the smirk that had made Jacob want to smash his face when they were boys.

"You're saying that Jacob flew about the universe on faith?"

"I'm not saying that. If you want answers, look inside. If you are happy with the way things are going, then don't."

"Speaking of faith," said Scott, "have you seen sales figures on Jacob's book? It's selling like wildfire in the colonies. Sheridan Mayfield may have an independence movement on his hands before he knows it." He smiled ruefully. "Sheridan's no politician. Fortunately St. Clair is."

Michlanski nodded. "It's hard to fight a myth and Jacob has taken on the attributes of a mythical hero. He has more than one birthplace. Several cities are claiming him. *Nobody* saw him die. There's no body. Of course, we know he plunged into the sun. But with no corpse, there's always a chance he didn't. He would've appreciated that: immortality as a folk hero of the spaceways."

"No, you're wrong, Sherry. Jacob would have preferred the kind of immortality where you don't die."

There was a knock on the door. It was Roger Ferdinand.

"Sorry to bother you, Mr. Scott. I know you're a busy U.N. commissioner. But I understand I have to see you on this matter—"

"Certainly, Mr. Ferdinand. Is it 'Inspector' or 'Director'?"

"I'm not with the FBI anymore. I work for the U.N. special investigations unit. We have reason to believe Horatius Krebs may be trying to ship out. I've been tracking him since he escaped me in San Diego. I have a U.N. warrant for him."

Scott shook his head emphatically. "The law says prior arrests or warrants do not apply to persons shipping on interstellar flights. The idea is to give everyone a clean slate."

"Even Horatius Krebs?"

"Even Horatius Krebs."

Ferdinand approached Scott and looked him in the eye. "Krebs was responsible for the death of your parents. After he helped murder them, he stole everything they worked for. Then he tried to kill off every person connected with your father who could tie him to the killings. Does that kind of man deserve a clean slate?"

Scott didn't answer, but turned away, in the disquieting, unconscious habit developed since he had starting wearing the vision prosthesis. It allowed him to gauge the feelings of others, without revealing his own.

Ferdinand went to the window that overlooked the line of would-be colonists. His mouth was working furiously. "There he is, big as day! Didn't bother to disguise himself. Lined up for Flight 555. For him, they should change it to 666. Mr. Scott, that man killed your parents."

Scott, his face hidden, didn't answer for a moment. "Ferdinand," he said, "I've known that Krebs killed Mom and Dad for quite some time." He walked over to the window where Ferdinand had watched the would-be colonists. "Perhaps even someone like Krebs deserves another chance, but that's not why I'm going to let him board the next flight."

He turned away from the window and started to walk out of the office, but then he stopped and seemed to contemplate something far away. "For the next thousand years or so, the colonies we humans make out in the stars will be some of the nastiest, most challenging frontiers you can imagine. There'll be squalor, heaven and hell. They'll need hard-driving men who'll stop at nothing. They'll need SOBs like Horatius Krebs. That's just where we're going to send him." Scott walked out of the room.

"Of course," said Michlanski. "There's no reason to send him to a nice place."

"You invented FTL, Michlanski," said Ferdinand, his frustration boiling to the surface. "What're you going to do with it? Your Sunside Project sold us a bill of goods. You said you'd solve earth's problems. You said you'd feed the world. Instead, you sent half the world's population running away from their problems. You call that saving the world? What do you have to say?"

"We lied, Mr. Ferdinand. We lied. And now, if you excuse me, I have to go play with my universe."

Michlanski left Ferdinand fuming. The idiot, thought Michlanski. He didn't see the big picture. Artificial photosynthesis, if perfected, would have been a temporary solution. Now man's food problems were solved because half the population would soon vanish into the star fields. Man was no longer confined to his home system. A new food source was, at best, a temporary solution. The stars were the solution of the ages.

And then, happily, all thoughts of Ferdinand, and other ordinary, little men, evaporated from his mind. He walked out onto the balcony, and in the bright, noontime day, he looked up into the sky and dreamed of the stars.